ADVENTURE TIME™

PLAYING WITH FIRE

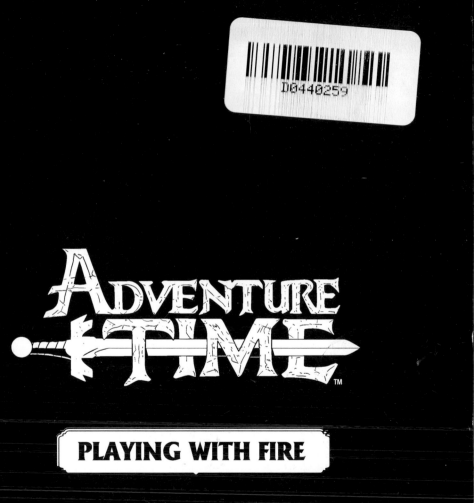

PUBLISHED BY KaBOOM!

ROSS RICHIE ~ CEO & Founder

MATT GAGNON ~ Editor-in-Chief

FILIP SABLIK ~ VP-Publishing & Marketing

LANCE KREITER ~ VP-Licensing & Merchandising

MATT NISSENBAUM ~ Senior Director of Sales & Marketing

PHIL BARBARO ~ Director of Finance

BRYCE CARLSON ~ Managing Editor

DAFNA PLEBAN ~ Editor

SHANNON WATTERS ~ Editor

ERIC HARBURN ~ Editor

CHRIS ROSA ~ Assistant Editor

ALEX GALER ~ Assistant Editor

WHITNEY LEOPARD ~ Assistant Editor

JASMINE AMIRI ~ Assistant Editor

STEPHANIE GONZAGA ~ Graphic Designer

KASSANDRA HELLER ~ Production Designer

MIKE LOPEZ ~ Production Designer

DEVIN FUNCHES ~ E-Commerce & Inventory Coordinator

VINCE FREDERICK ~ Event Coordinator

BRIANNA HART ~ Executive Assistant

ADVENTURE TIME: PLAYING WITH FIRE — April 2013. Published by KaBOOM!, a division of Boom Entertainment, Inc. ADVENTURE TIME, CARTOON NETWORK, the logos, and all related characters and elements are trademarks of and © Cartoon Network. (S13) All rights reserved. KaBOOM!™ and the KaBOOM! logo are trademarks of Boom Entertainment, Inc., registered in various countries and categories. All characters, events, and institutions depicted herein are fictional. Any similarity between any of the names, characters, persons, events, and/or institutions in this publication to actual names, characters, and persons, whether living or dead, events, and/or institutions is unintended and purely coincidental. KaBOOM! does not read or accept unsolicited submissions of ideas, stories, or artwork.

For information regarding the CPSIA on this printed material, call: (203) 595-3636 and provide reference #RICH – 475279. A catalog record of this book is available from OCLC and from the KaBOOM! website, www.kaboom-studios.com, on the Librarians page.

BOOM! Studios, 5670 Wilshire Boulevard, Suite 450, Los Angeles, CA 90036-5679. Printed in USA. First Printing. ISBN: 978-1-60886-325-9

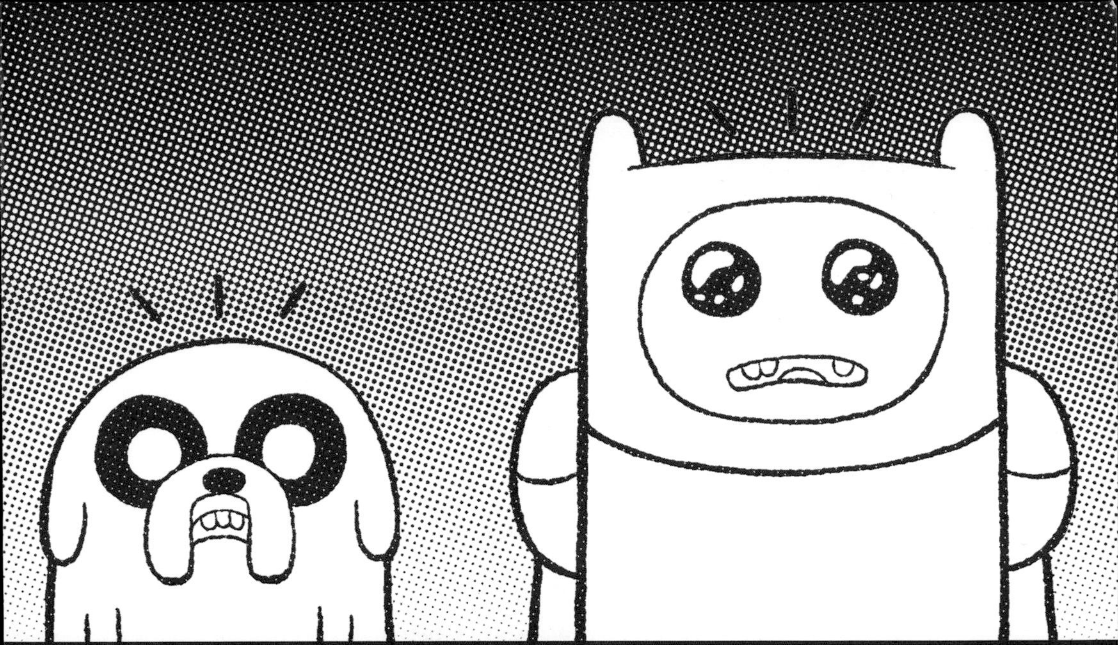

Created by Pendleton Ward

Written by Danielle Corsetto

Illustrated by Zack Sterling

Additional Pencils by JJ Harrison

Inks by Stephanie Hocutt

Tones by Amanda Lafrenais

Letters by Mad Rupert

"Adventure Time with BMO!" by Meredith McClaren

Tones by Amanda Lafrenais

Cover by Stephanie Gonzaga

Colors by Kassandra Heller

Assistant Editor: Whitney Leopard

Editor: Shannon Watters

Designer: Stephanie Gonzaga

With Special Thanks to Marisa Marionakis, Rick Blanco, Curtis Lelash, Laurie Halal-Ono, Keith Mack, Kelly Crews and the wonderful folks at Cartoon Network.

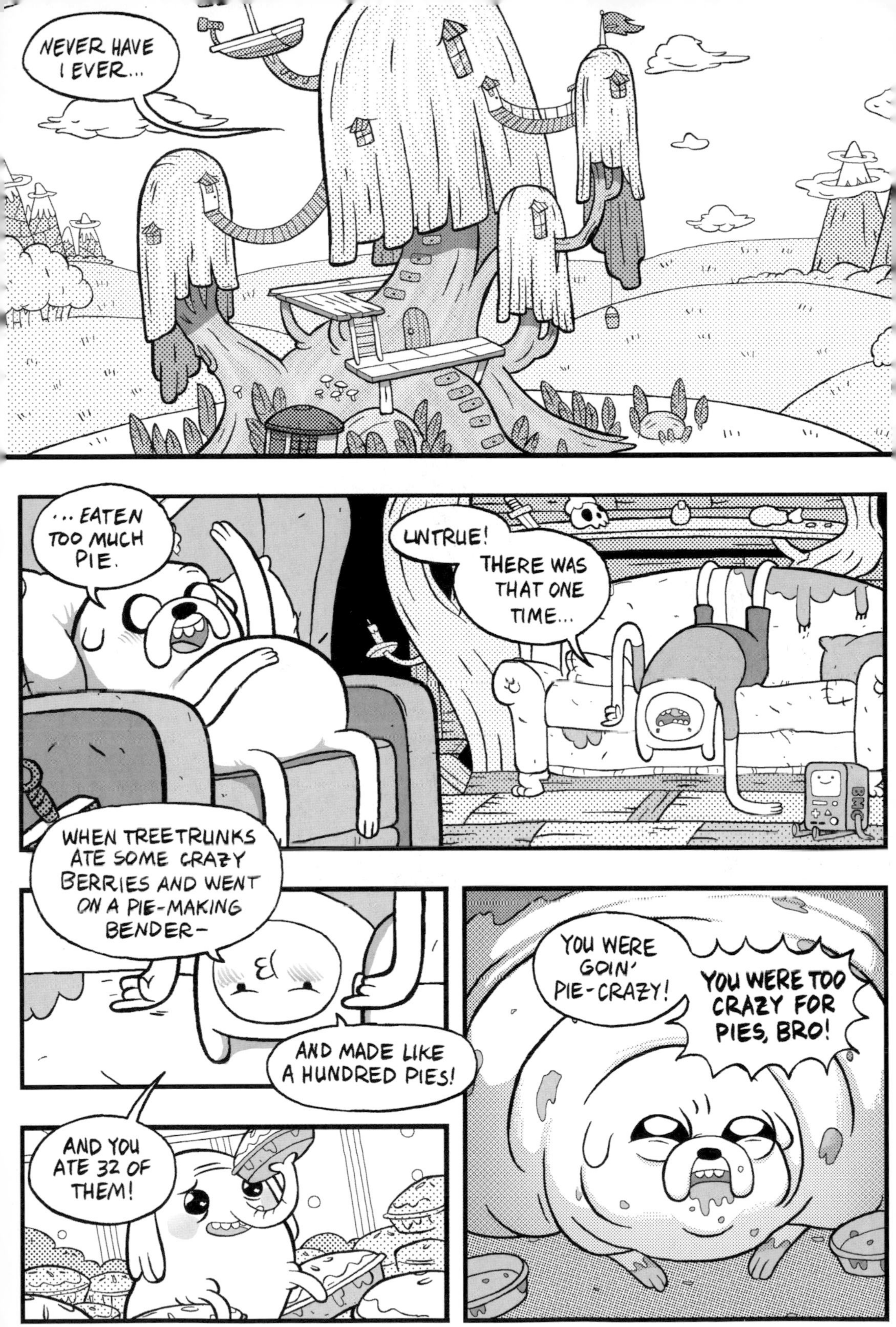
NEVER HAVE I EVER...
...EATEN TOO MUCH PIE.
UNTRUE!
THERE WAS THAT ONE TIME...
WHEN TREETRUNKS ATE SOME CRAZY BERRIES AND WENT ON A PIE-MAKING BENDER–
AND MADE LIKE A HUNDRED PIES!
AND YOU ATE 32 OF THEM!
YOU WERE GOIN' PIE-CRAZY!
YOU WERE TOO CRAZY FOR PIES, BRO!
BMO

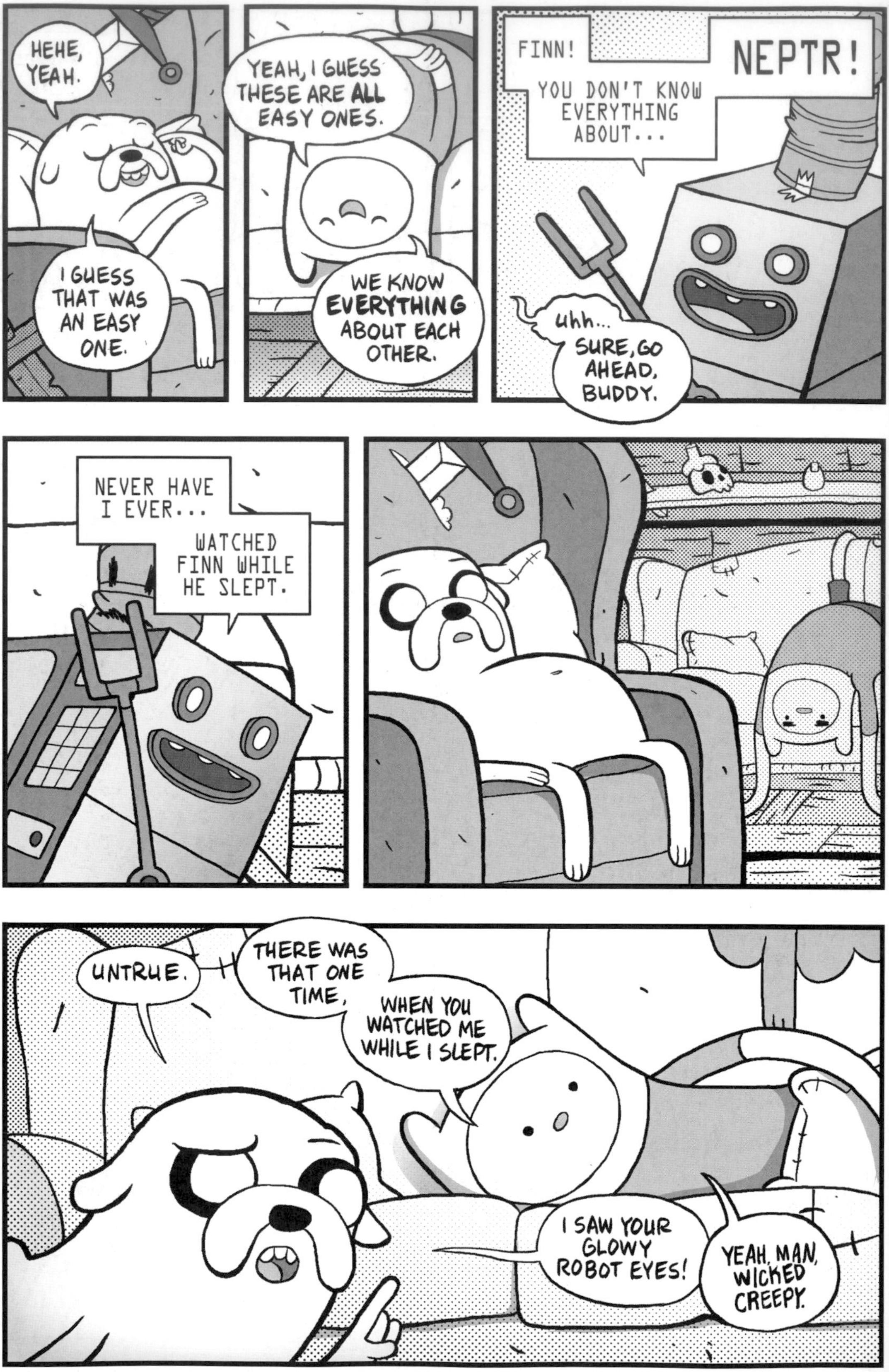
HEHE, YEAH.
I GUESS THAT WAS AN EASY ONE.
YEAH, I GUESS THESE ARE ALL EASY ONES.
WE KNOW EVERYTHING ABOUT EACH OTHER.
FINN!
NEPTR!
YOU DON'T KNOW EVERYTHING ABOUT...
uhh... SURE, GO AHEAD, BUDDY.
NEVER HAVE I EVER...
WATCHED FINN WHILE HE SLEPT.
UNTRUE.
THERE WAS THAT ONE TIME,
WHEN YOU WATCHED ME WHILE I SLEPT.
I SAW YOUR GLOWY ROBOT EYES!
YEAH, MAN, WICKED CREEPY.

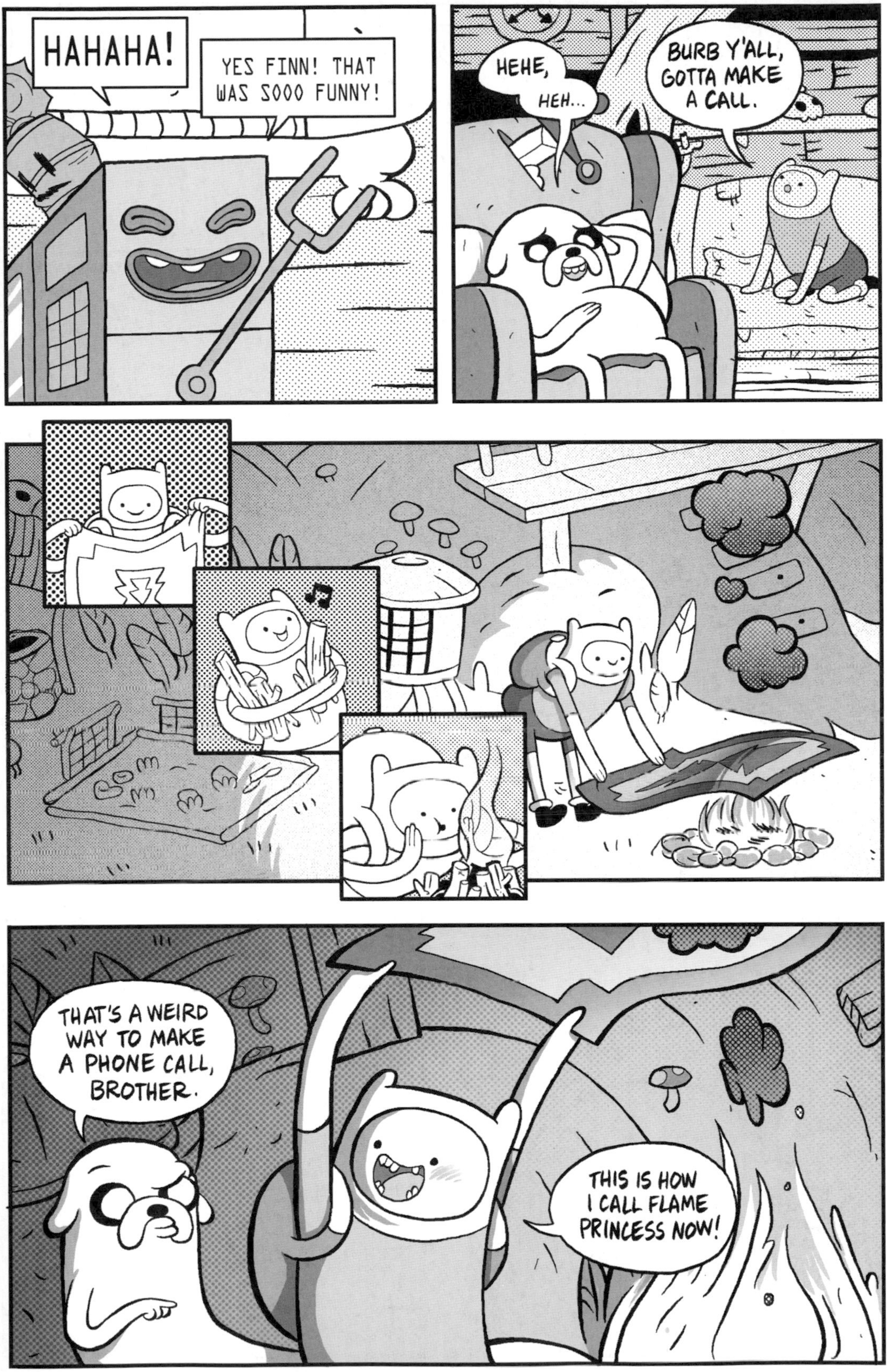
HAHAHA!
YES FINN! THAT WAS SOOO FUNNY!
HEHE,
HEH...
BURB Y'ALL, GOTTA MAKE A CALL.
THAT'S A WEIRD WAY TO MAKE A PHONE CALL, BROTHER.
THIS IS HOW I CALL FLAME PRINCESS NOW!

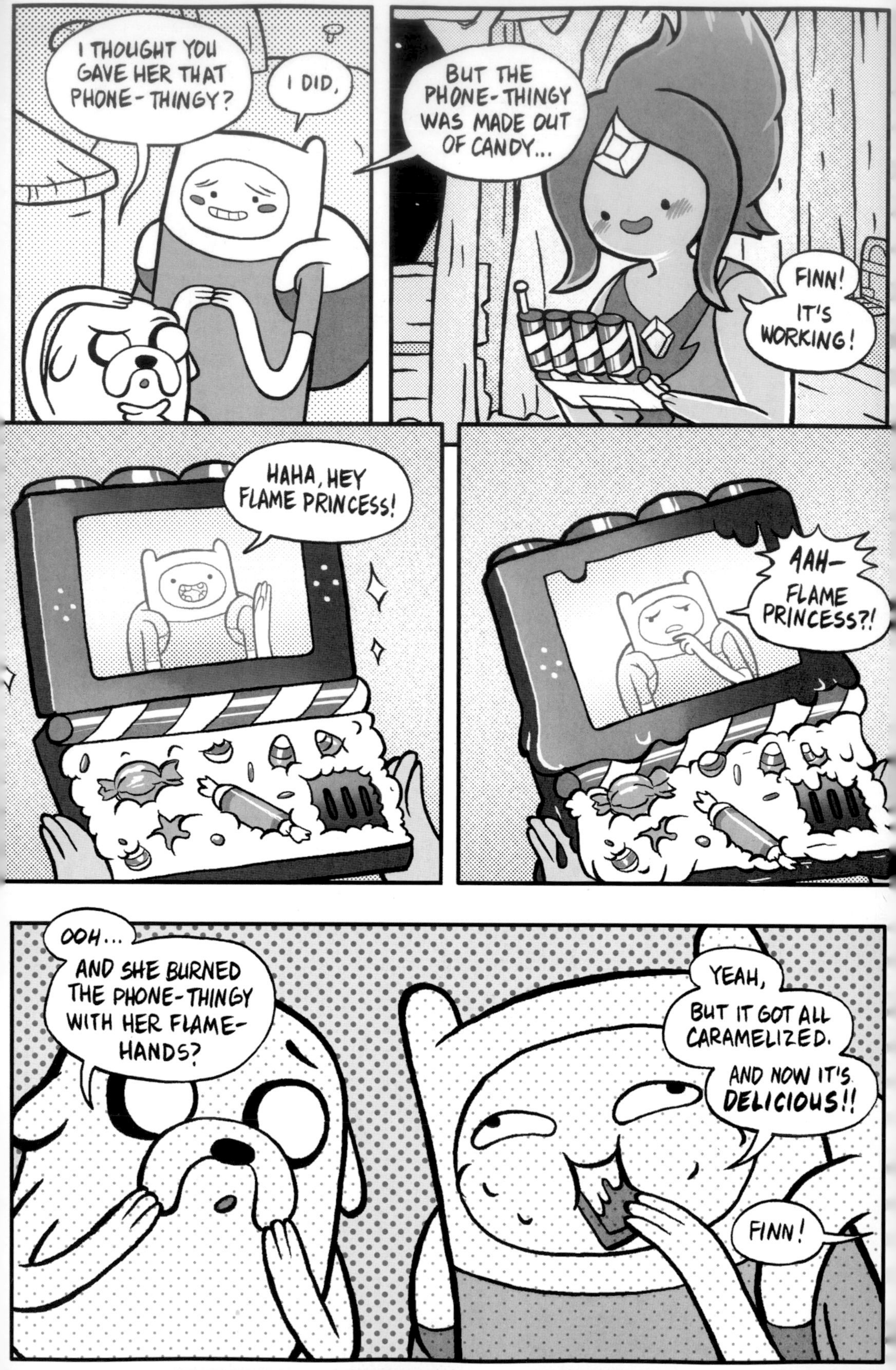
I THOUGHT YOU GAVE HER THAT PHONE-THINGY?
I DID,
BUT THE PHONE-THINGY WAS MADE OUT OF CANDY...
FINN! IT'S WORKING!
HAHA, HEY FLAME PRINCESS!
AAH- FLAME PRINCESS?!
OOH...
AND SHE BURNED THE PHONE-THINGY WITH HER FLAME-HANDS?
YEAH,
BUT IT GOT ALL CARAMELIZED.
AND NOW IT'S DELICIOUS!!
FINN!

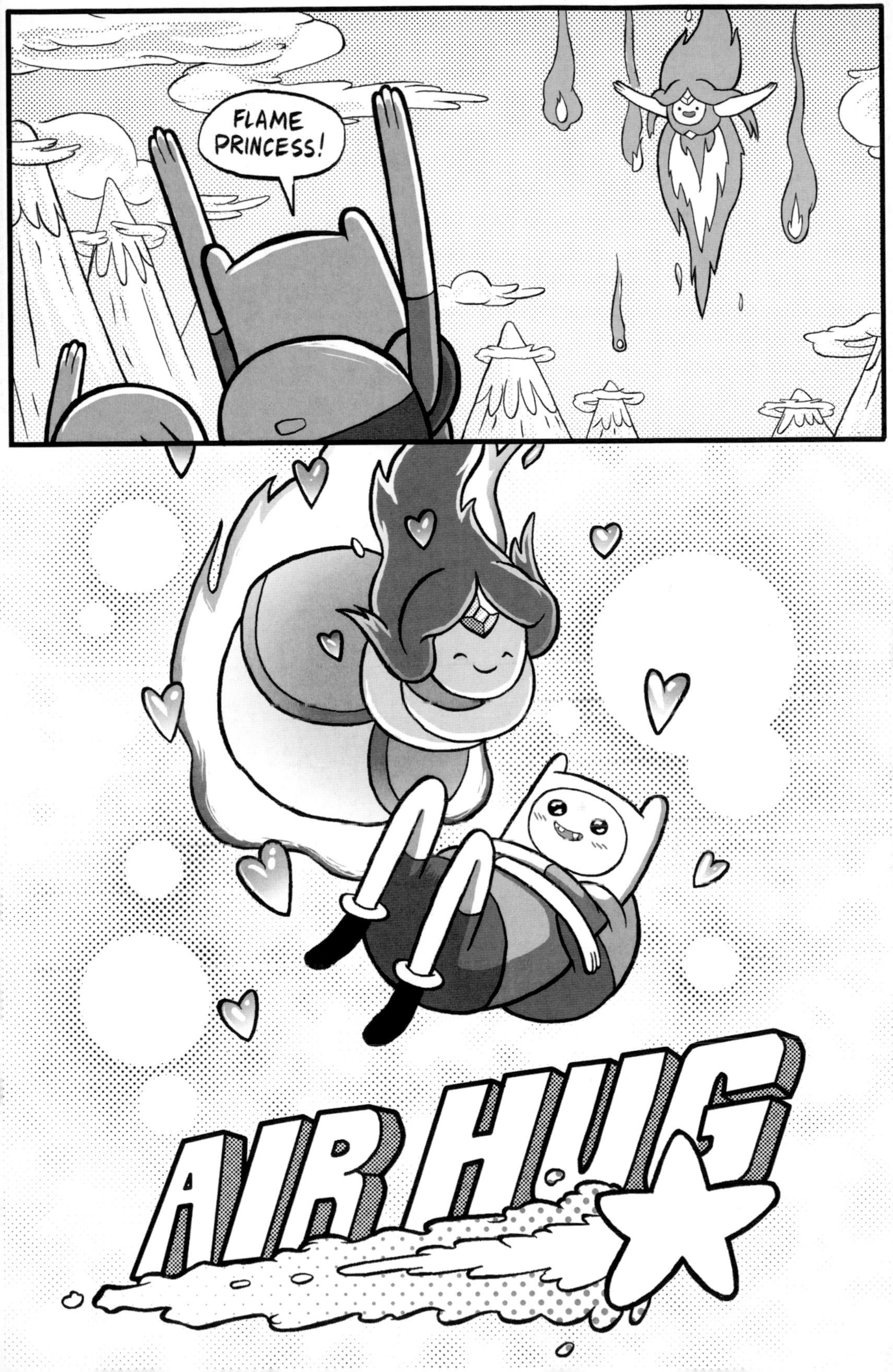
FLAME PRINCESS!
AIR HUG

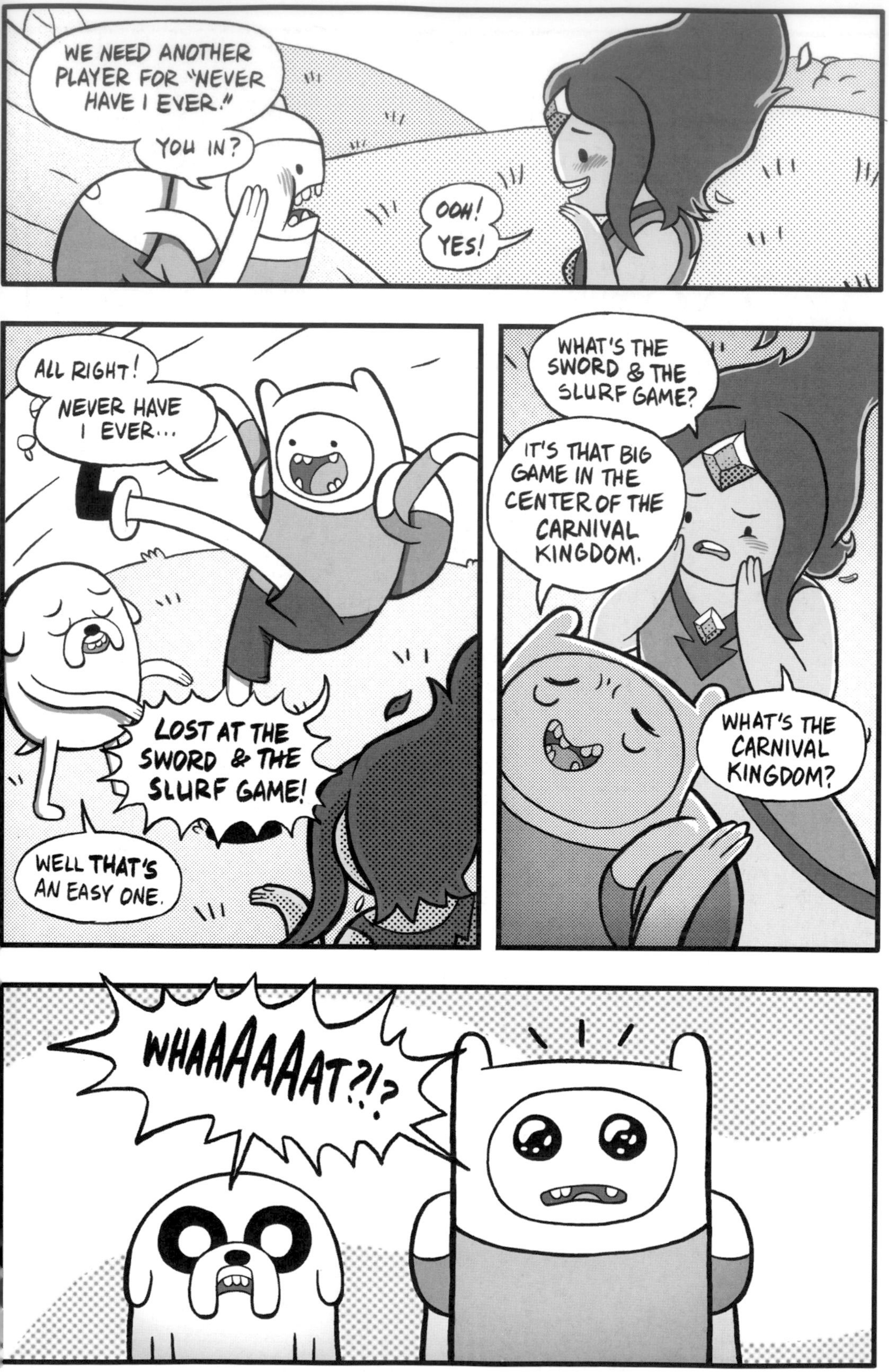

WE NEED ANOTHER PLAYER FOR "NEVER HAVE I EVER."
YOU IN?
OOH! YES!
ALL RIGHT!
NEVER HAVE I EVER...
LOST AT THE SWORD & THE SLURF GAME!
WELL THAT'S AN EASY ONE.
WHAT'S THE SWORD & THE SLURF GAME?
IT'S THAT BIG GAME IN THE CENTER OF THE CARNIVAL KINGDOM.
WHAT'S THE CARNIVAL KINGDOM?
WHAAAAAAAT?!?

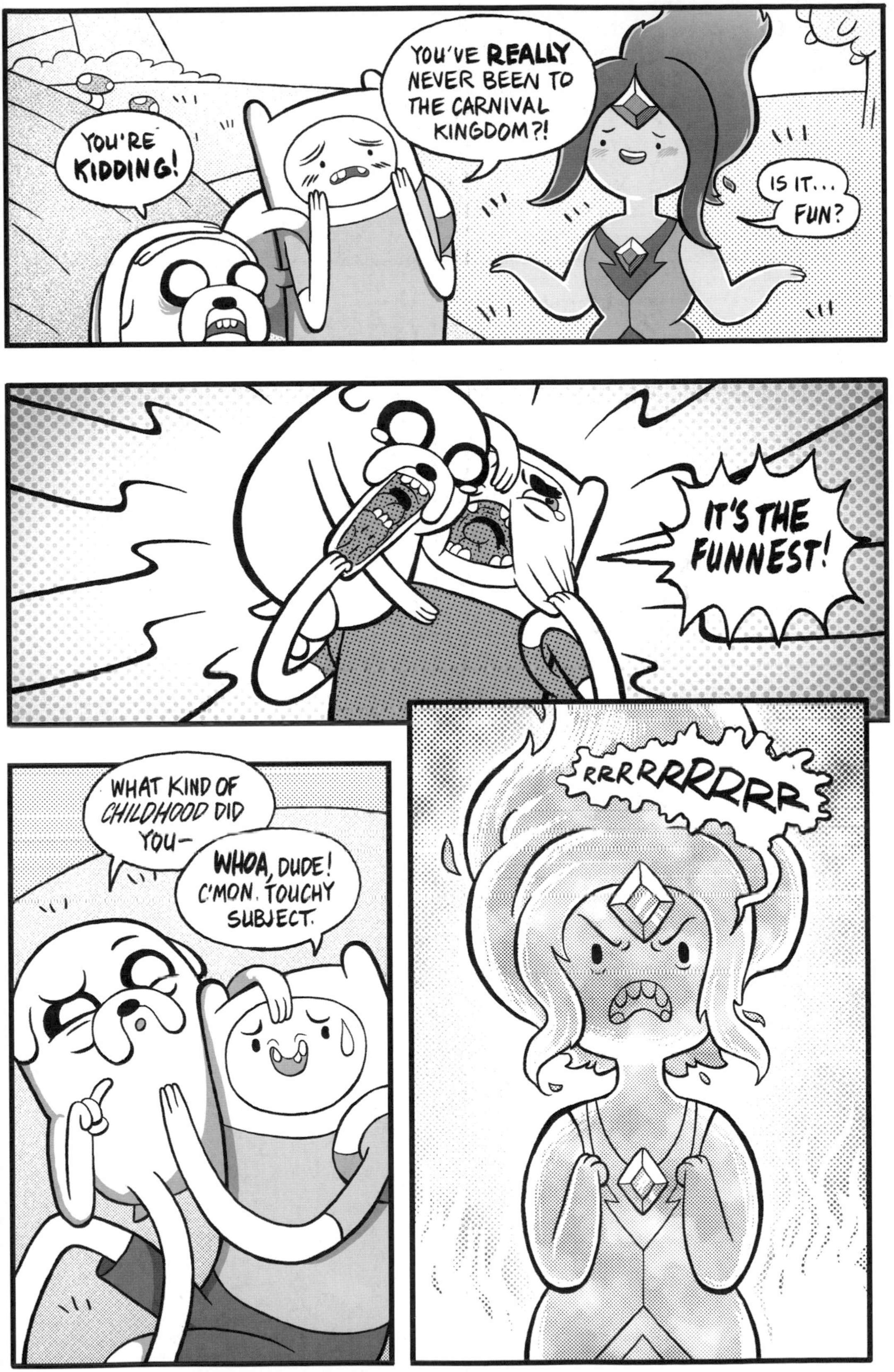
YOU'RE KIDDING!
YOU'VE REALLY NEVER BEEN TO THE CARNIVAL KINGDOM?!
IS IT... FUN?
IT'S THE FUNNEST!
WHAT KIND OF CHILDHOOD DID YOU–
WHOA, DUDE! C'MON. TOUCHY SUBJECT.
RRRRRRRRRR

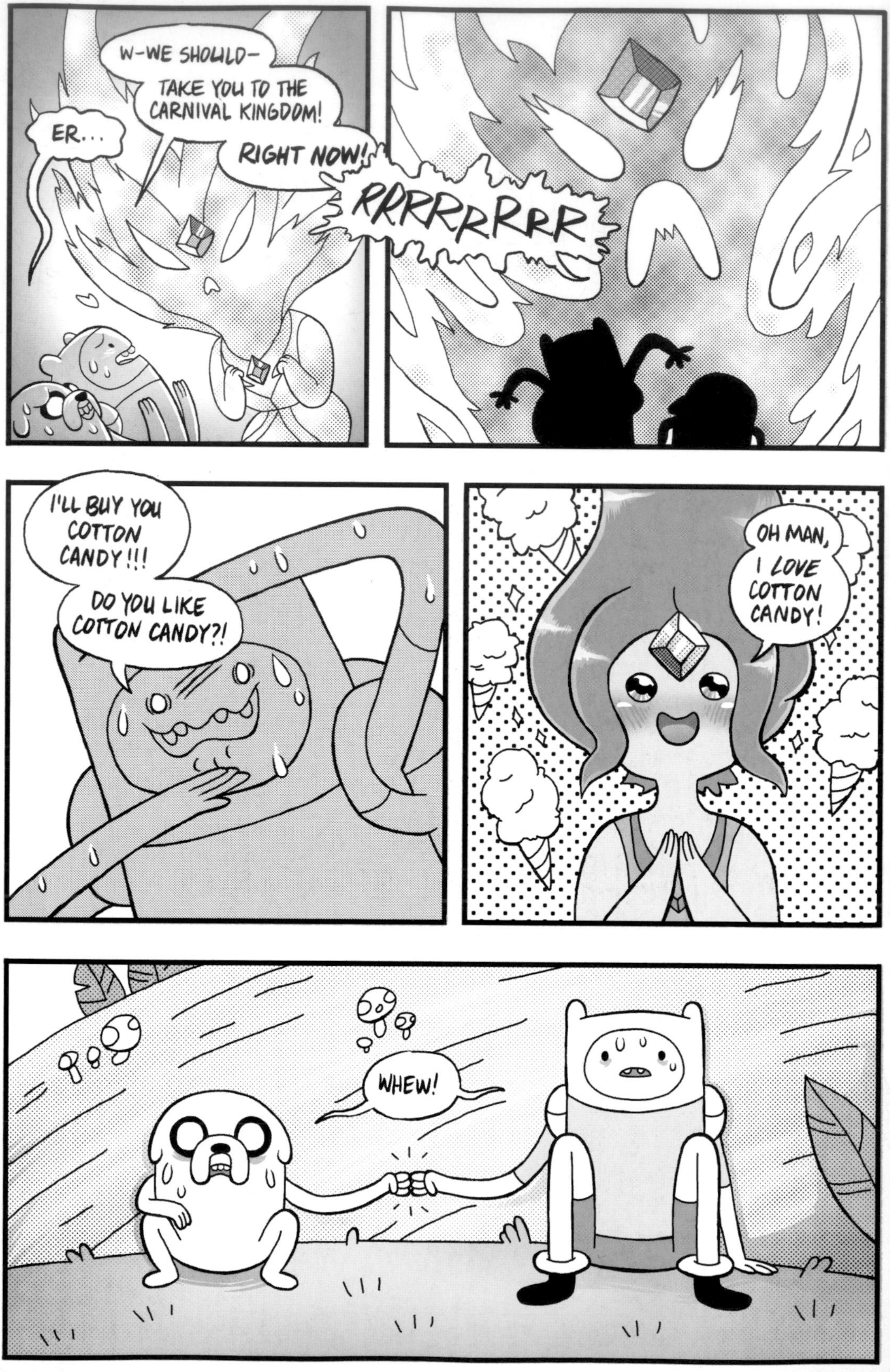
W-WE SHOULD-
TAKE YOU TO THE CARNIVAL KINGDOM!
ER...
RIGHT NOW!
RRRRRRRR
I'LL BUY YOU COTTON CANDY!!!
DO YOU LIKE COTTON CANDY?!
OH MAN, I LOVE COTTON CANDY!
WHEW!

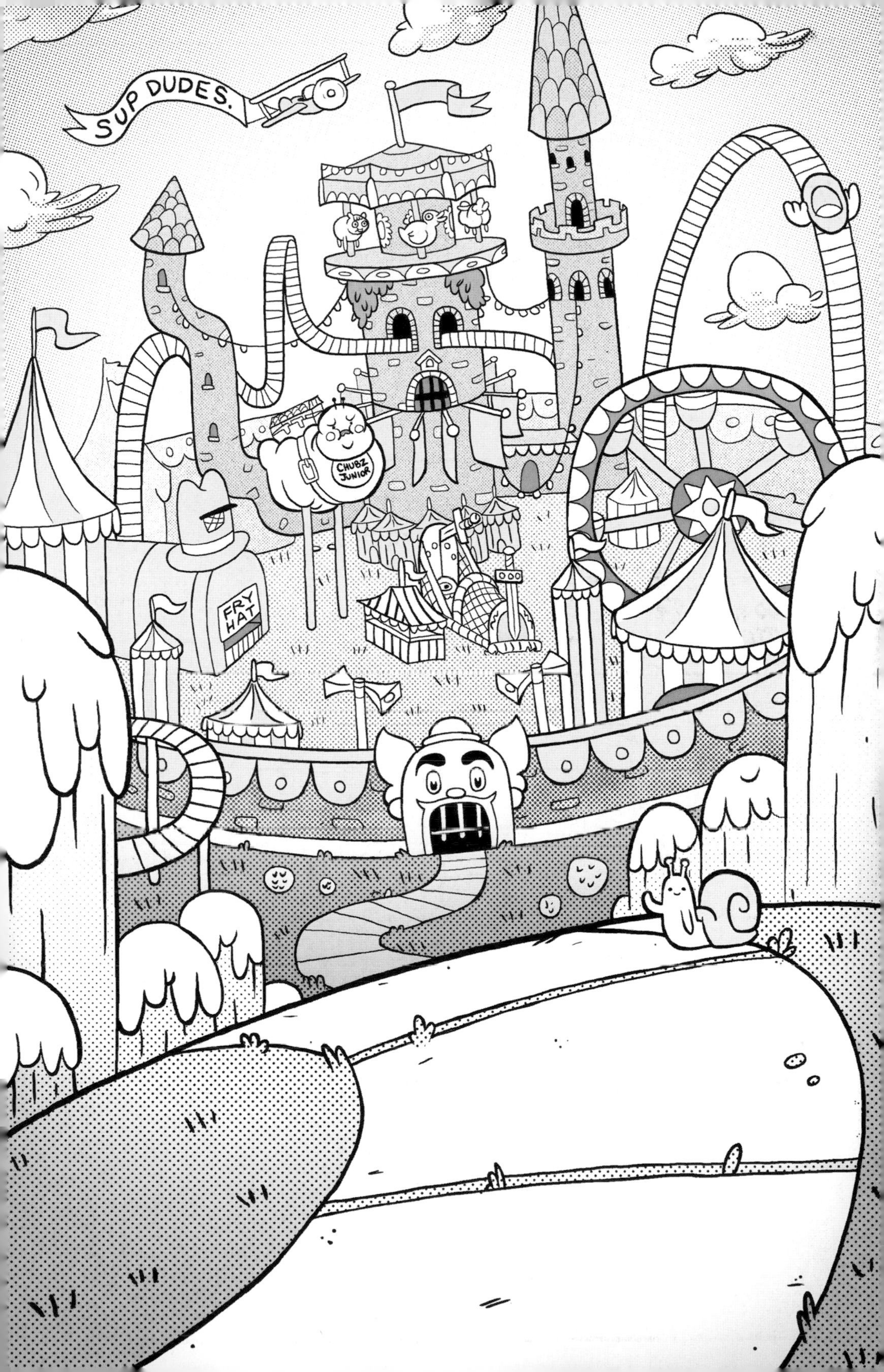

SUP DUDES.
CHUBZ JUNIOR
FRY HAT

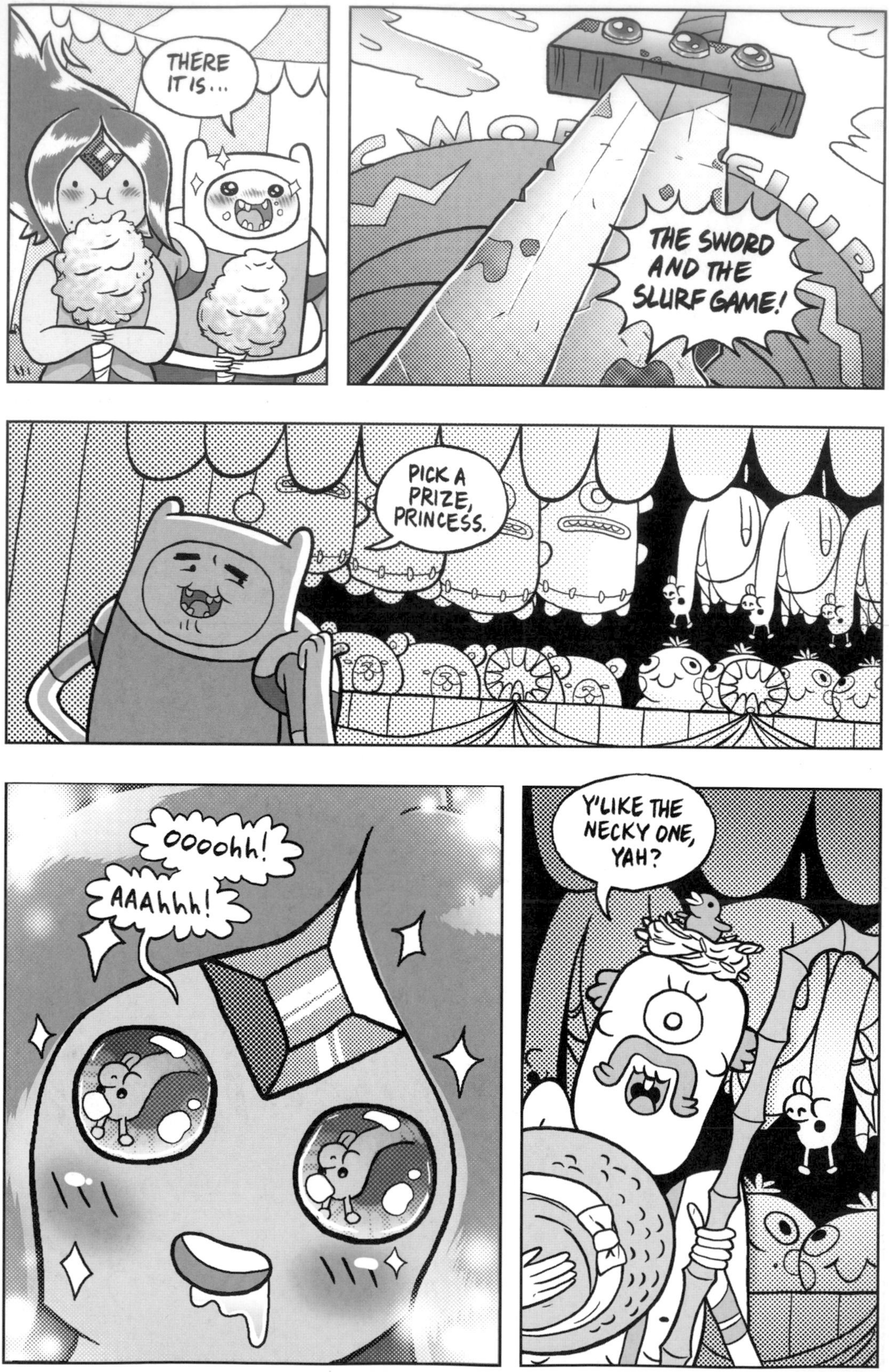
THERE IT IS...
THE SWORD AND THE SLURF GAME!
PICK A PRIZE, PRINCESS.
OOOOhh!
AAAhhh!
Y'LIKE THE NECKY ONE, YAH?

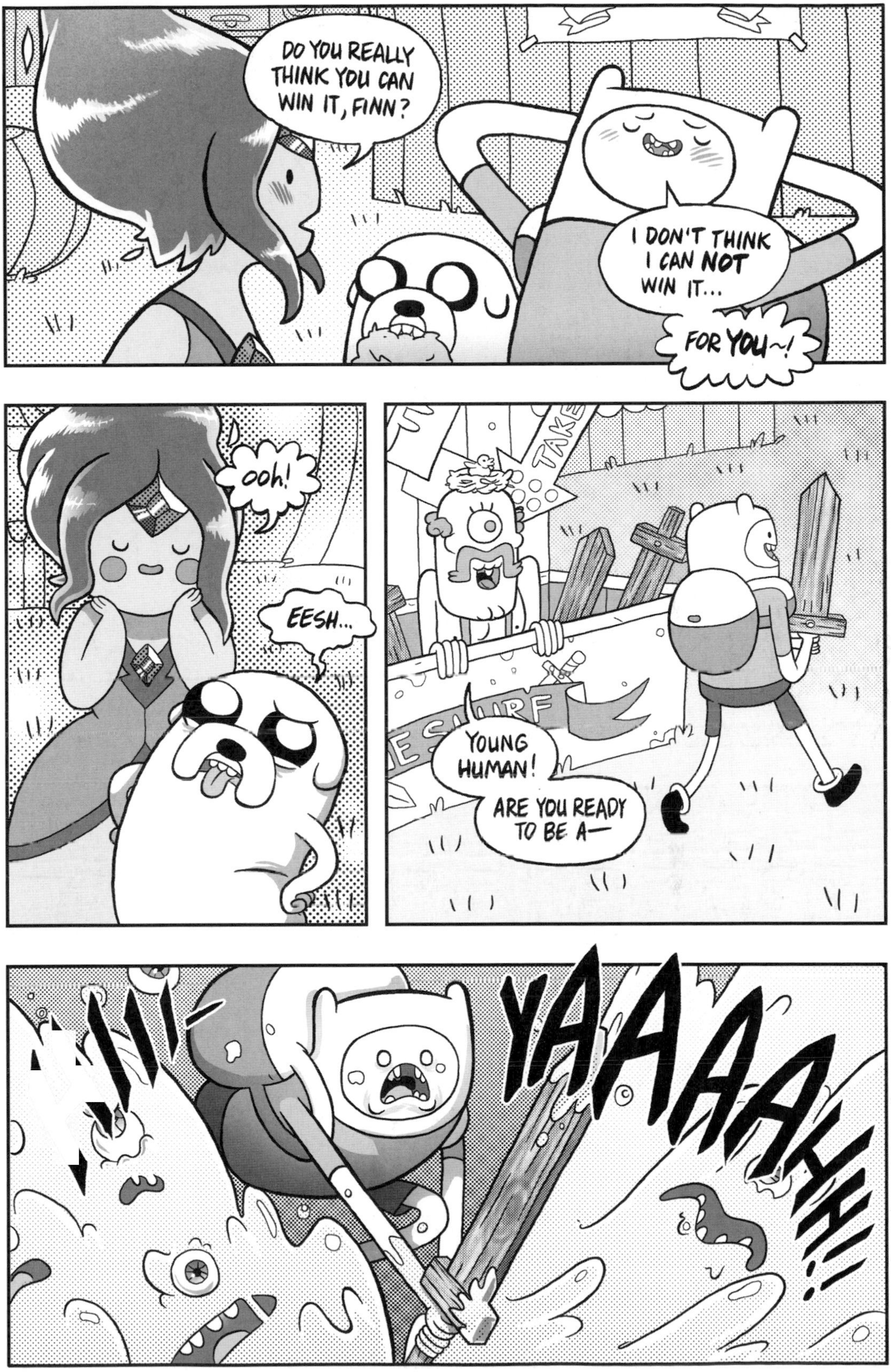
DO YOU REALLY THINK YOU CAN WIN IT, FINN?
I DON'T THINK I CAN NOT WIN IT...
FOR YOU~!
OOH!
EESH...
YOUNG HUMAN!
ARE YOU READY TO BE A—
YAAAAHH!!!

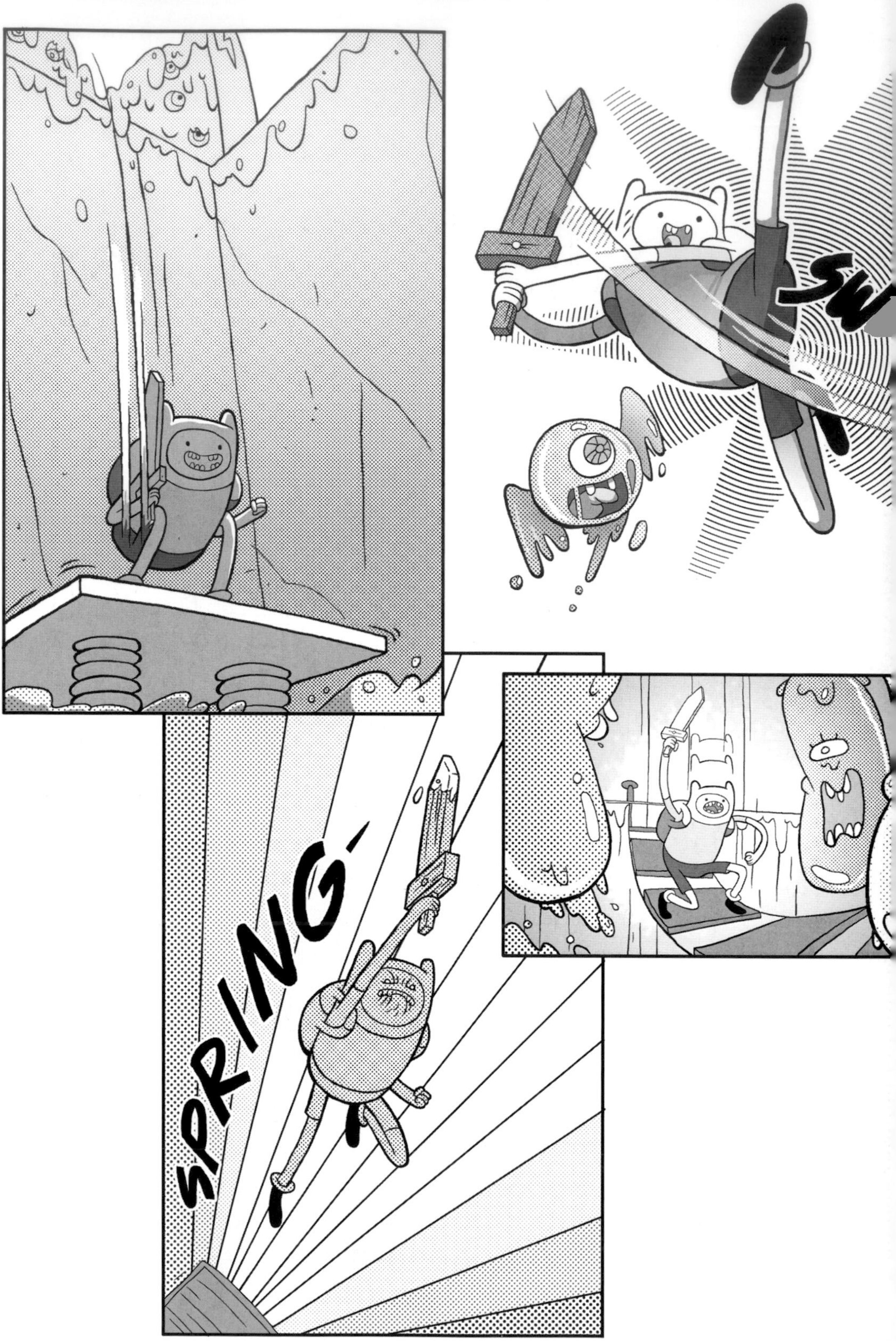

SW
SPRING-

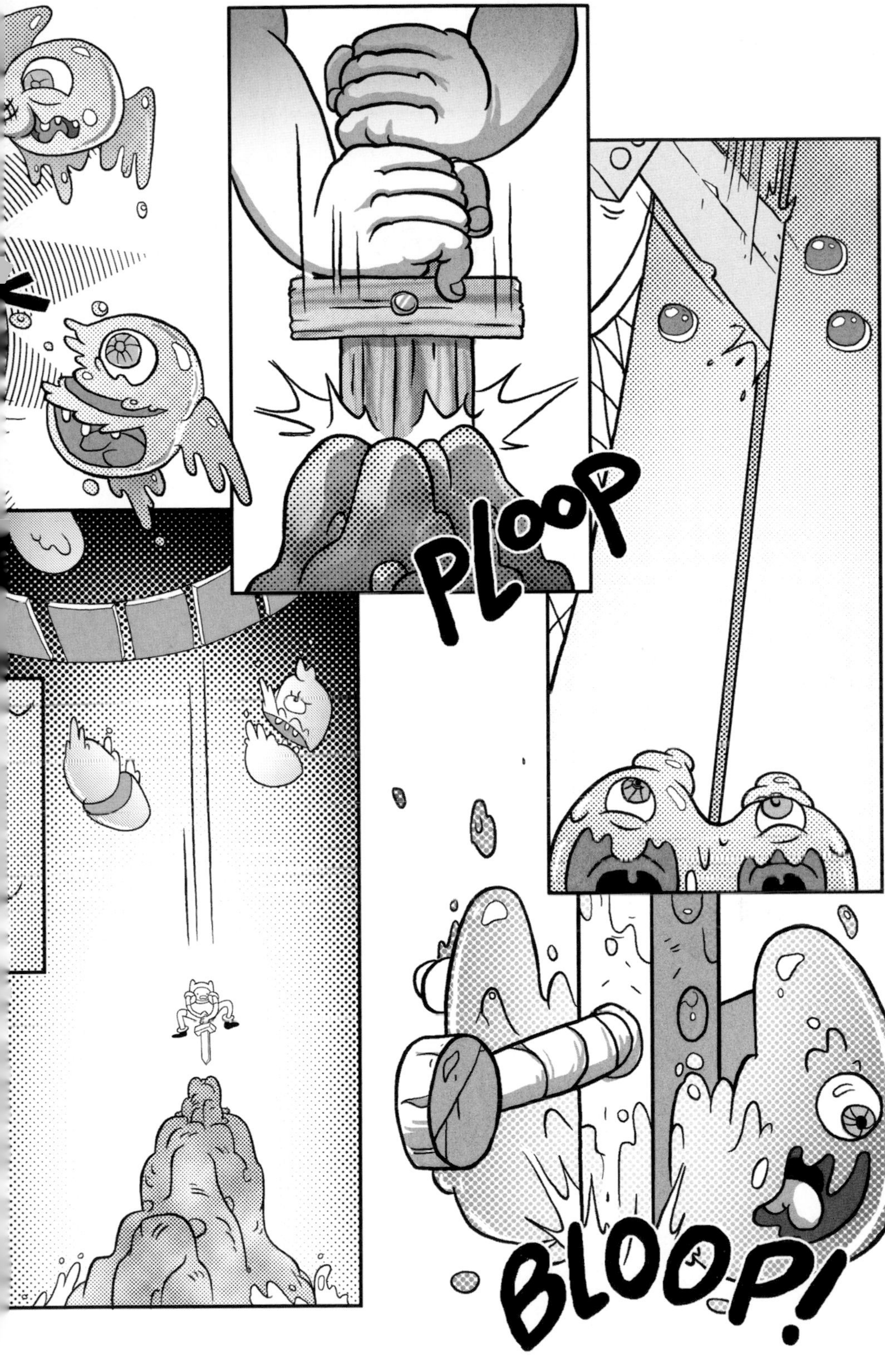
PLOOP
BLOOP!

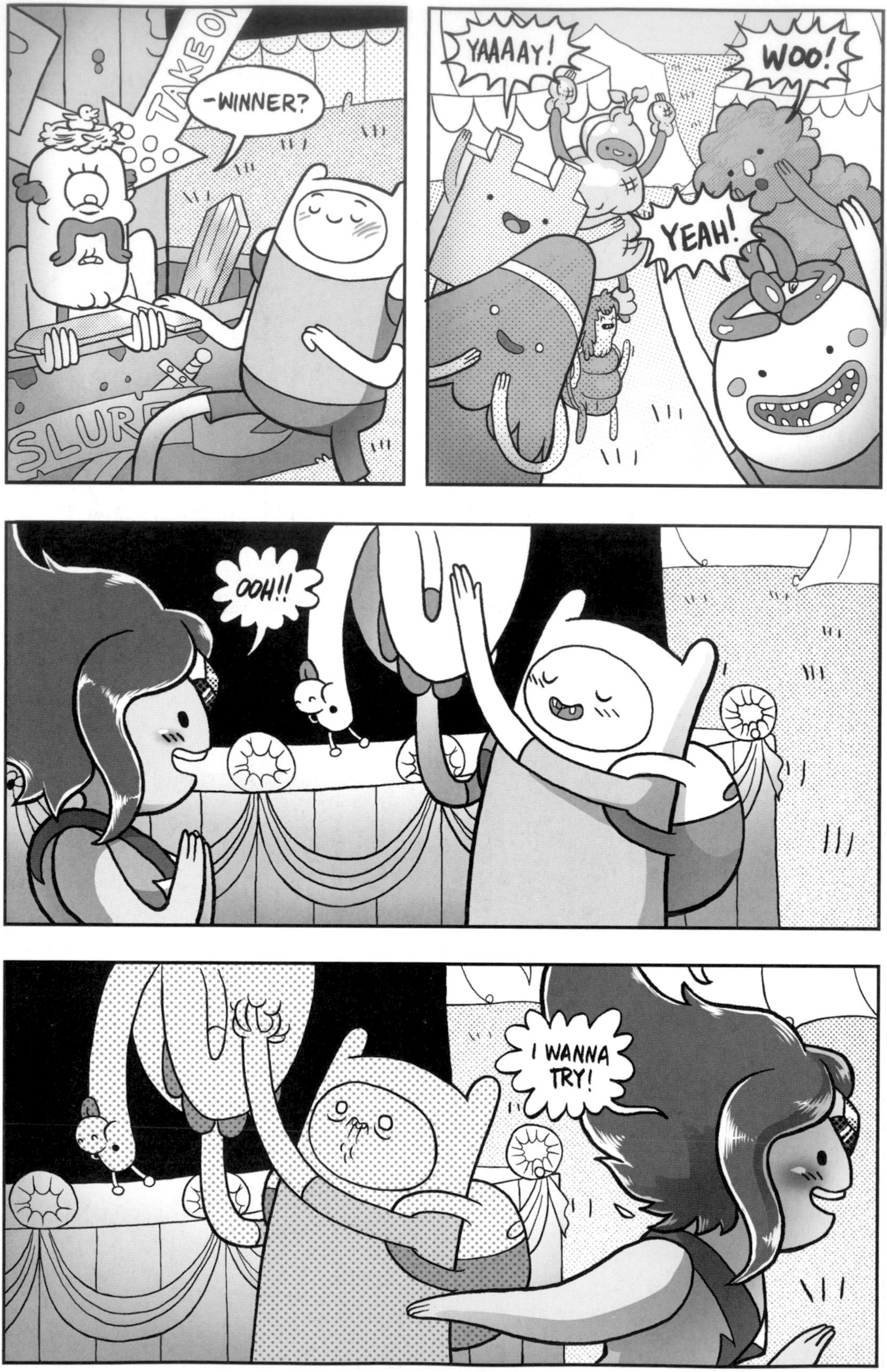
TAKE OV
-WINNER?
SLUR
YAAAAY!
WOO!
YEAH!
OOH!!
I WANNA TRY!

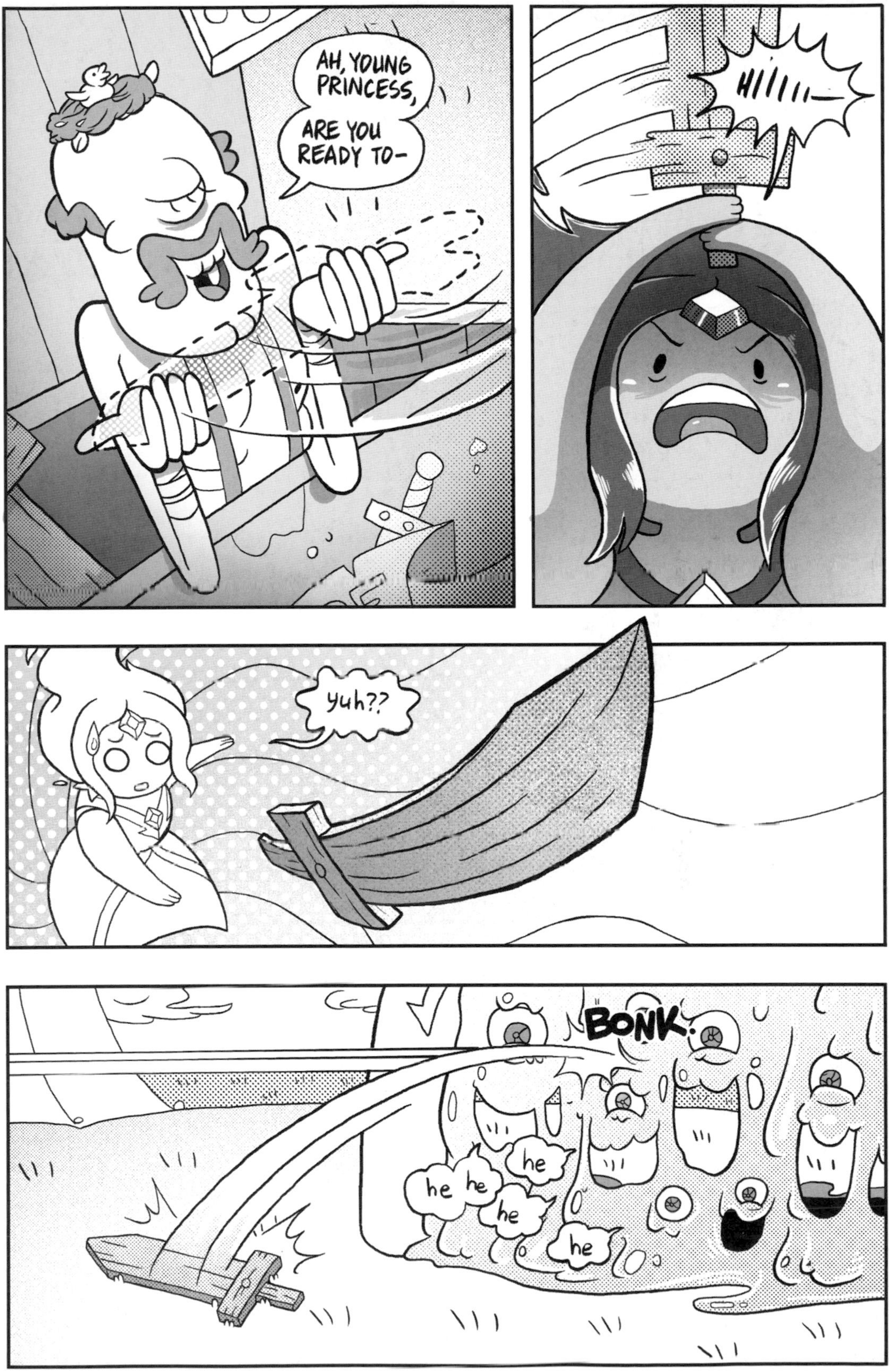
AH, YOUNG PRINCESS,
ARE YOU READY TO-
HI!!!!—
yuh??
BONK.
he
he
he
he
he

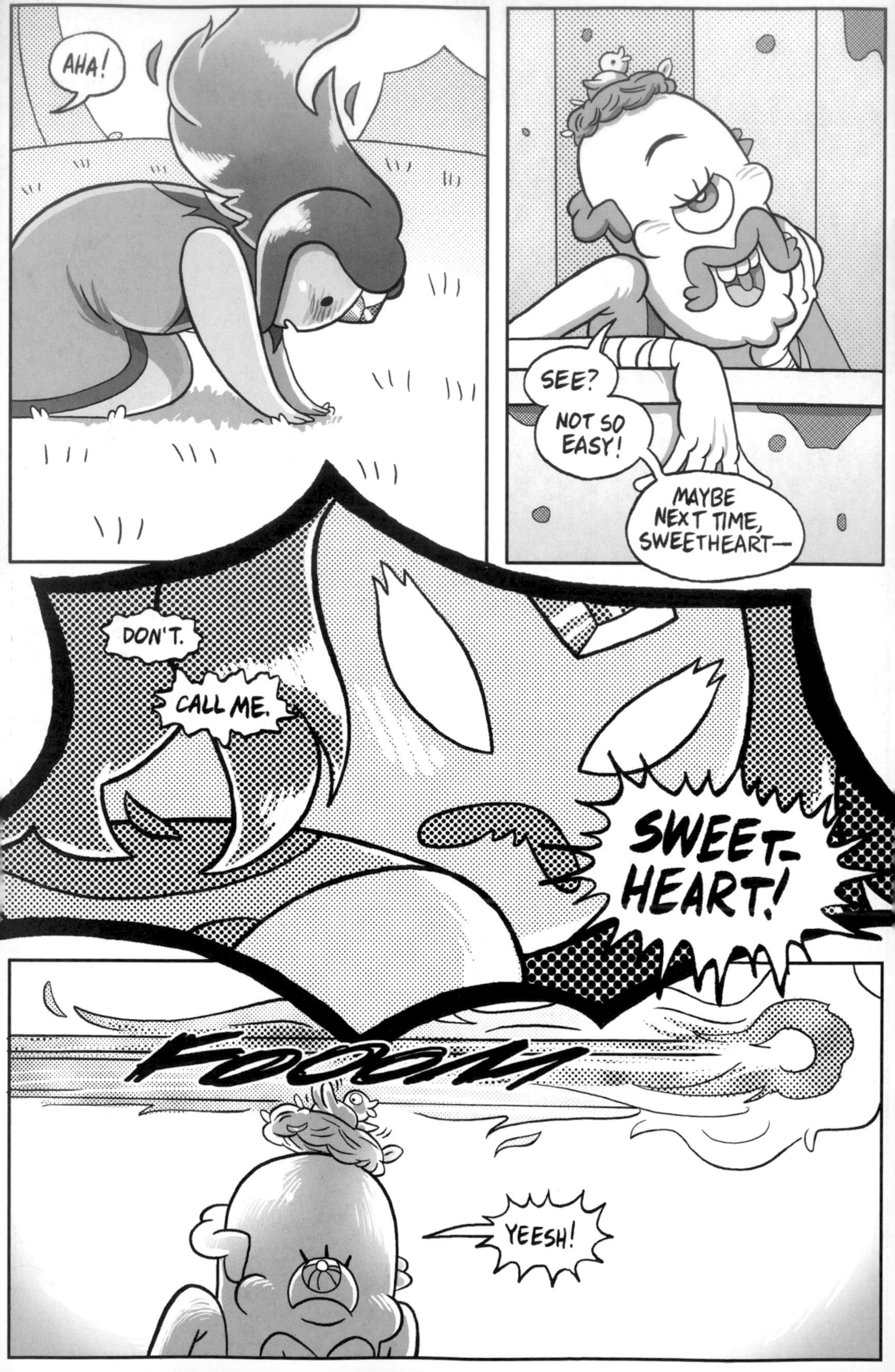
AHA!
SEE?
NOT SO EASY!
MAYBE NEXT TIME, SWEETHEART—
DON'T.
CALL ME.
SWEET-HEART!
KOOOM
YEESH!

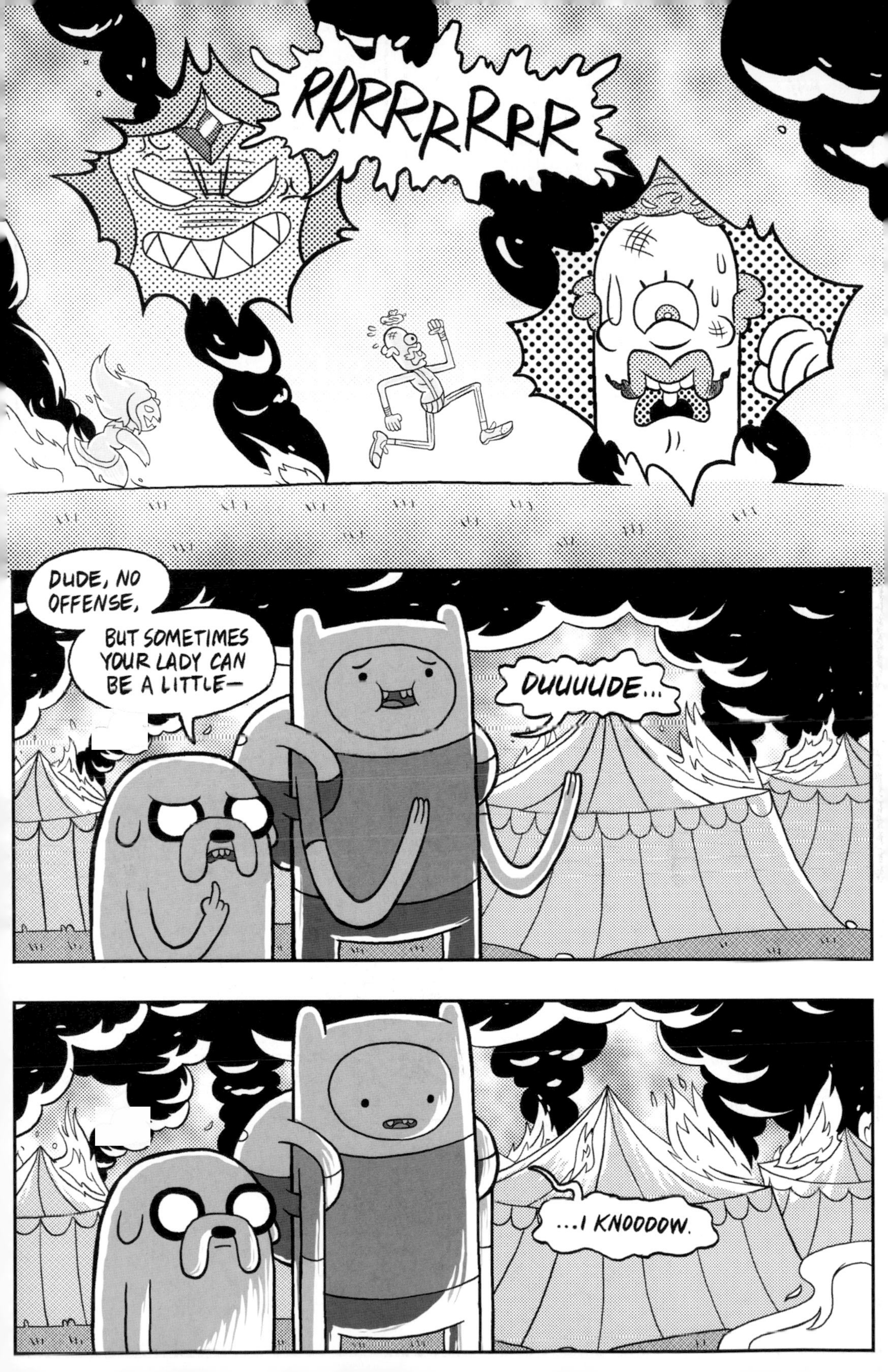
RRRRRRRRR
DUDE, NO OFFENSE,
BUT SOMETIMES YOUR LADY CAN BE A LITTLE—
DUUUUDE...
...I KNOOOOW.

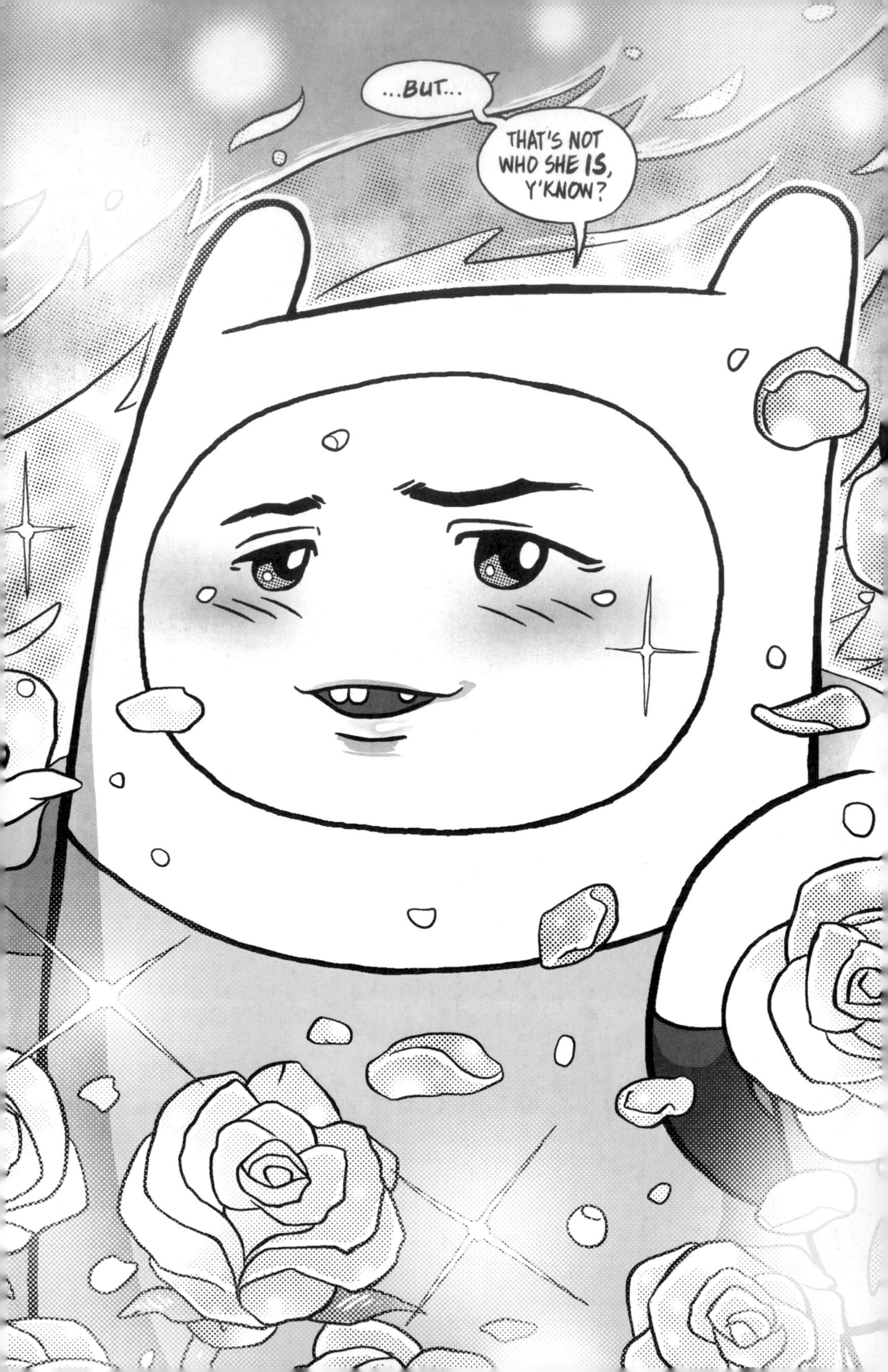
...BUT...
THAT'S NOT WHO SHE IS, Y'KNOW?

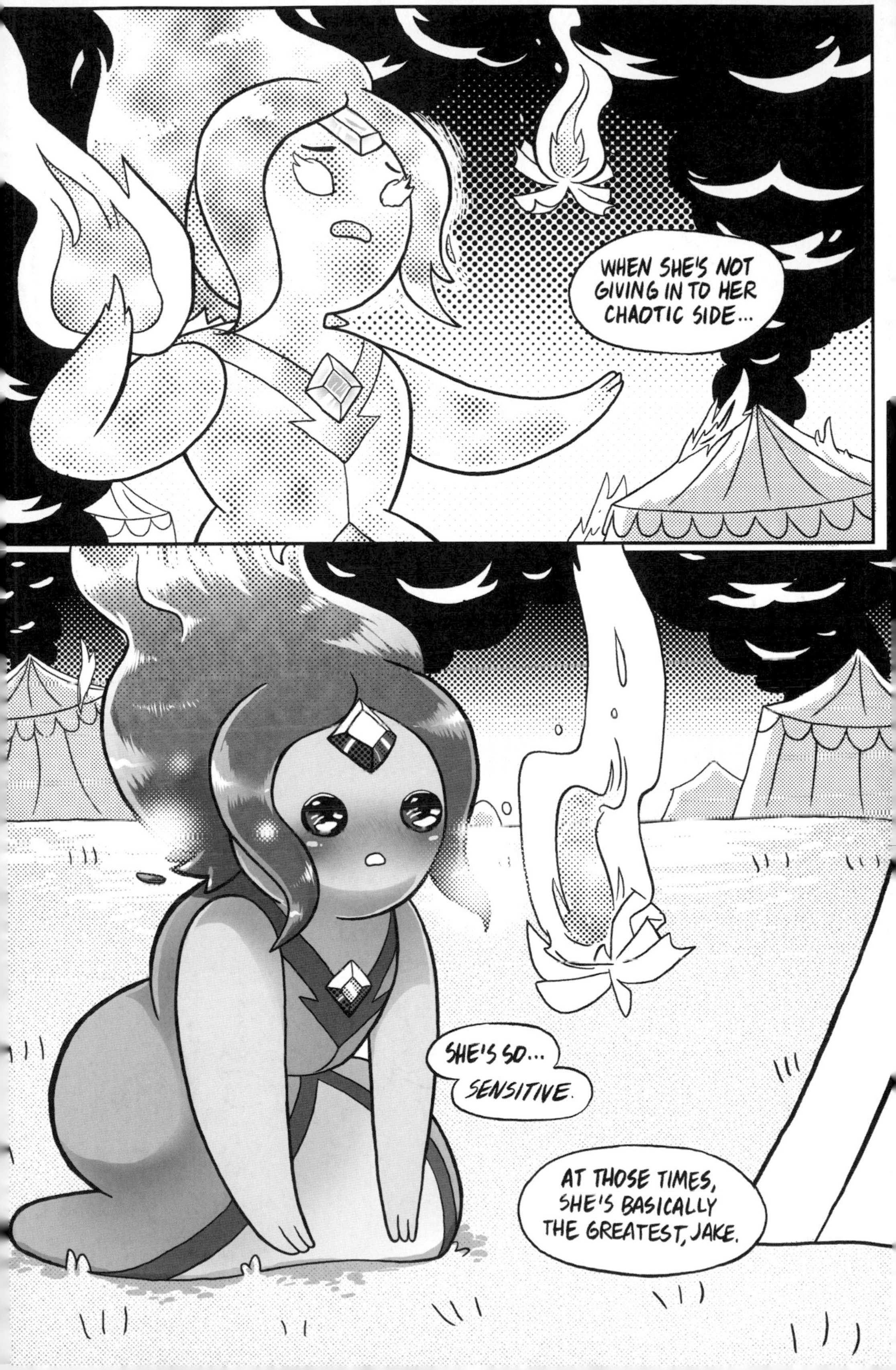
WHEN SHE'S NOT GIVING IN TO HER CHAOTIC SIDE...
SHE'S SO... SENSITIVE.
AT THOSE TIMES, SHE'S BASICALLY THE GREATEST, JAKE.

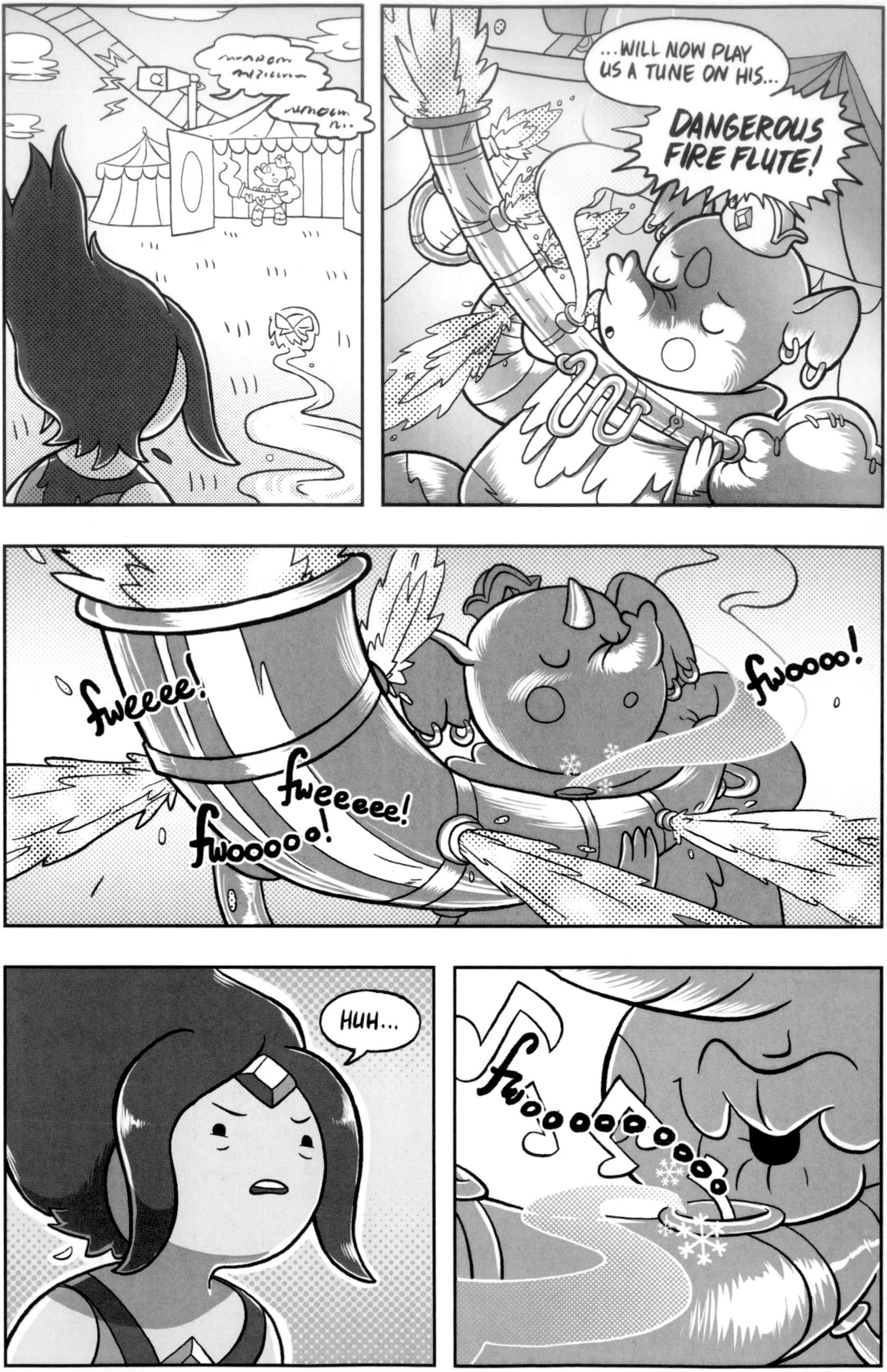
...WILL NOW PLAY US A TUNE ON HIS...
DANGEROUS FIRE FLUTE!
fweeee!
fwoooo!
fweeeee!
fwooooo!
HUH...
fwooooooooo

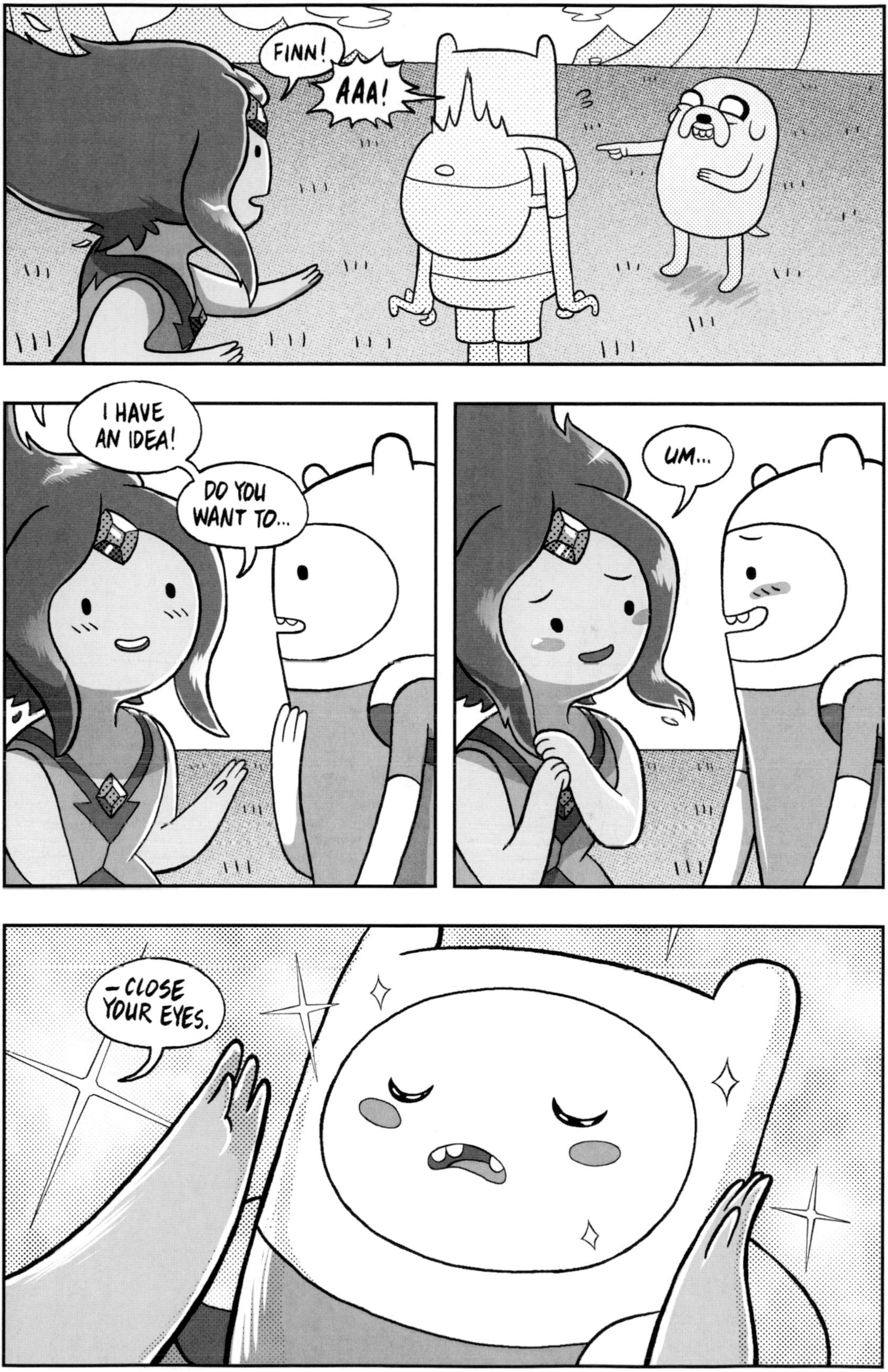
FINN!
AAA!
I HAVE AN IDEA!
DO YOU WANT TO...
UM...
–CLOSE YOUR EYES.

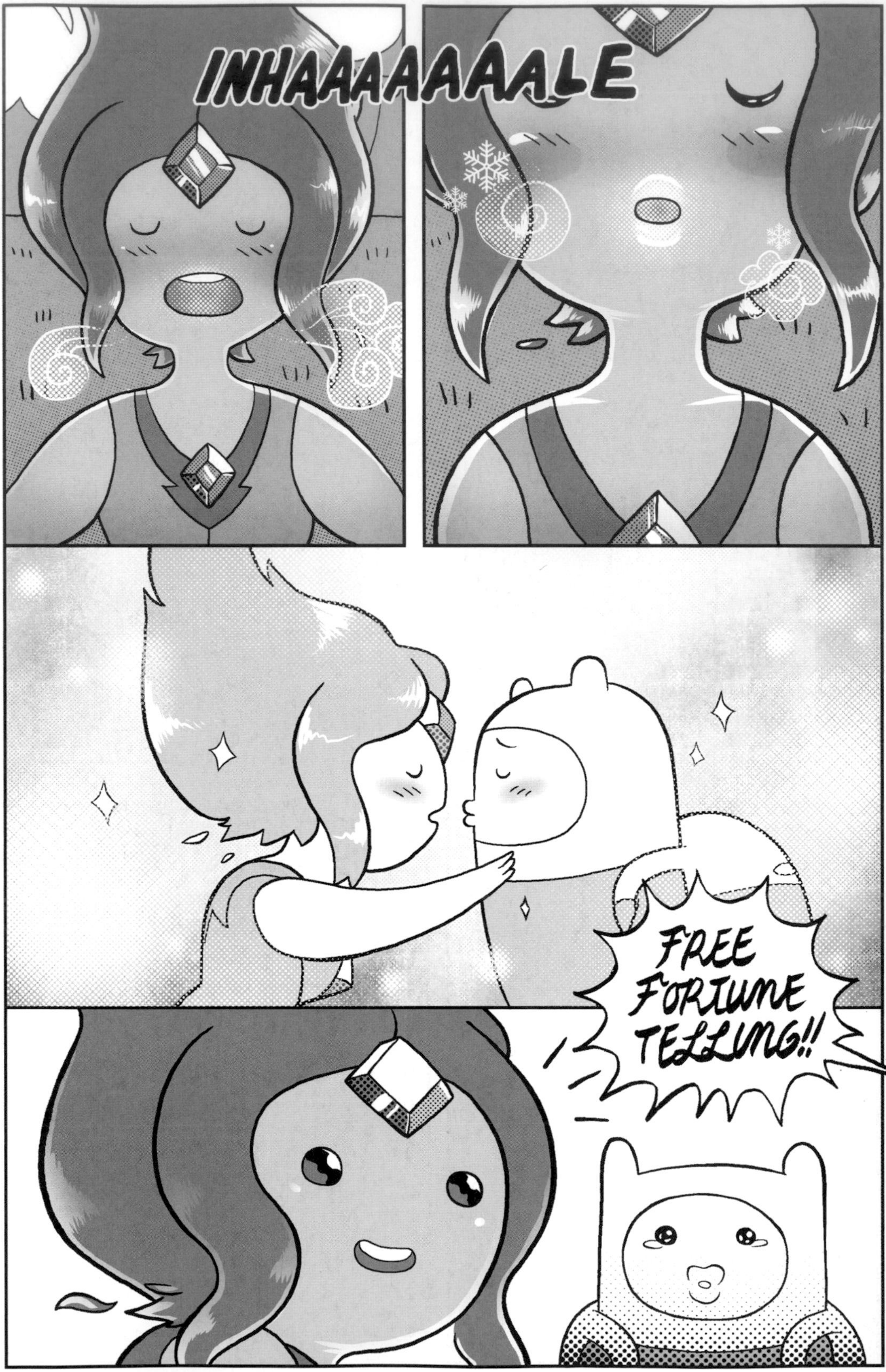
INHAAAAAAAALE
FREE FORTUNE TELLING!!

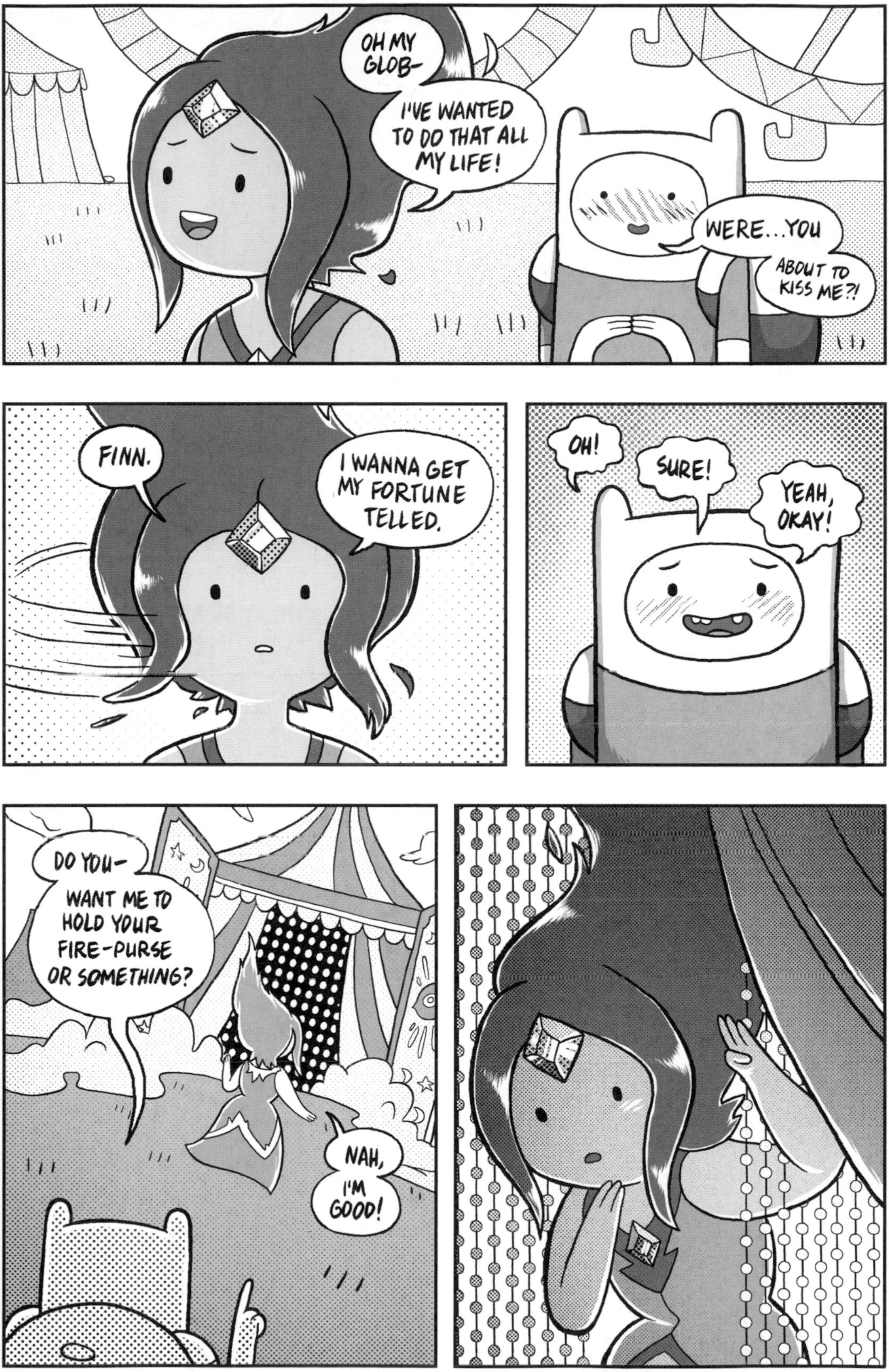
OH MY GLOB-
I'VE WANTED TO DO THAT ALL MY LIFE!
WERE...YOU
ABOUT TO KISS ME?!
FINN.
I WANNA GET MY FORTUNE TELLED.
OH!
SURE!
YEAH, OKAY!
DO YOU-
WANT ME TO HOLD YOUR FIRE-PURSE OR SOMETHING?
NAH, I'M GOOD!

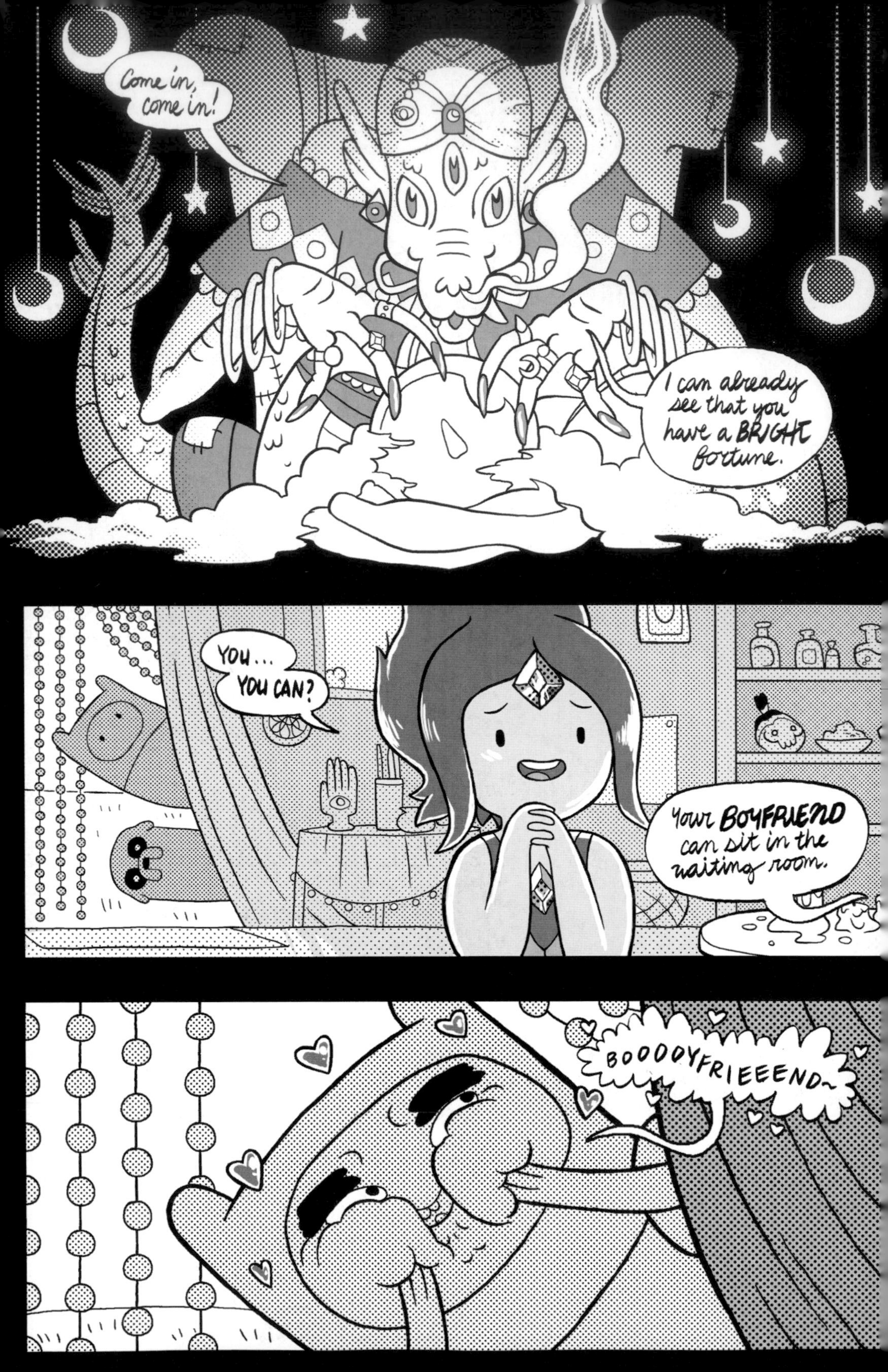
Come in, come in!
I can already see that you have a BRIGHT fortune.
YOU... YOU CAN?
Your BOYFRIEND can sit in the waiting room.
BOODDDYFRIEEEEND~

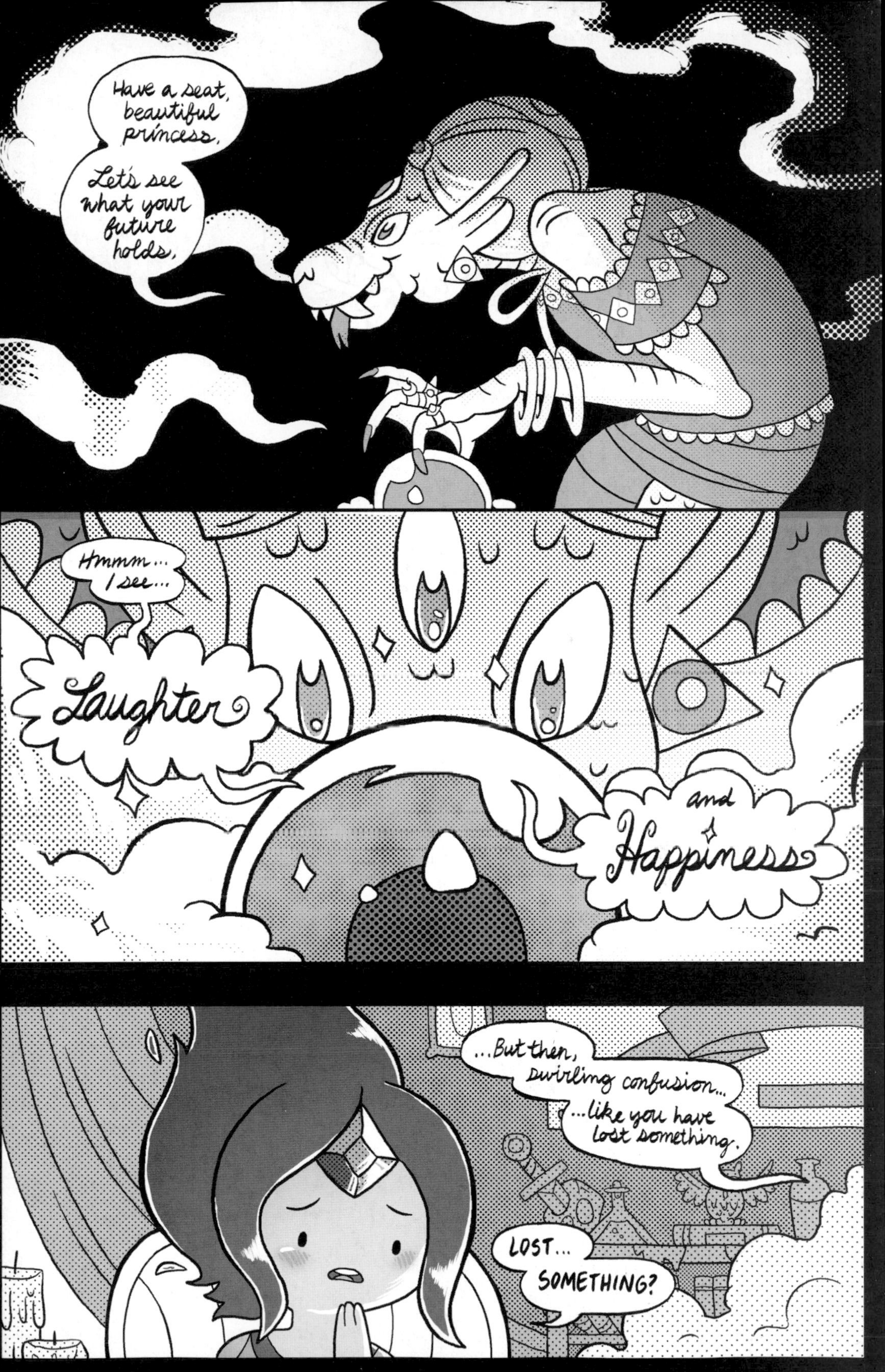

Have a seat, beautiful princess.
Let's see what your future holds.
Hmmm... I see...
Laughter
and Happiness
...But then, swirling confusion...
...like you have lost something.
LOST... SOMETHING?

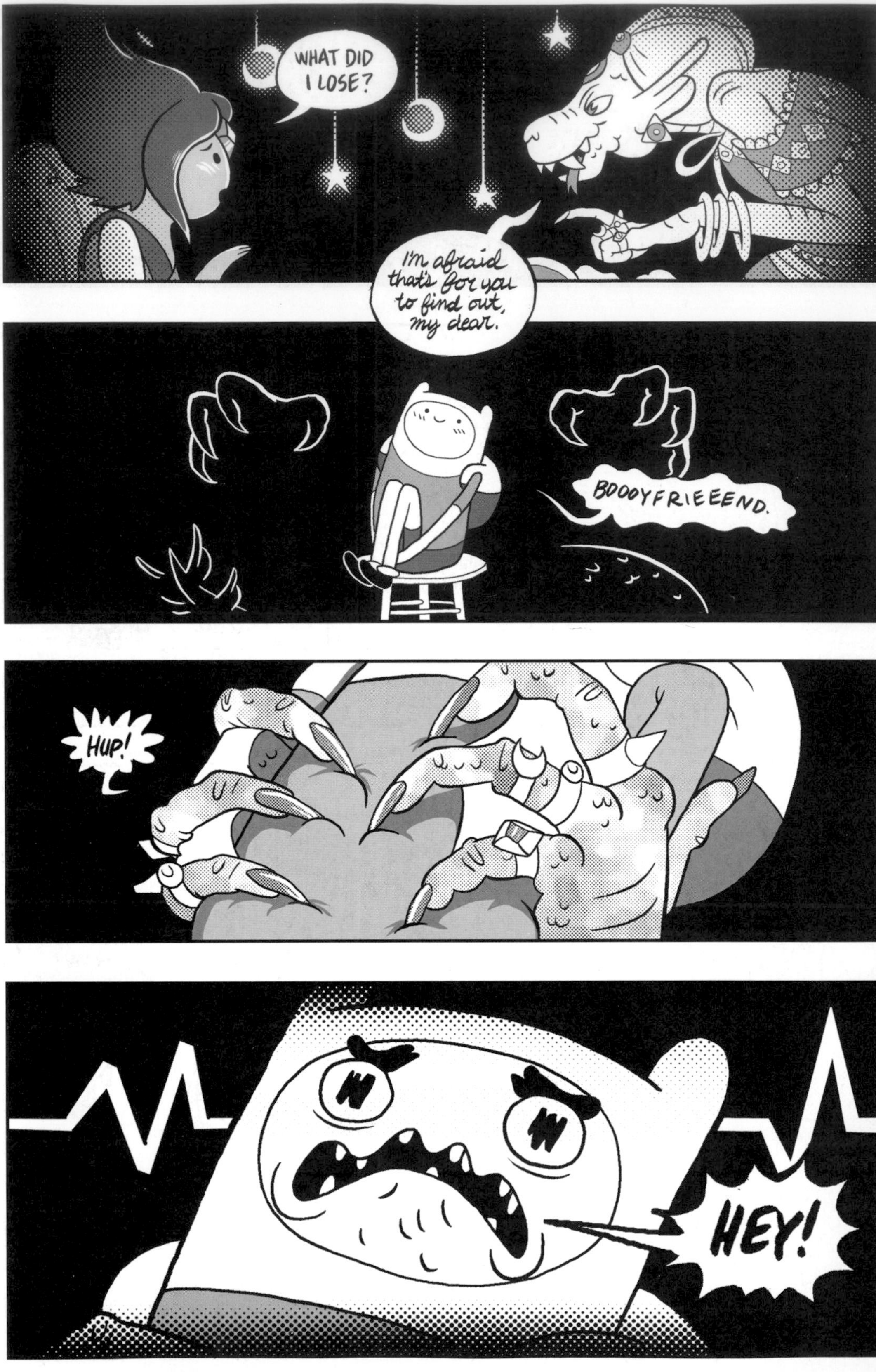
WHAT DID I LOSE?
I'm afraid that's for you to find out, my dear.
BOOOYFRIEEEND.
HUP!
HEY!

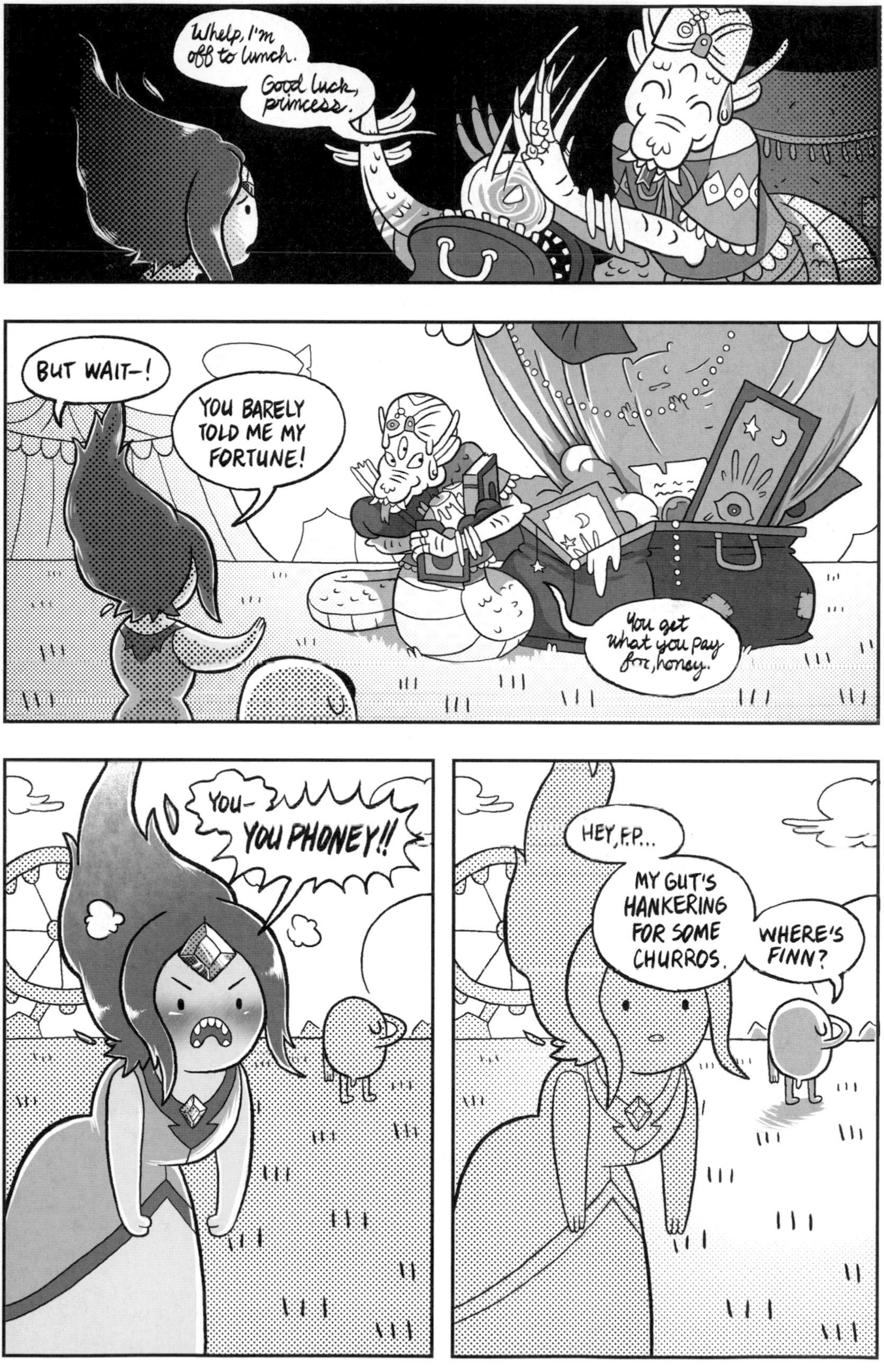
Whelp, I'm off to lunch.
Good luck, princess.
BUT WAIT—!
YOU BARELY TOLD ME MY FORTUNE!
You get what you pay for, honey.
YOU— YOU PHONEY!!
HEY, F.P...
MY GUT'S HANKERING FOR SOME CHURROS.
WHERE'S FINN?

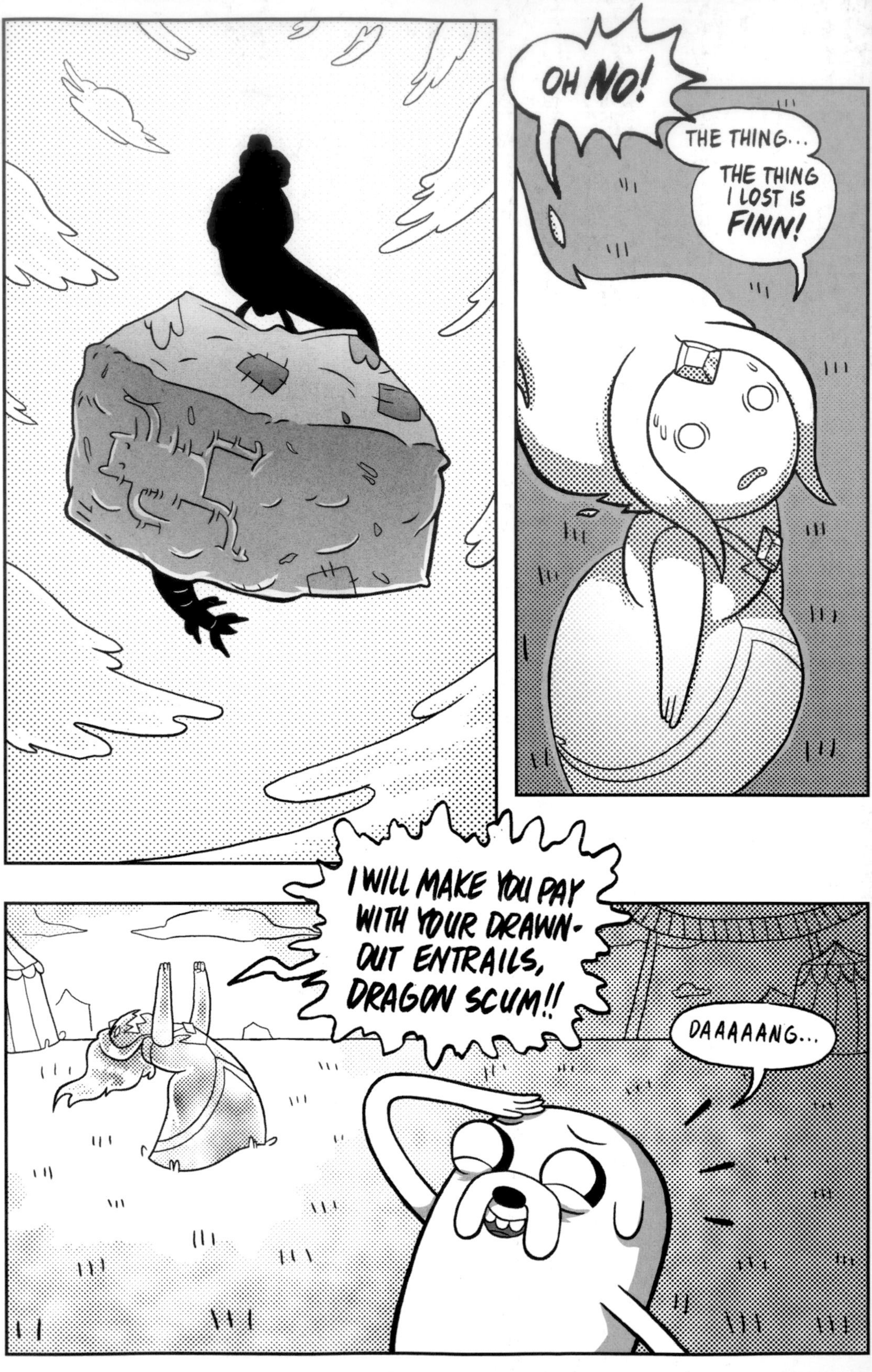
OH NO!
THE THING...
THE THING I LOST IS FINN!
I WILL MAKE YOU PAY WITH YOUR DRAWN-OUT ENTRAILS, DRAGON SCUM!!
DAAAAANG...

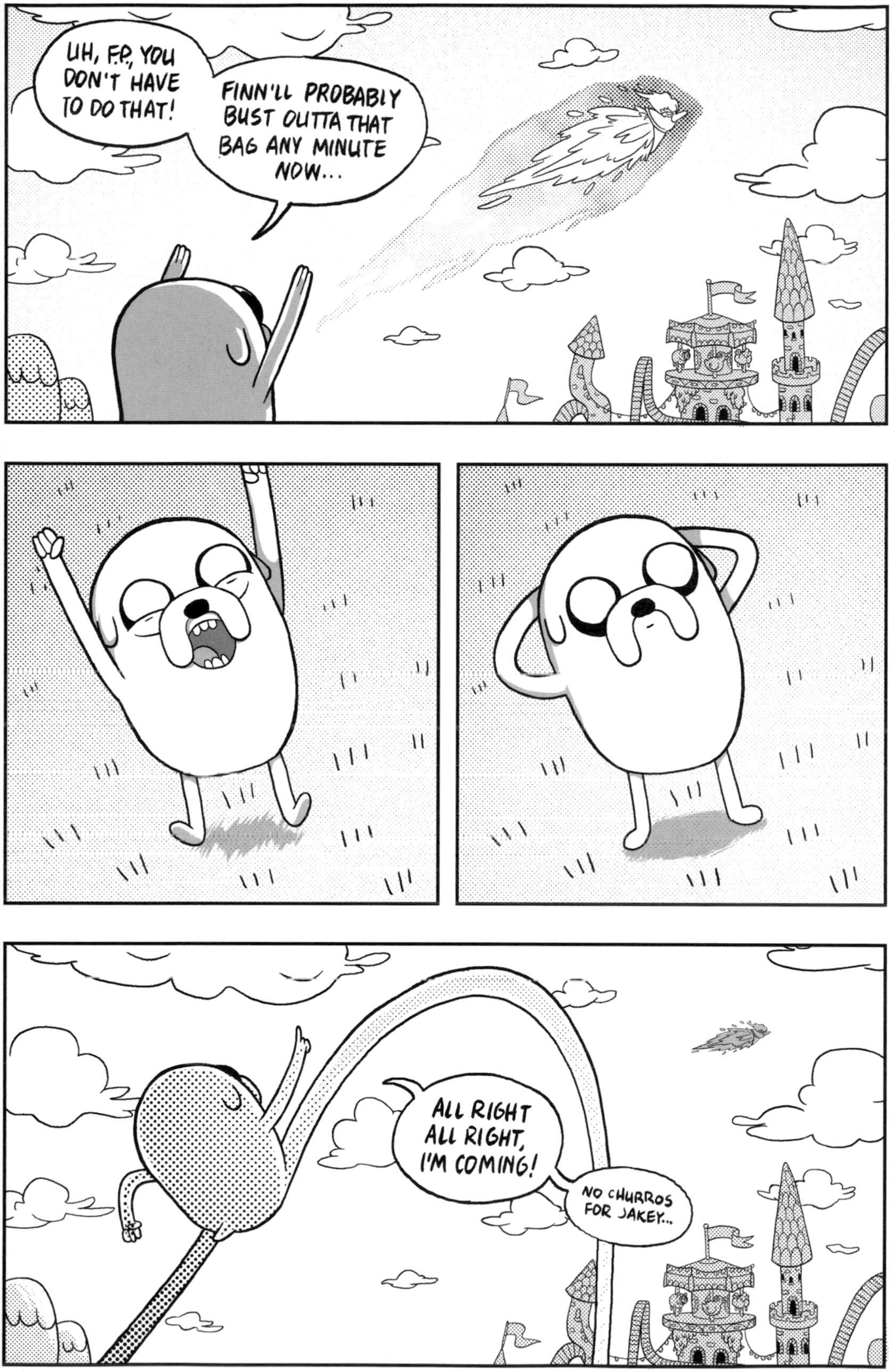
UH, F.P., YOU DON'T HAVE TO DO THAT!
FINN'LL PROBABLY BUST OUTTA THAT BAG ANY MINUTE NOW...
ALL RIGHT ALL RIGHT, I'M COMING!
NO CHURROS FOR JAKEY...

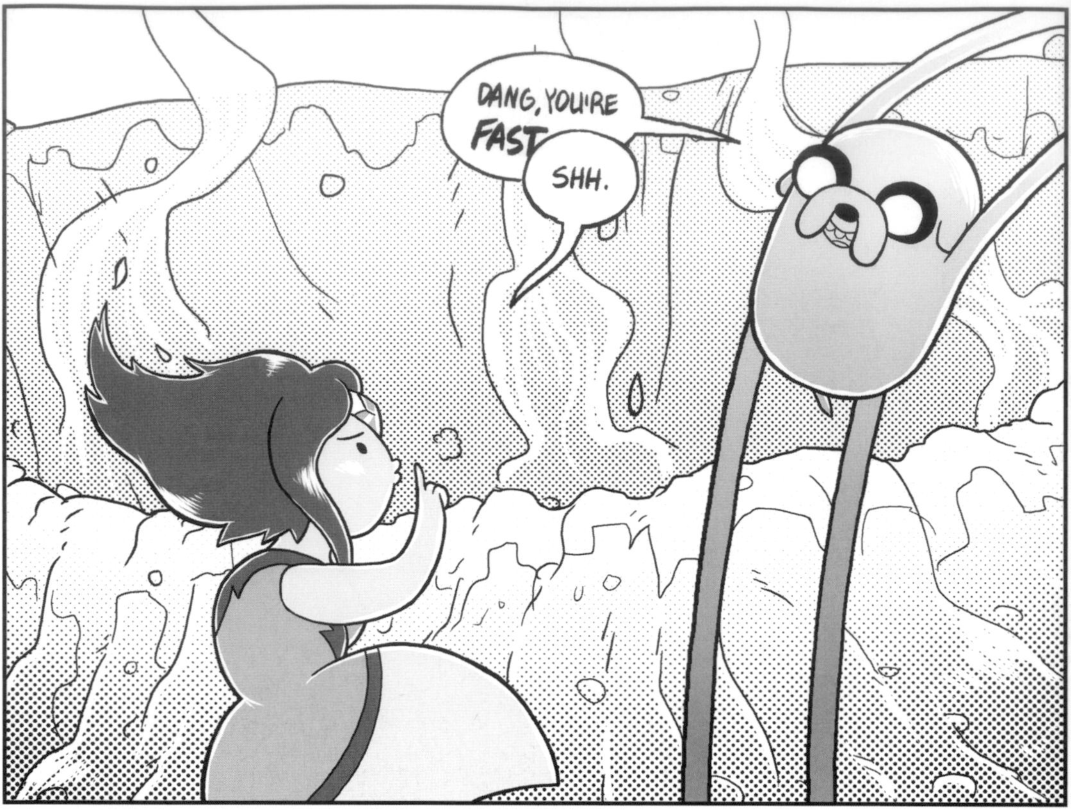
DANG, YOU'RE FAST.
SHH.

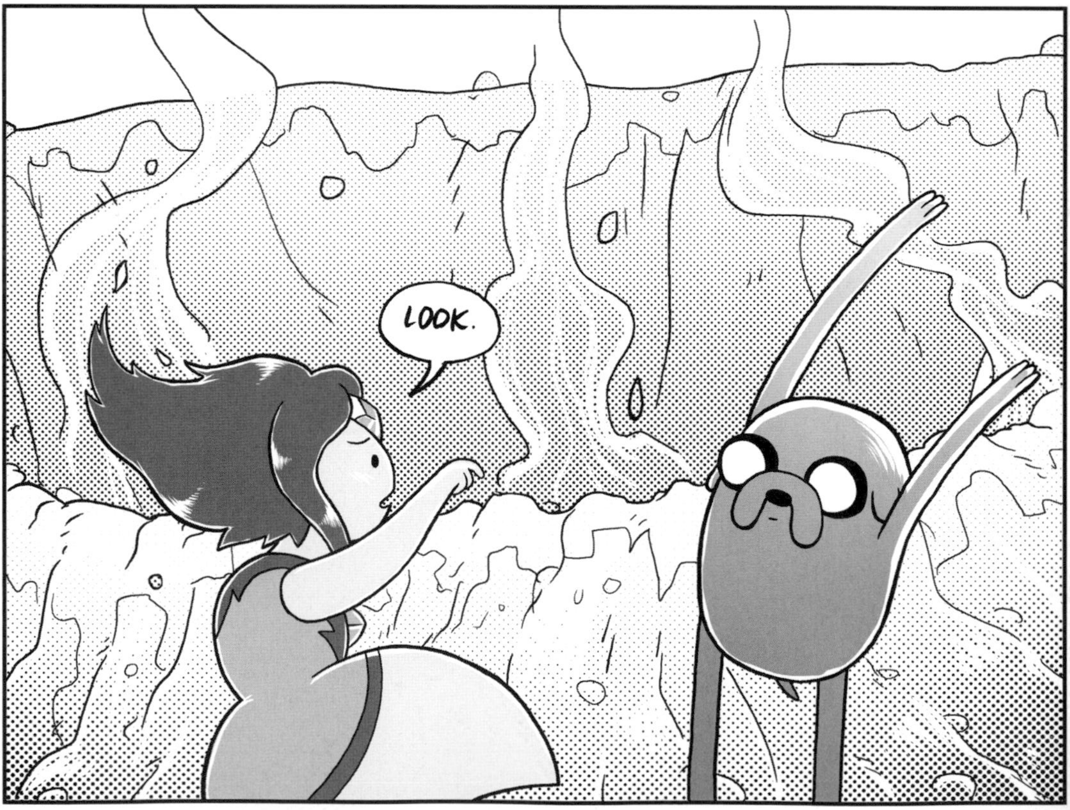
LOOK.

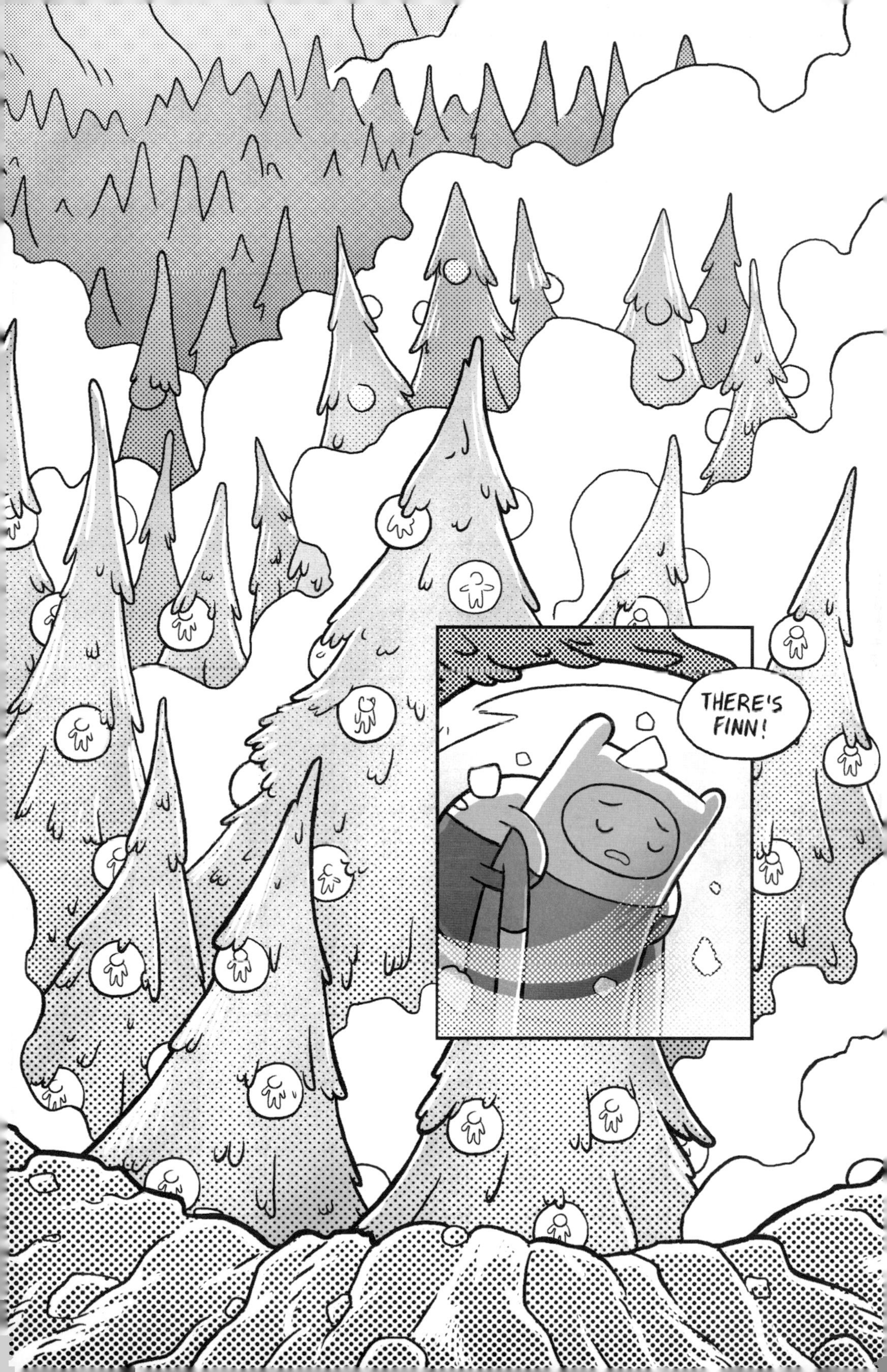
THERE'S FINN!

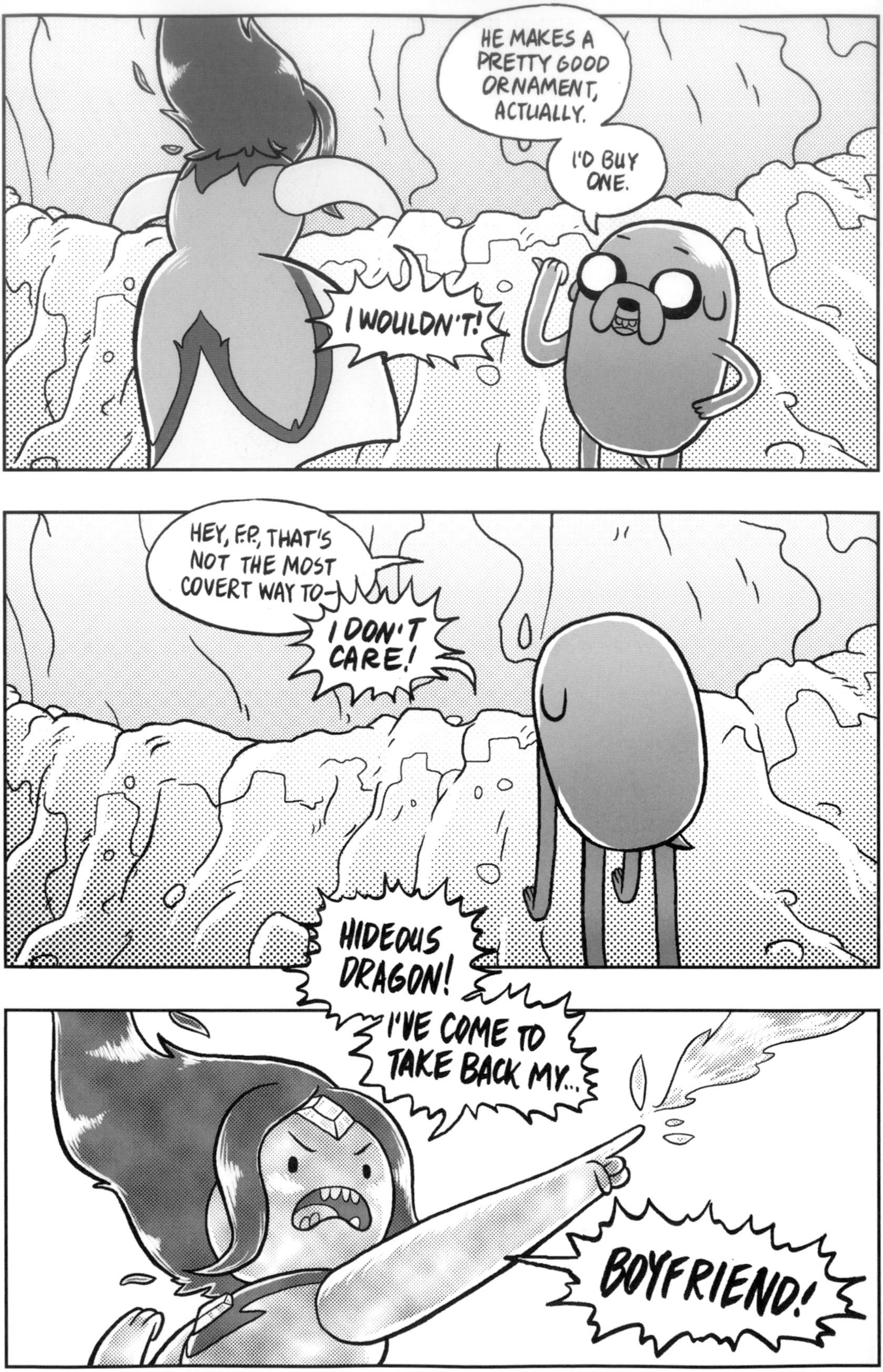

HE MAKES A PRETTY GOOD ORNAMENT, ACTUALLY.
I'D BUY ONE.
I WOULDN'T!
HEY, F.P., THAT'S NOT THE MOST COVERT WAY TO–
I DON'T CARE!
HIDEOUS DRAGON!
I'VE COME TO TAKE BACK MY...
BOYFRIEND!

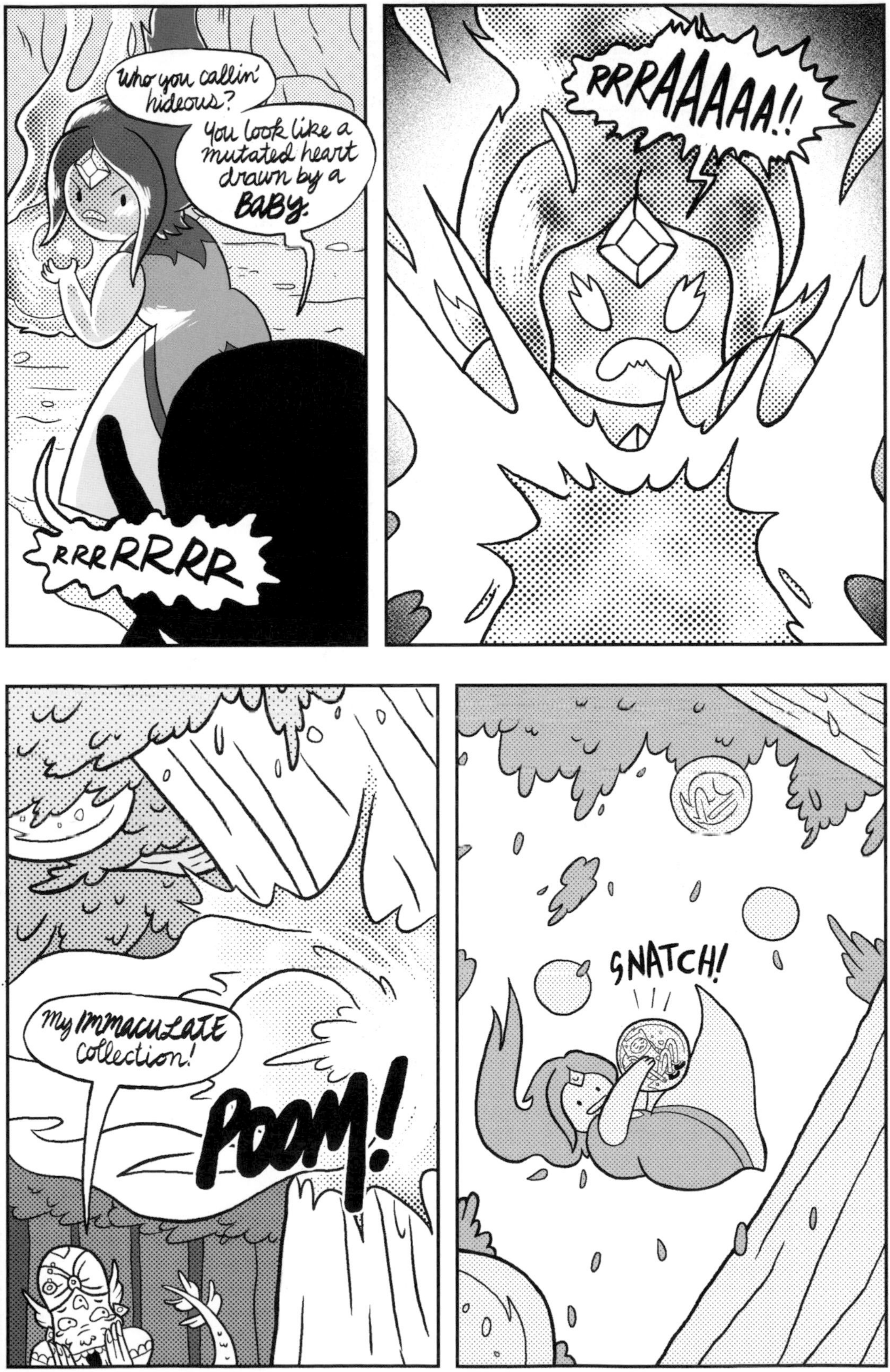

Who you callin' hideous?
You look like a mutated heart drawn by a BABY.
RRRRRRR
RRRAAAAAA!!
My IMMACULATE collection!
POOM!
SNATCH!

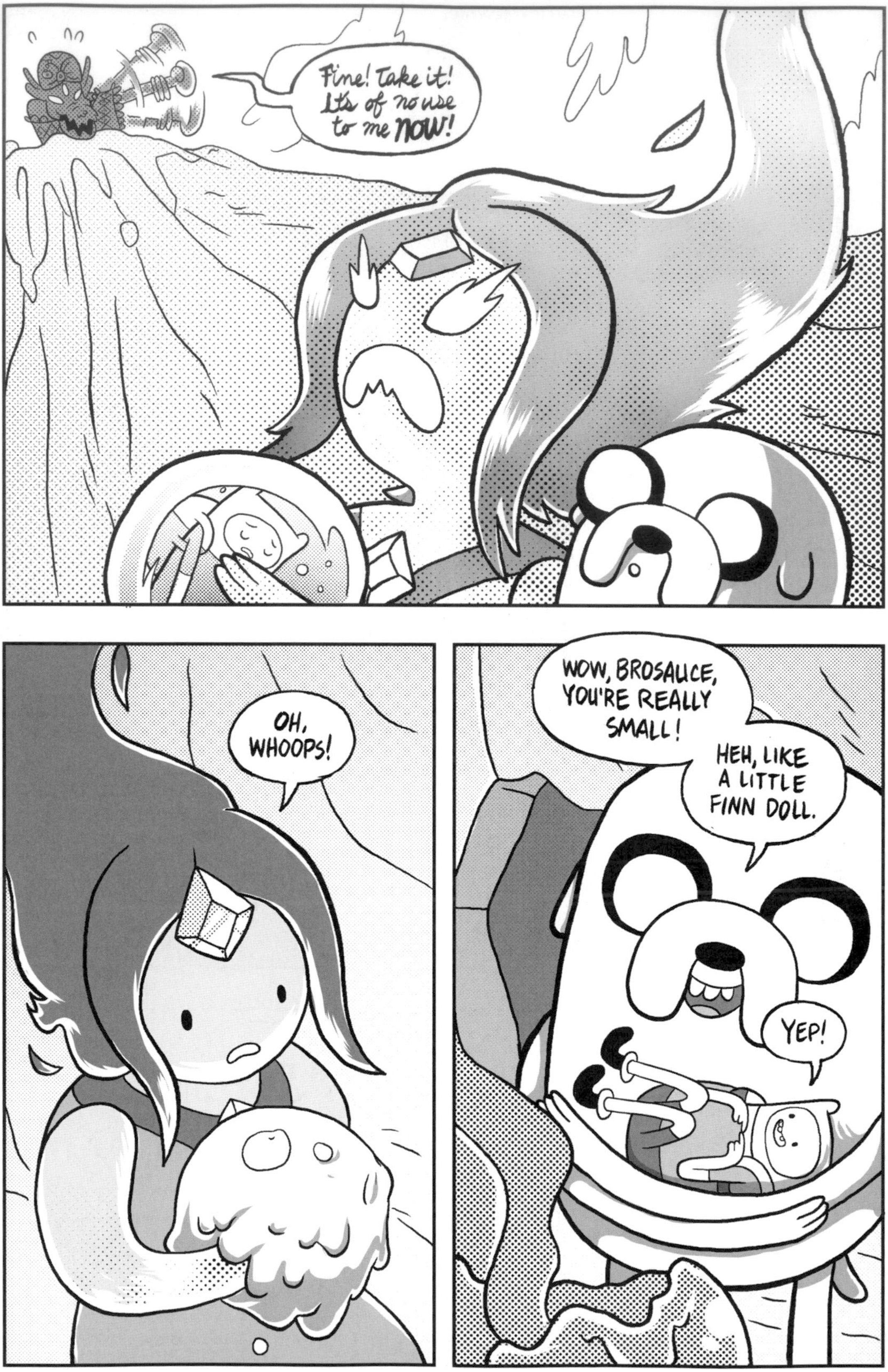
Fine! Take it! It's of no use to me NOW!
OH, WHOOPS!
WOW, BROSAUCE, YOU'RE REALLY SMALL!
HEH, LIKE A LITTLE FINN DOLL.
YEP!

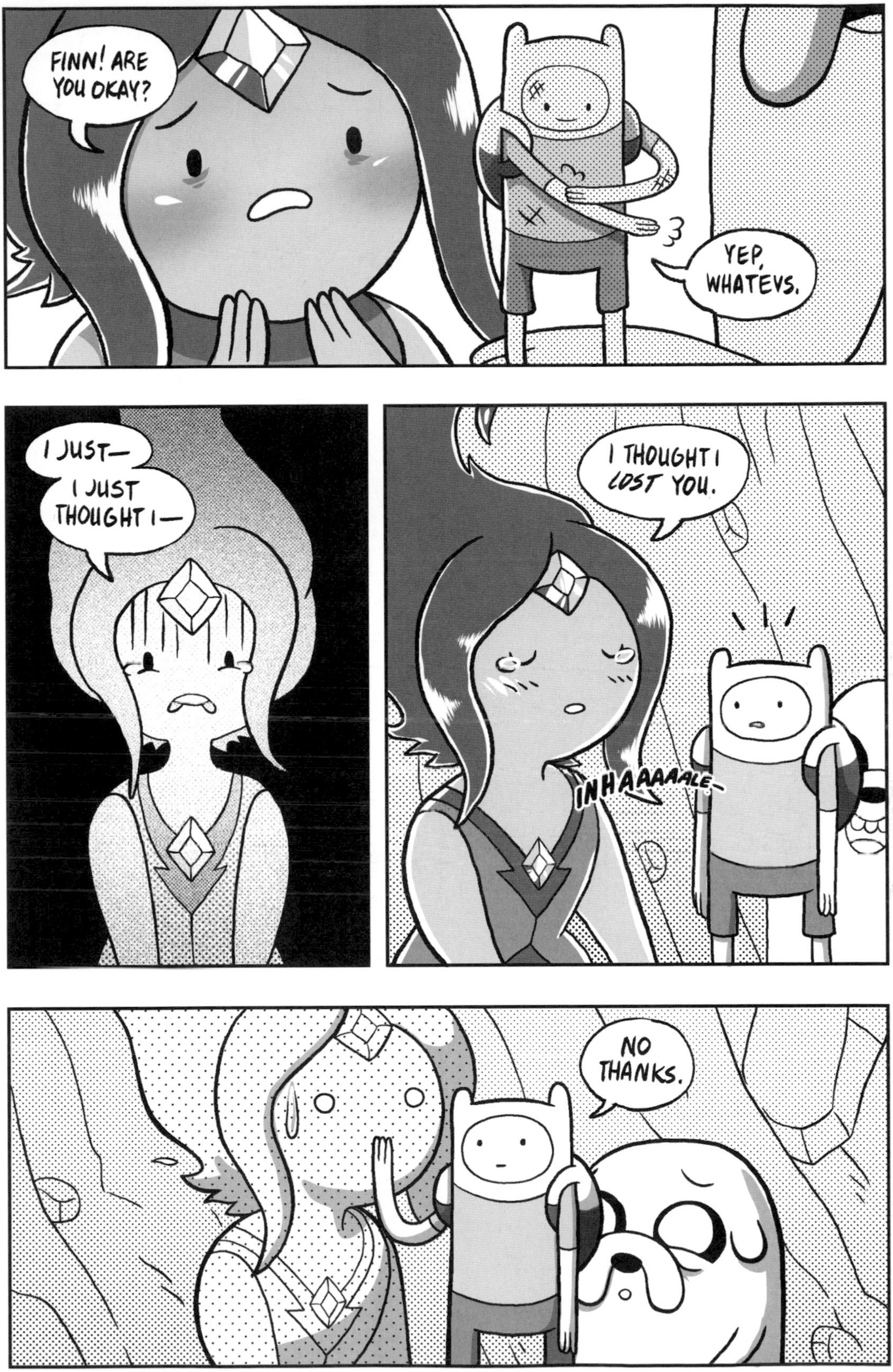
FINN! ARE YOU OKAY?
YEP, WHATEVS.
I JUST—
I JUST THOUGHT I—
I THOUGHT I LOST YOU.
INHAAAAALE—
NO THANKS.

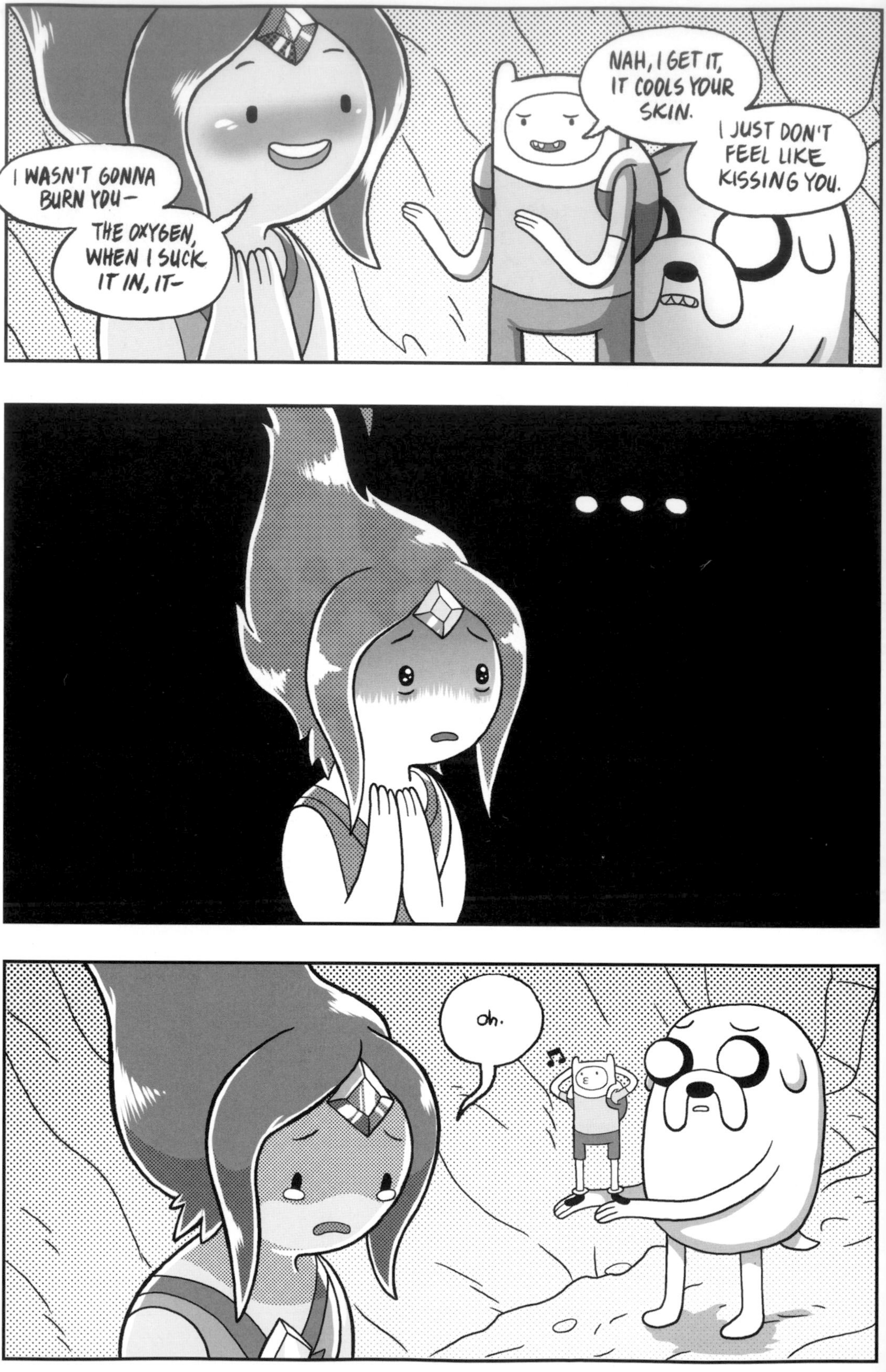
I WASN'T GONNA BURN YOU–
THE OXYGEN, WHEN I SUCK IT IN, IT–
NAH, I GET IT, IT COOLS YOUR SKIN.
I JUST DON'T FEEL LIKE KISSING YOU.
...
oh.

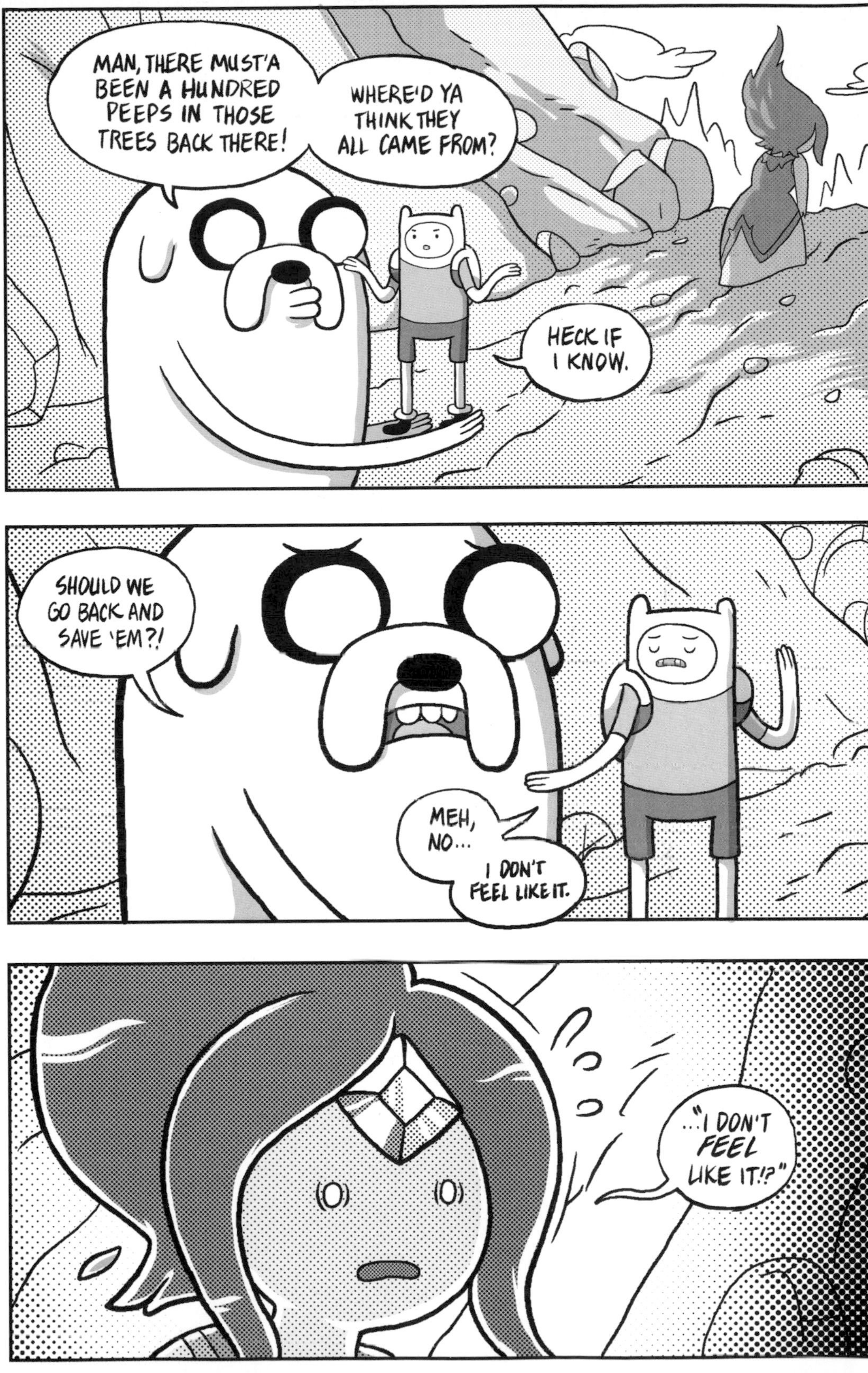
MAN, THERE MUST'A BEEN A HUNDRED PEEPS IN THOSE TREES BACK THERE!
WHERE'D YA THINK THEY ALL CAME FROM?
HECK IF I KNOW.
SHOULD WE GO BACK AND SAVE 'EM?!
MEH, NO...
I DON'T FEEL LIKE IT.
..."I DON'T FEEL LIKE IT!?"

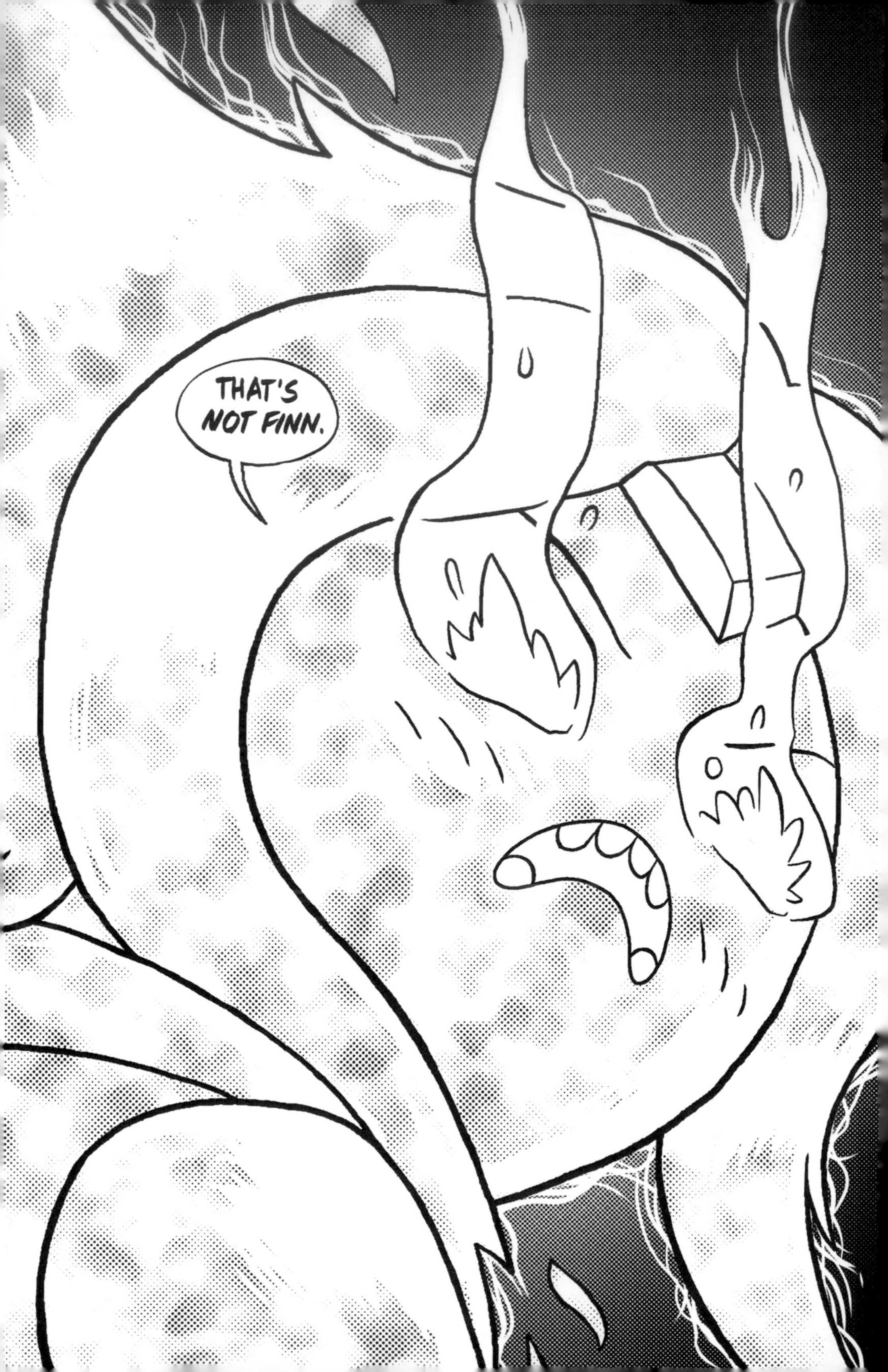
THAT'S NOT FINN.

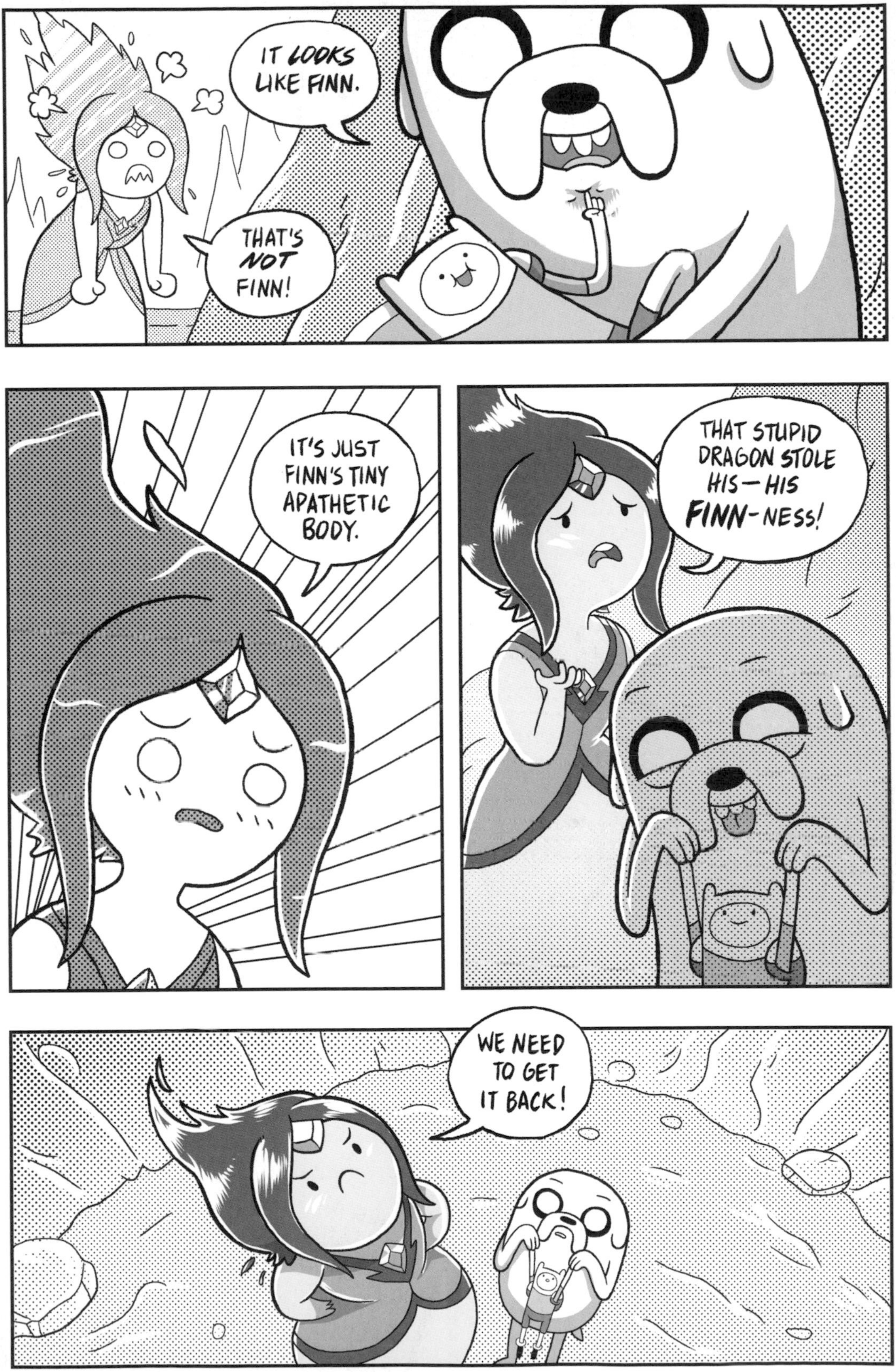
IT LOOKS LIKE FINN.
THAT'S NOT FINN!
IT'S JUST FINN'S TINY APATHETIC BODY.
THAT STUPID DRAGON STOLE HIS— HIS FINN-NESS!
WE NEED TO GET IT BACK!

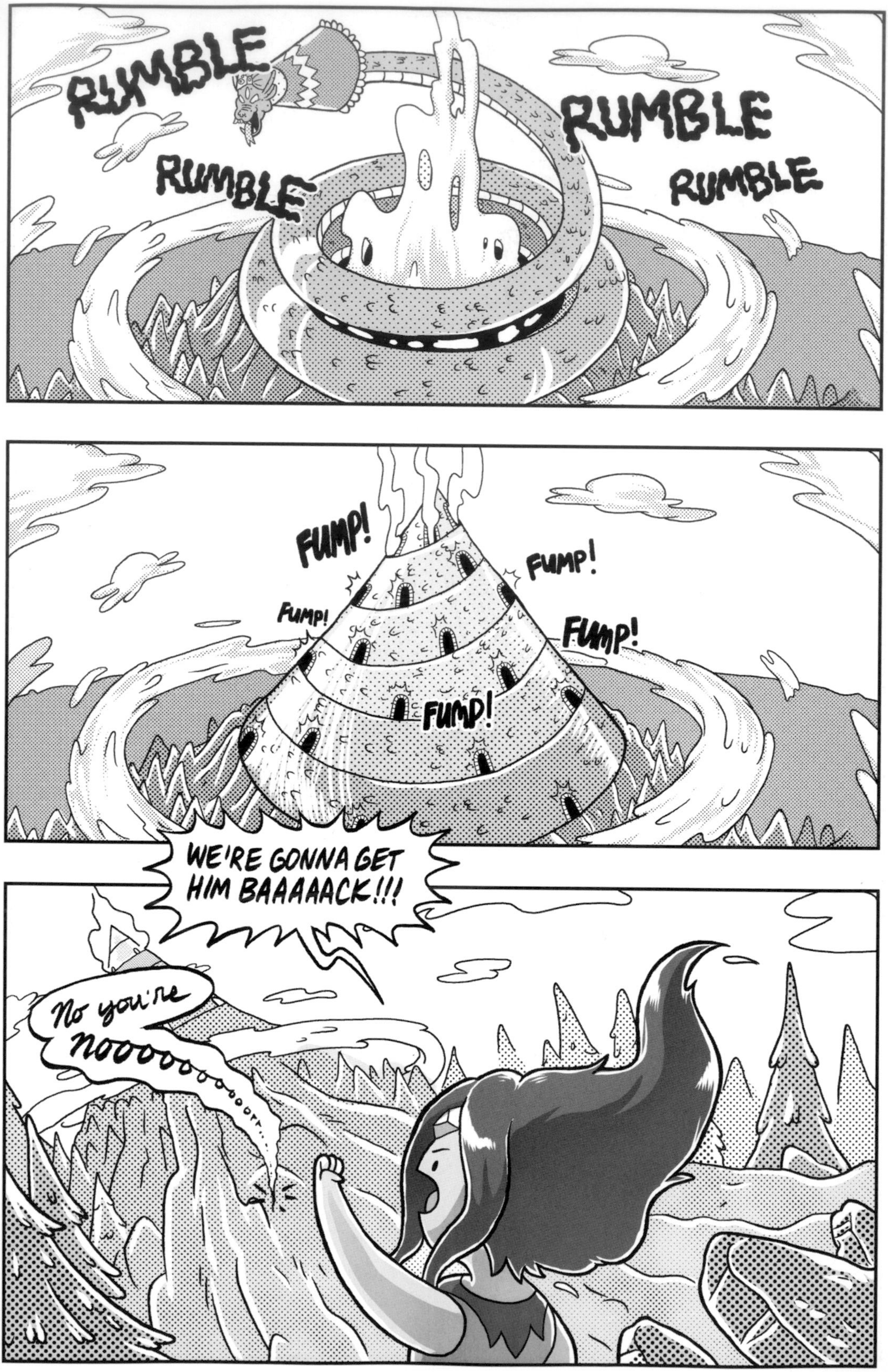
RUMBLE
RUMBLE
RUMBLE
RUMBLE
FUMP!
FUMP!
FUMP!
FUMP!
FUMP!
WE'RE GONNA GET HIM BAAAAACK!!!
No you're nooooooooooooorrr...

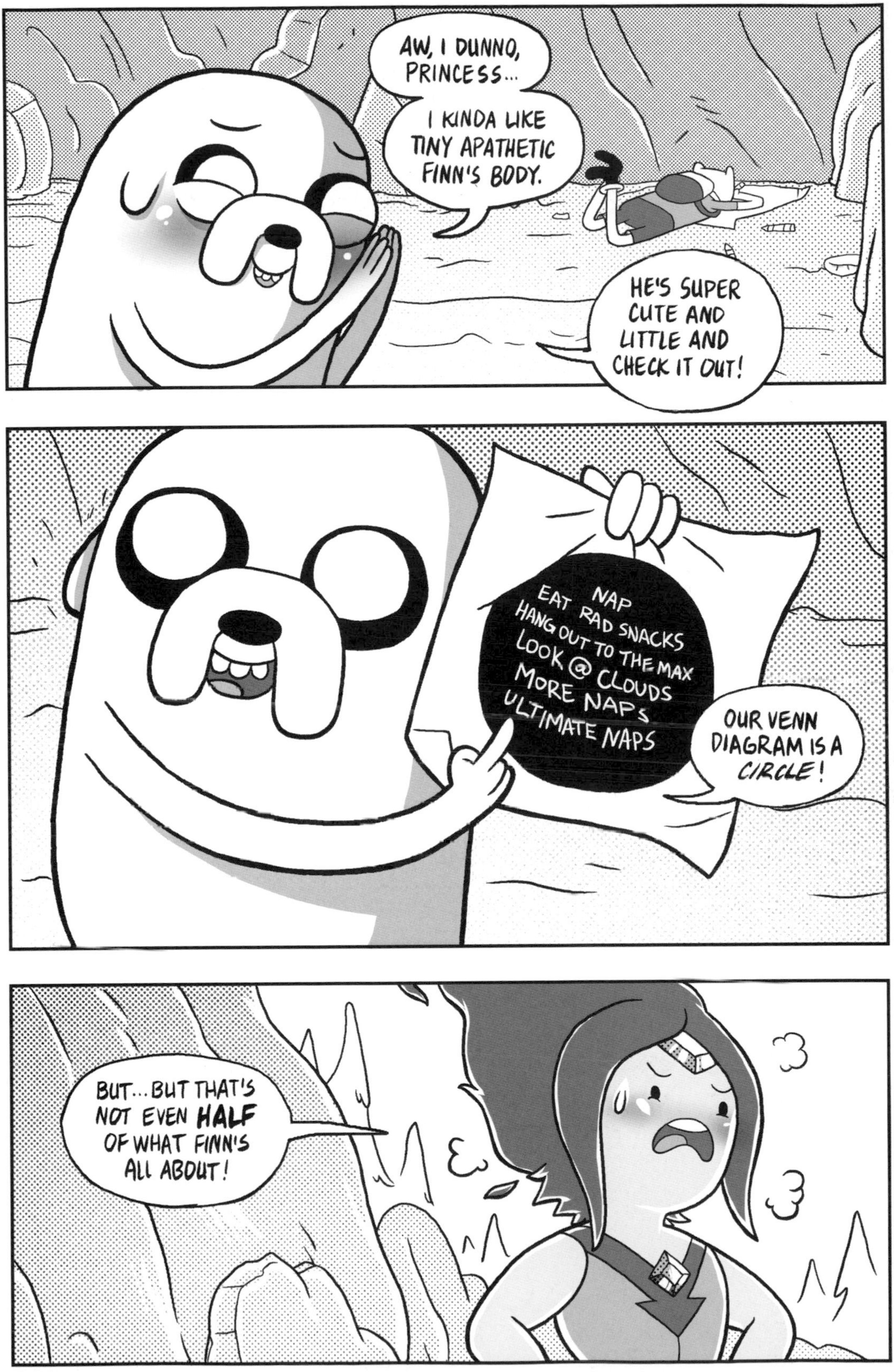
AW, I DUNNO, PRINCESS...
I KINDA LIKE TINY APATHETIC FINN'S BODY.
HE'S SUPER CUTE AND LITTLE AND CHECK IT OUT!
NAP
EAT RAD SNACKS
HANG OUT TO THE MAX
LOOK @ CLOUDS
MORE NAPS
ULTIMATE NAPS
OUR VENN DIAGRAM IS A CIRCLE!
BUT... BUT THAT'S NOT EVEN HALF OF WHAT FINN'S ALL ABOUT!

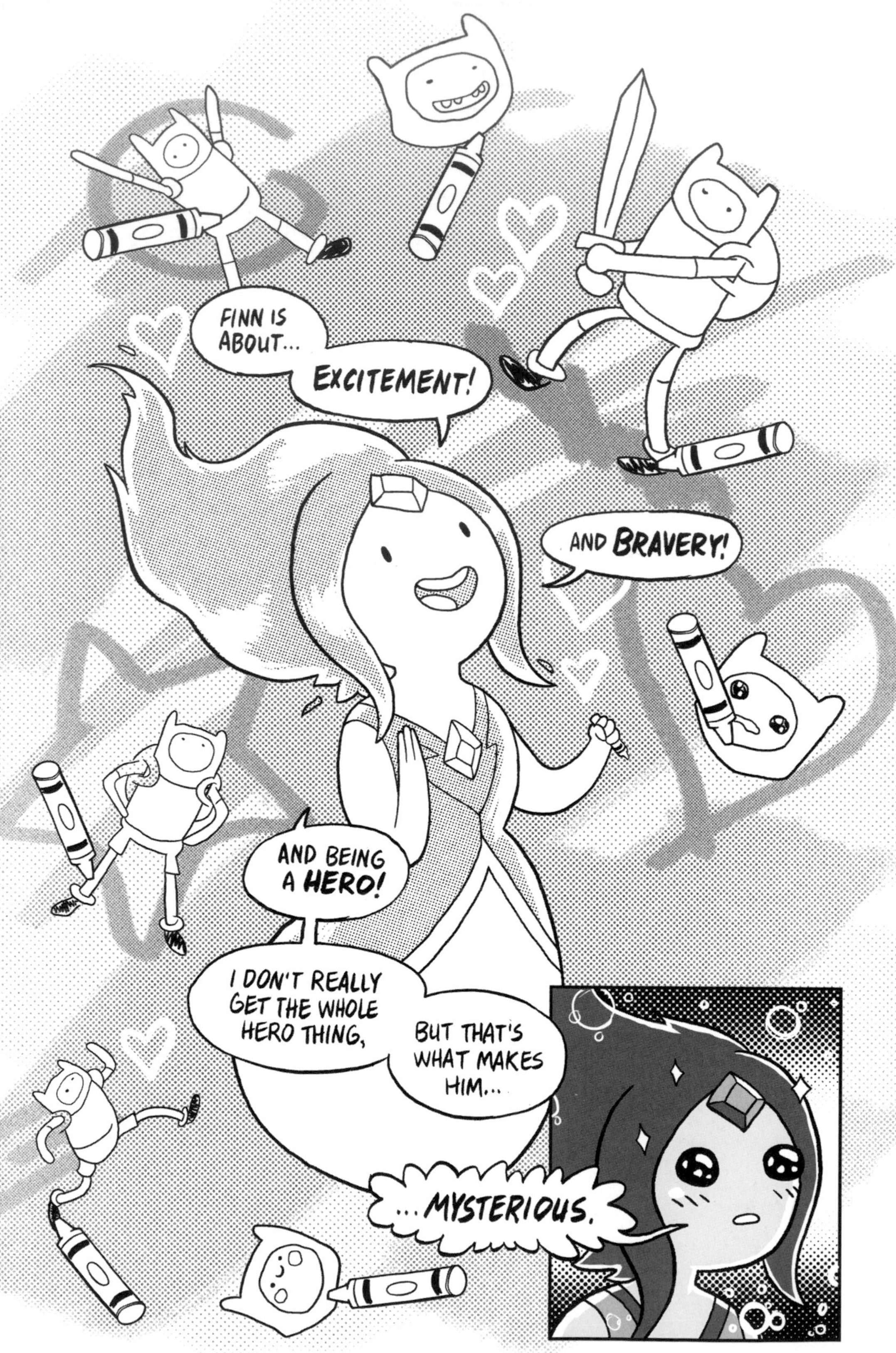
FINN IS ABOUT...
EXCITEMENT!
AND BRAVERY!
AND BEING A HERO!
I DON'T REALLY GET THE WHOLE HERO THING,
BUT THAT'S WHAT MAKES HIM...
...MYSTERIOUS.

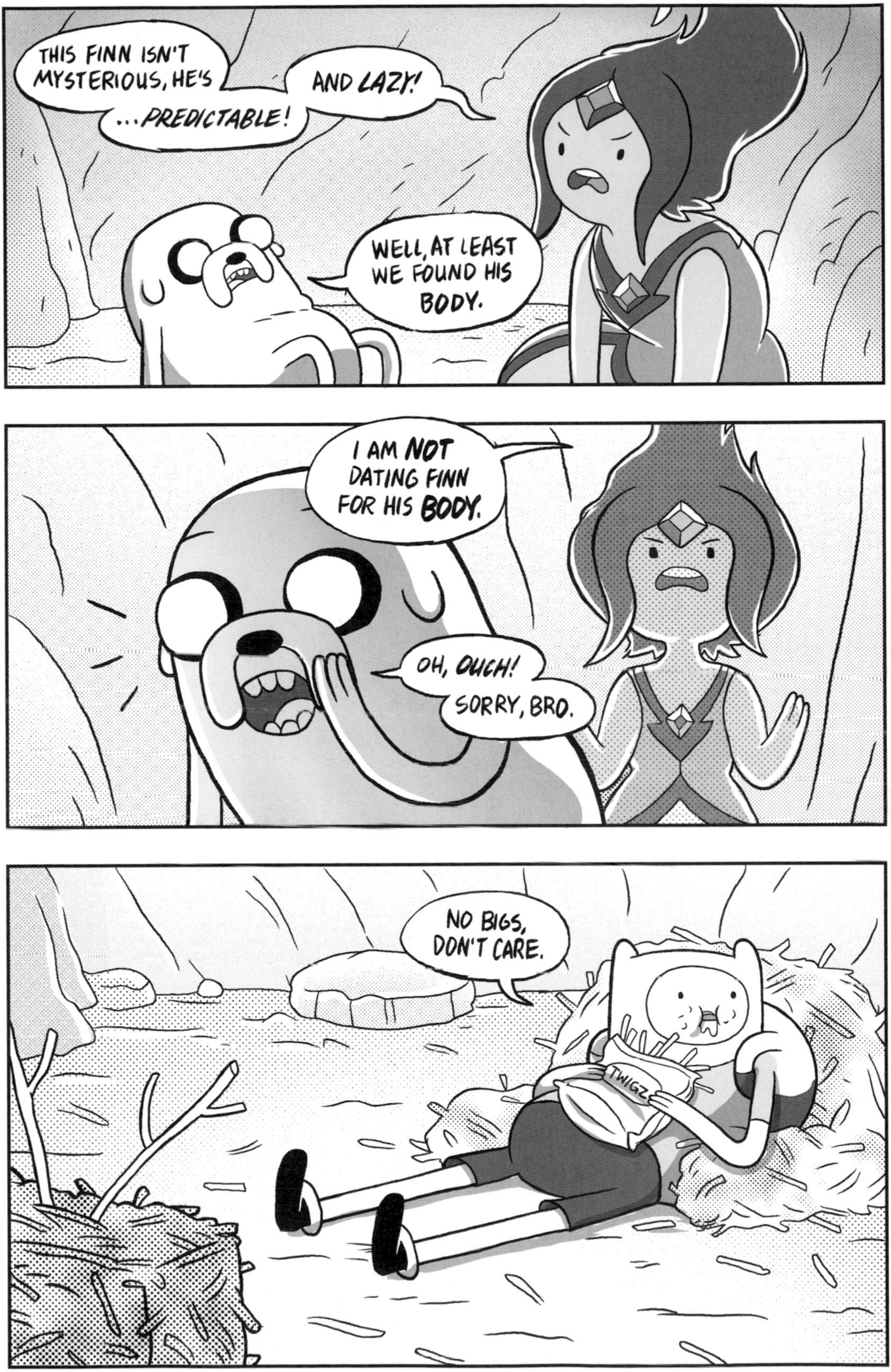
THIS FINN ISN'T MYSTERIOUS, HE'S
...PREDICTABLE!
AND LAZY!
WELL, AT LEAST WE FOUND HIS BODY.
I AM NOT DATING FINN FOR HIS BODY.
OH, OUCH!
SORRY, BRO.
NO BIGS, DON'T CARE.
TWIGZ

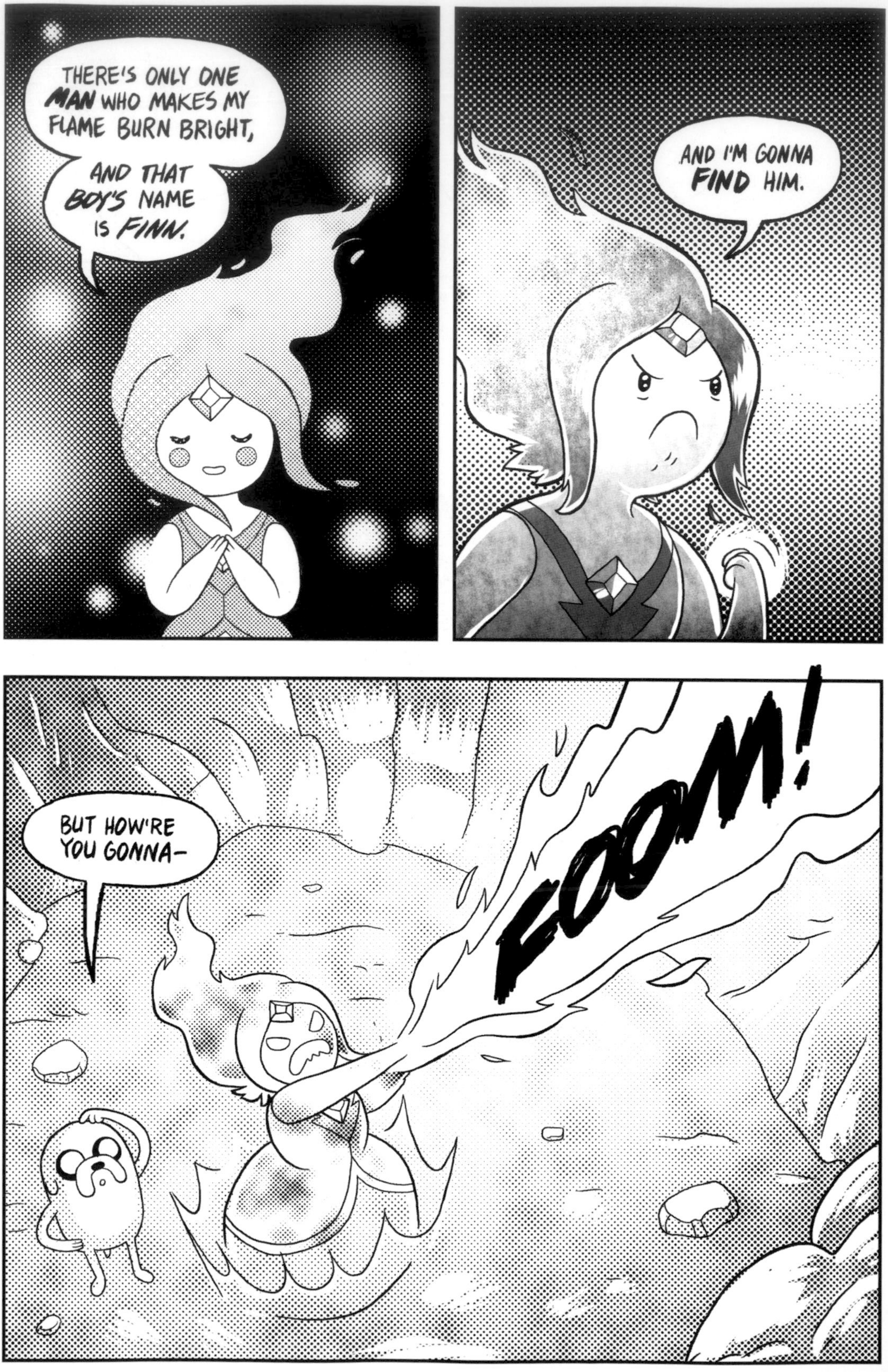
THERE'S ONLY ONE MAN WHO MAKES MY FLAME BURN BRIGHT,
AND THAT BOY'S NAME IS FINN.
AND I'M GONNA FIND HIM.
BUT HOW'RE YOU GONNA-
FOOOM!

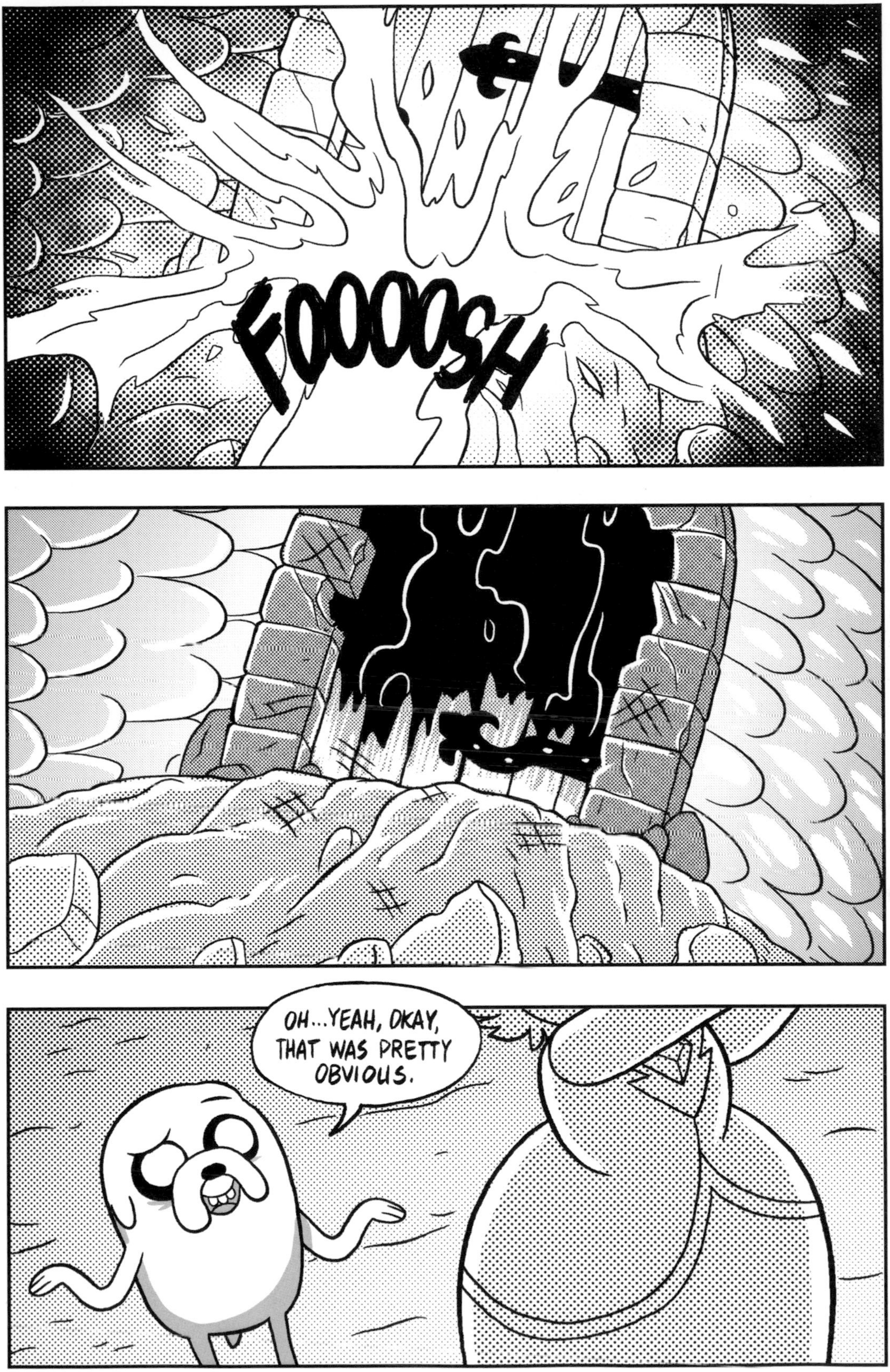
FOOOOSH
OH...YEAH, OKAY, THAT WAS PRETTY OBVIOUS.

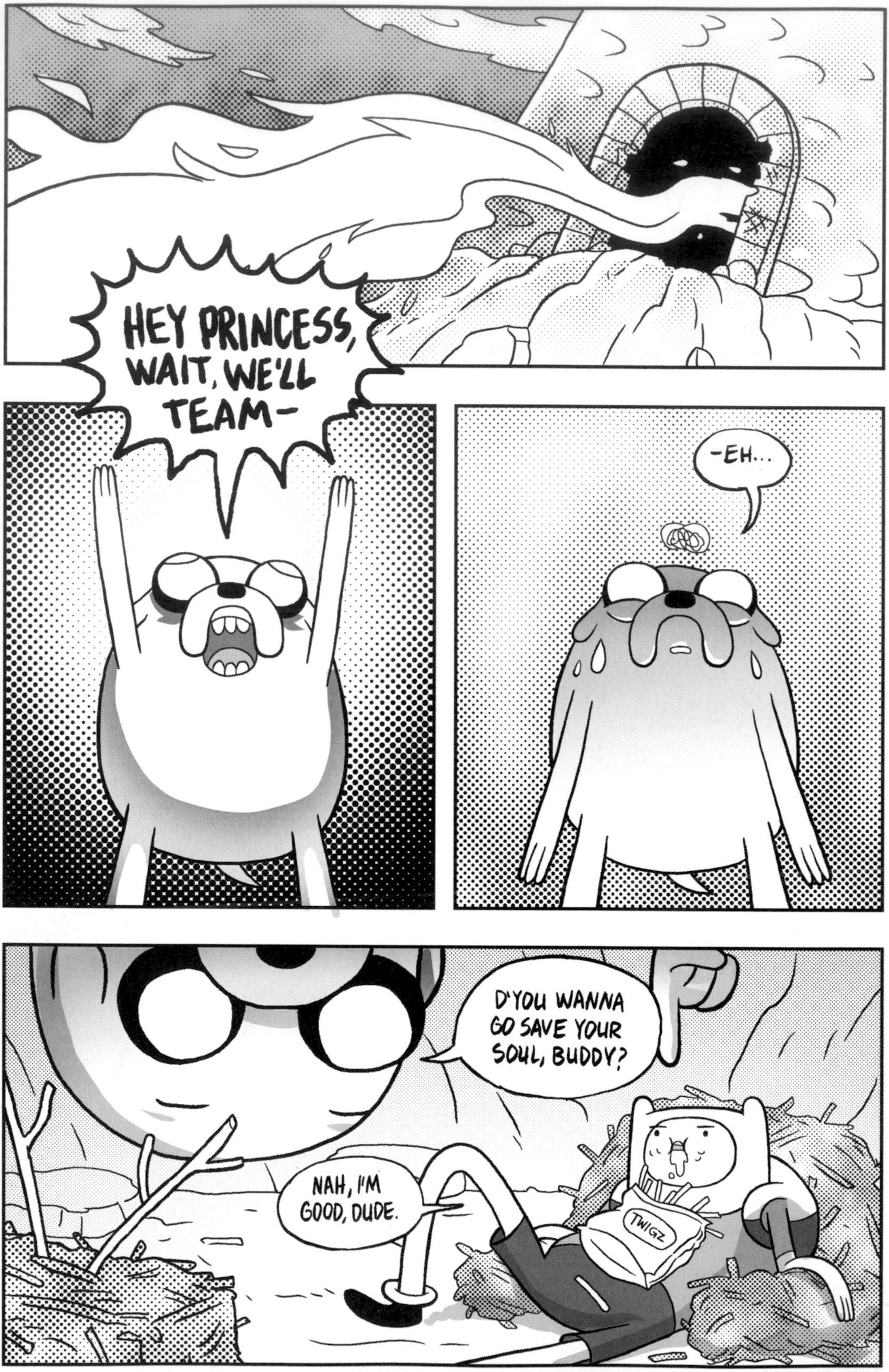
HEY PRINCESS, WAIT, WE'LL TEAM-
-EH...
D'YOU WANNA GO SAVE YOUR SOUL, BUDDY?
NAH, I'M GOOD, DUDE.
TWIGZ

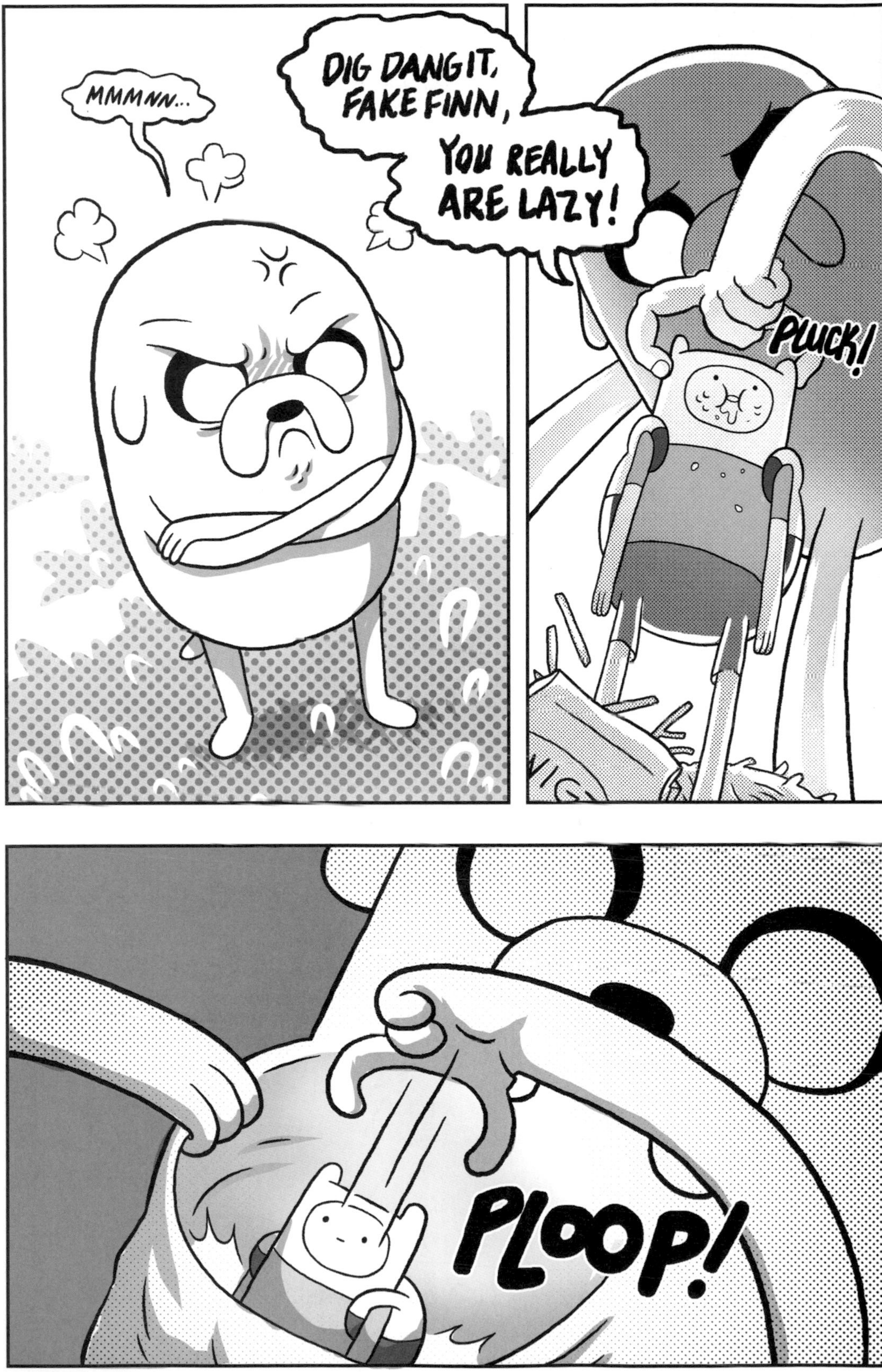
MMMNN...
DIG DANGIT, FAKE FINN,
YOU REALLY ARE LAZY!
PLUCK!
PLOOP!

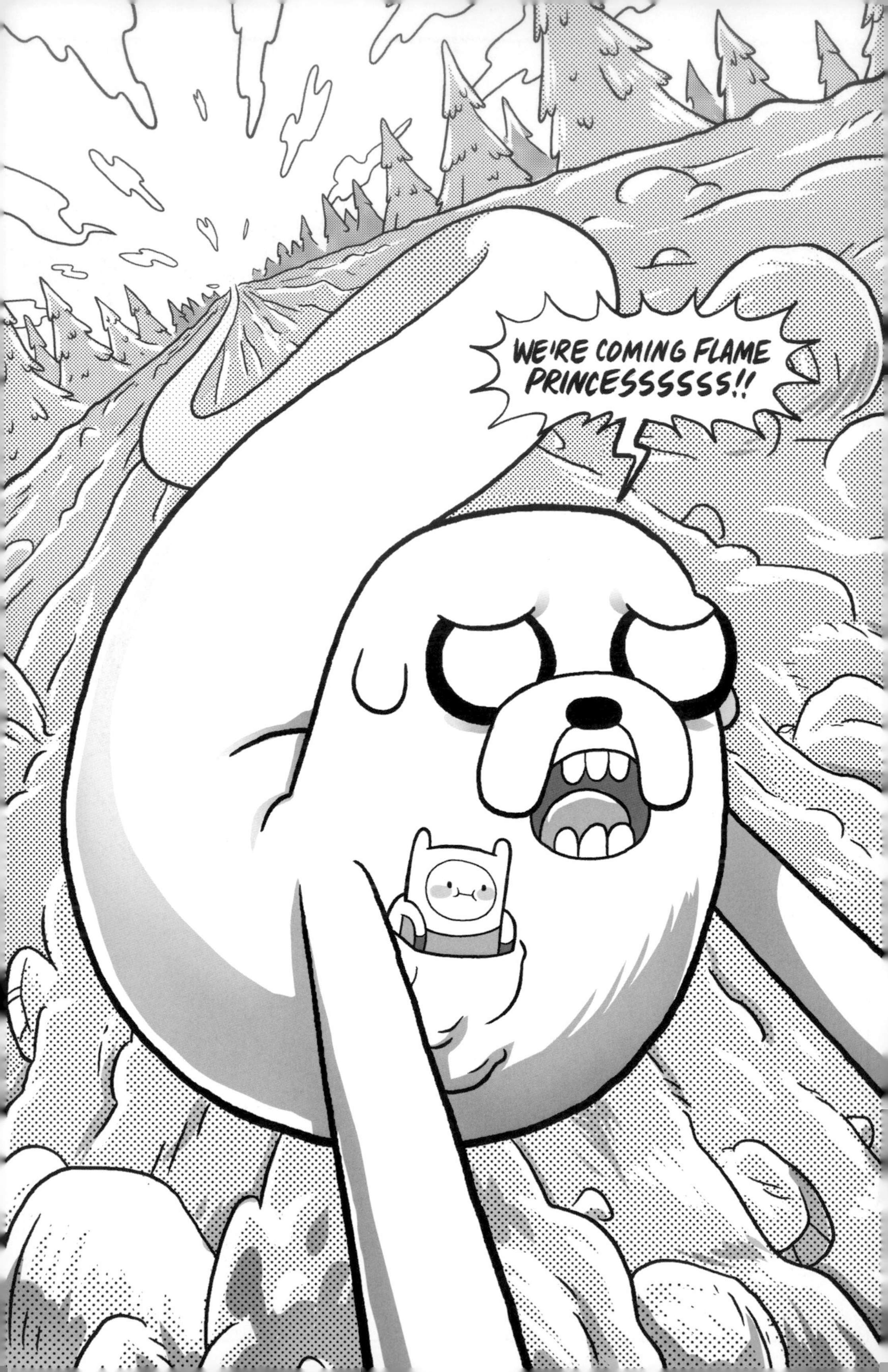
WE'RE COMING FLAME PRINCESSSSSS!!

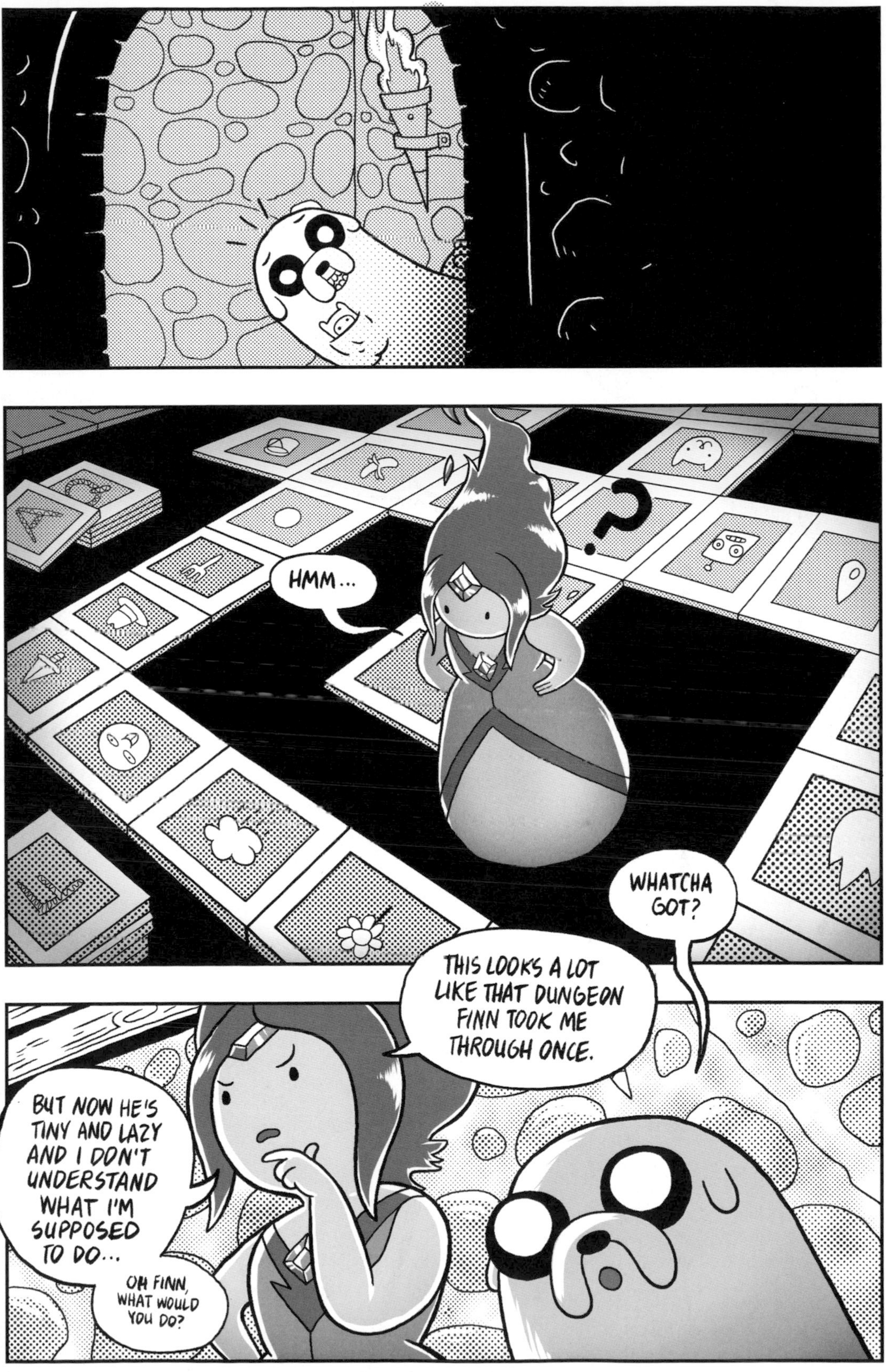
HMM...
WHATCHA GOT?
THIS LOOKS A LOT LIKE THAT DUNGEON FINN TOOK ME THROUGH ONCE.
BUT NOW HE'S TINY AND LAZY AND I DON'T UNDERSTAND WHAT I'M SUPPOSED TO DO...
OH FINN, WHAT WOULD YOU DO?

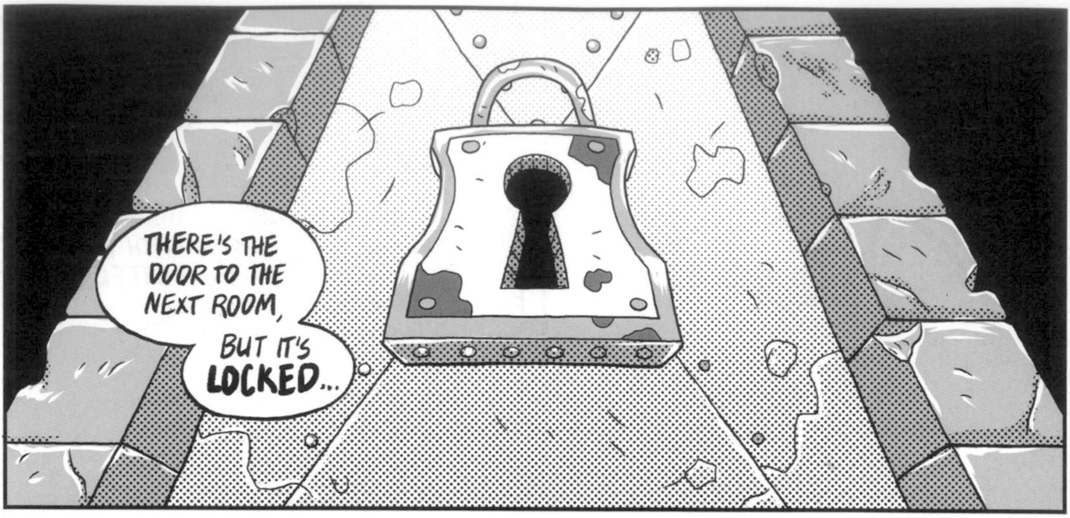
THERE'S THE DOOR TO THE NEXT ROOM,
BUT IT'S LOCKED...

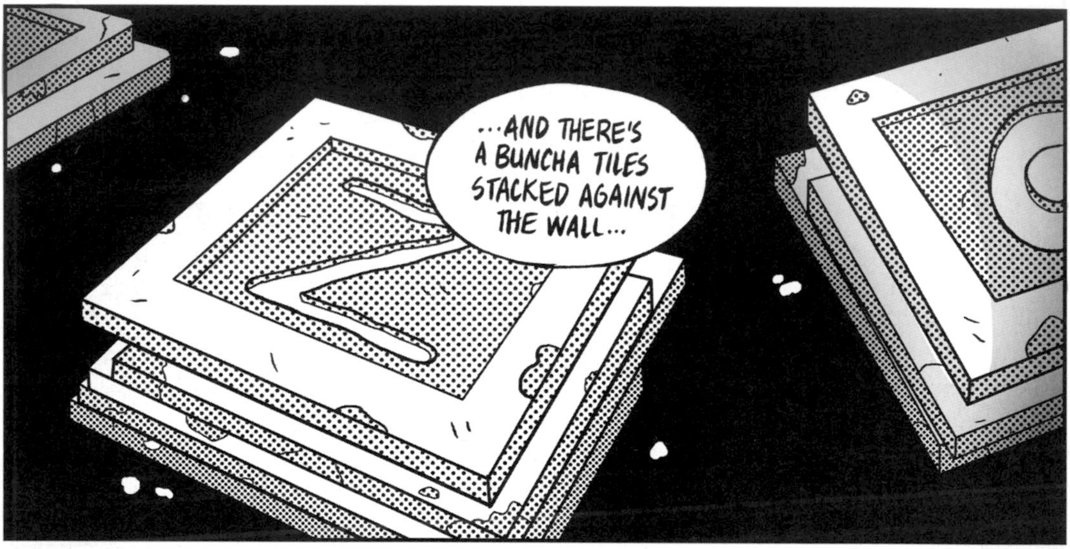
...AND THERE'S A BUNCHA TILES STACKED AGAINST THE WALL...

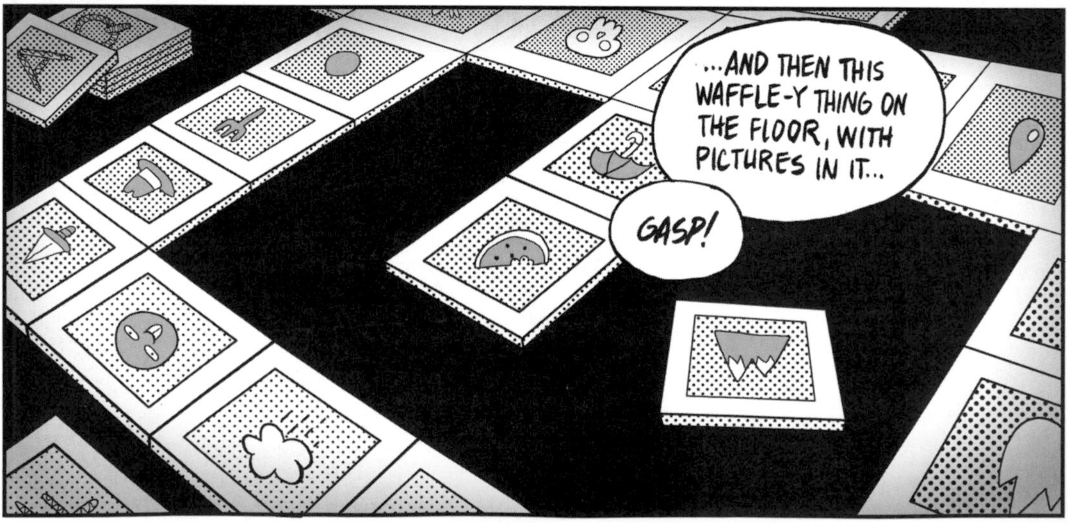
...AND THEN THIS WAFFLE-Y THING ON THE FLOOR, WITH PICTURES IN IT...
GASP!

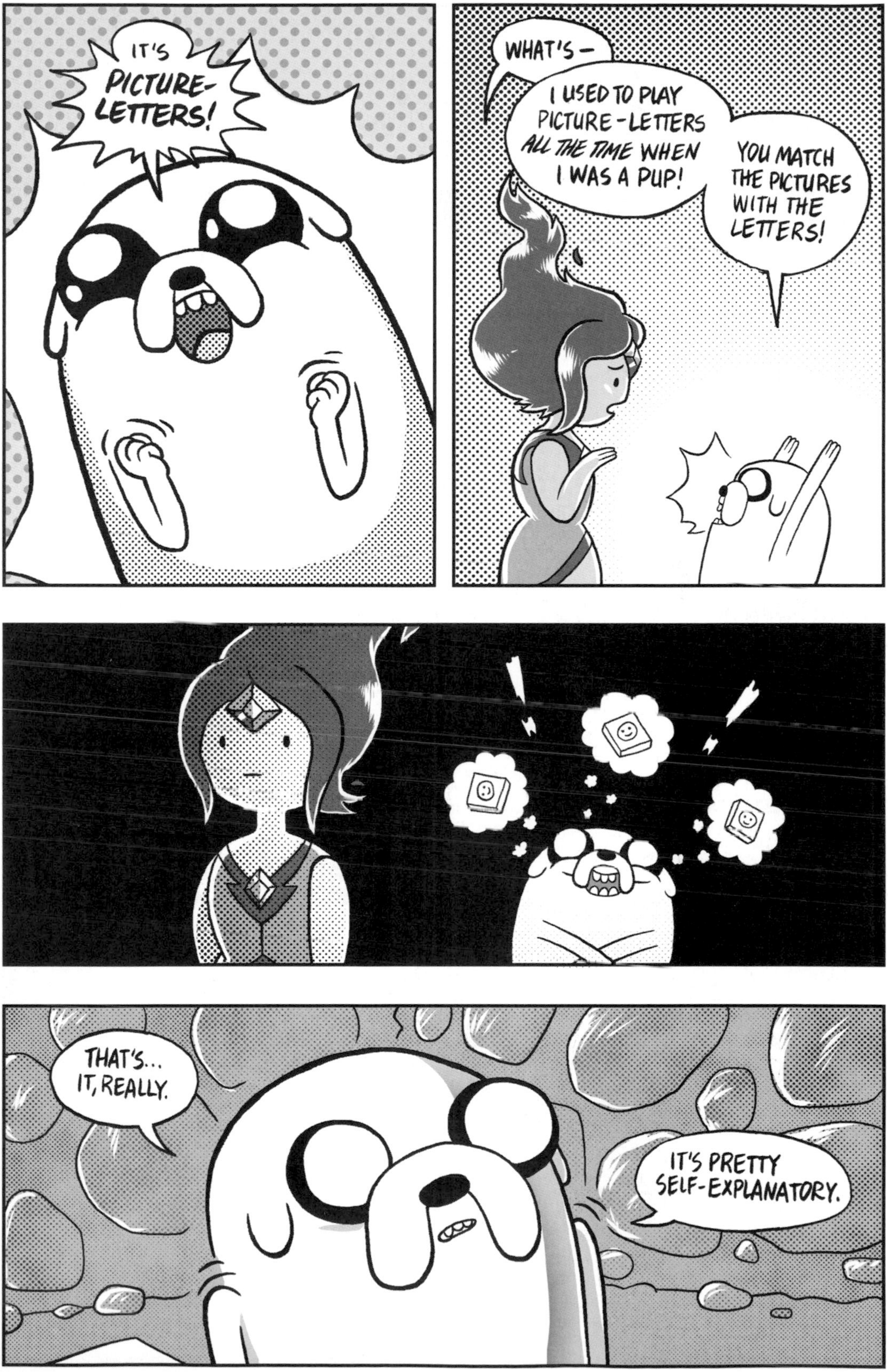
IT'S PICTURE-LETTERS!
WHAT'S —
I USED TO PLAY PICTURE-LETTERS *ALL THE TIME* WHEN I WAS A PUP!
YOU MATCH THE PICTURES WITH THE LETTERS!
THAT'S... IT, REALLY.
IT'S PRETTY SELF-EXPLANATORY.

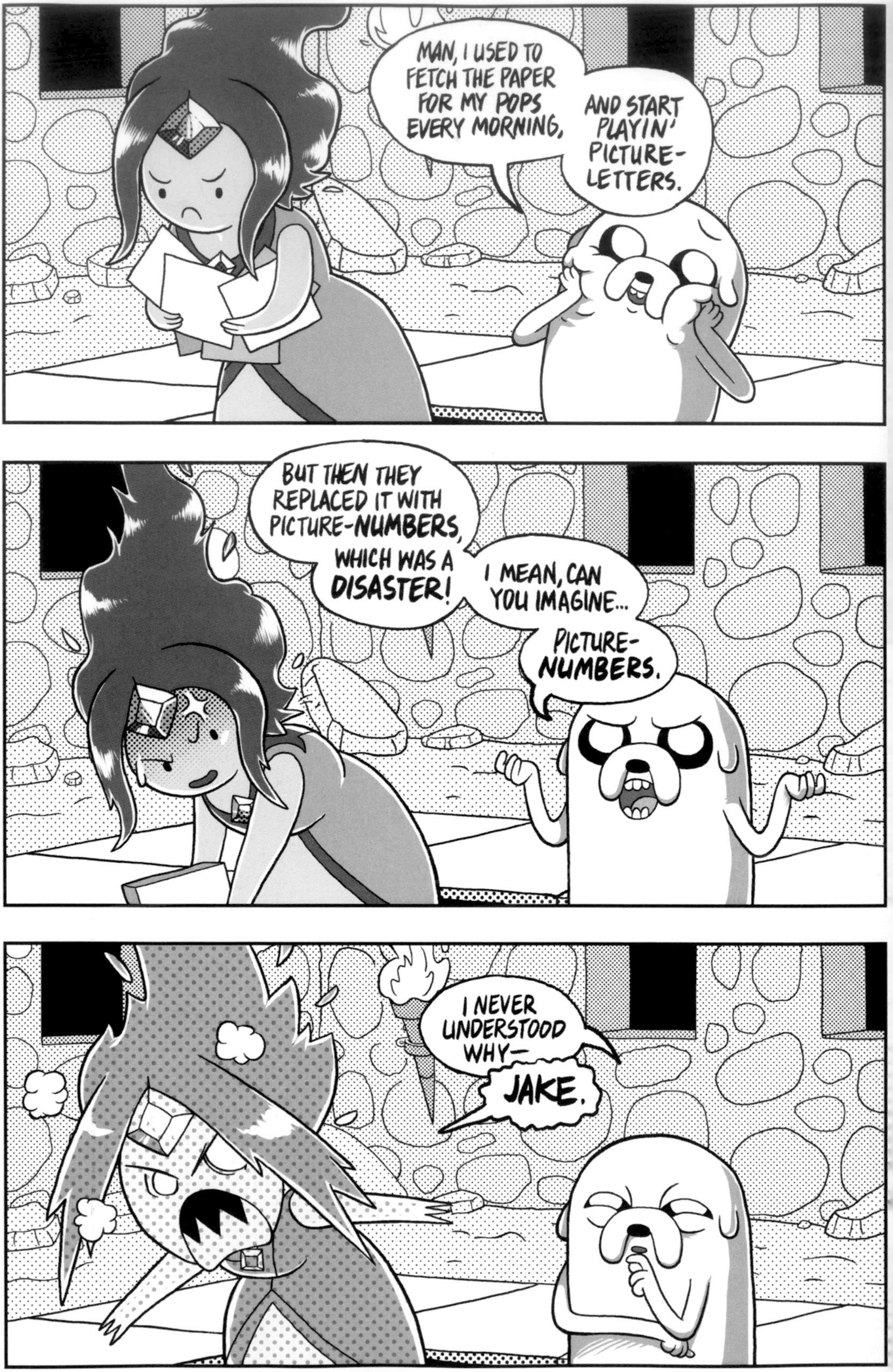
MAN, I USED TO FETCH THE PAPER FOR MY POPS EVERY MORNING,
AND START PLAYIN' PICTURE-LETTERS.
BUT THEN THEY REPLACED IT WITH PICTURE-NUMBERS,
WHICH WAS A DISASTER!
I MEAN, CAN YOU IMAGINE...
PICTURE-NUMBERS.
I NEVER UNDERSTOOD WHY—
JAKE.

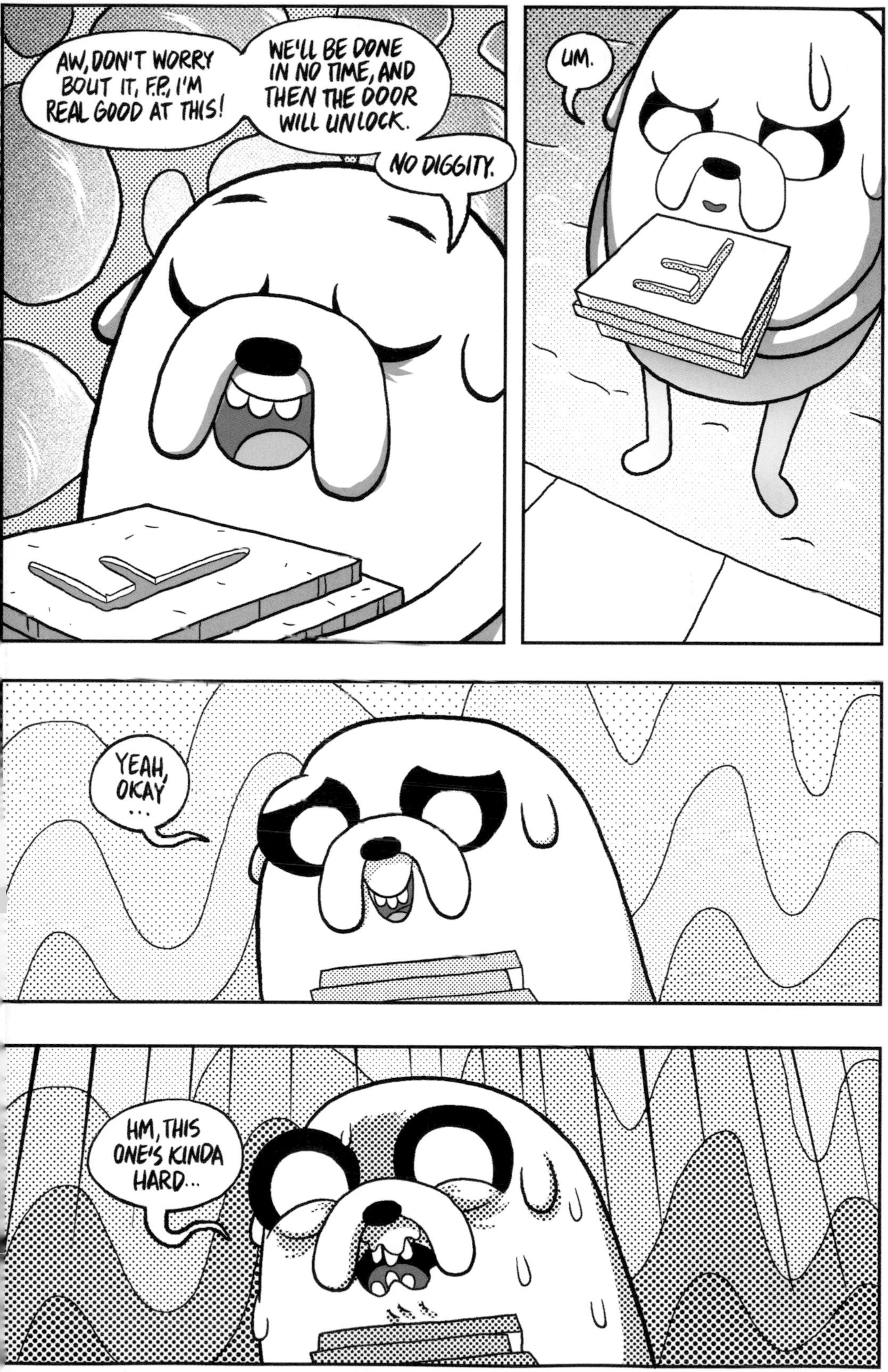
AW, DON'T WORRY BOUT IT, F.P., I'M REAL GOOD AT THIS!
WE'LL BE DONE IN NO TIME, AND THEN THE DOOR WILL UNLOCK.
NO DIGGITY.
UM.
YEAH, OKAY ...
HM, THIS ONE'S KINDA HARD...

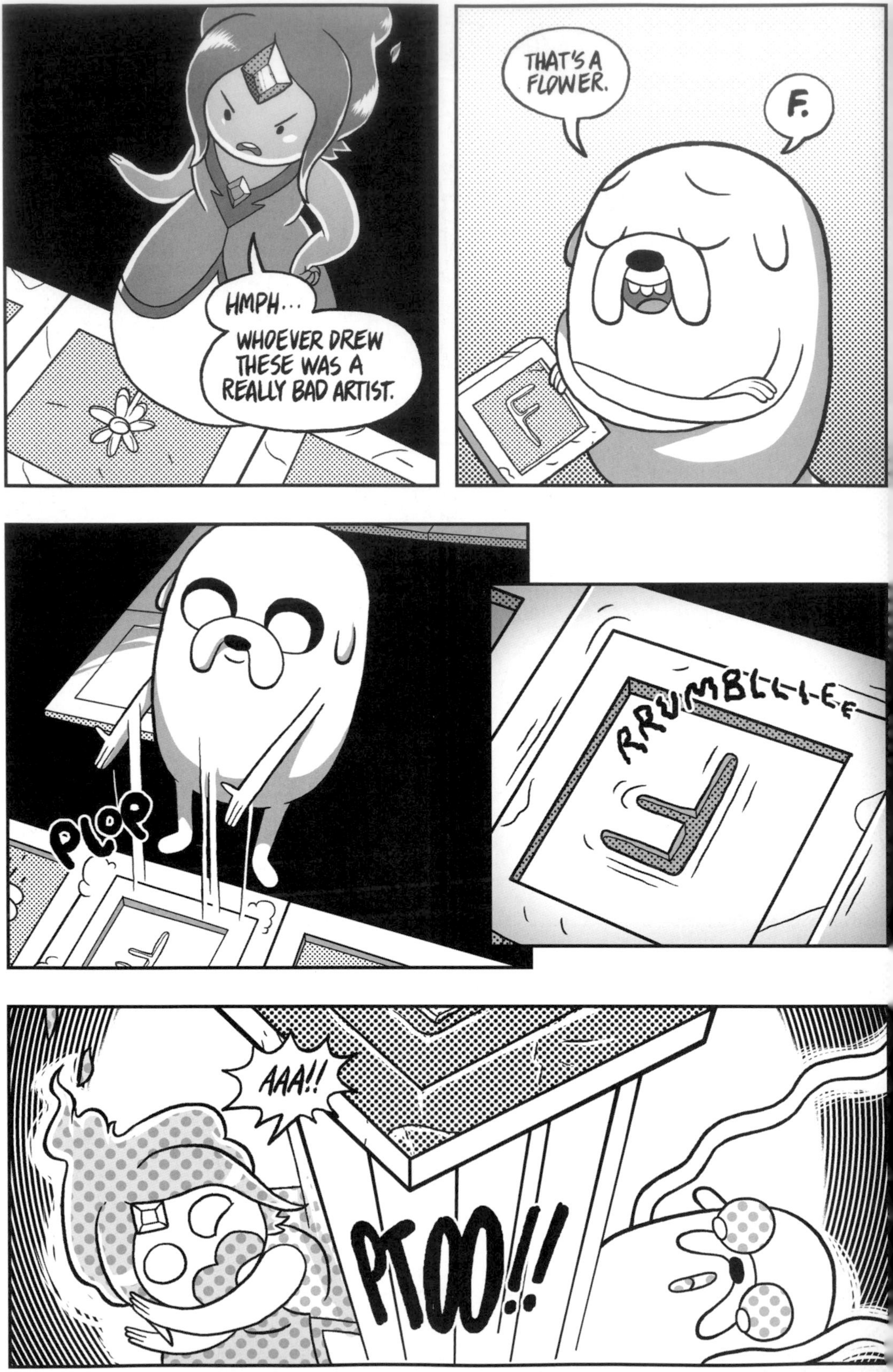
HMPH...
WHOEVER DREW THESE WAS A REALLY BAD ARTIST.
THAT'S A FLOWER.
F.
PLOP
RRUMBLLLEE
AAA!!
PTOO!!

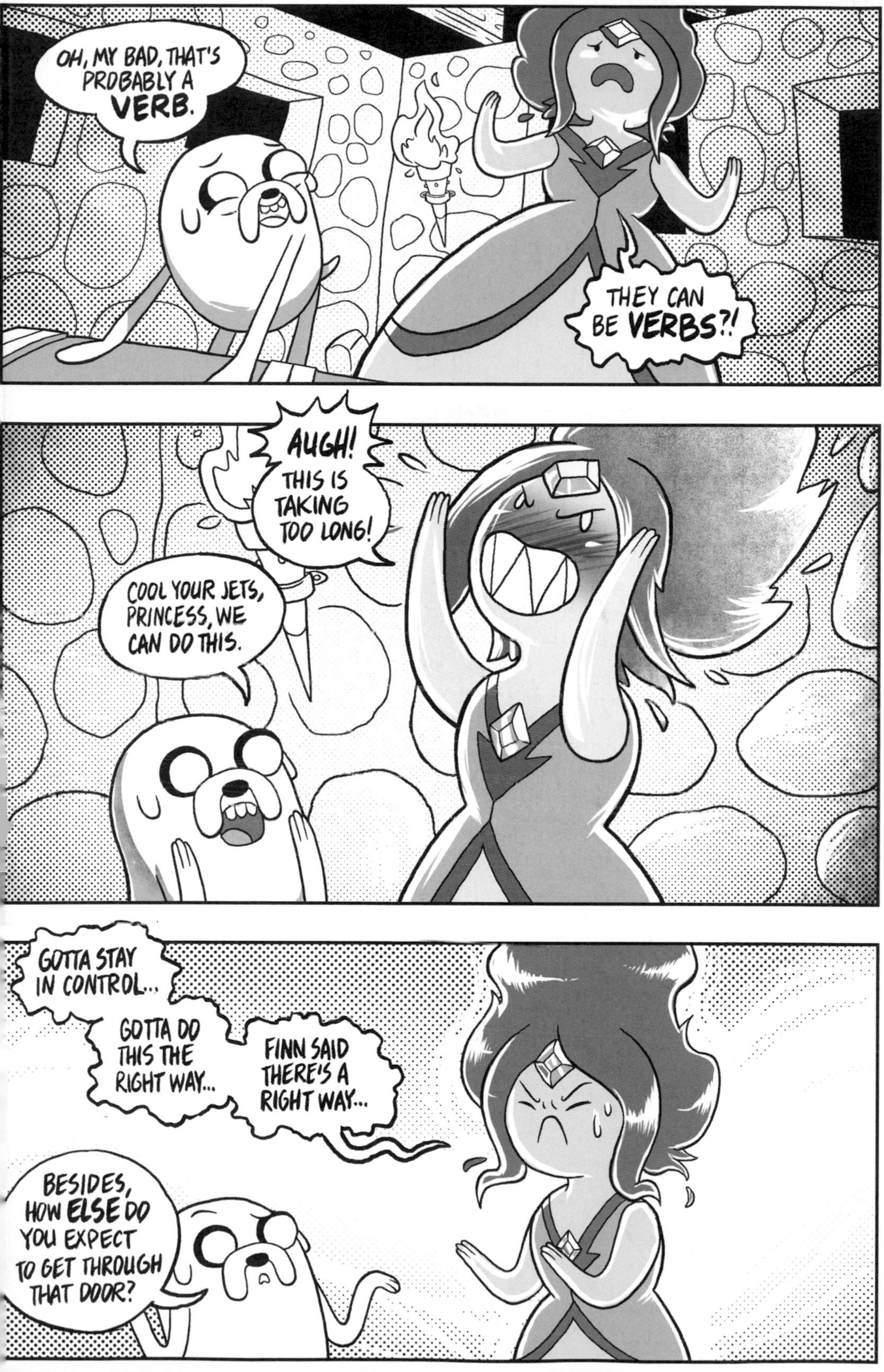
OH, MY BAD, THAT'S PROBABLY A VERB.
THEY CAN BE VERBS?!
AUGH! THIS IS TAKING TOO LONG!
COOL YOUR JETS, PRINCESS, WE CAN DO THIS.
GOTTA STAY IN CONTROL...
GOTTA DO THIS THE RIGHT WAY...
FINN SAID THERE'S A RIGHT WAY...
BESIDES, HOW ELSE DO YOU EXPECT TO GET THROUGH THAT DOOR?

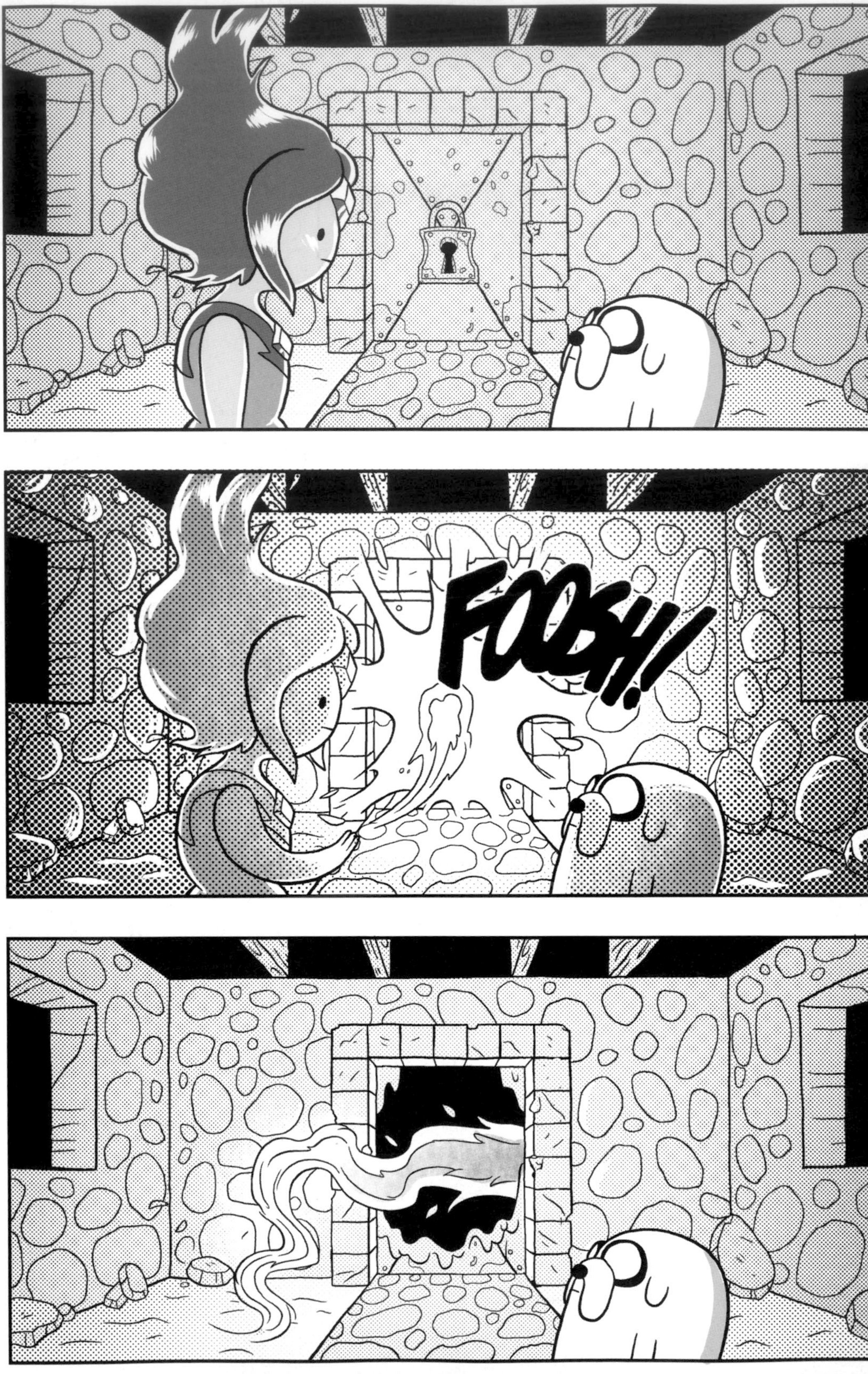
FOOSH!!

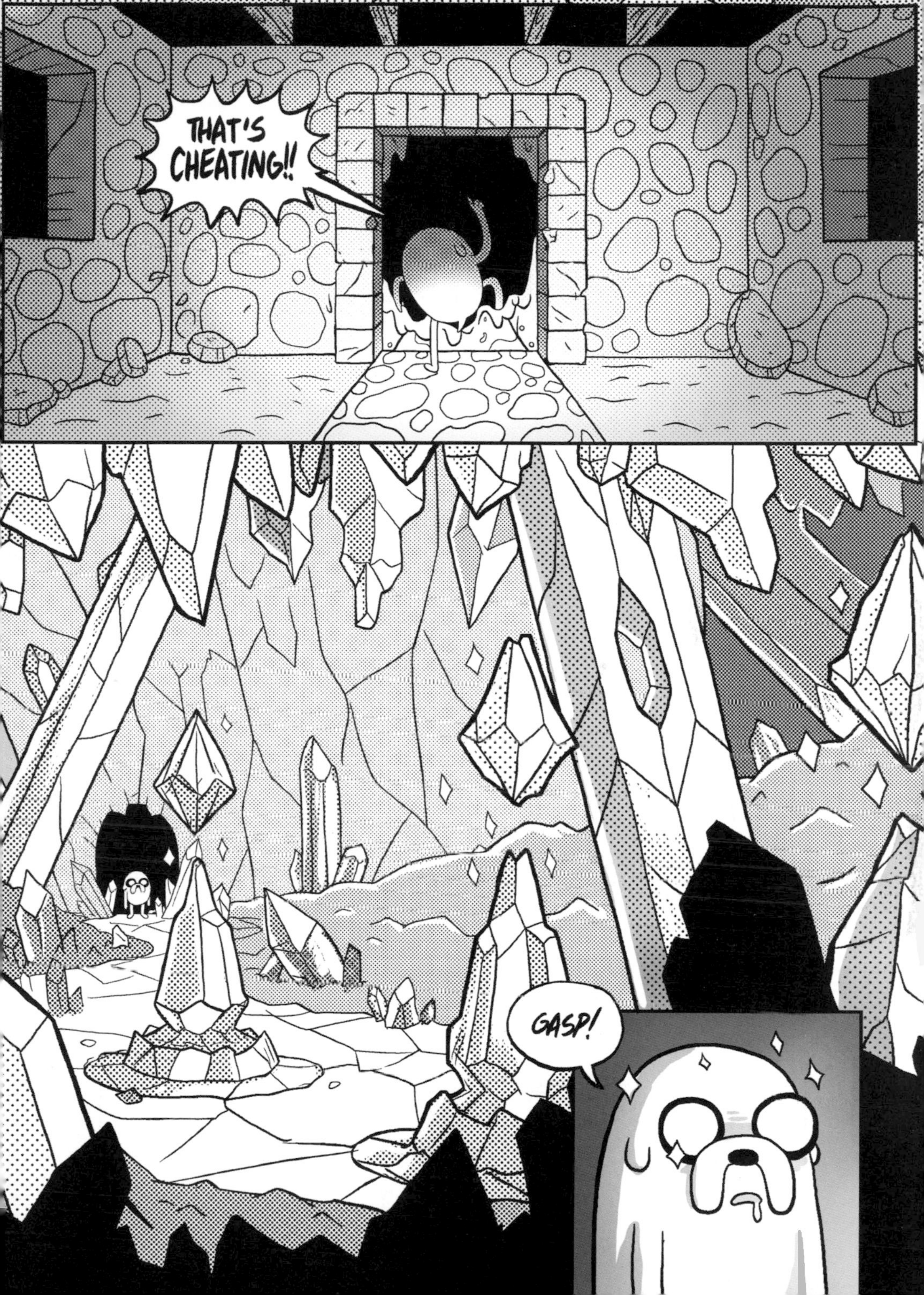
THAT'S CHEATING!!
GASP!

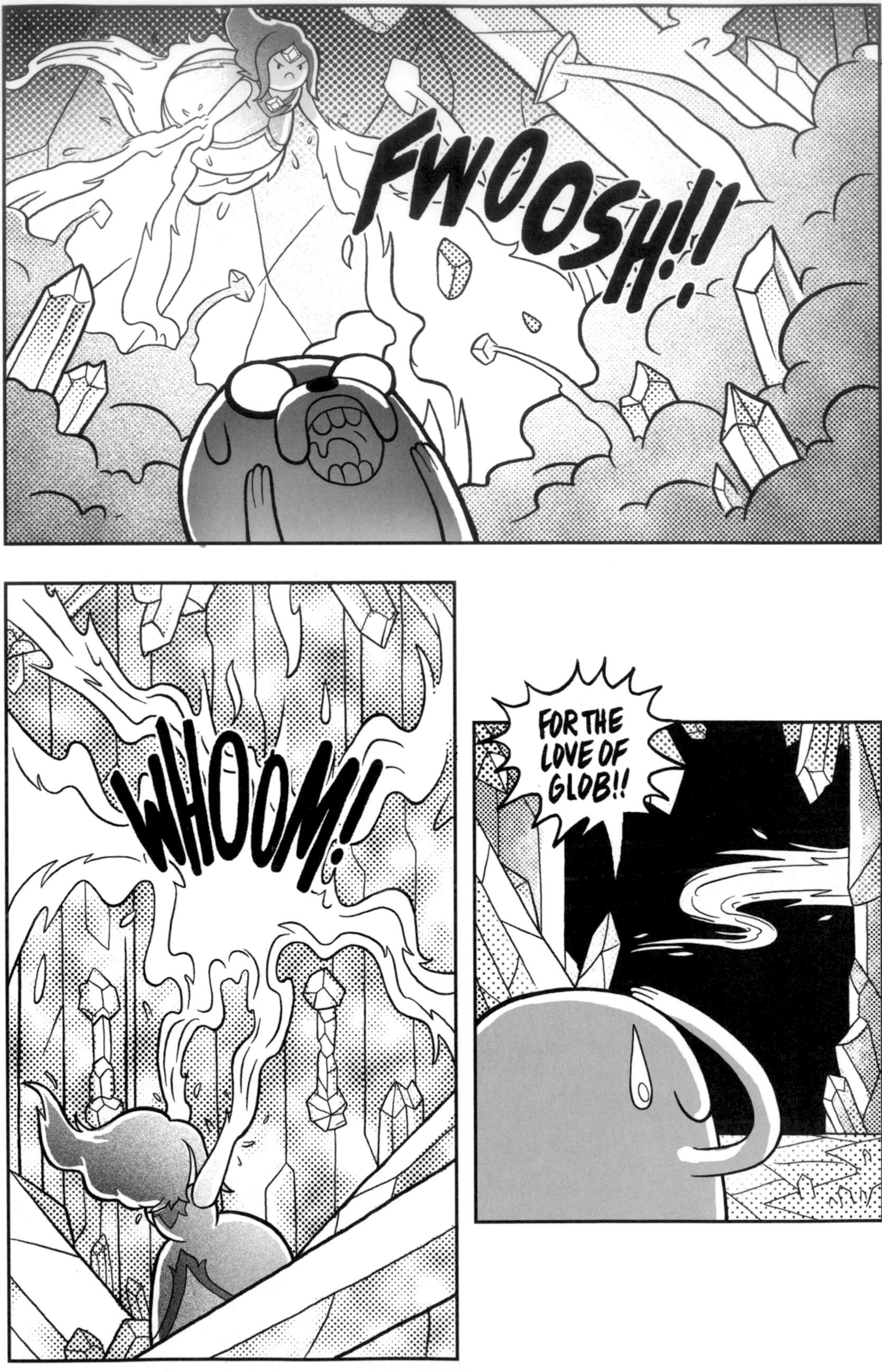
FWOOSH!!
WHOOM!
FOR THE LOVE OF GLOB!!

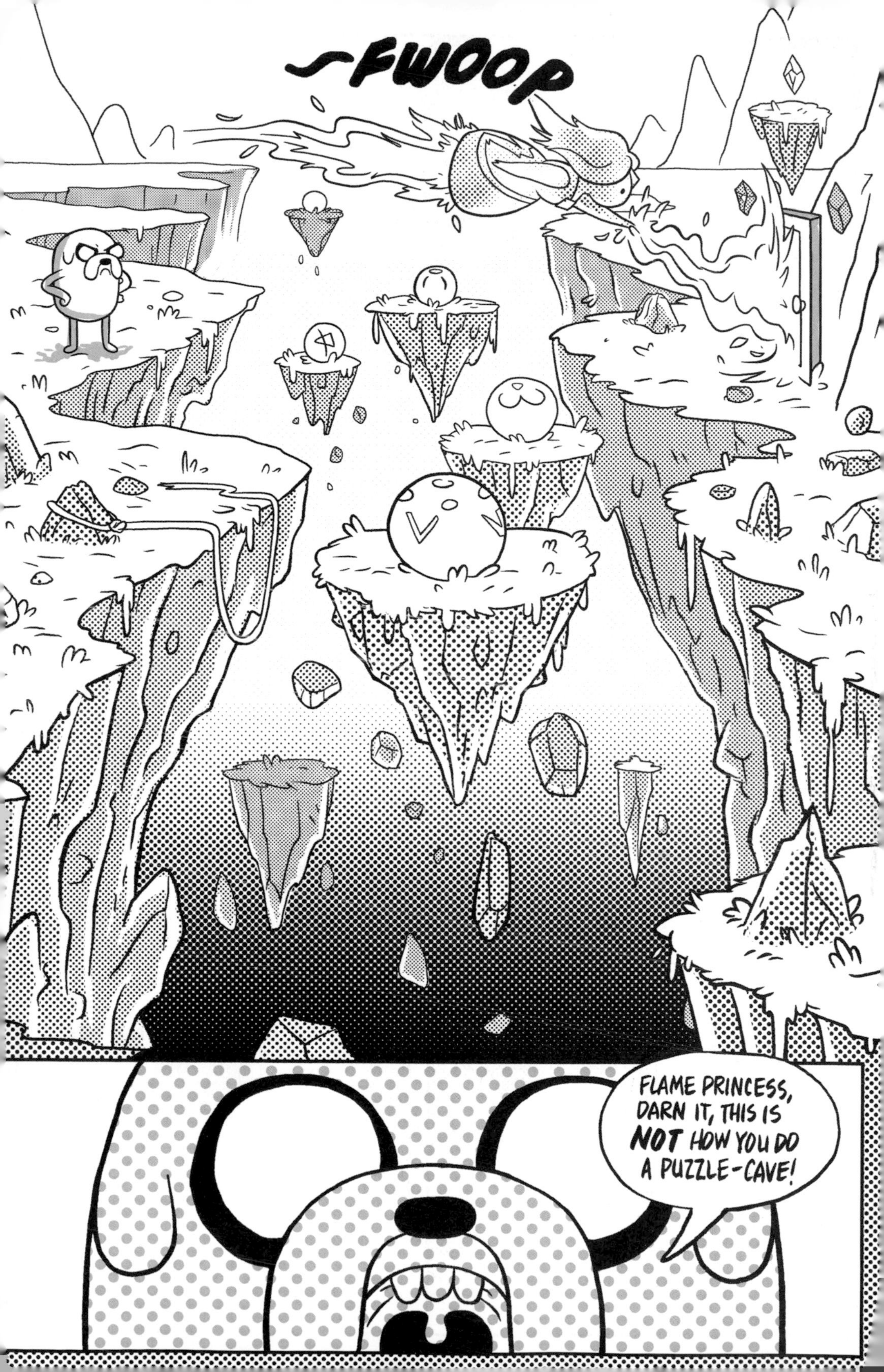
FWOOP
FLAME PRINCESS, DARN IT, THIS IS NOT HOW YOU DO A PUZZLE-CAVE!

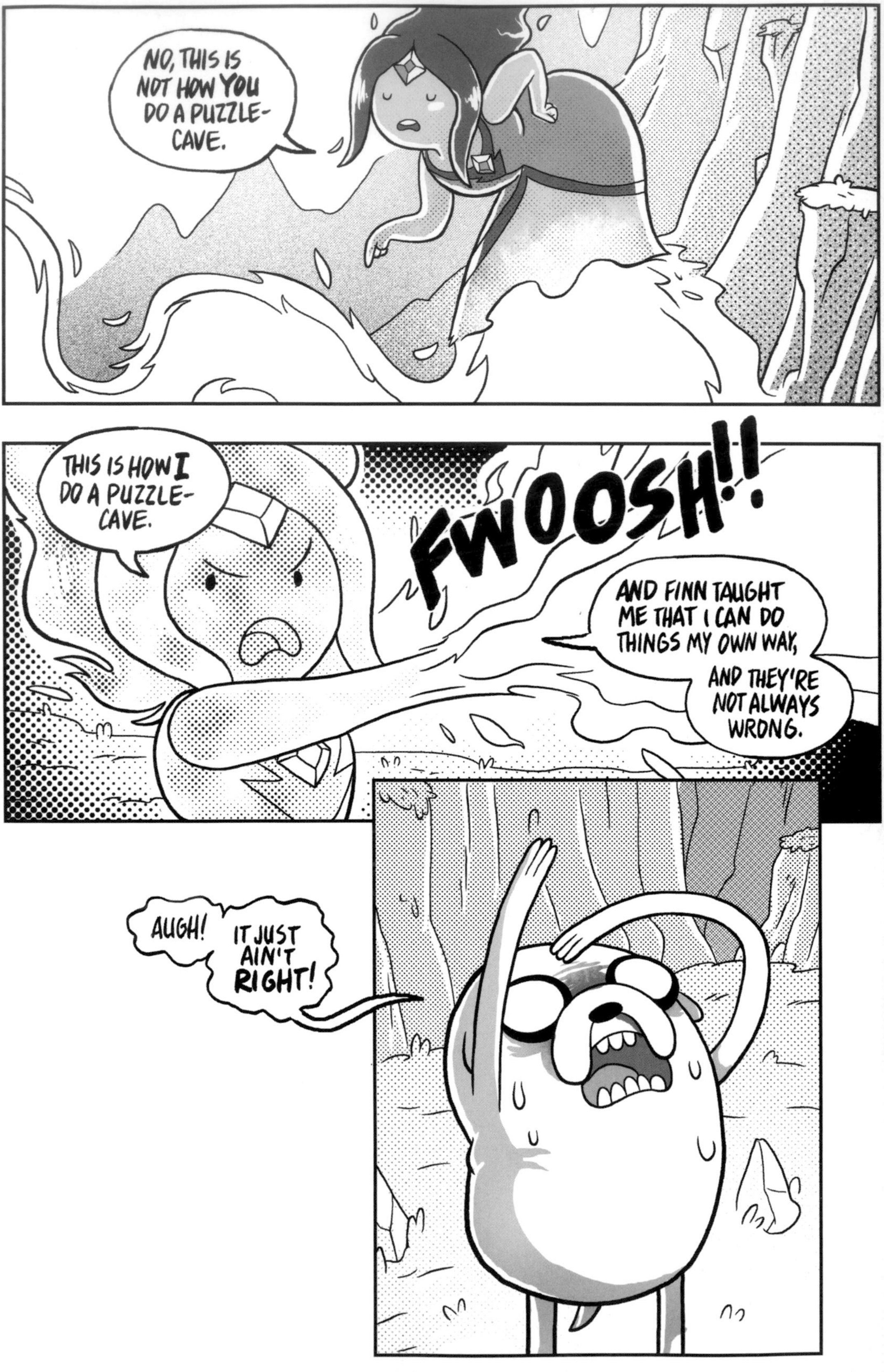
NO, THIS IS NOT HOW YOU DO A PUZZLE-CAVE.
THIS IS HOW I DO A PUZZLE-CAVE.
FWOOSH!!
AND FINN TAUGHT ME THAT I CAN DO THINGS MY OWN WAY,
AND THEY'RE NOT ALWAYS WRONG.
AUGH!
IT JUST AIN'T RIGHT!

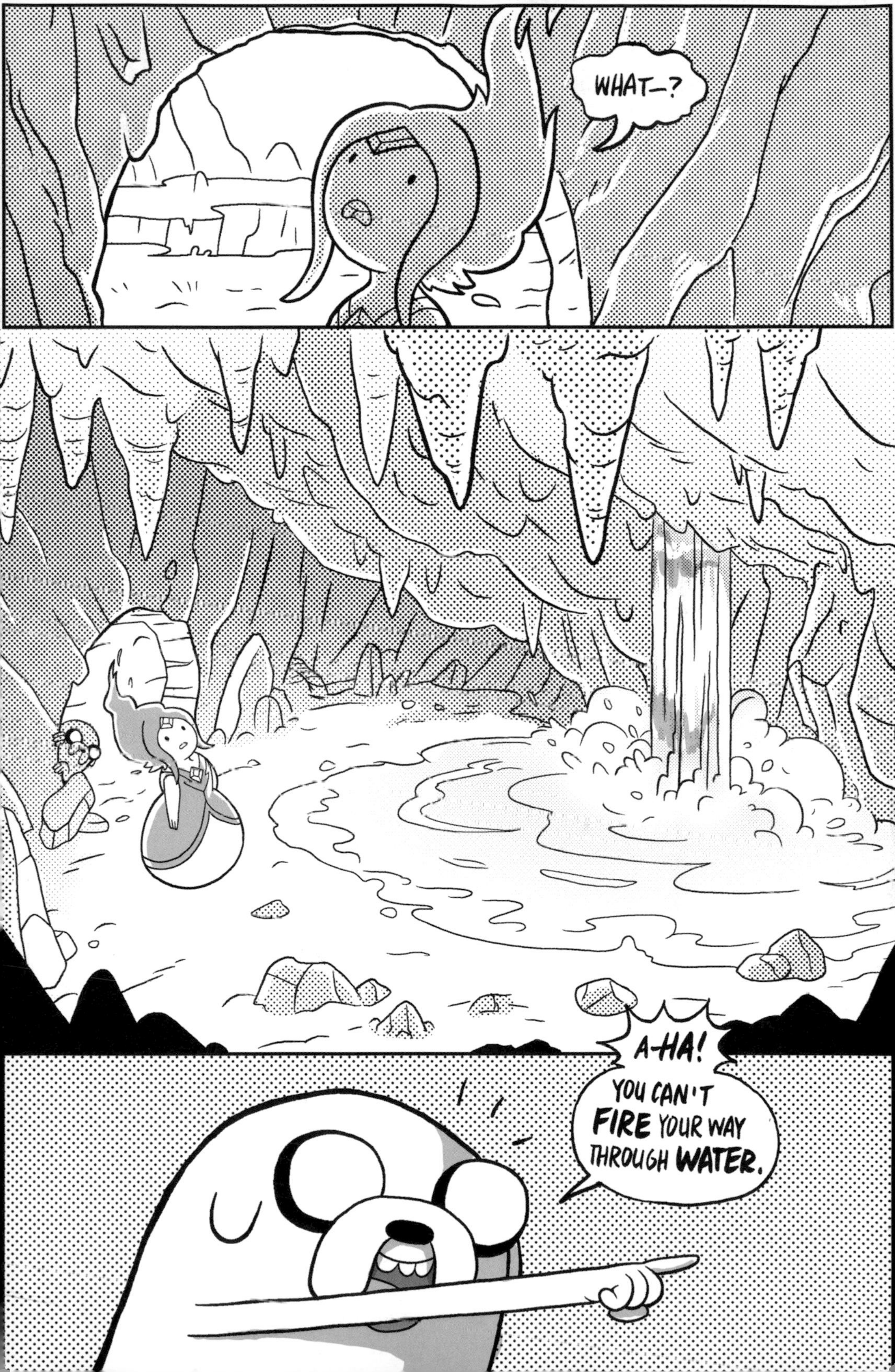
WHAT—?
A-HA!
YOU CAN'T FIRE YOUR WAY THROUGH WATER.

FOOO—

AAAAAAaa!!

TSsssss

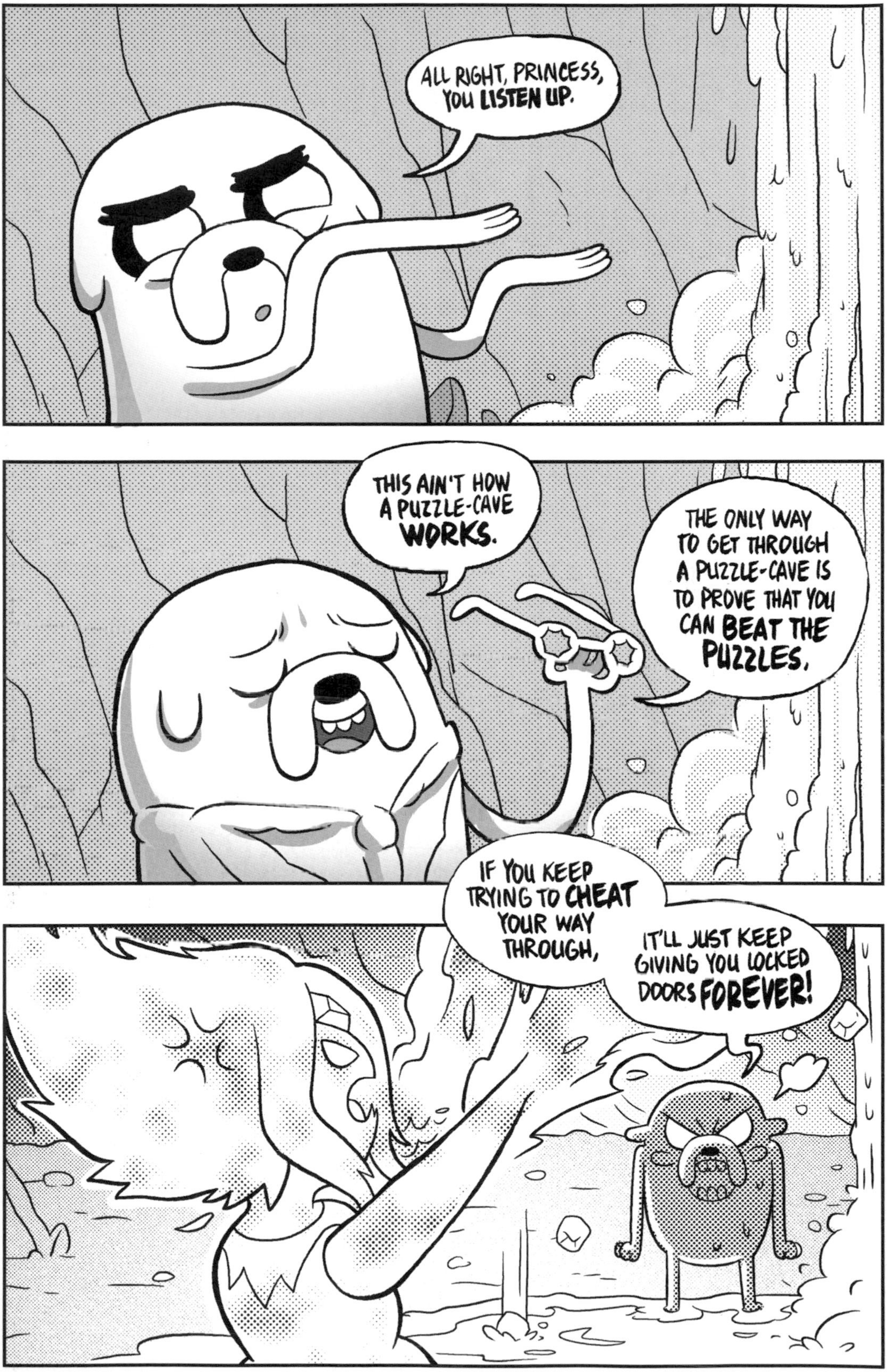
ALL RIGHT, PRINCESS, YOU LISTEN UP.
THIS AIN'T HOW A PUZZLE-CAVE WORKS.
THE ONLY WAY TO GET THROUGH A PUZZLE-CAVE IS TO PROVE THAT YOU CAN BEAT THE PUZZLES.
IF YOU KEEP TRYING TO CHEAT YOUR WAY THROUGH,
IT'LL JUST KEEP GIVING YOU LOCKED DOORS FOREVER!

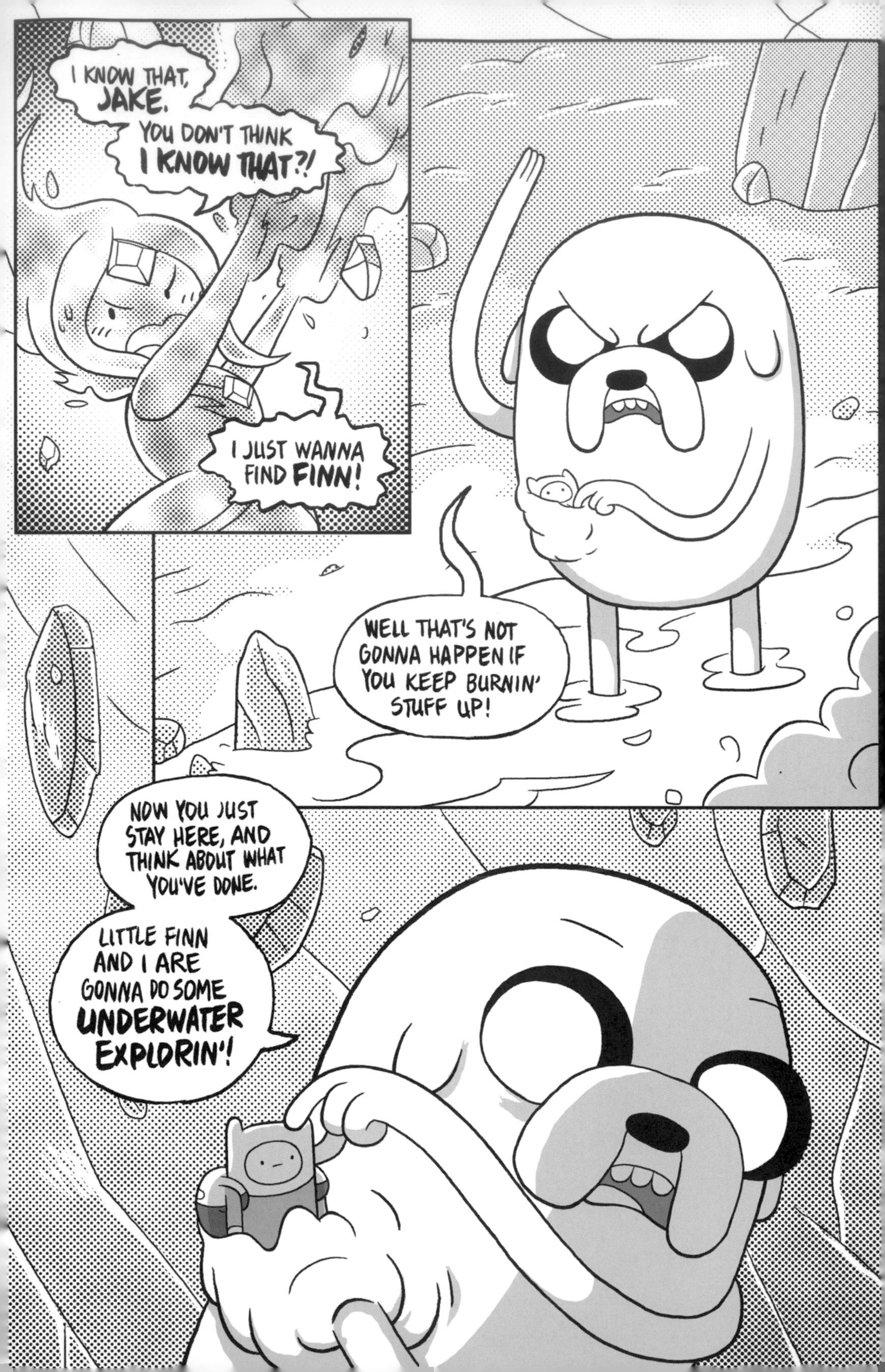
I KNOW THAT, JAKE.
YOU DON'T THINK I KNOW THAT?!
I JUST WANNA FIND FINN!
WELL THAT'S NOT GONNA HAPPEN IF YOU KEEP BURNIN' STUFF UP!
NOW YOU JUST STAY HERE, AND THINK ABOUT WHAT YOU'VE DONE.
LITTLE FINN AND I ARE GONNA DO SOME UNDERWATER EXPLORIN'!

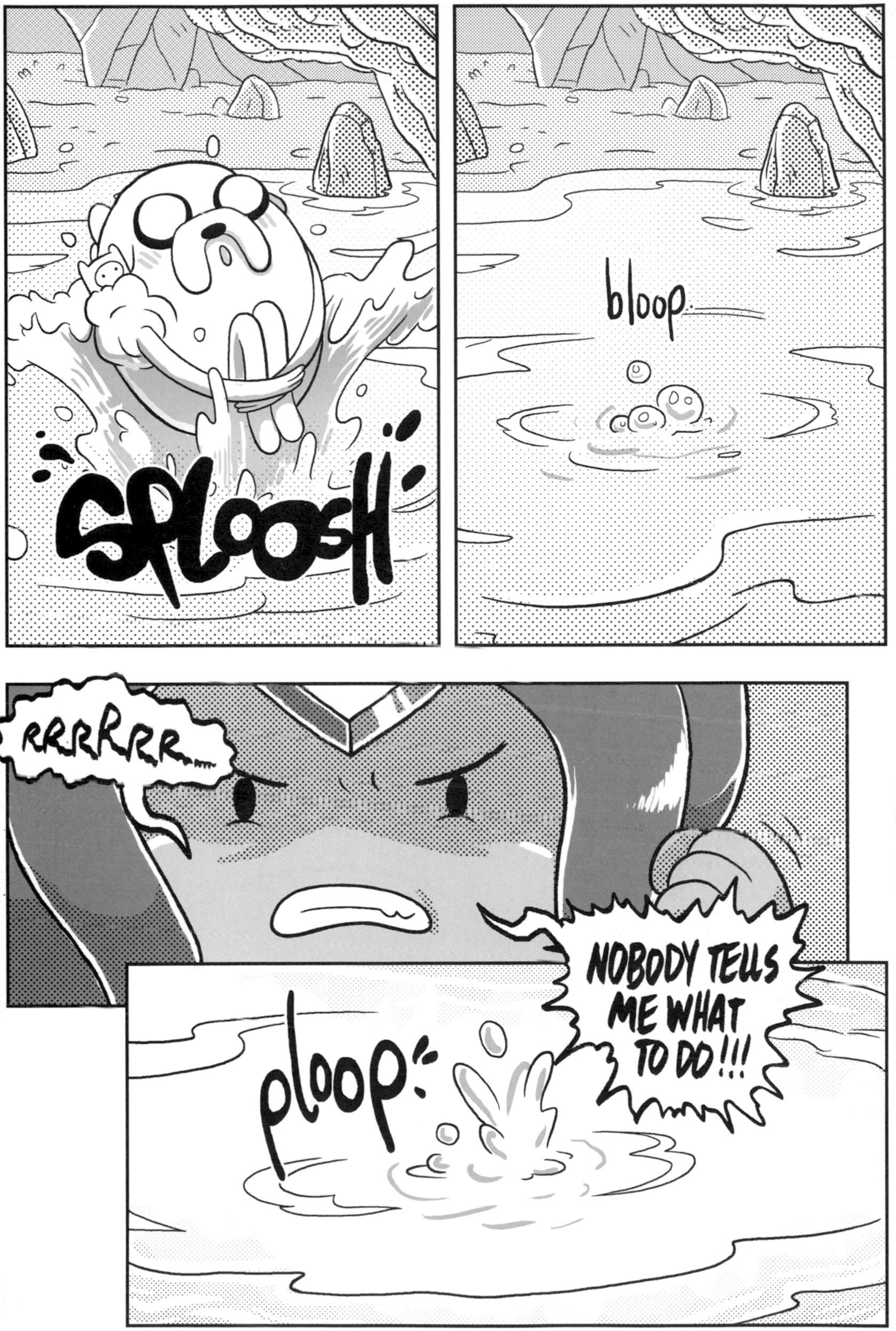
SPLOOSH
bloop
RRRRRR...
NOBODY TELLS ME WHAT TO DO!!!
ploop

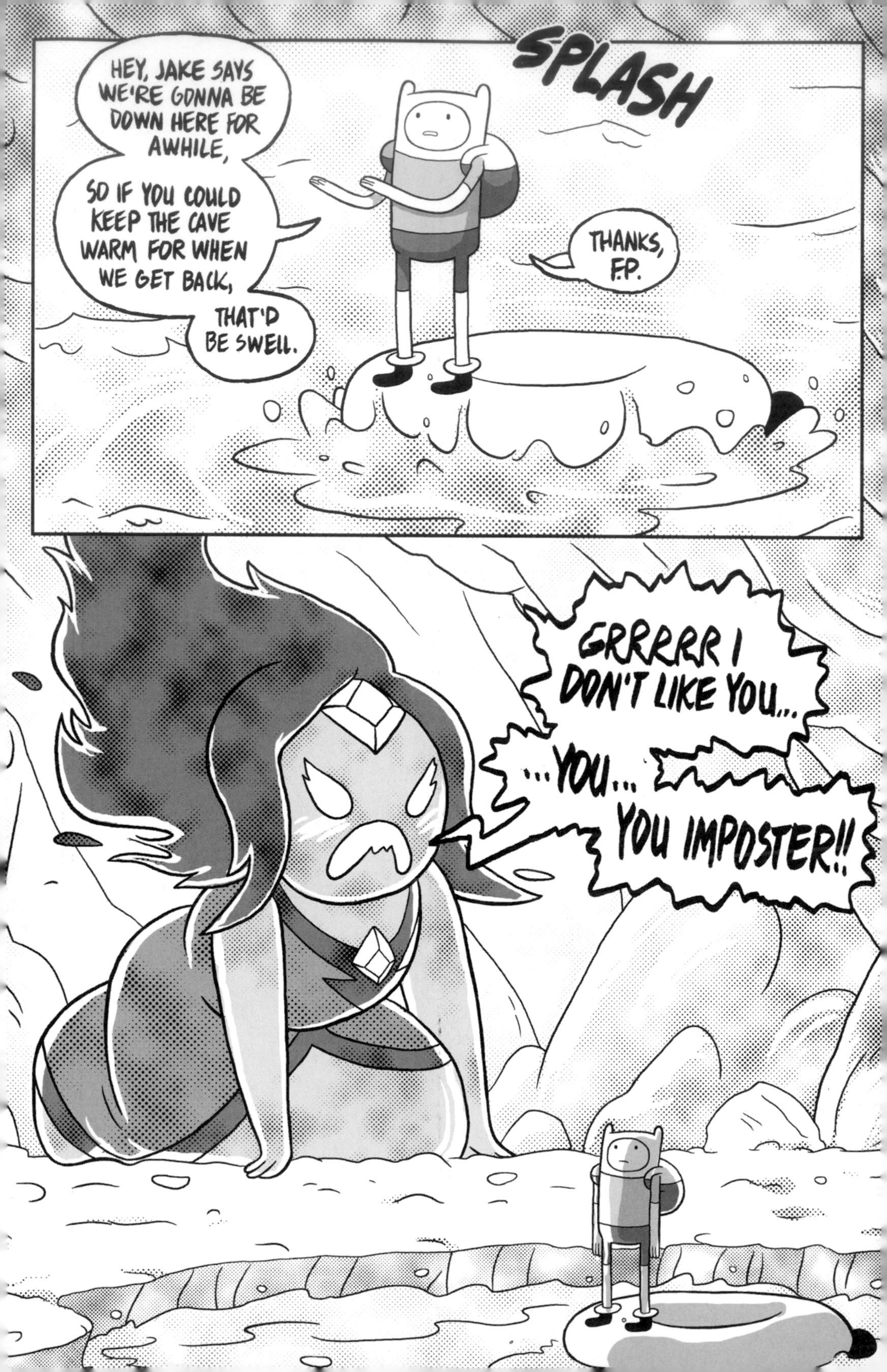
SPLASH
HEY, JAKE SAYS WE'RE GONNA BE DOWN HERE FOR AWHILE,
SO IF YOU COULD KEEP THE CAVE WARM FOR WHEN WE GET BACK,
THAT'D BE SWELL.
THANKS, F.P.
GRRRRR I DON'T LIKE YOU...
...YOU...
YOU IMPOSTER!!

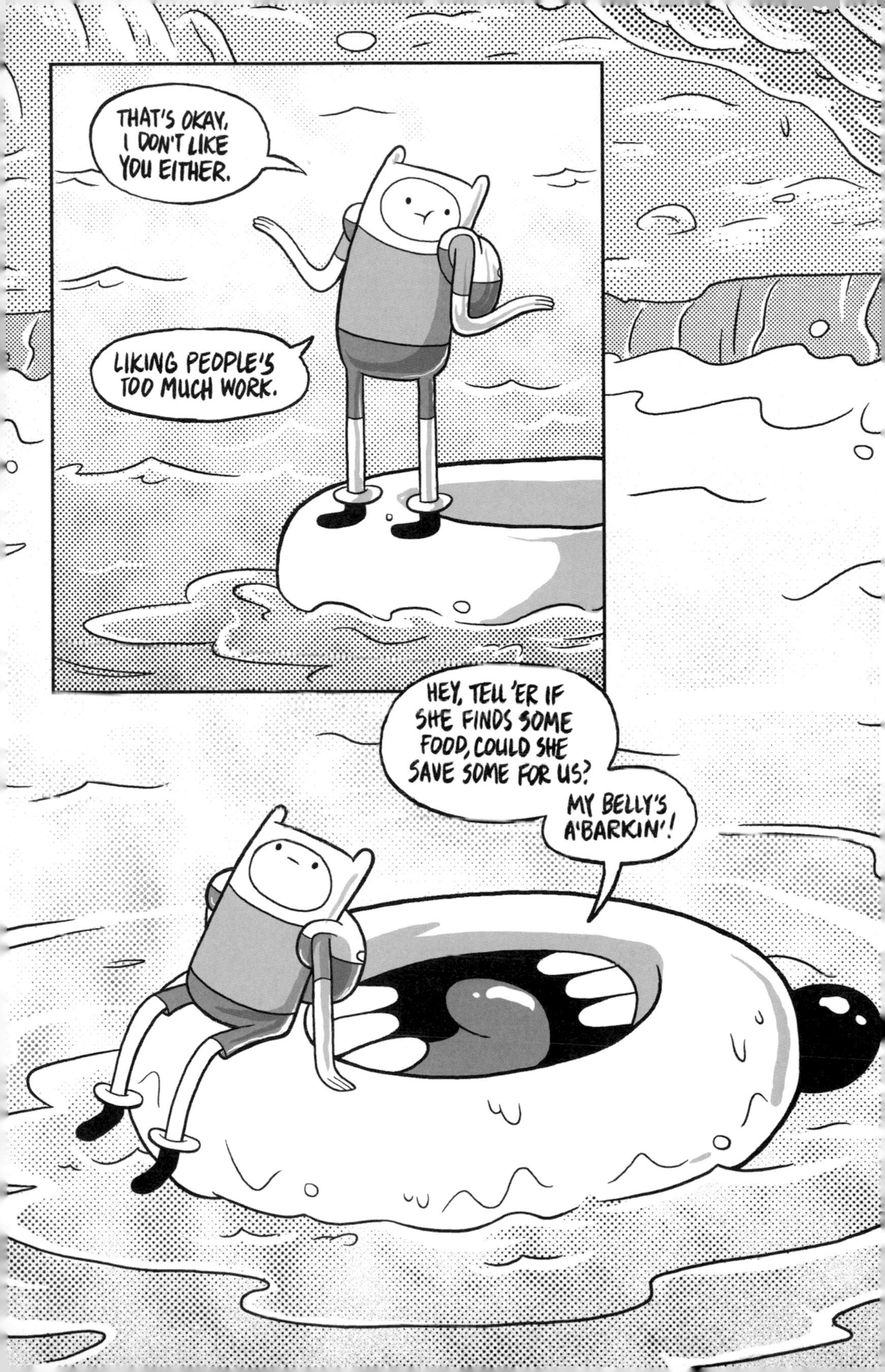
THAT'S OKAY, I DON'T LIKE YOU EITHER.
LIKING PEOPLE'S TOO MUCH WORK.
HEY, TELL 'ER IF SHE FINDS SOME FOOD, COULD SHE SAVE SOME FOR US?
MY BELLY'S A'BARKIN'!

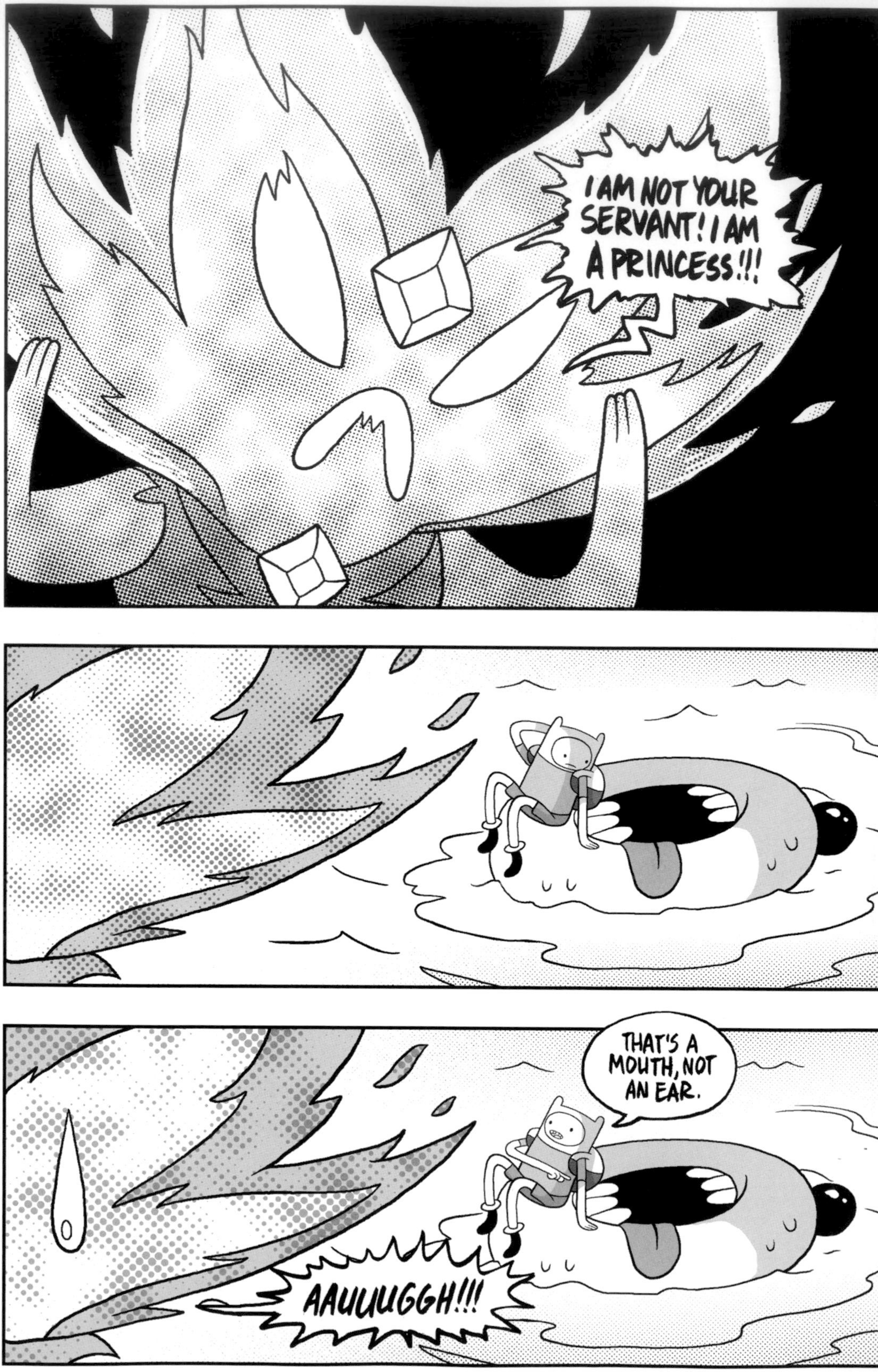
I AM NOT YOUR SERVANT! I AM A PRINCESS!!!
THAT'S A MOUTH, NOT AN EAR.
AAUUUGGH!!!

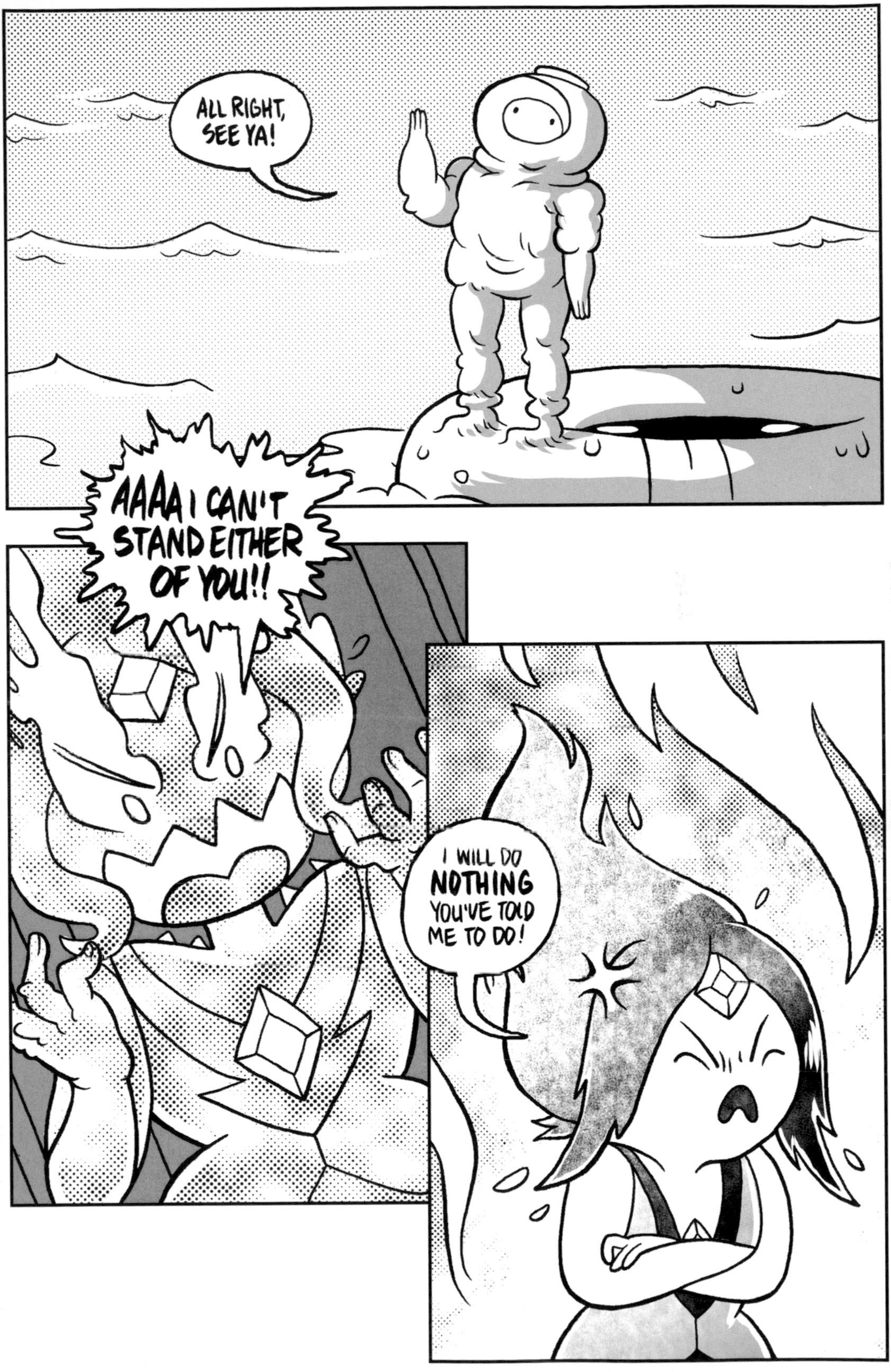
ALL RIGHT, SEE YA!
AAAA I CAN'T STAND EITHER OF YOU!!
I WILL DO **NOTHING** YOU'VE TOLD ME TO DO!

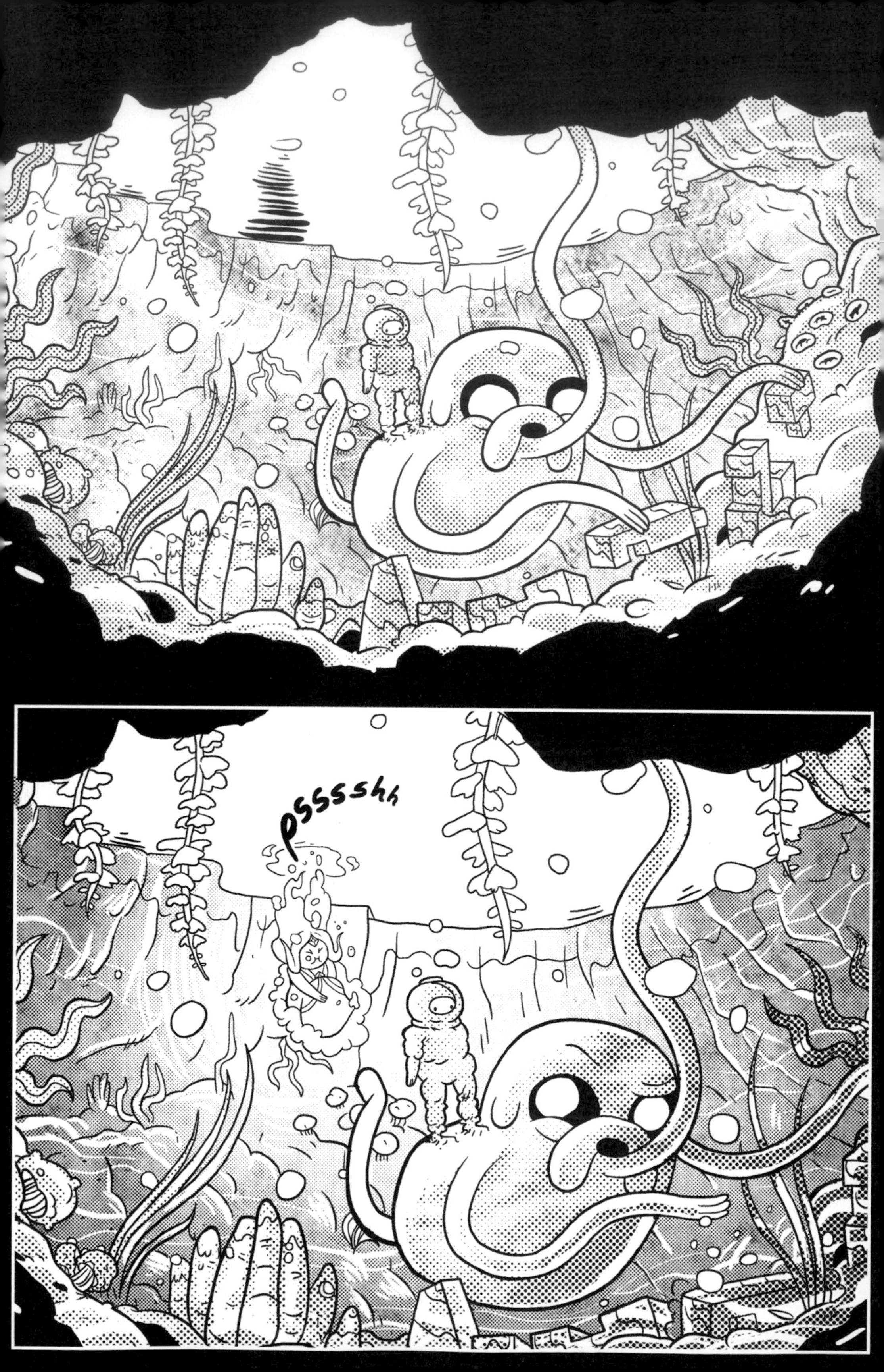
PSSSSHH

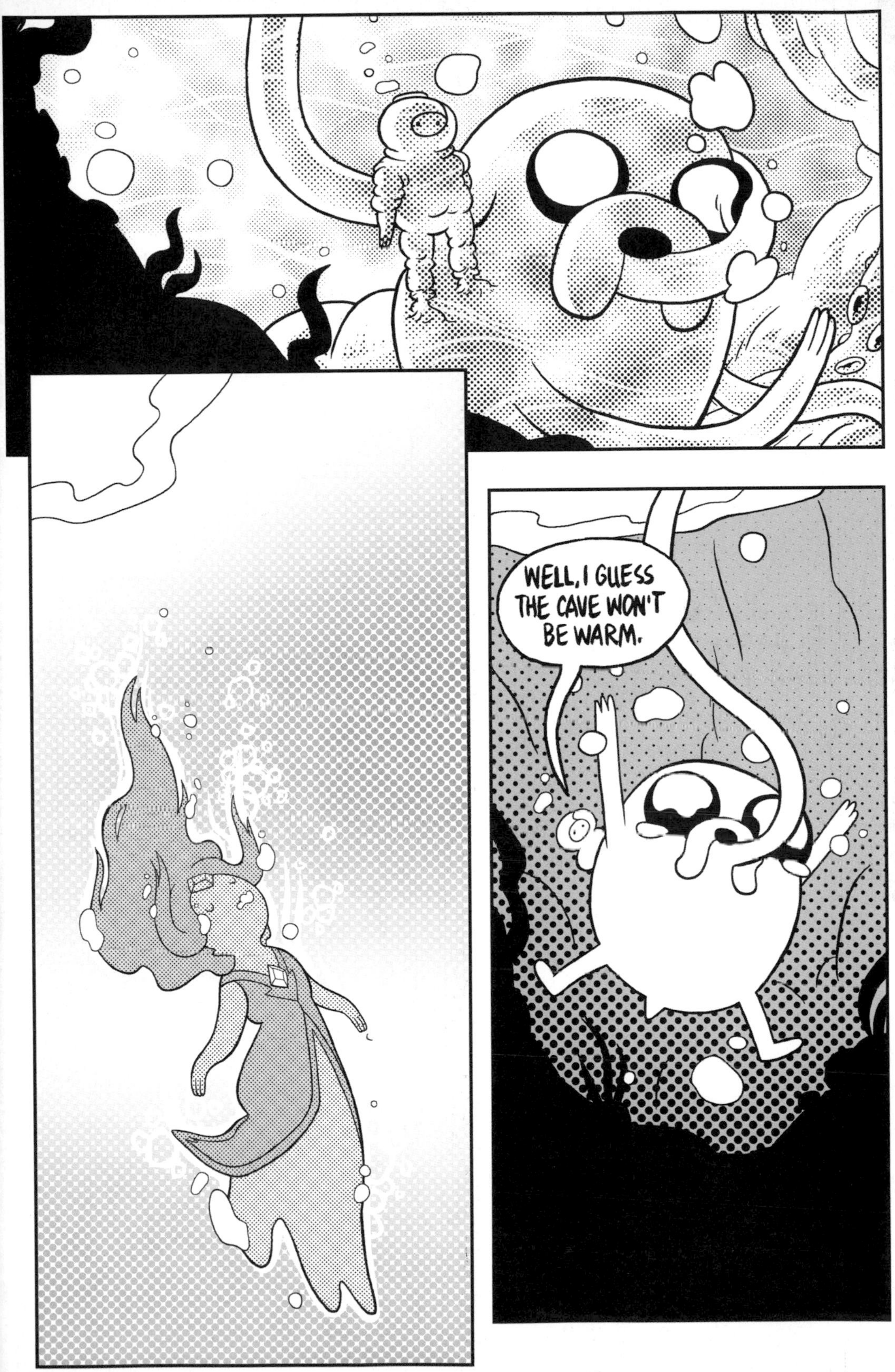
WELL, I GUESS THE CAVE WON'T BE WARM.

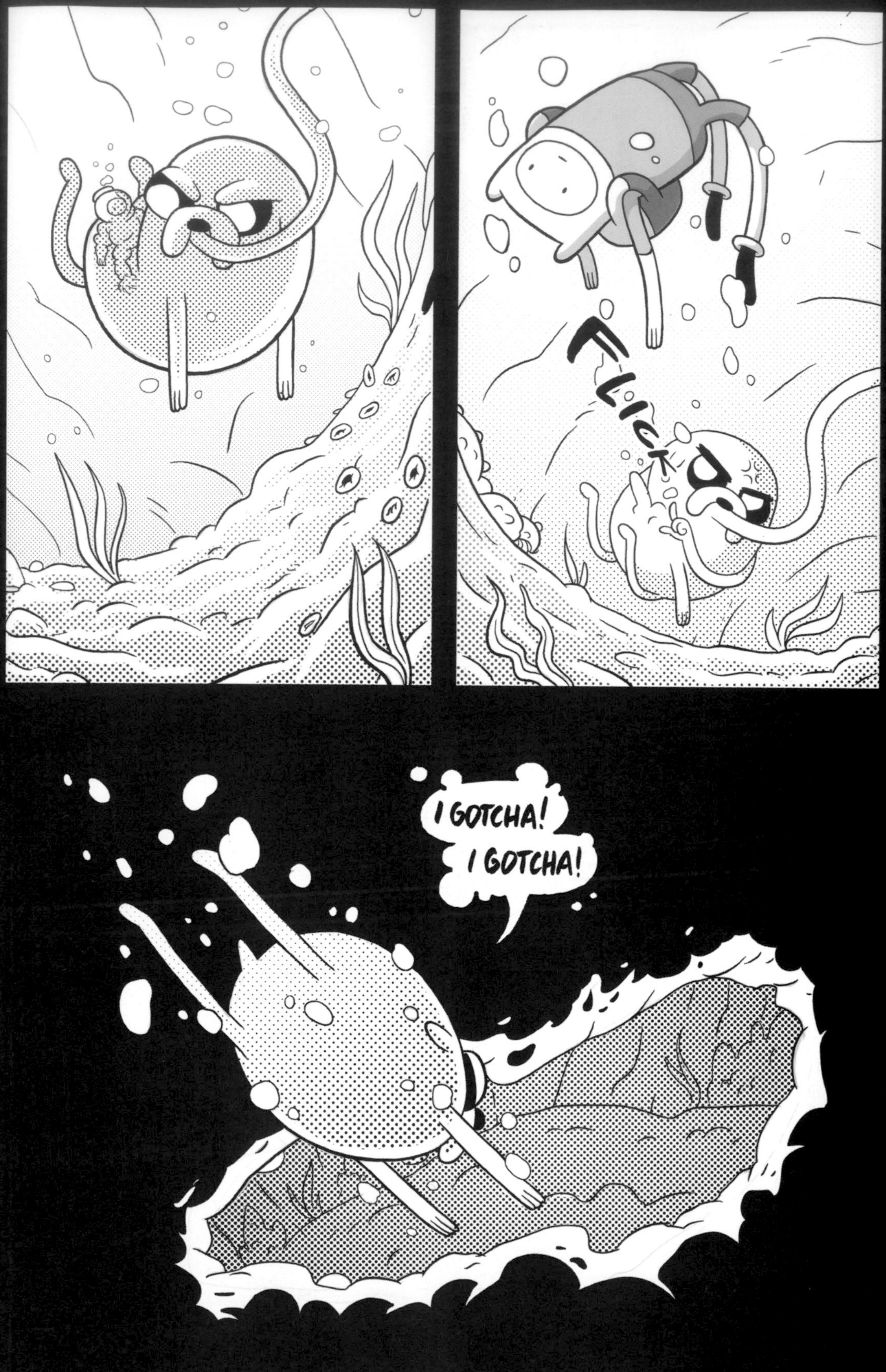
FLICK
I GOTCHA! I GOTCHA!

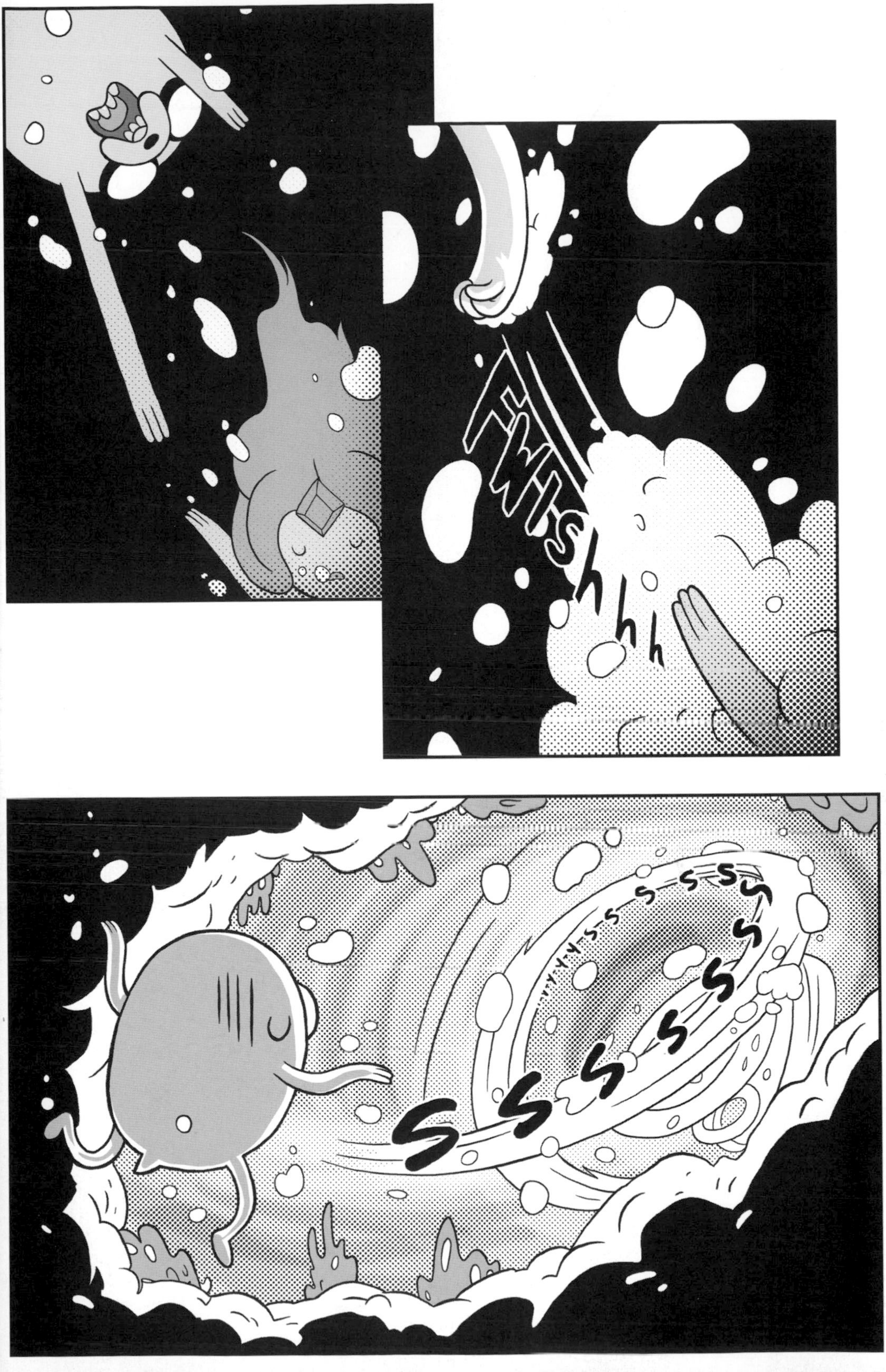
FWIShhhh
SSSSSSSSS-S-S-S-S

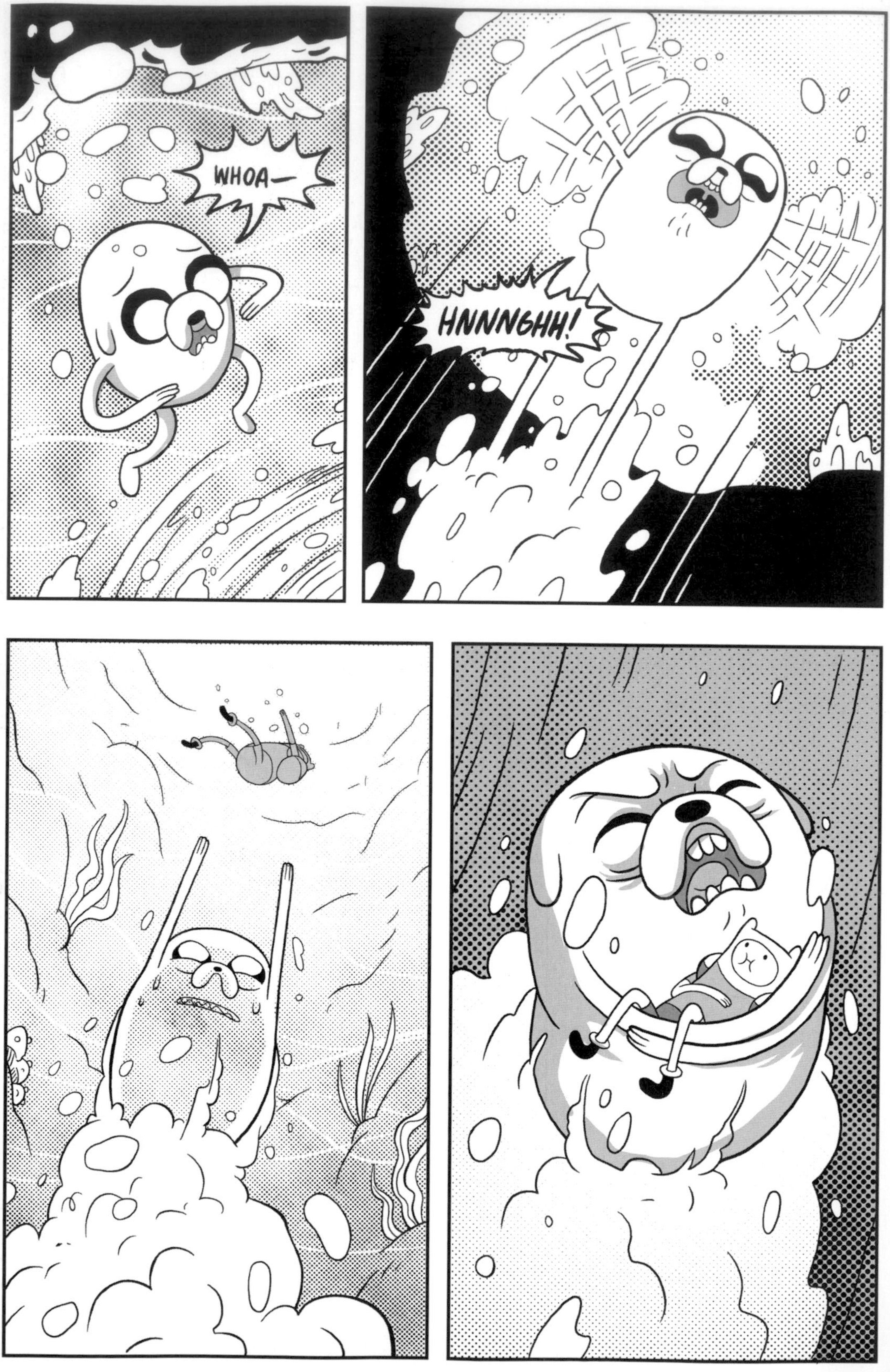
WHOA—
HNNNGHH!

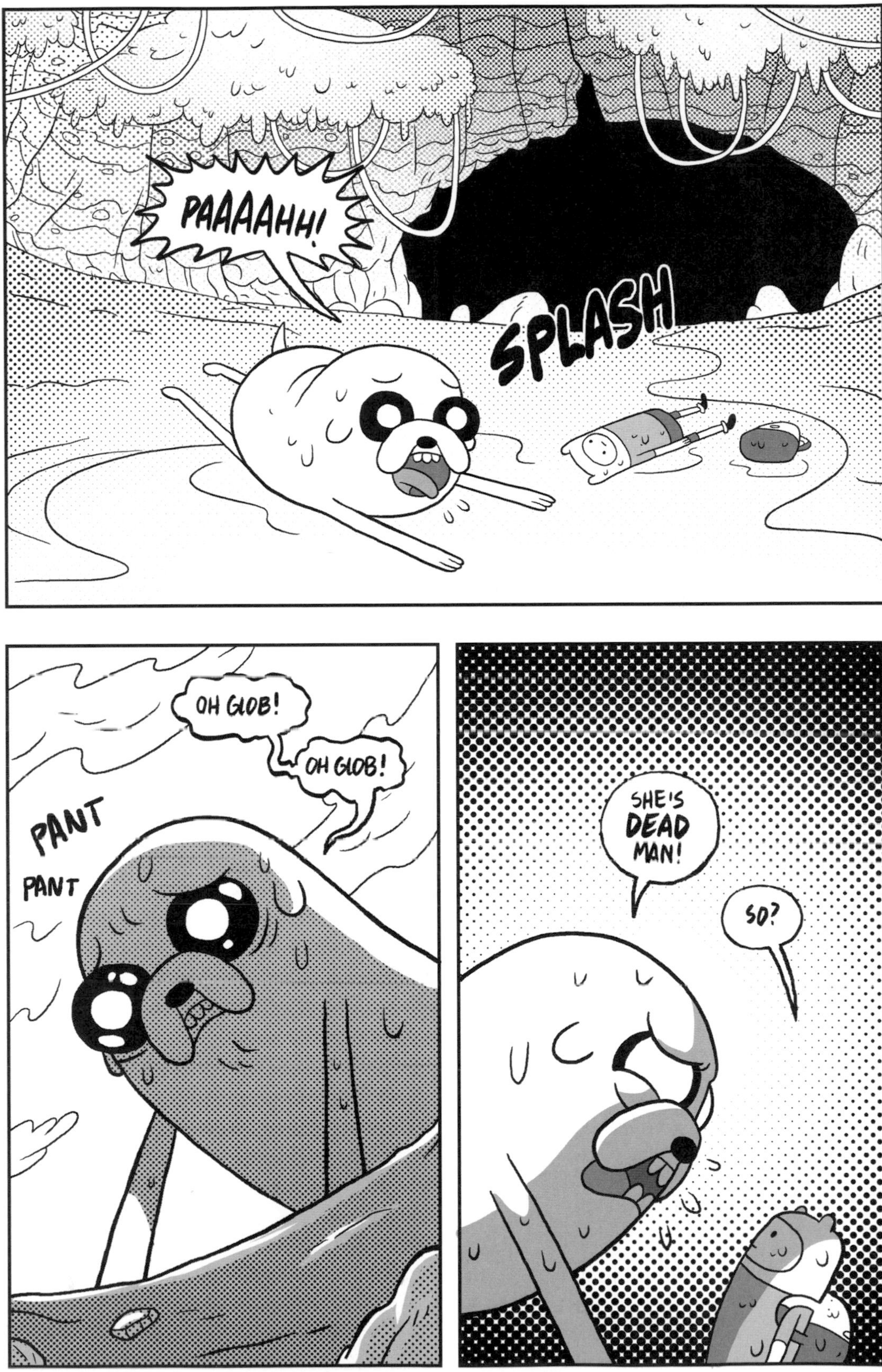
PAAAAHH!
SPLASH
OH GLOB!
OH GLOB!
PANT
PANT
SHE'S DEAD MAN!
SO?

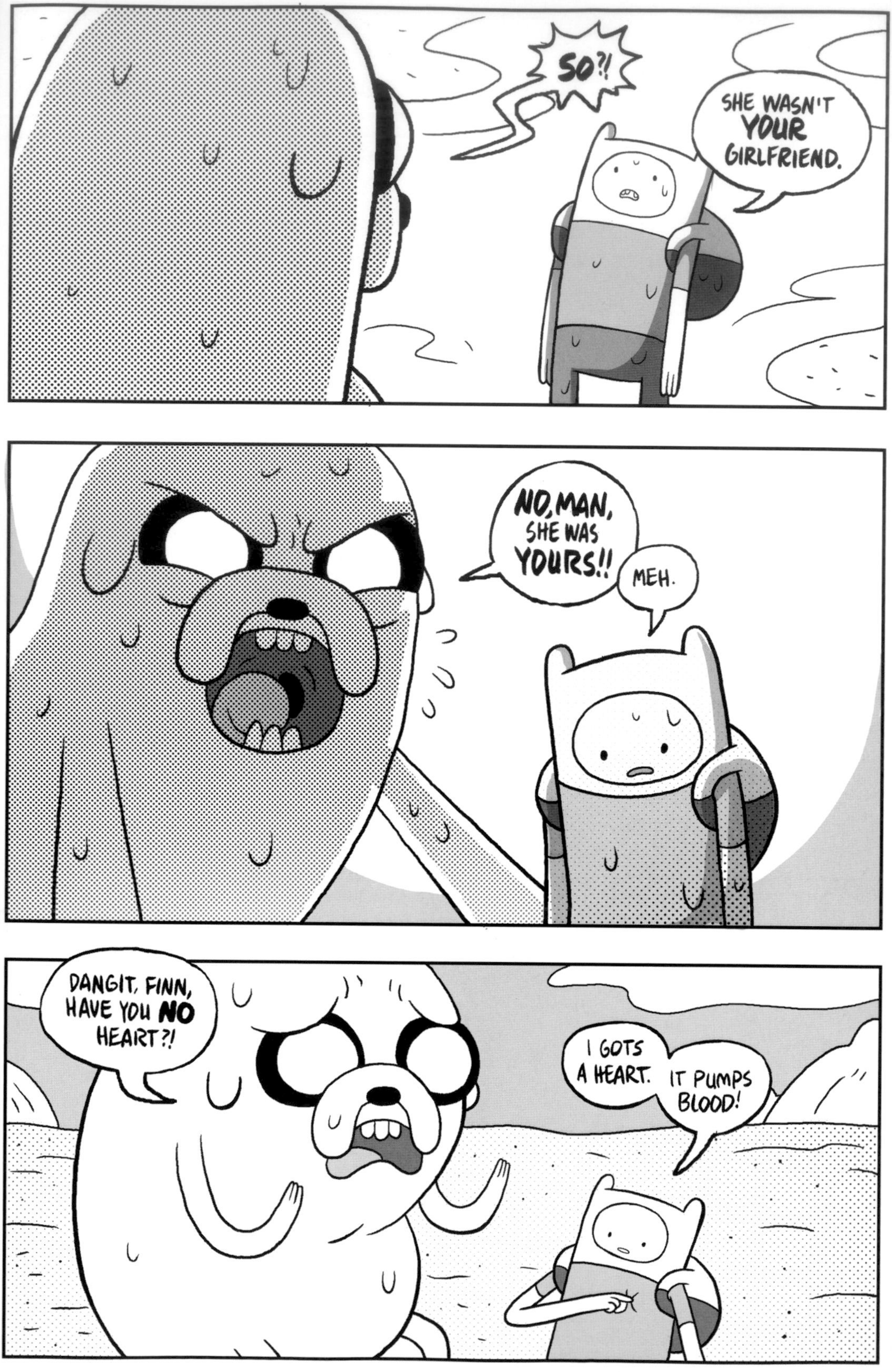
SO?!
SHE WASN'T YOUR GIRLFRIEND.
NO, MAN, SHE WAS YOURS!!
MEH.
DANGIT, FINN, HAVE YOU NO HEART?!
I GOTS A HEART.
IT PUMPS BLOOD!

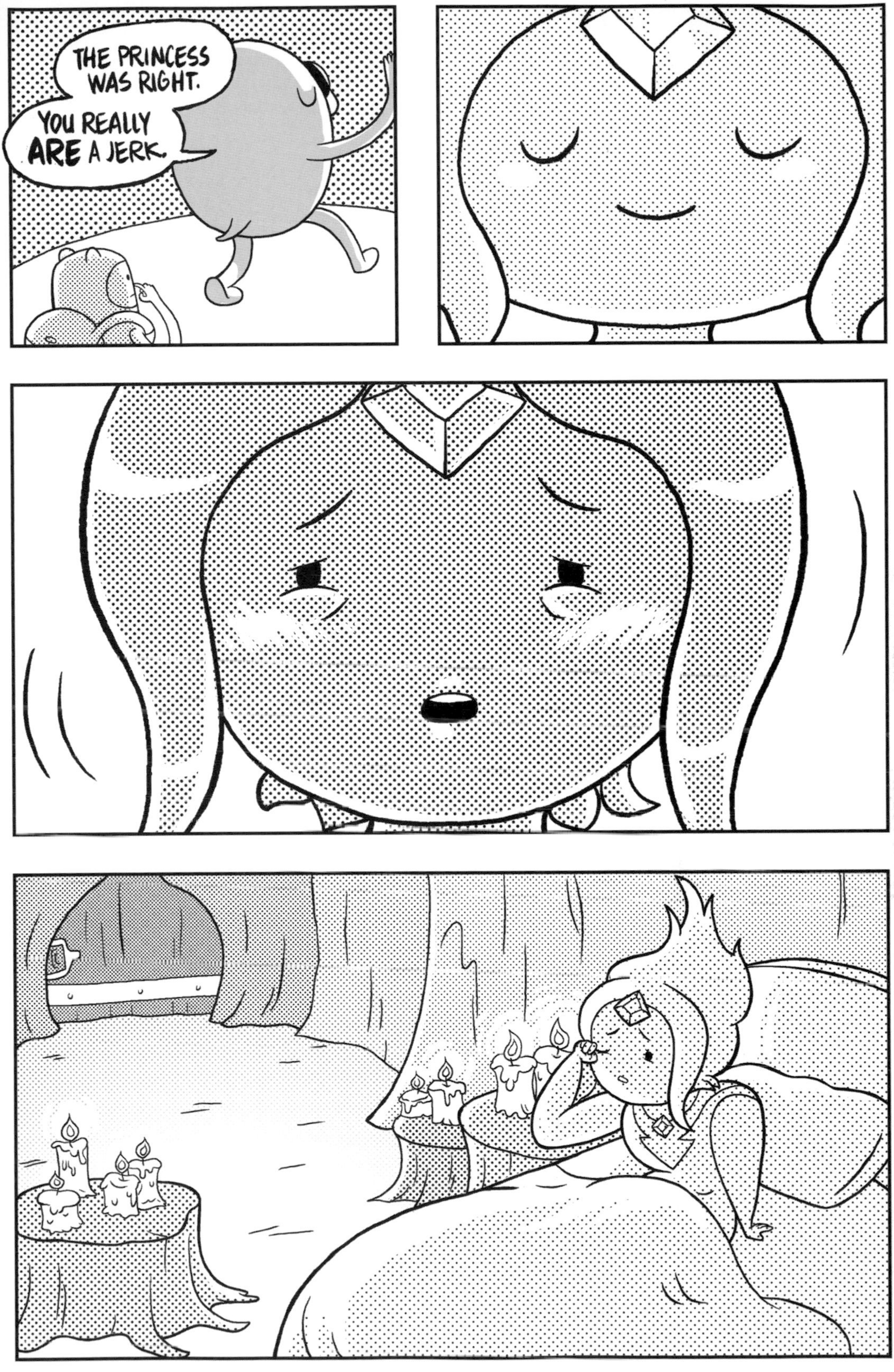
THE PRINCESS WAS RIGHT.
YOU REALLY ARE A JERK.

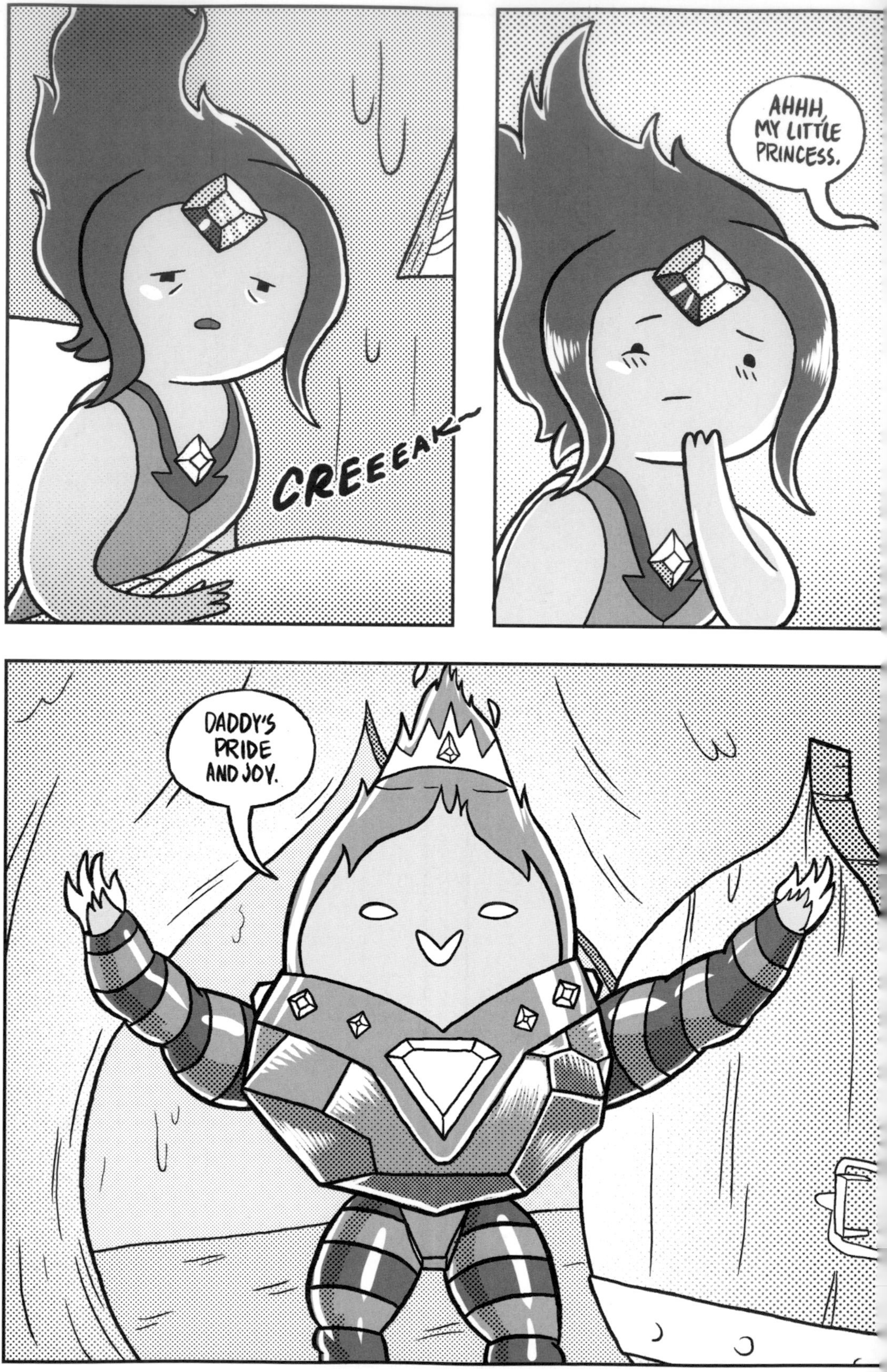
CREEEAK~
AHHH, MY LITTLE PRINCESS.
DADDY'S PRIDE AND JOY.

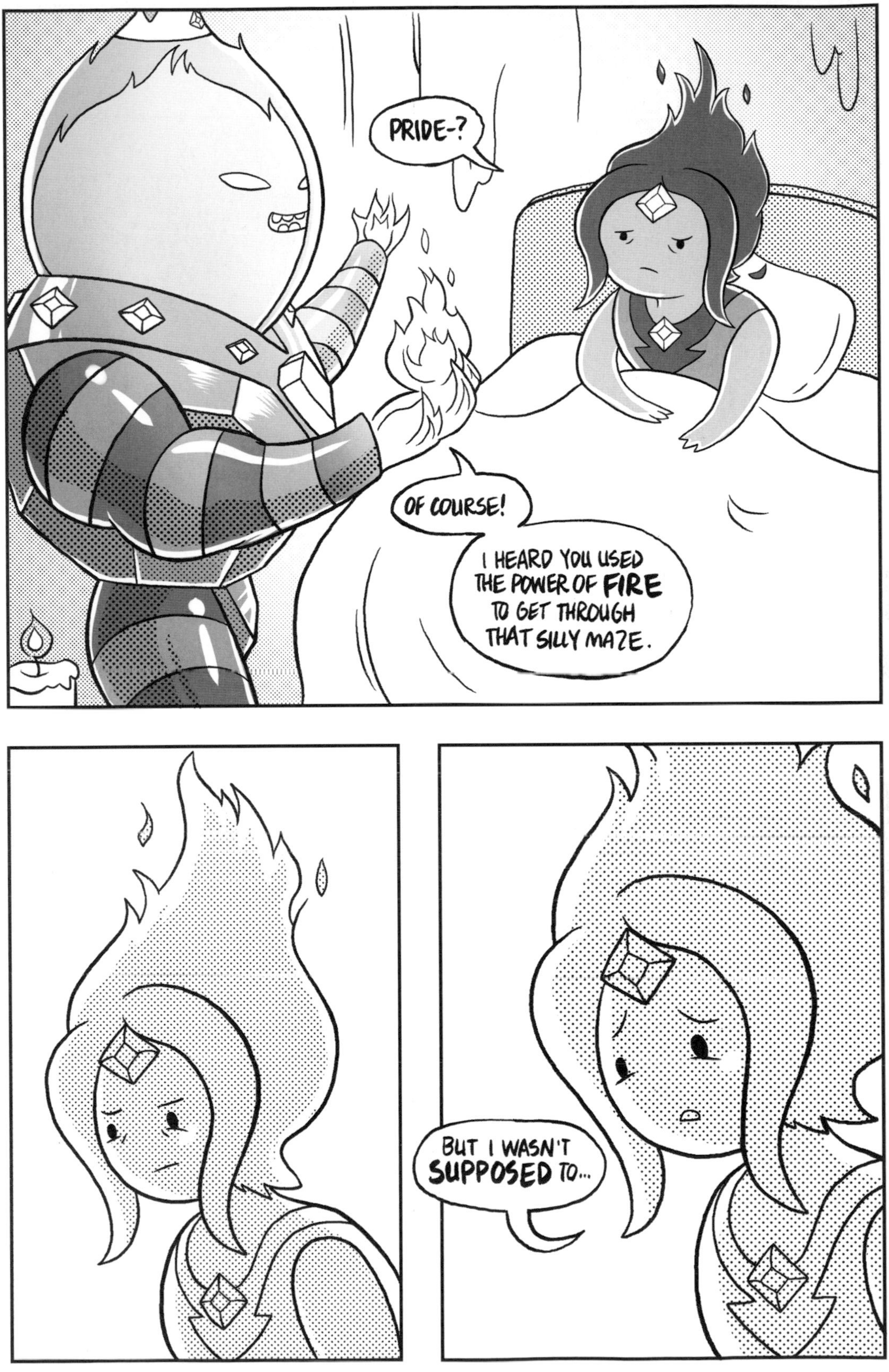
PRIDE-?
OF COURSE!
I HEARD YOU USED THE POWER OF FIRE TO GET THROUGH THAT SILLY MAZE.
BUT I WASN'T SUPPOSED TO...

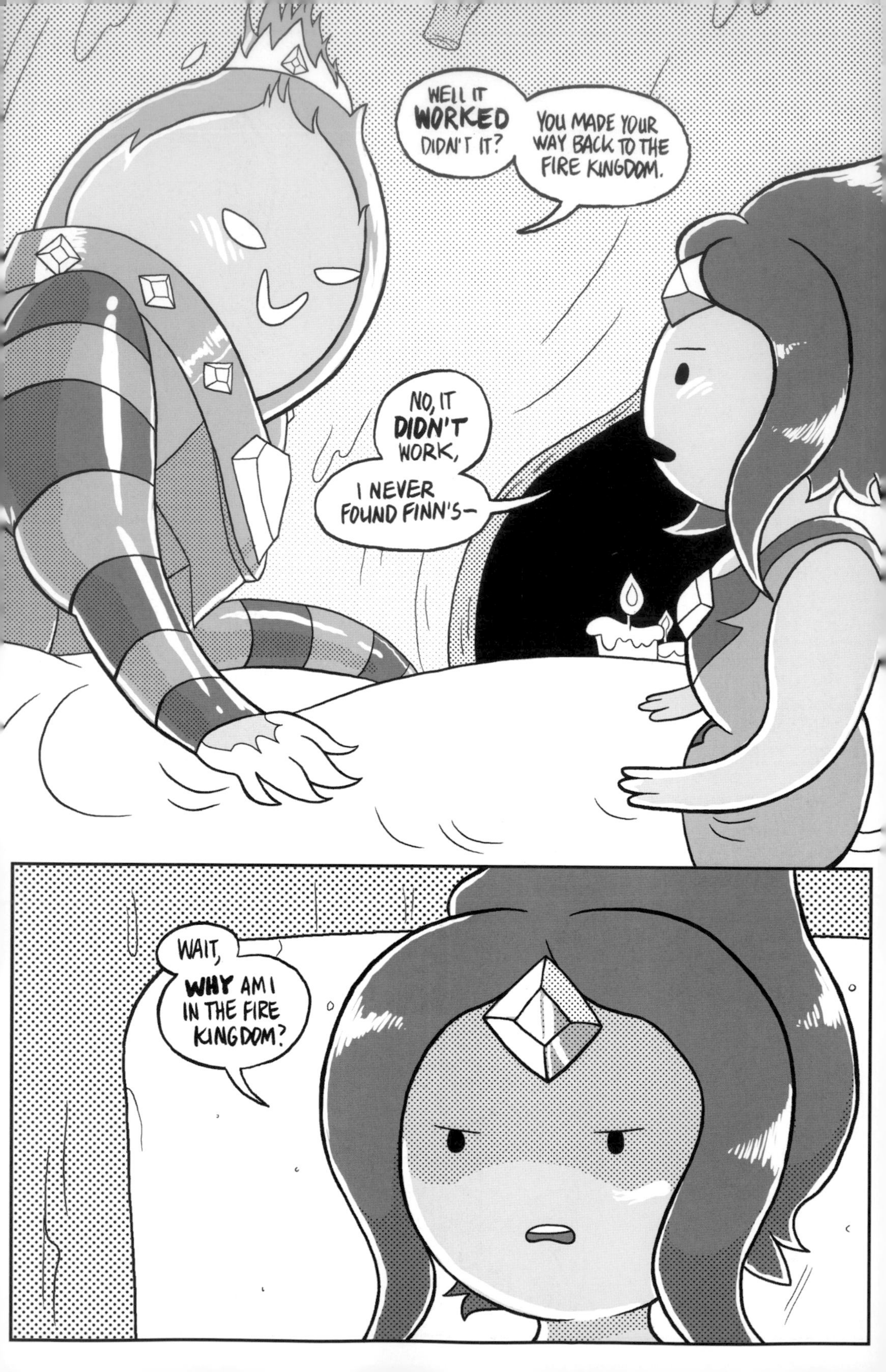
WELL IT WORKED DIDN'T IT?
YOU MADE YOUR WAY BACK TO THE FIRE KINGDOM.
NO, IT DIDN'T WORK,
I NEVER FOUND FINN'S—
WAIT, WHY AM I IN THE FIRE KINGDOM?

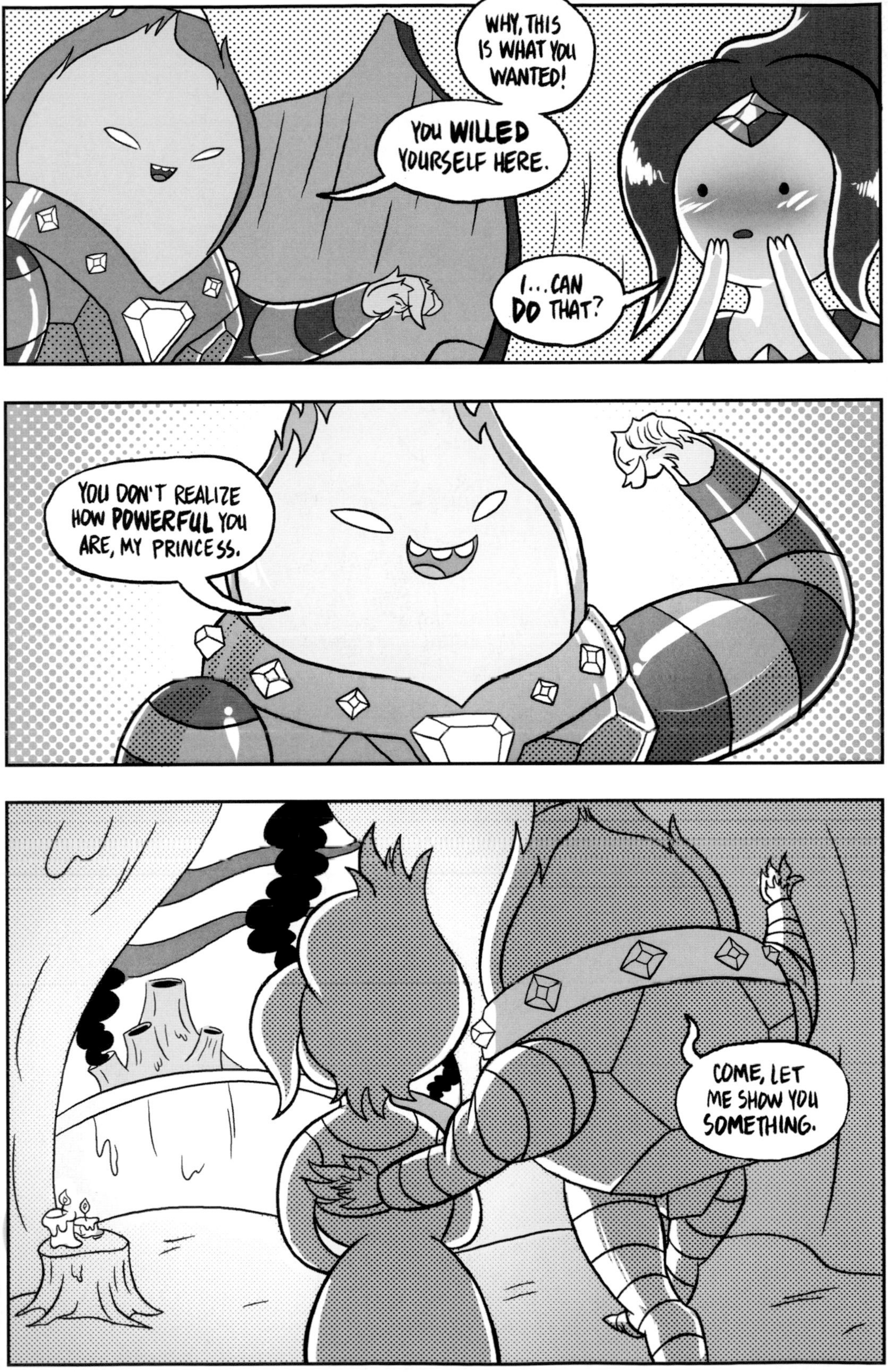
WHY, THIS IS WHAT YOU WANTED!
YOU WILLED YOURSELF HERE.
I...CAN DO THAT?
YOU DON'T REALIZE HOW POWERFUL YOU ARE, MY PRINCESS.
COME, LET ME SHOW YOU SOMETHING.

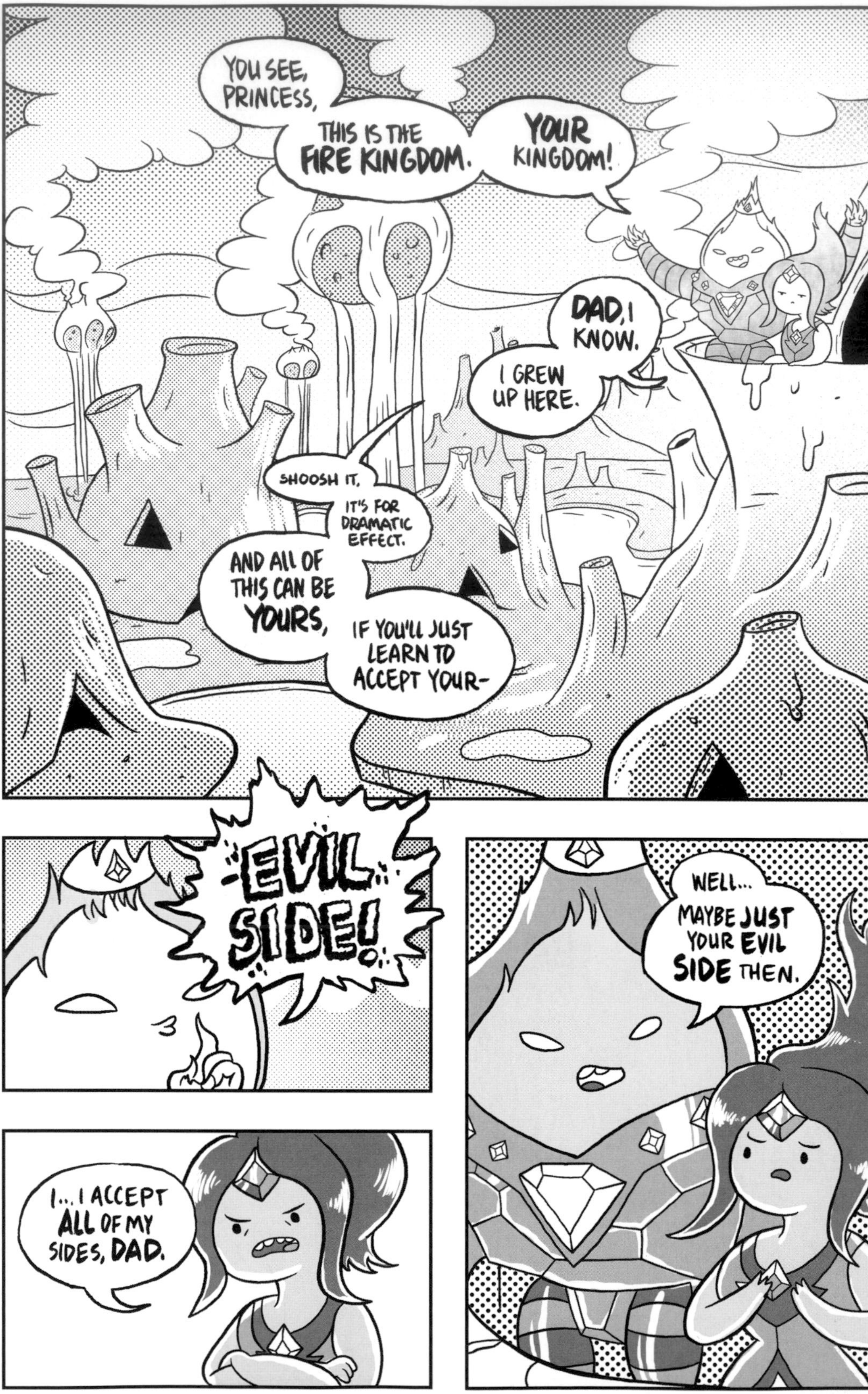
YOU SEE, PRINCESS,
THIS IS THE FIRE KINGDOM.
YOUR KINGDOM!
DAD, I KNOW.
I GREW UP HERE.
SHOOSH IT.
IT'S FOR DRAMATIC EFFECT.
AND ALL OF THIS CAN BE YOURS,
IF YOU'LL JUST LEARN TO ACCEPT YOUR-
EVIL SIDE!
WELL... MAYBE JUST YOUR EVIL SIDE THEN.
I... I ACCEPT ALL OF MY SIDES, DAD.

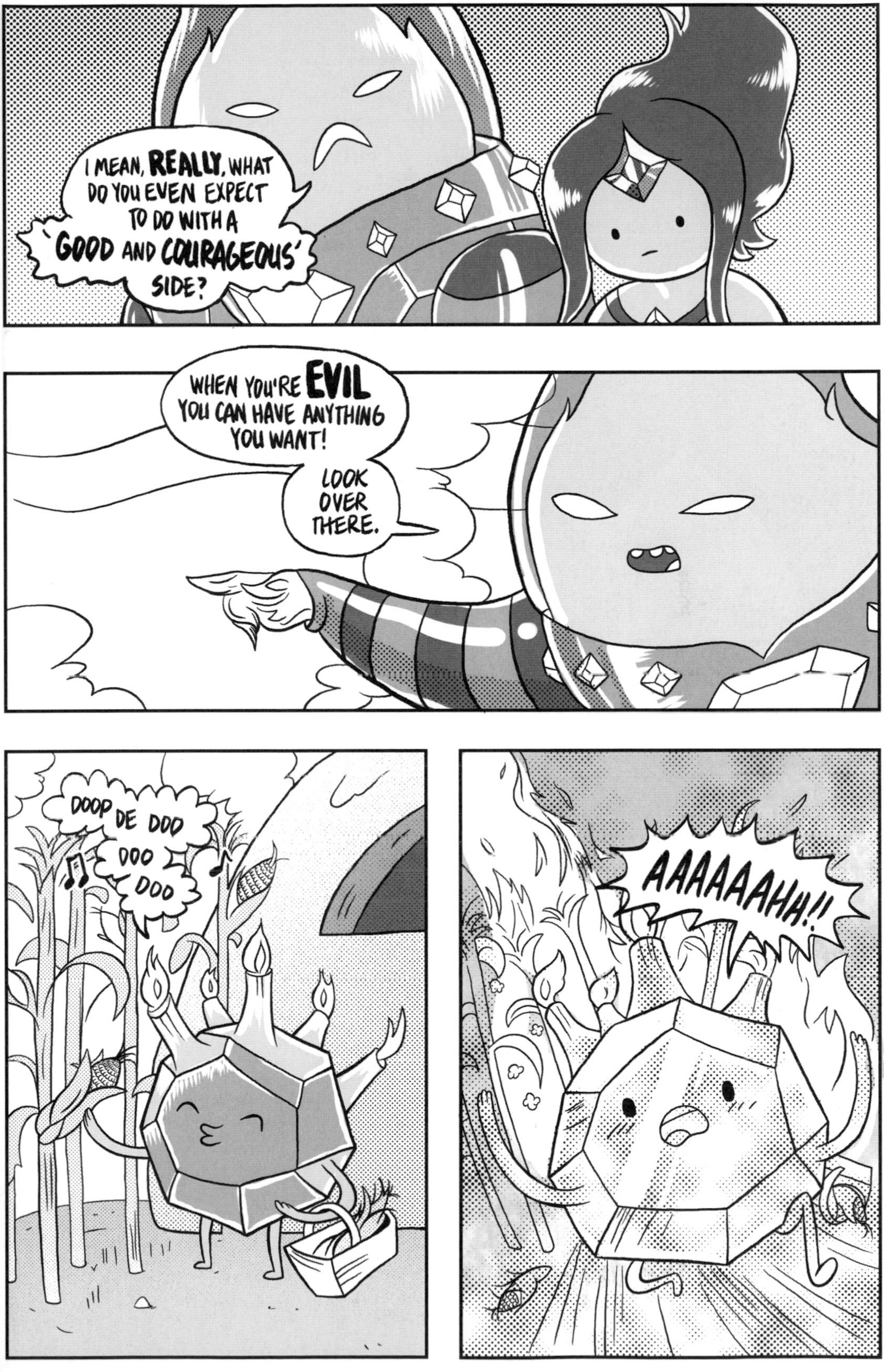
I MEAN, REALLY, WHAT DO YOU EVEN EXPECT TO DO WITH A 'GOOD AND COURAGEOUS' SIDE?
WHEN YOU'RE EVIL YOU CAN HAVE ANYTHING YOU WANT!
LOOK OVER THERE.
DOOP DE DOO DOO DOO
AAAAAAHH!!

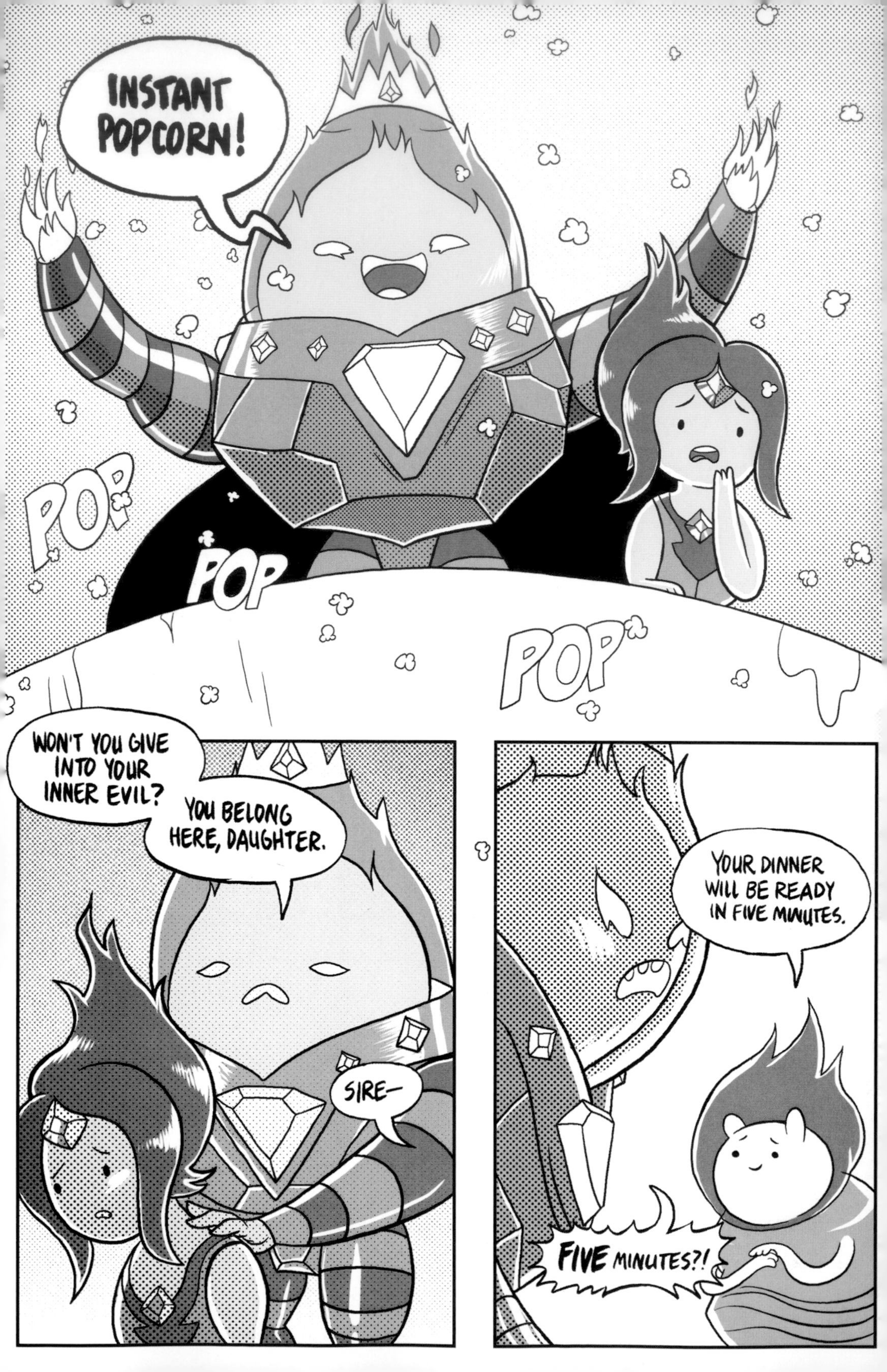

INSTANT POPCORN!
POP
POP
POP
WON'T YOU GIVE INTO YOUR INNER EVIL?
YOU BELONG HERE, DAUGHTER.
SIRE—
YOUR DINNER WILL BE READY IN FIVE MINUTES.
FIVE MINUTES?!

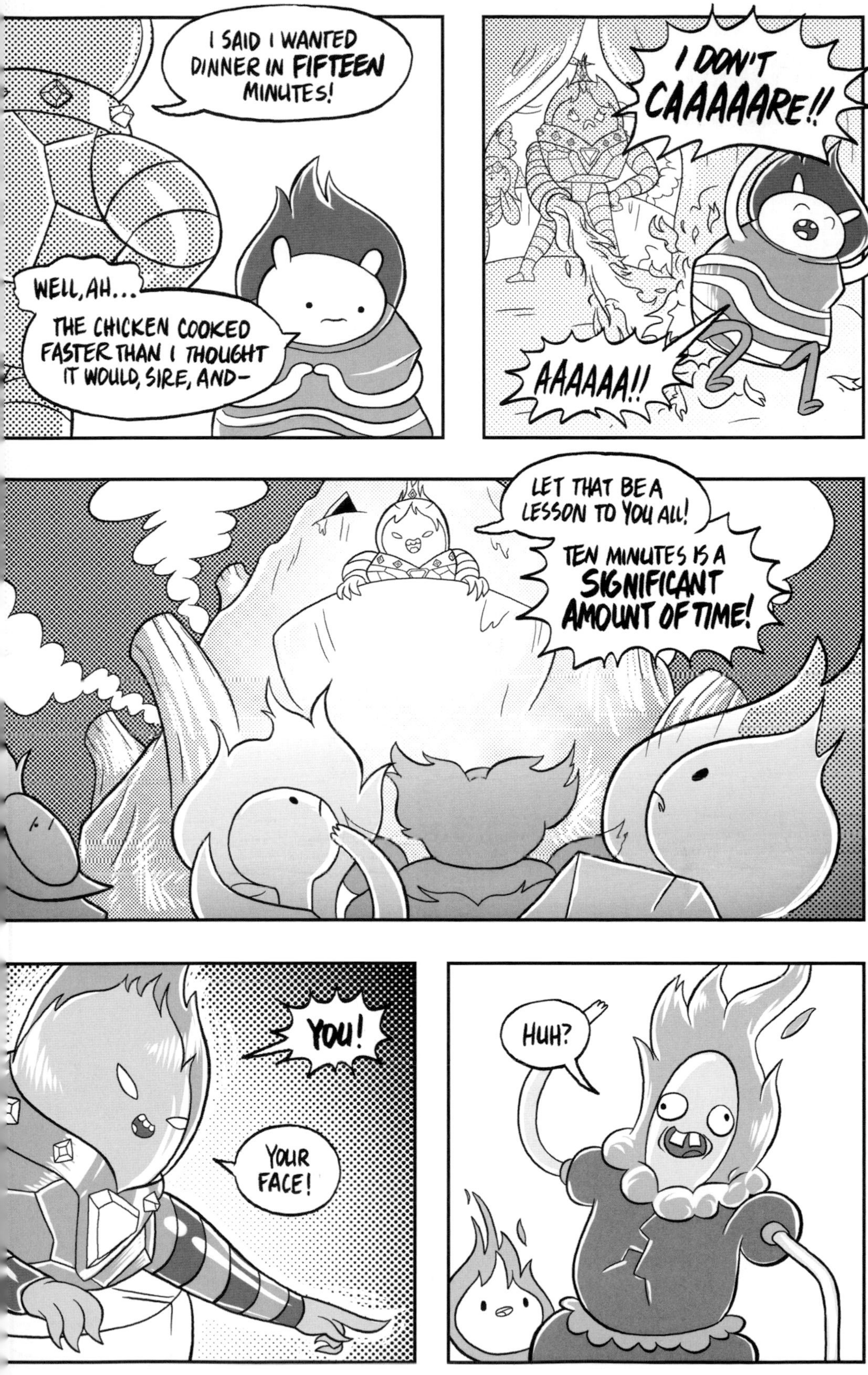
I SAID I WANTED DINNER IN FIFTEEN MINUTES!
WELL, AH...
THE CHICKEN COOKED FASTER THAN I THOUGHT IT WOULD, SIRE, AND–
I DON'T CAAAAARE!!
AAAAAA!!
LET THAT BE A LESSON TO YOU ALL!
TEN MINUTES IS A SIGNIFICANT AMOUNT OF TIME!
YOU!
YOUR FACE!
HUH?

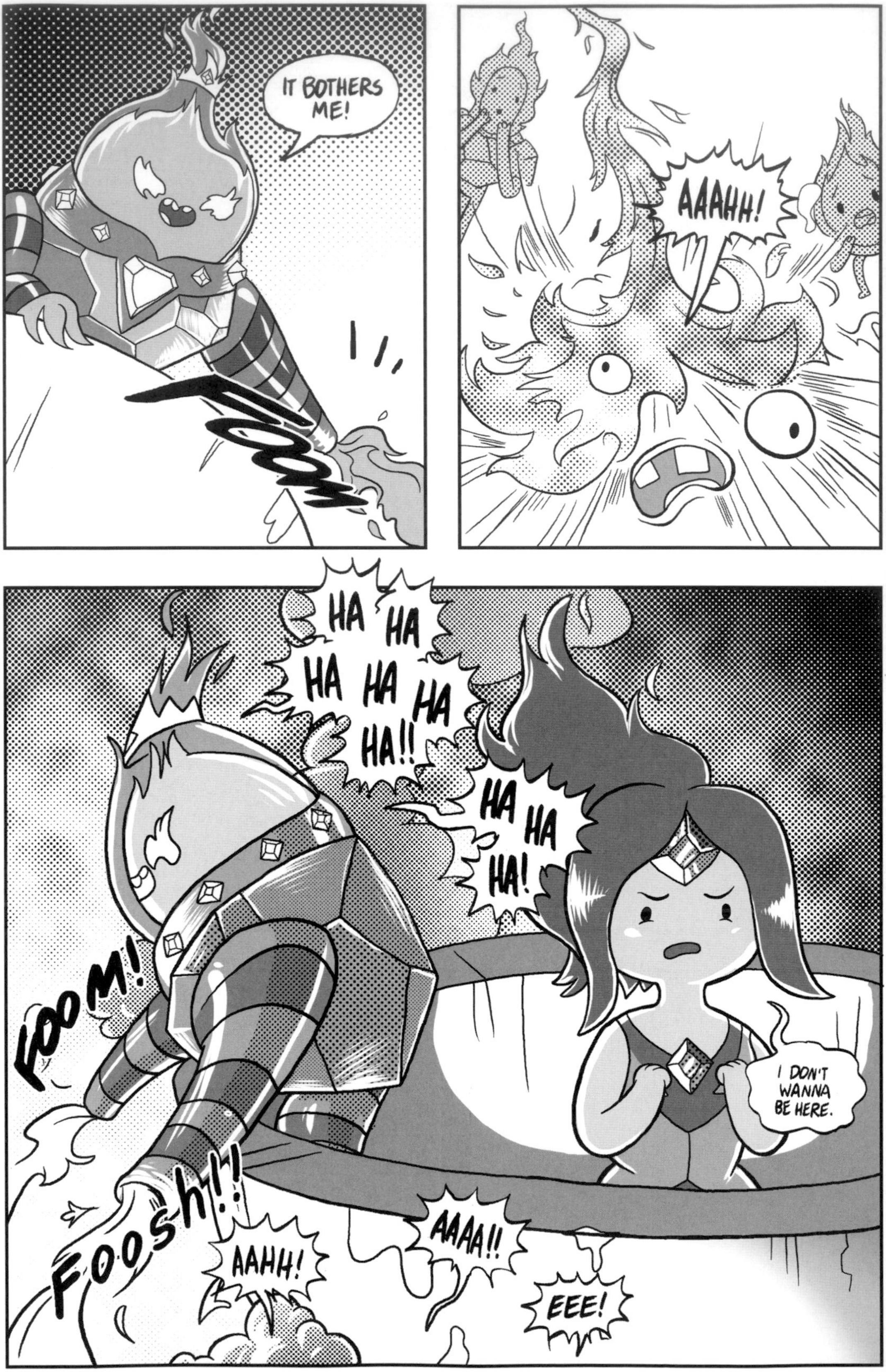

IT BOTHERS ME!
FOOM
AAAHH!
HA HA HA HA HA HA!!
HA HA HA!
FOOM!
I DON'T WANNA BE HERE.
FOOSH!!
AAHH!
AAAA!!
EEE!

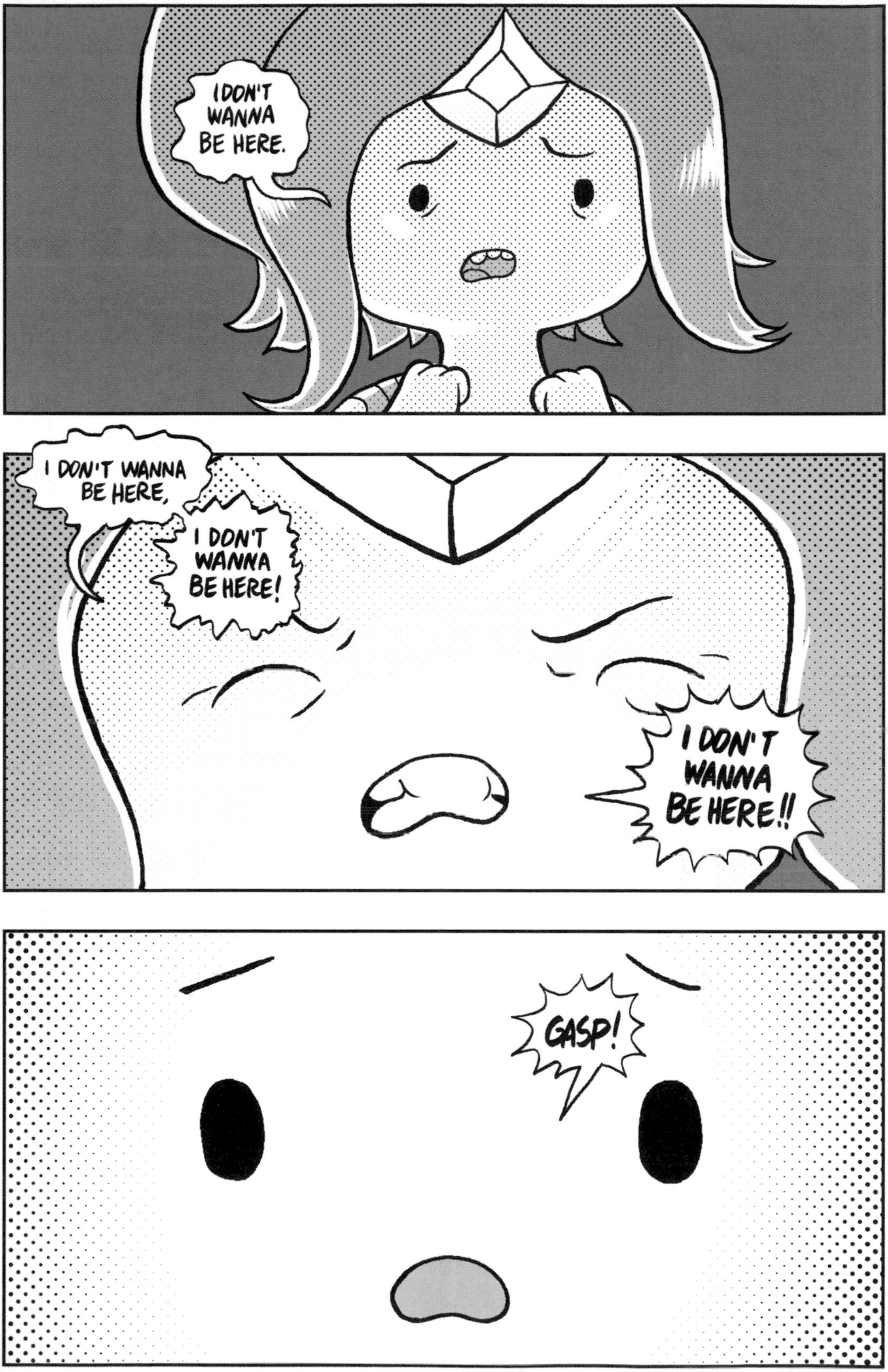
I DON'T WANNA BE HERE.
I DON'T WANNA BE HERE,
I DON'T WANNA BE HERE!
I DON'T WANNA BE HERE!!
GASP!

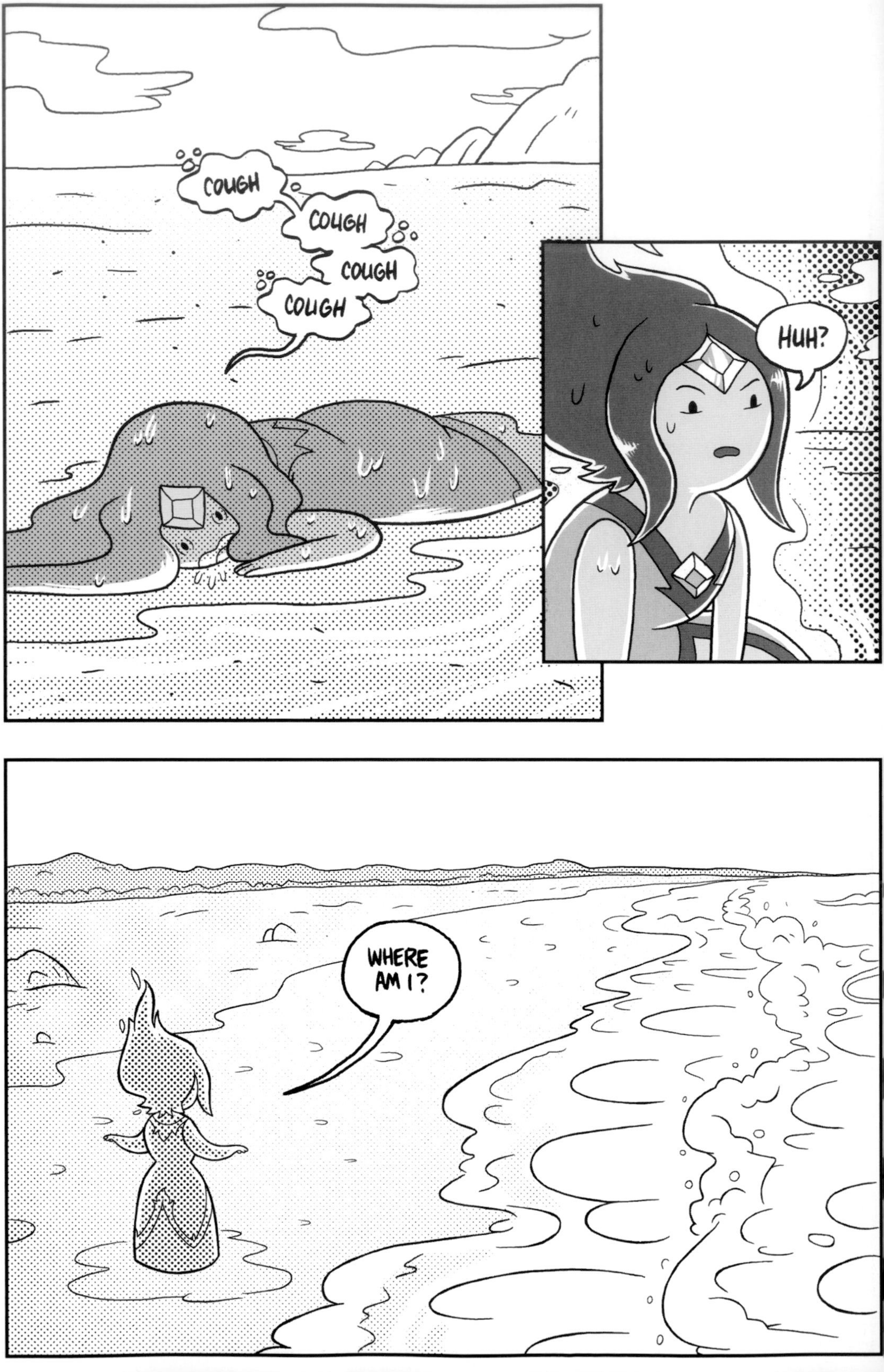
COUGH
COUGH
COUGH
COUGH
HUH?
WHERE AM I?

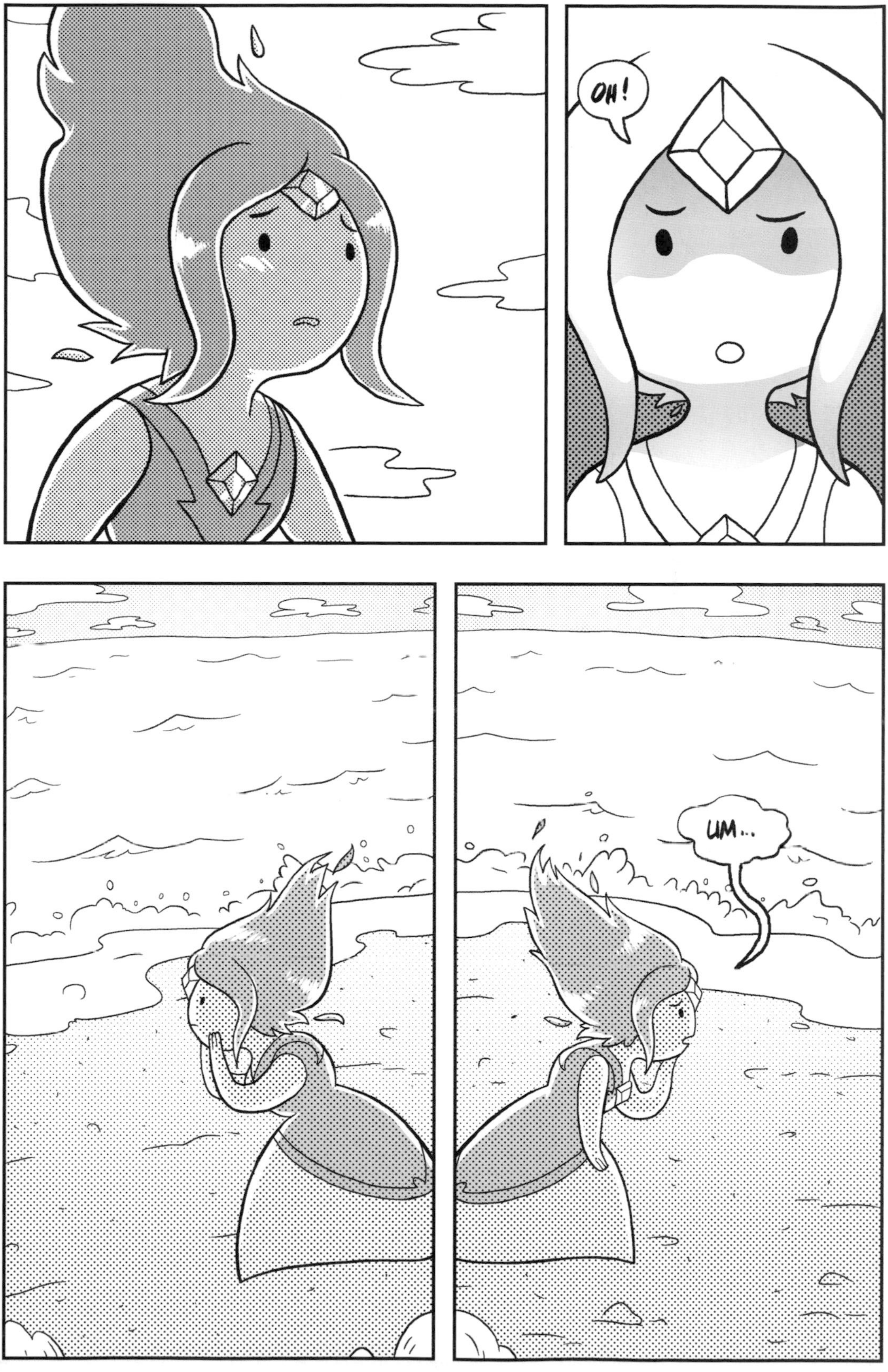
OH!
UM...

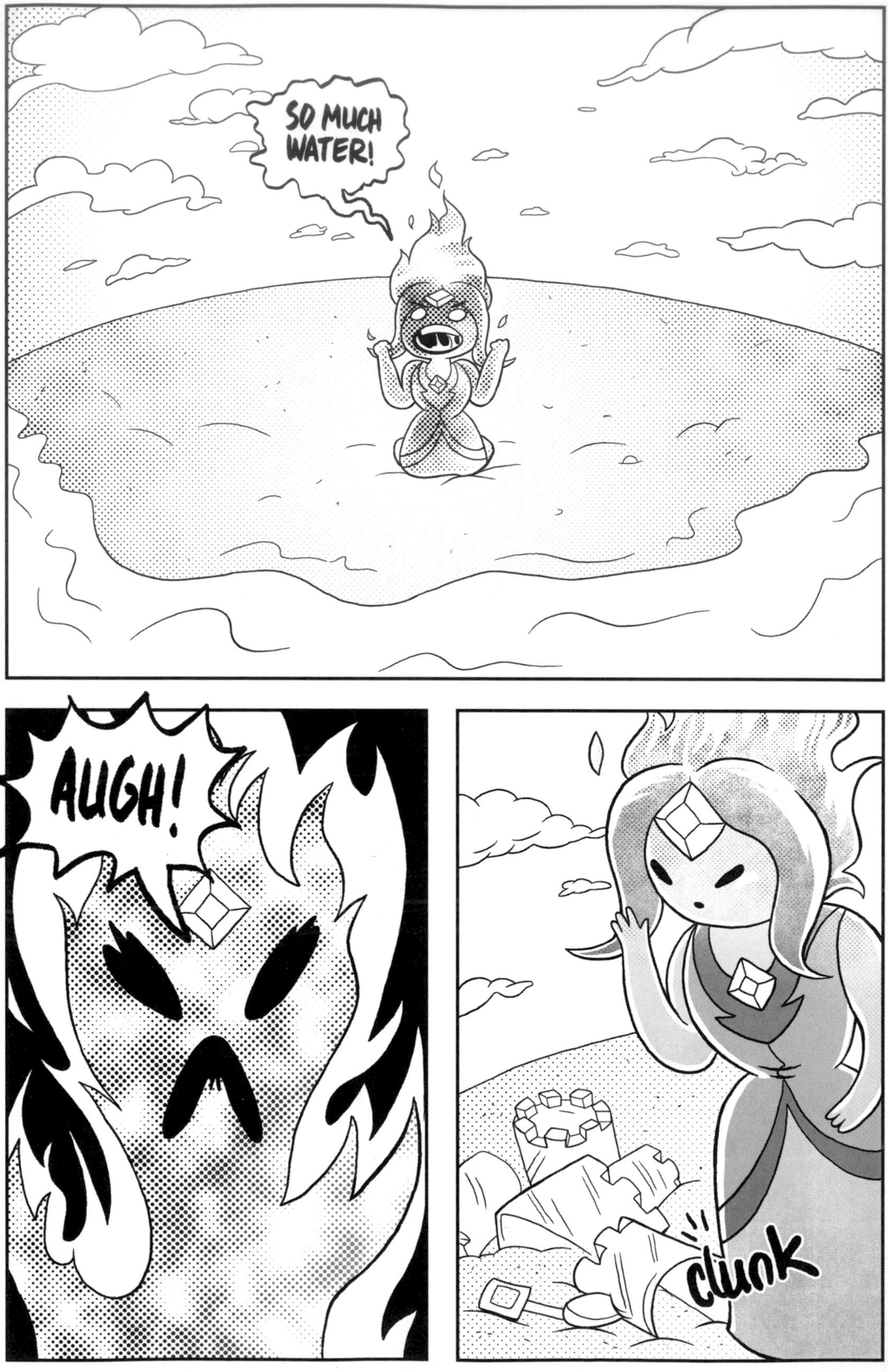
SO MUCH WATER!
AUGH!
clunk

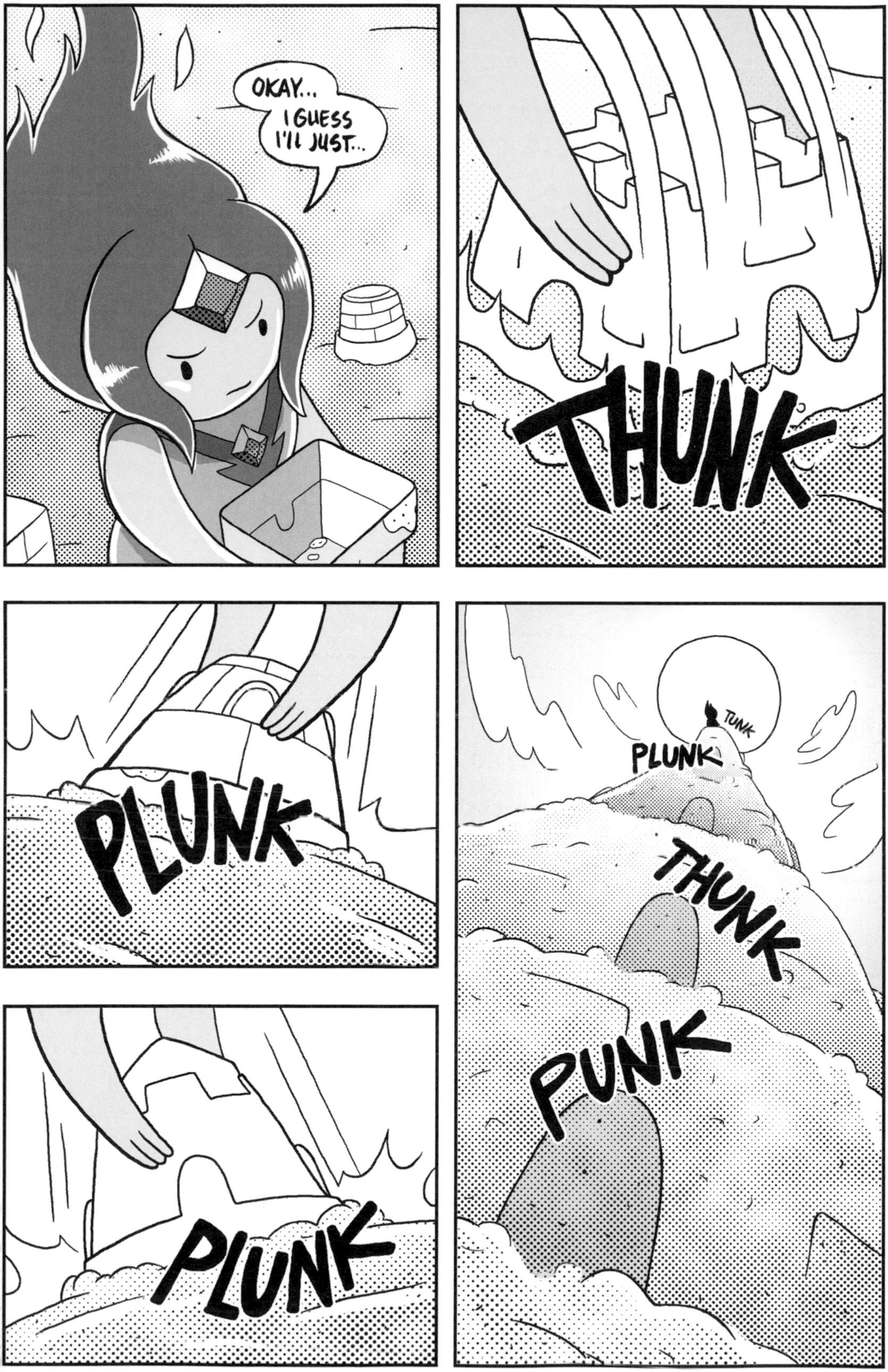
OKAY... I GUESS I'LL JUST...
THUNK
PLUNK
PLUNK
TUNK
PLUNK
THUNK
PUNK

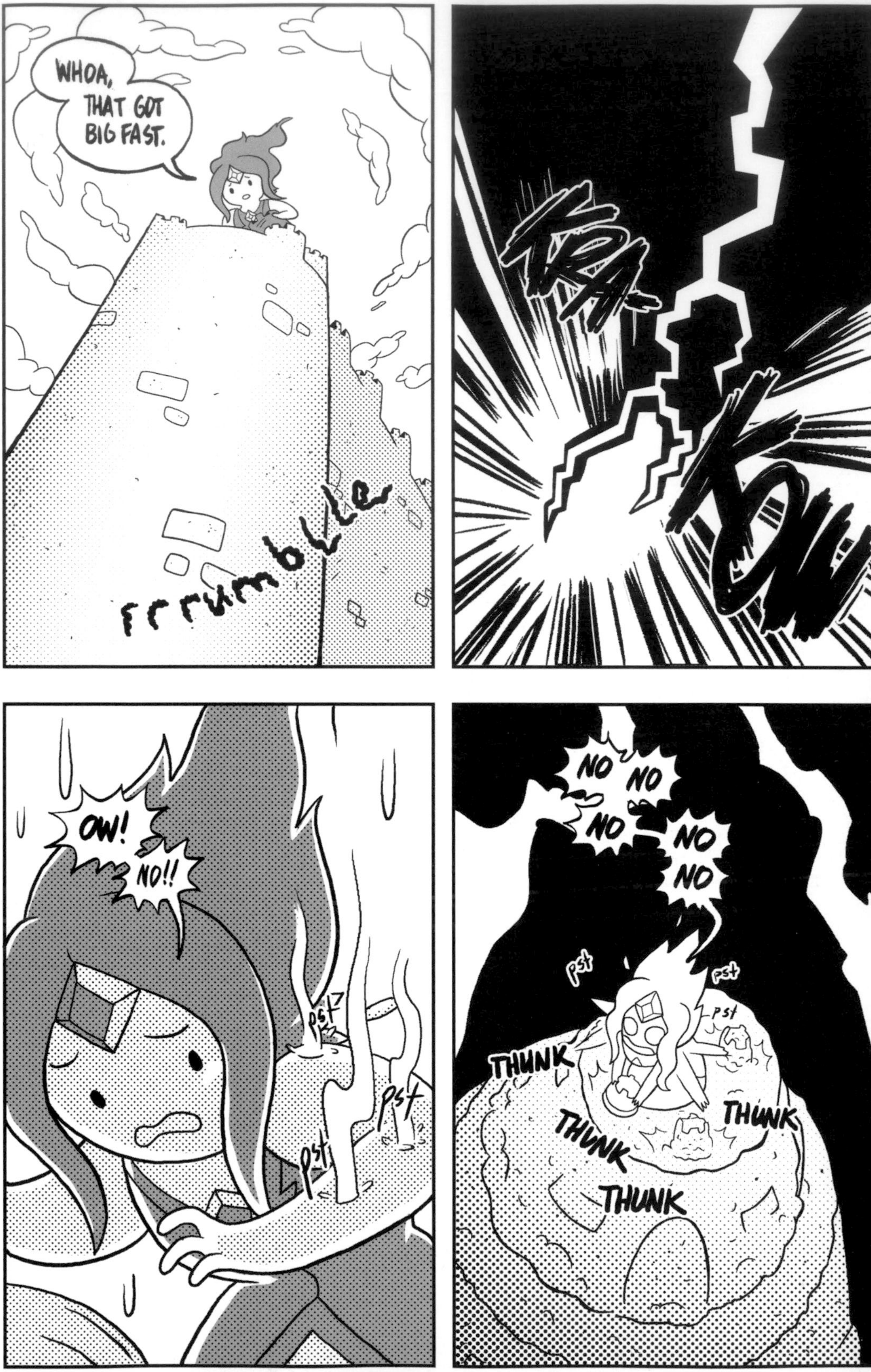
WHOA, THAT GOT BIG FAST.
frrumble
KRA-KOW
OW!
NO!!
pst
pst
pst
NO NO NO
NO NO
pst
pst
pst
THUNK
THUNK
THUNK
THUNK

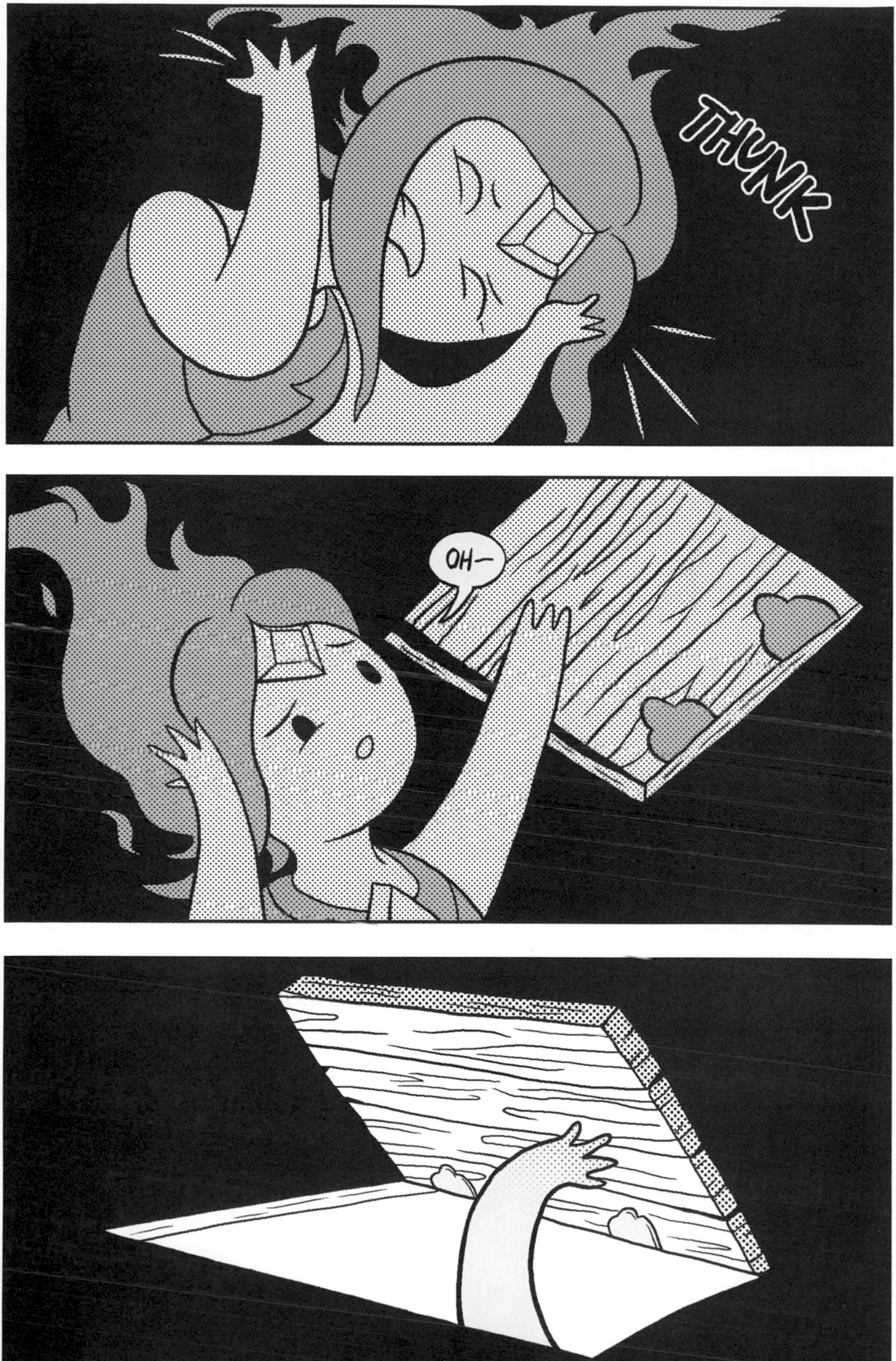
THUNK
OH—

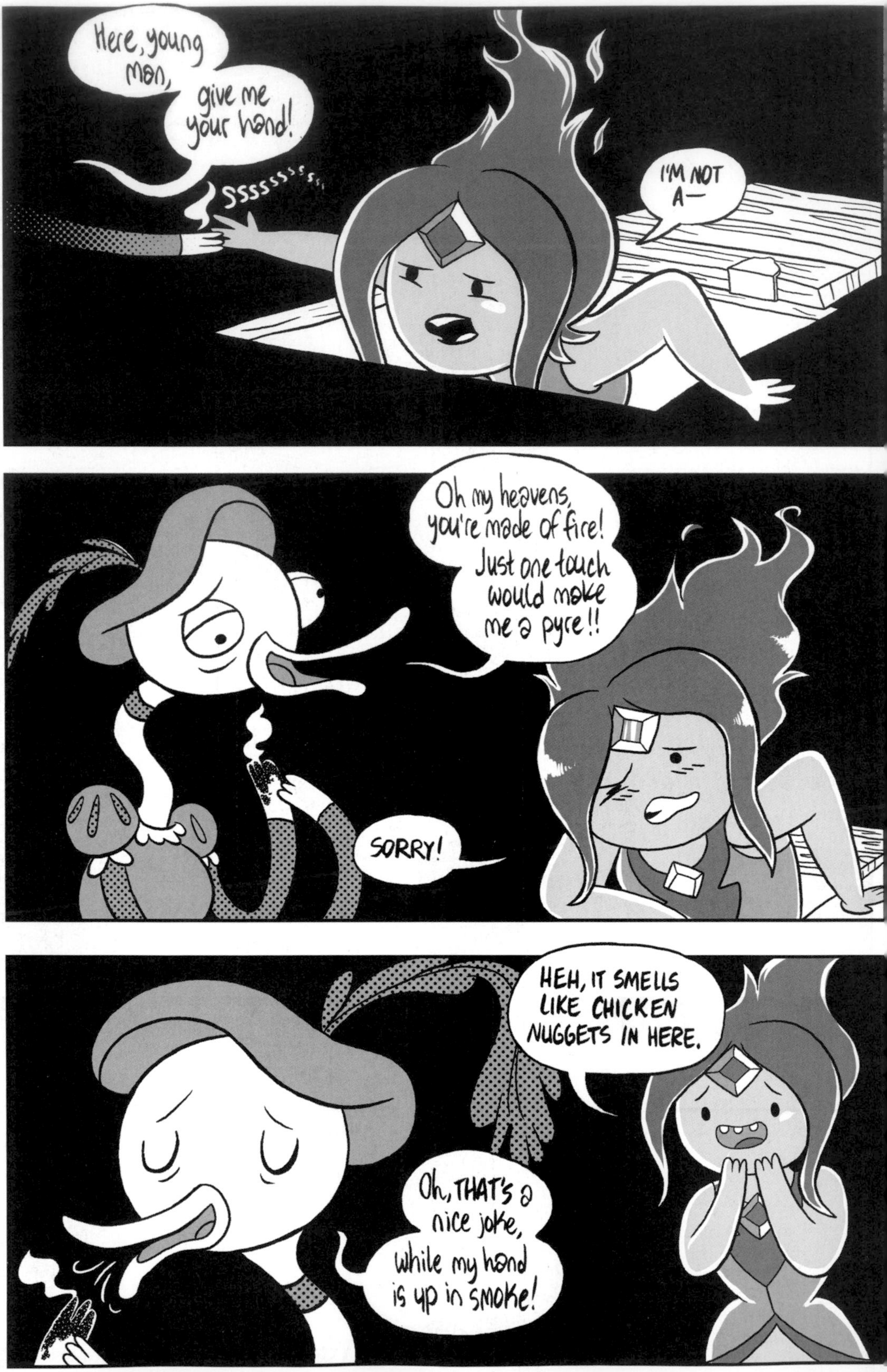
Here, young man, give me your hand!
SSSSSSSSSS
I'M NOT A—
Oh my heavens, you're made of fire! Just one touch would make me a pyre!!
SORRY!
HEH, IT SMELLS LIKE CHICKEN NUGGETS IN HERE.
Oh, THAT'S a nice joke, while my hand is up in smoke!

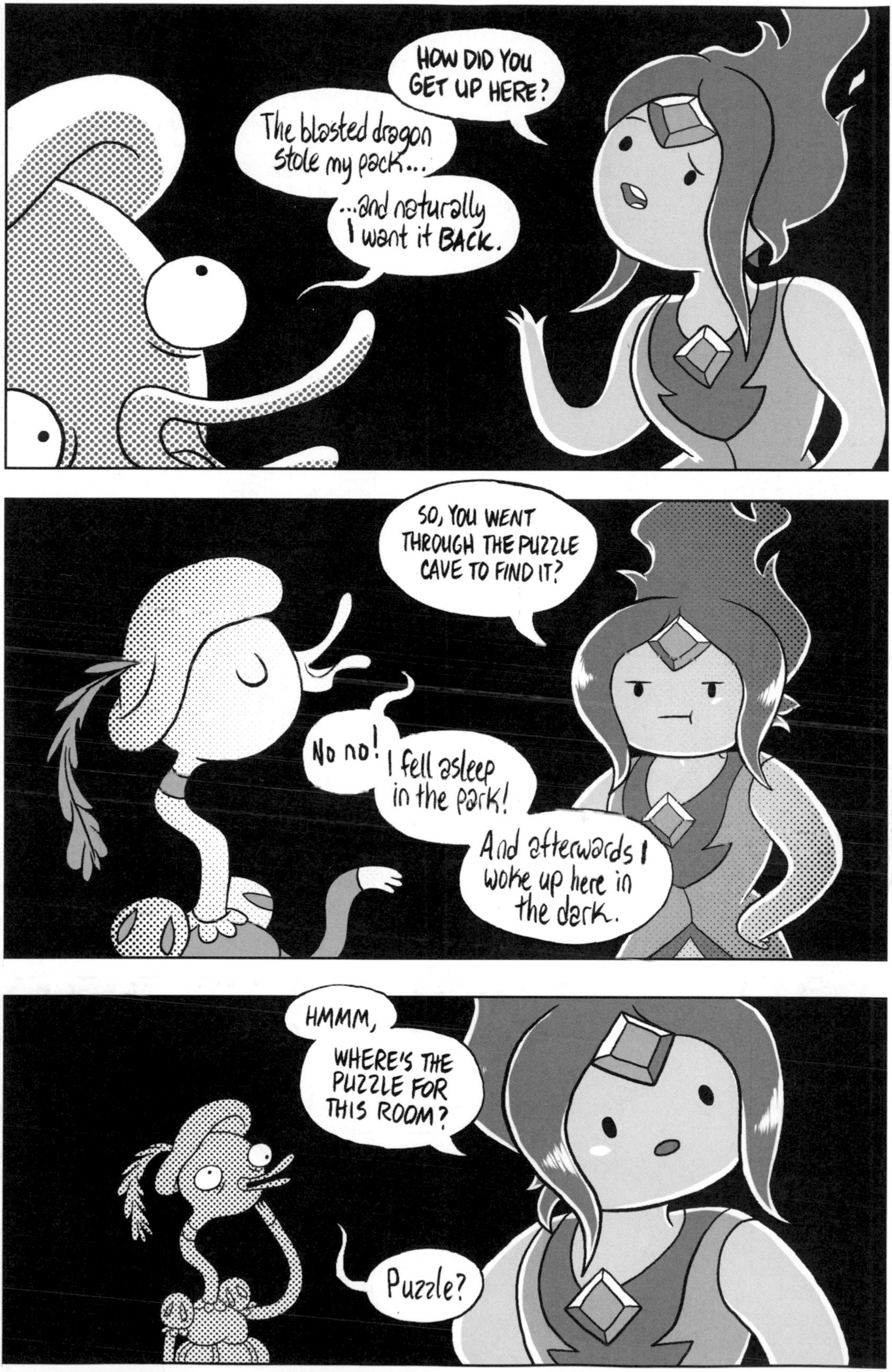
HOW DID YOU GET UP HERE?
The blasted dragon stole my pack...
...and naturally I want it BACK.
SO, YOU WENT THROUGH THE PUZZLE CAVE TO FIND IT?
No no! I fell asleep in the park!
And afterwards I woke up here in the dark.
HMMM,
WHERE'S THE PUZZLE FOR THIS ROOM?
Puzzle?

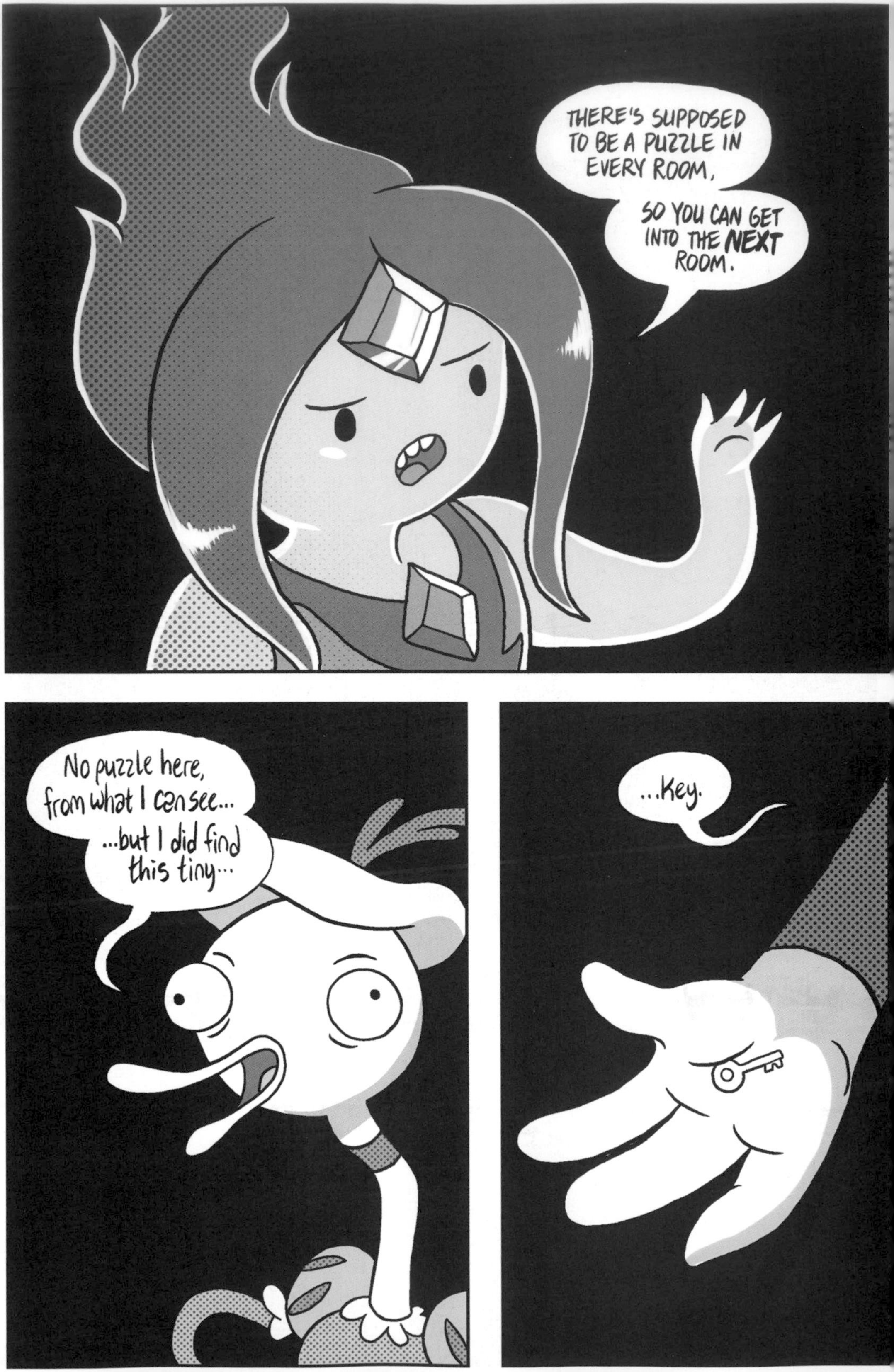
THERE'S SUPPOSED TO BE A PUZZLE IN EVERY ROOM,
SO YOU CAN GET INTO THE NEXT ROOM.
No puzzle here, from what I can see...
...but I did find this tiny...
...Key.

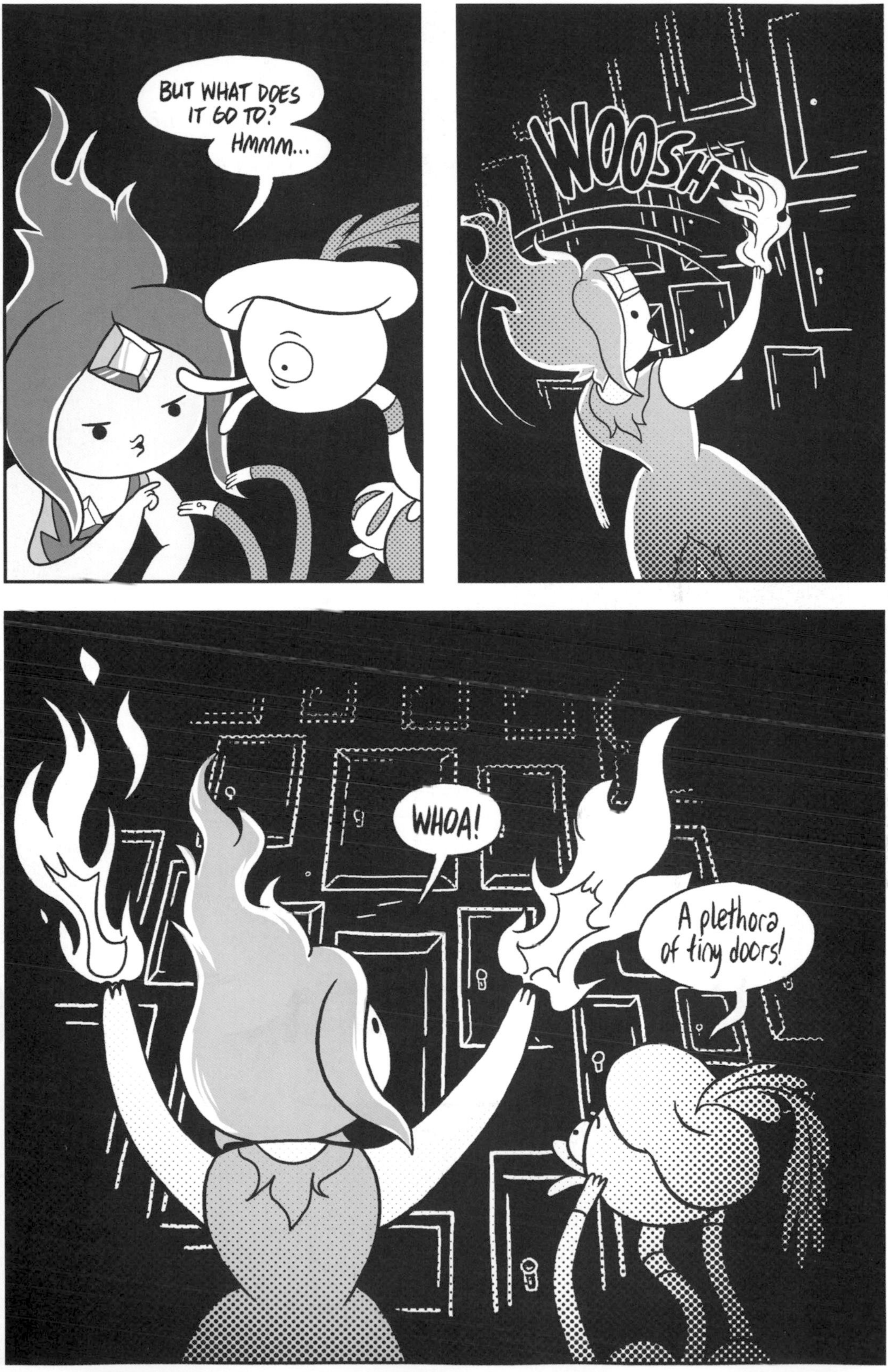
BUT WHAT DOES IT GO TO? HMMM...
WOOSH
WHOA!
A plethora of tiny doors!

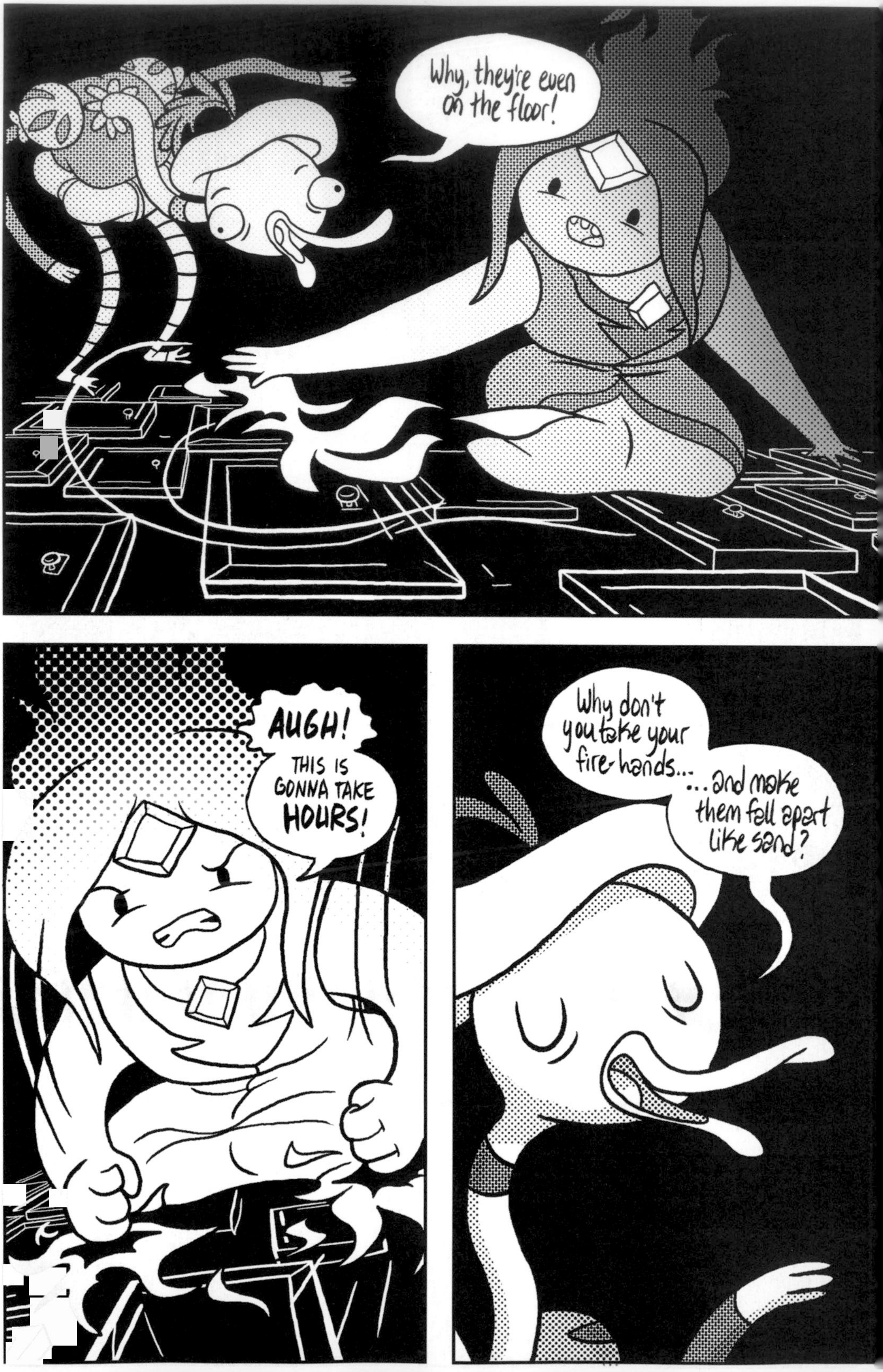
Why, they're even on the floor!
AUGH!
THIS IS GONNA TAKE HOURS!
Why don't you take your fire-hands...
...and make them fall apart like sand?

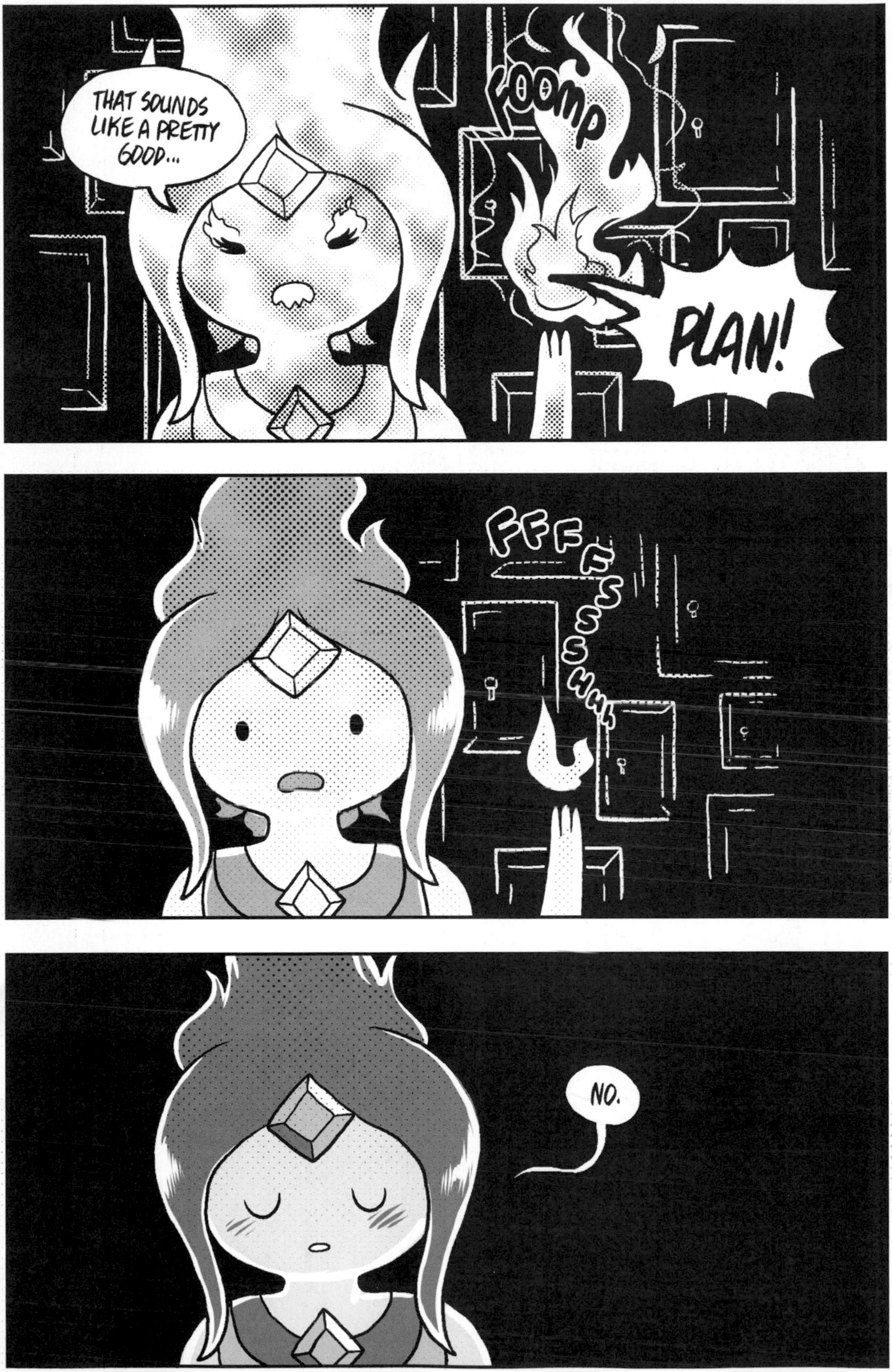

THAT SOUNDS LIKE A PRETTY GOOD...
FOOMP
PLAN!
FFFFSSSSHHh
NO.

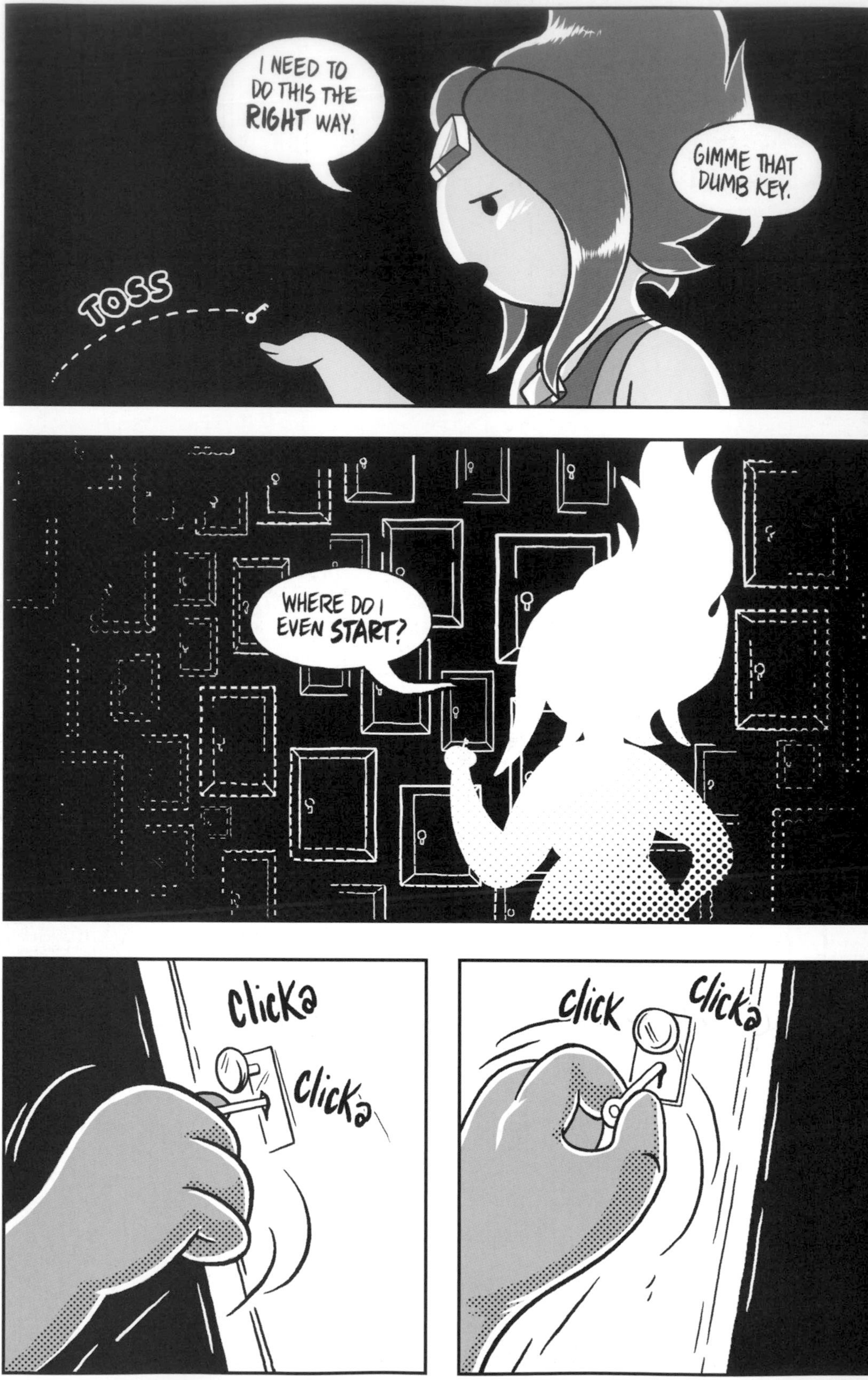
I NEED TO DO THIS THE RIGHT WAY.
GIMME THAT DUMB KEY.
TOSS
WHERE DO I EVEN START?
Clicka
Clicka
Click
Clicka

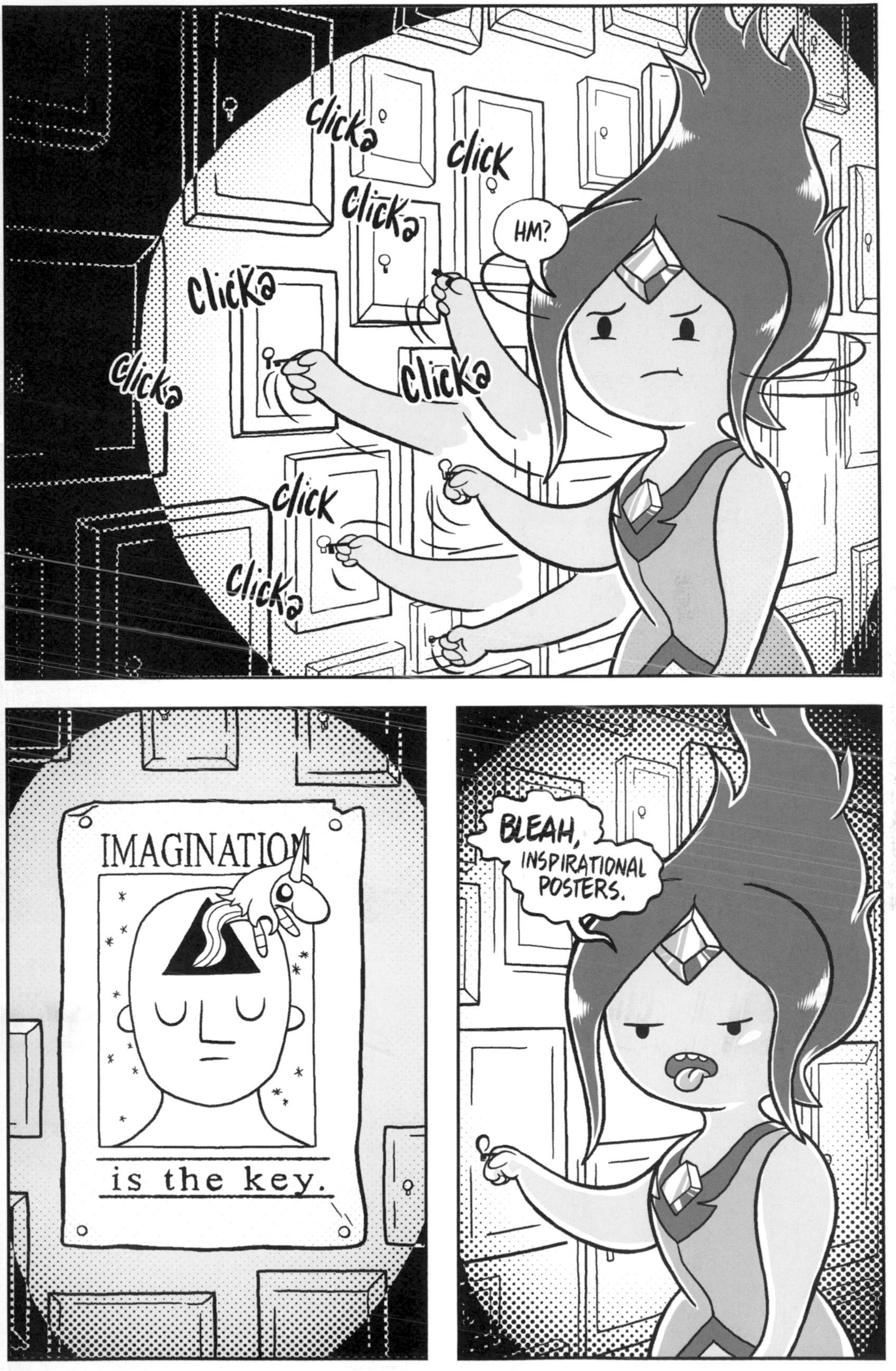

CLICKA
CLICK
CLICKA
HM?
CLICKA
CLICKA
CLICKA
CLICK
CLICKA
IMAGINATION
is the key.
BLEAH, INSPIRATIONAL POSTERS.

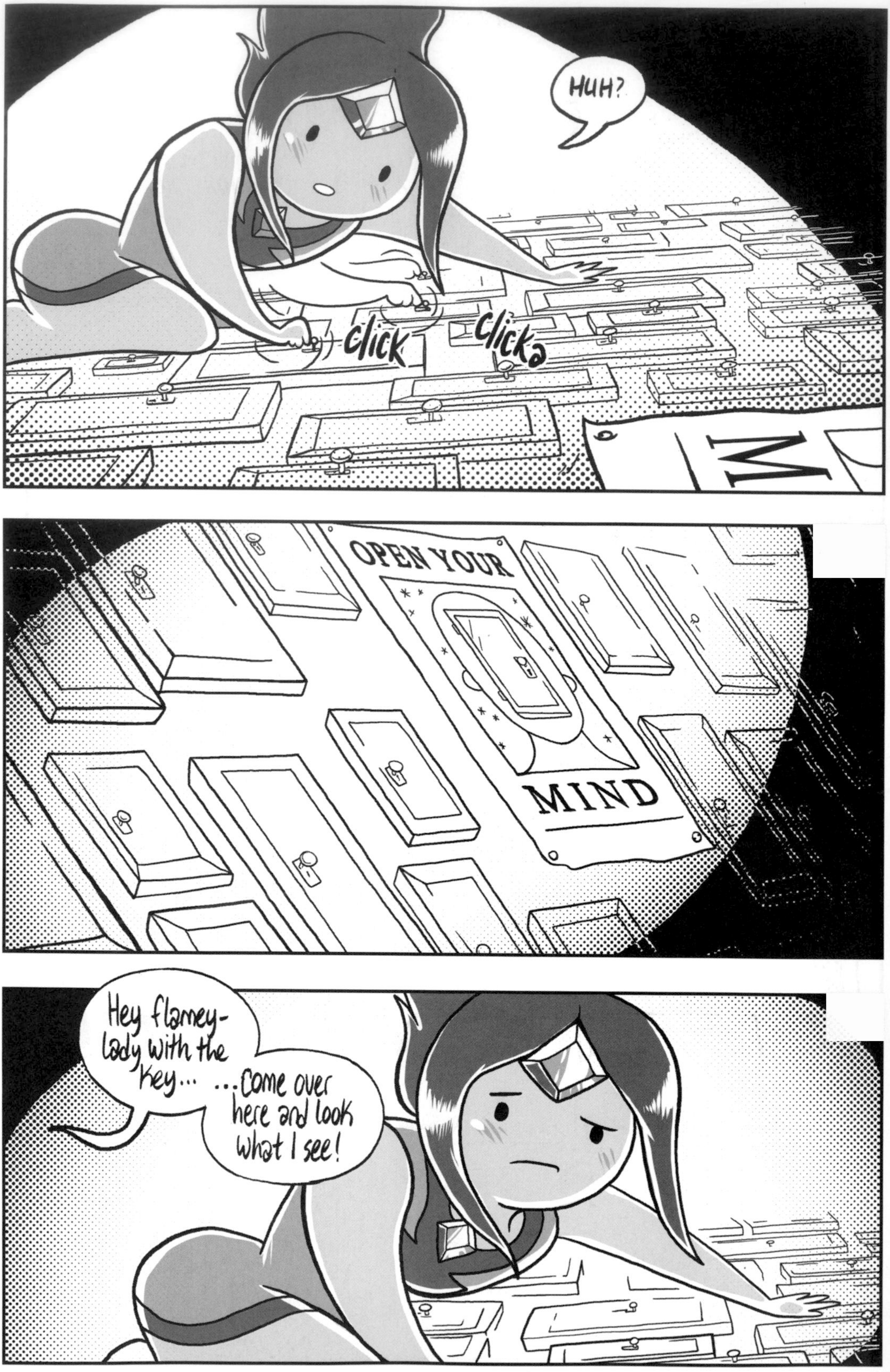
HUH?
CLICK
CLICKA
M
OPEN YOUR
MIND
Hey flamey-lady with the key...
...come over here and look what I see!

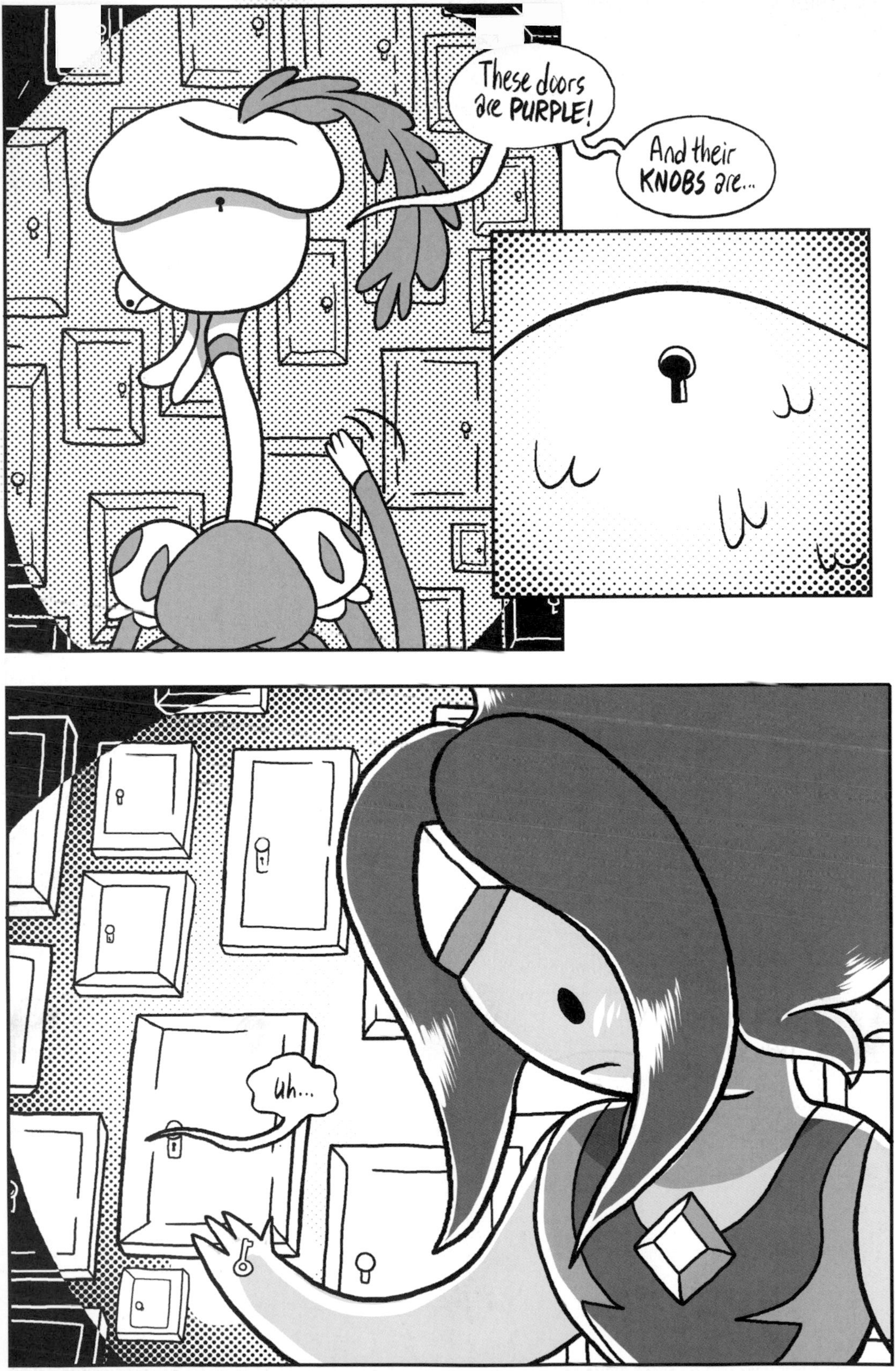
These doors are PURPLE!
And their KNOBS are...
uh...

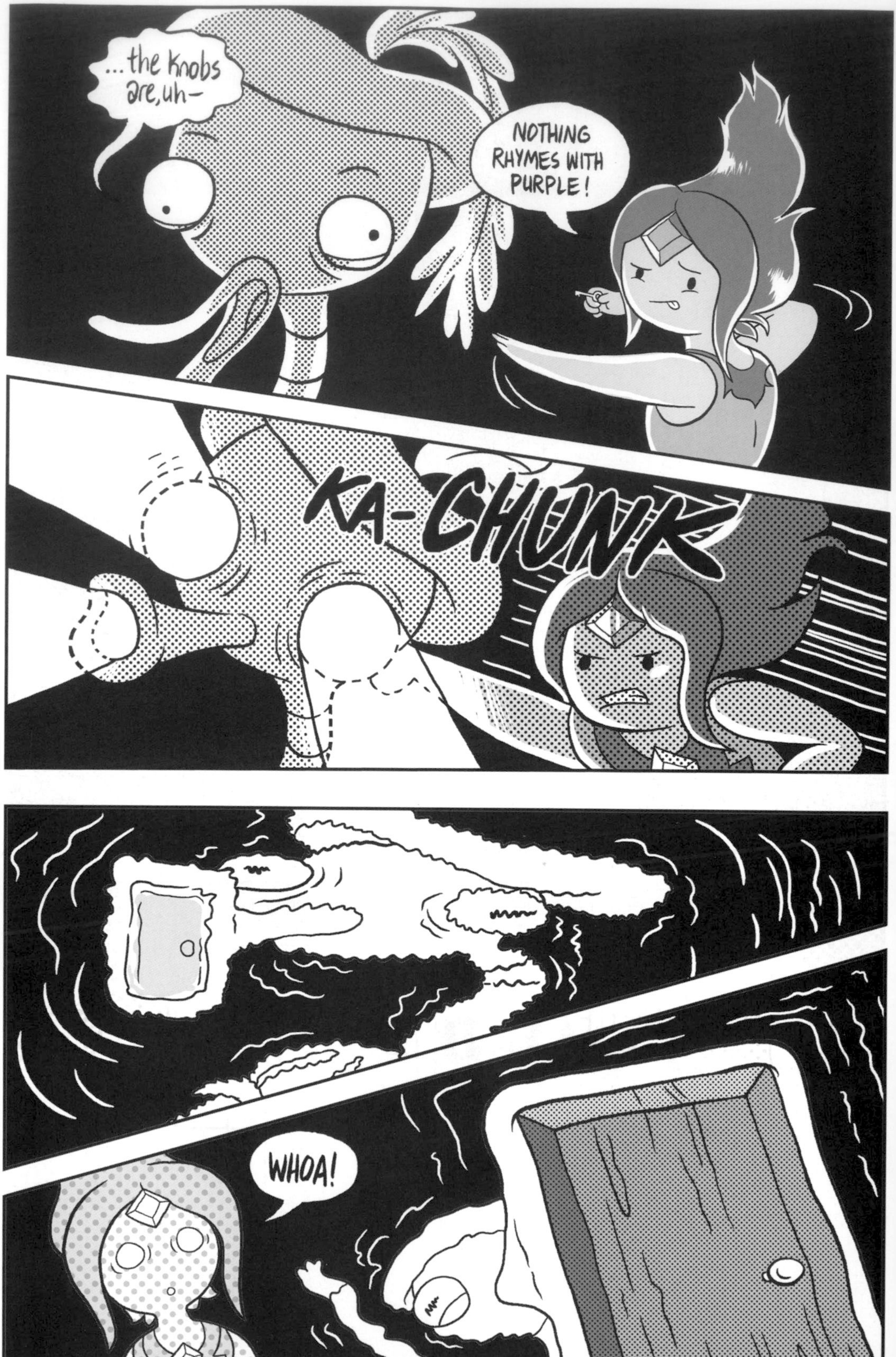
...the knobs are, uh-
NOTHING RHYMES WITH PURPLE!
KA-CHUNK
WHOA!

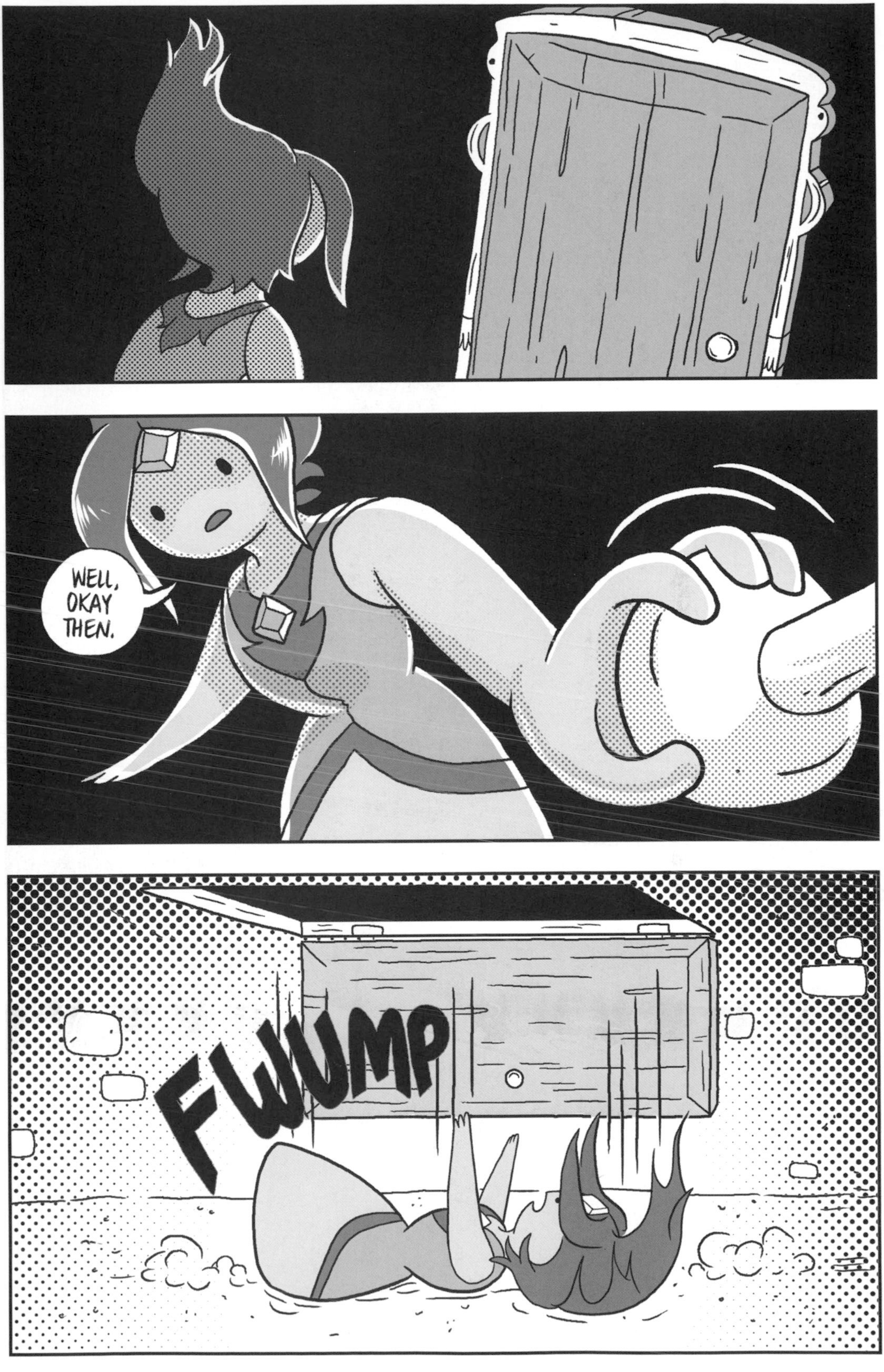
WELL, OKAY THEN.
FWUMP

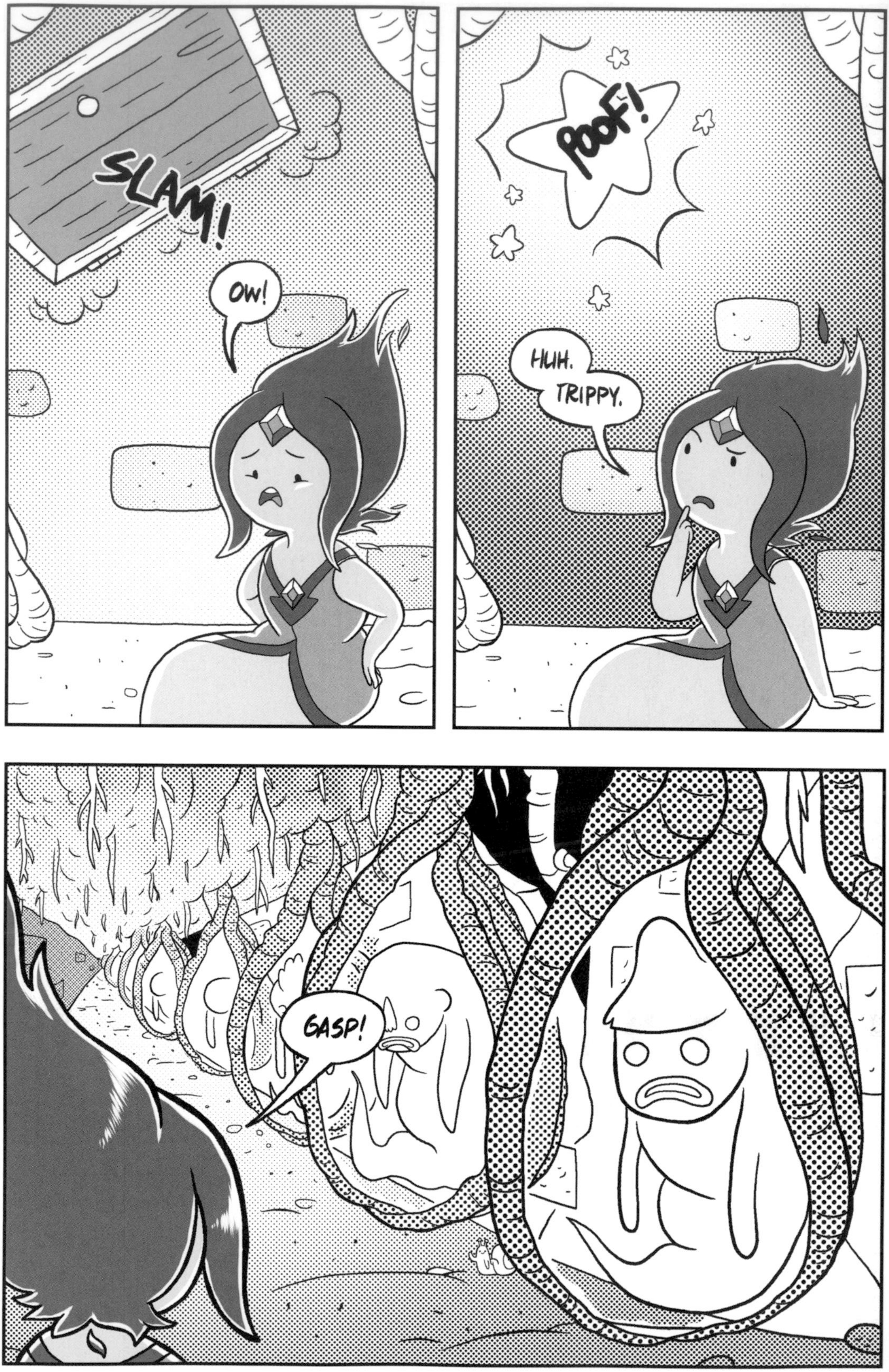
SLAM!
OW!
POOF!
HUH. TRIPPY.
GASP!

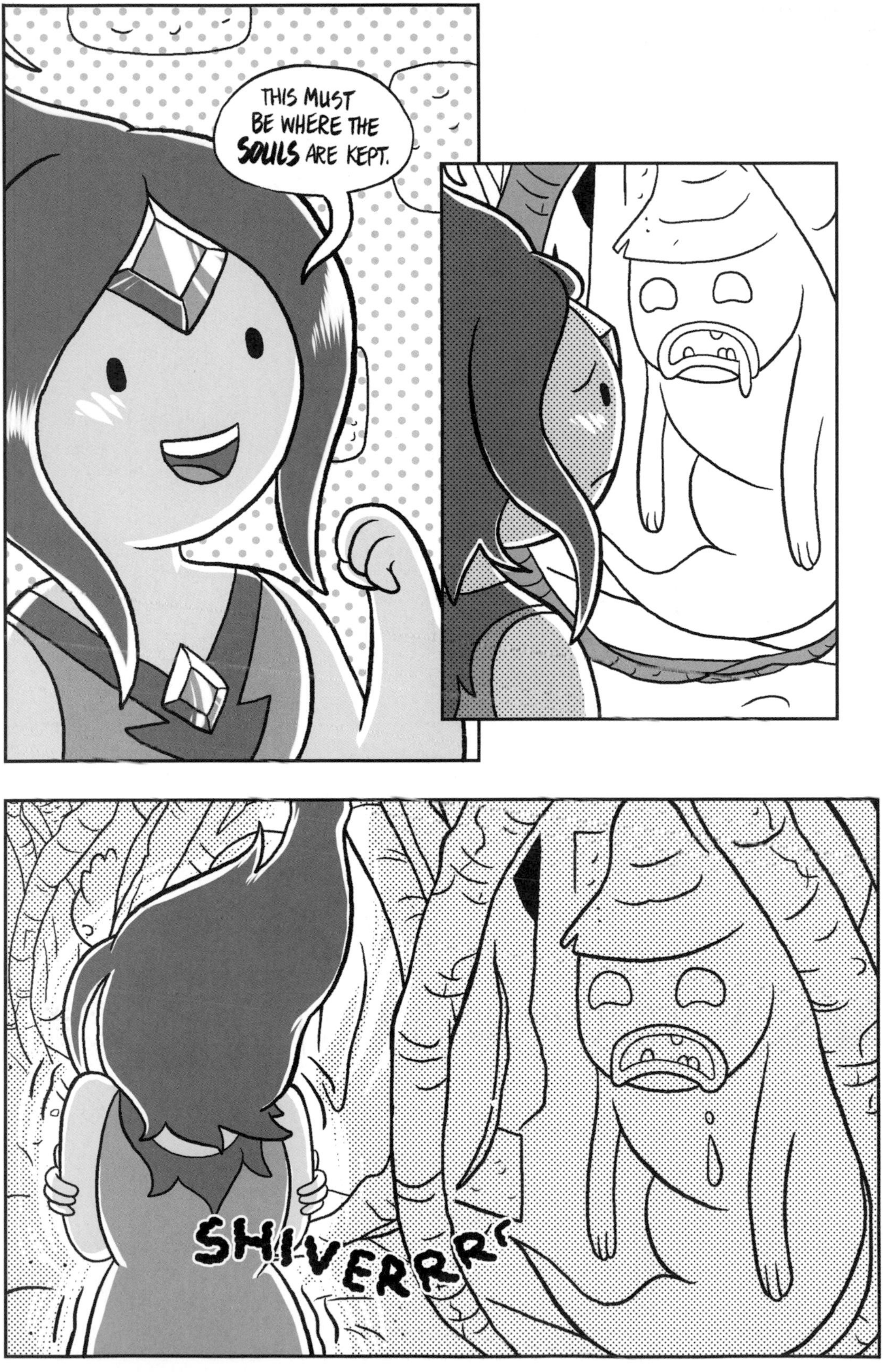
THIS MUST BE WHERE THE SOULS ARE KEPT.
SHIVERRR

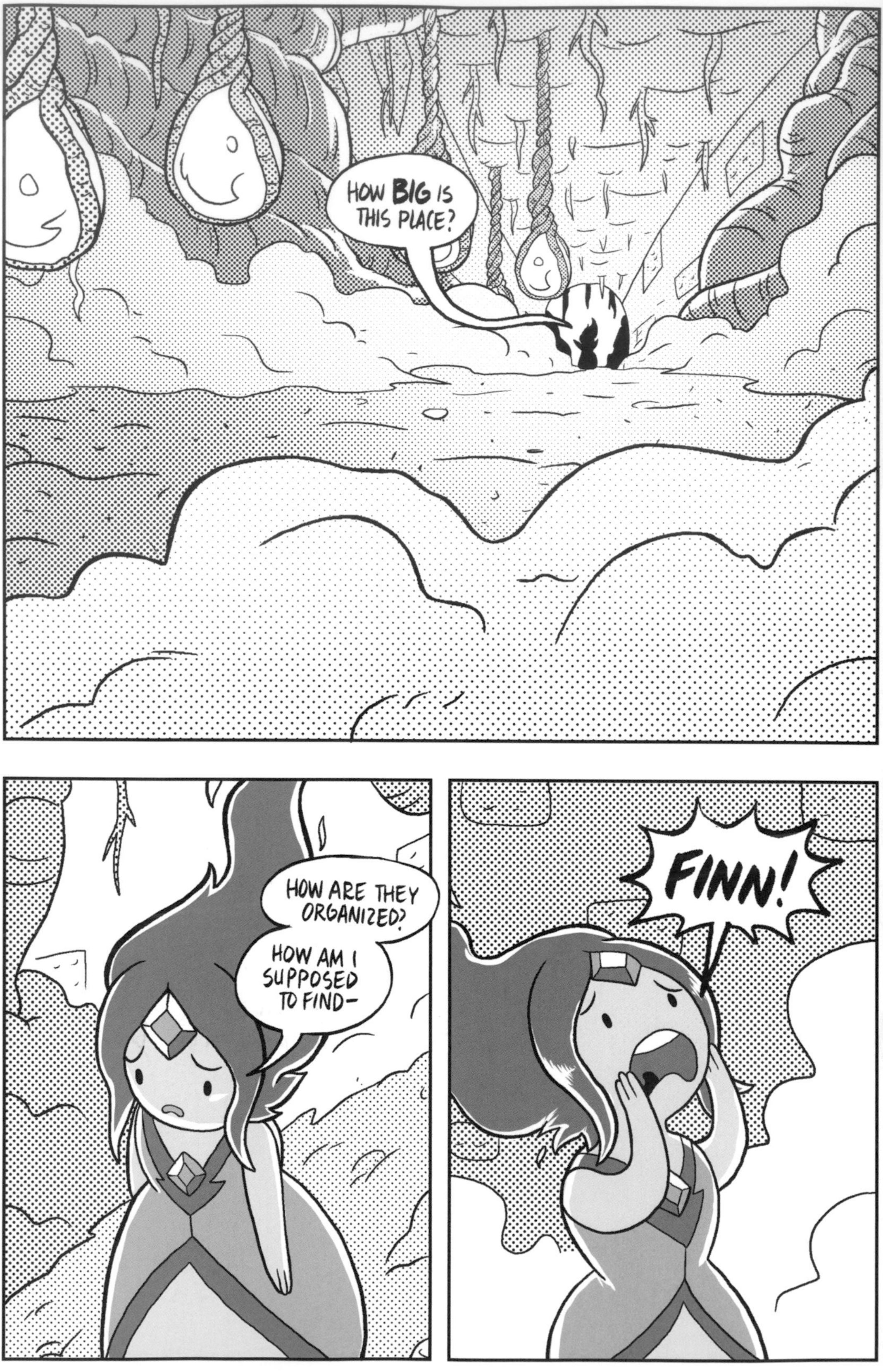
HOW BIG IS THIS PLACE?
HOW ARE THEY ORGANIZED?
HOW AM I SUPPOSED TO FIND-
FINN!

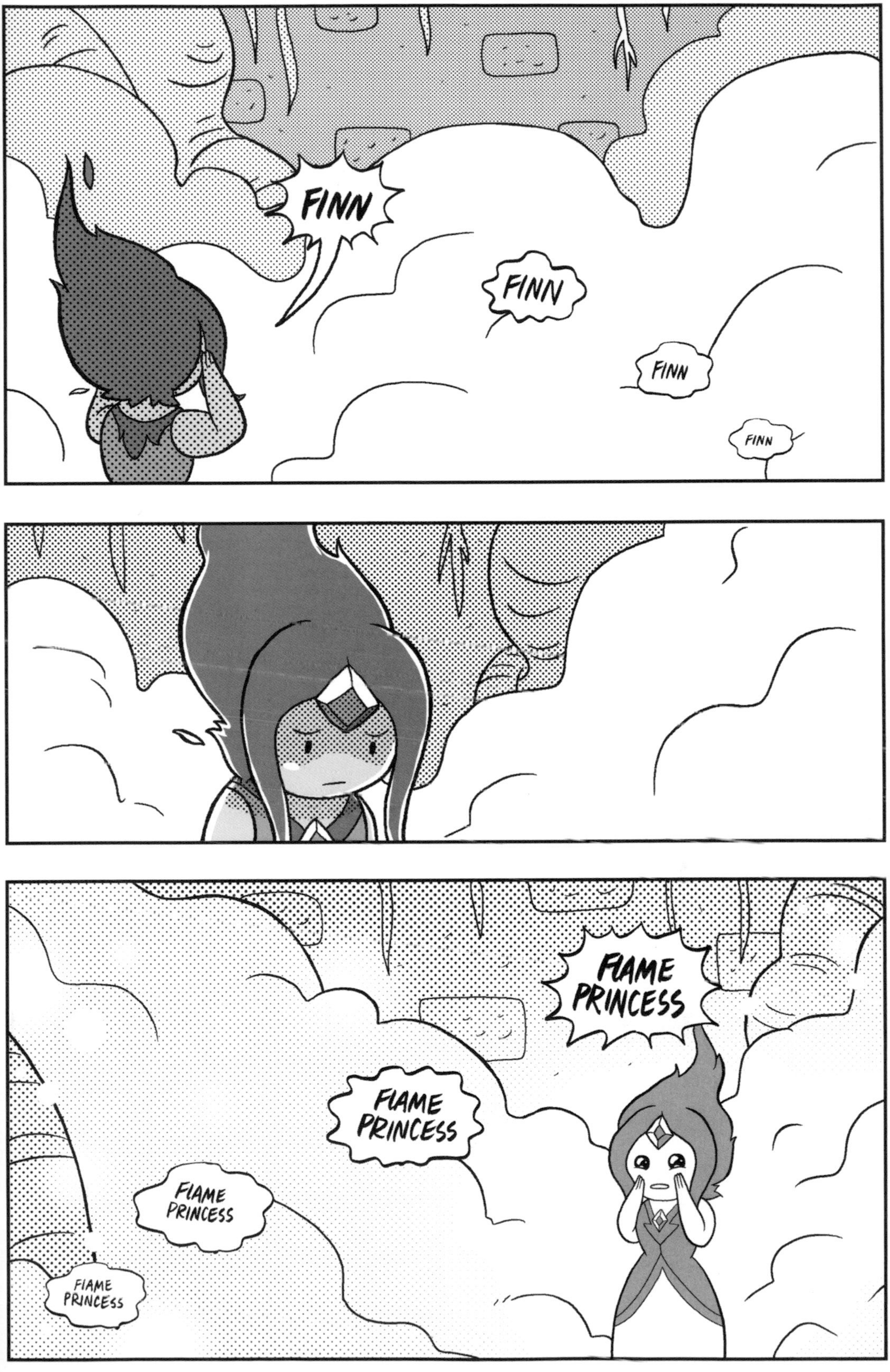
FINN
FINN
FINN
FINN
FLAME PRINCESS
FLAME PRINCESS
FLAME PRINCESS
FLAME PRINCESS

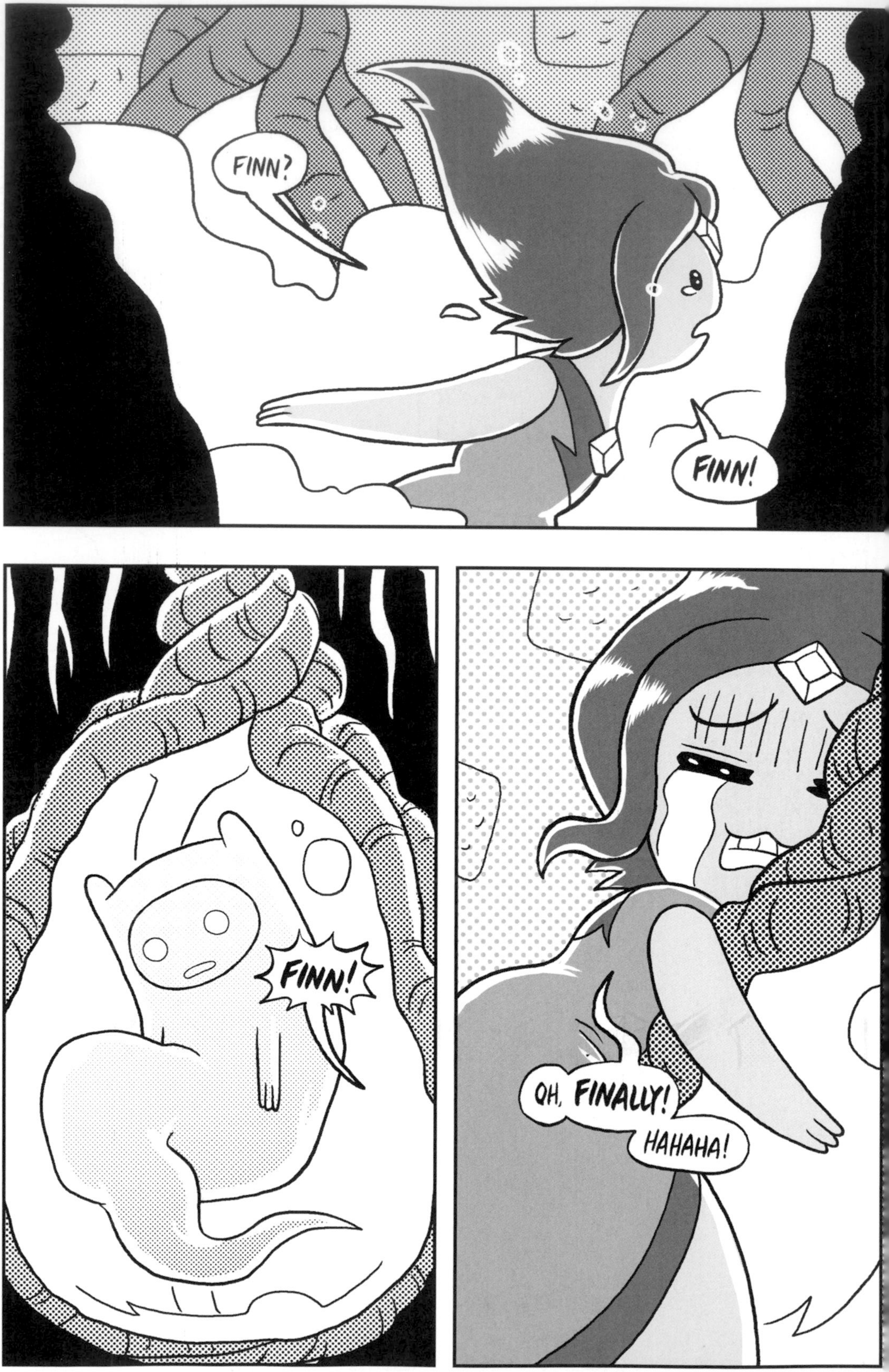
FINN?
FINN!
FINN!
OH, FINALLY!
HAHAHA!

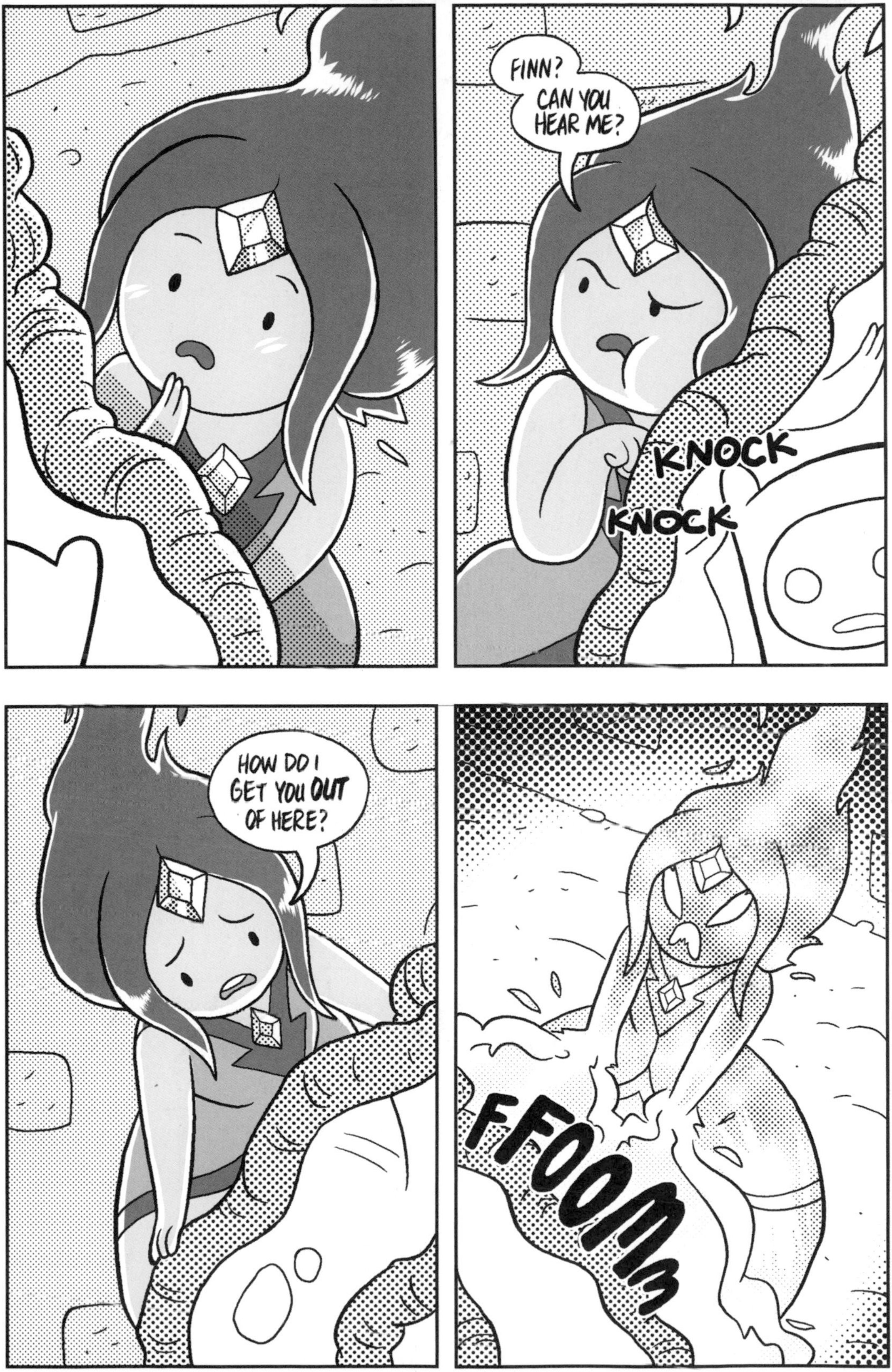

FINN? CAN YOU HEAR ME?
KNOCK
KNOCK
HOW DO I GET YOU OUT OF HERE?
FFOOMM

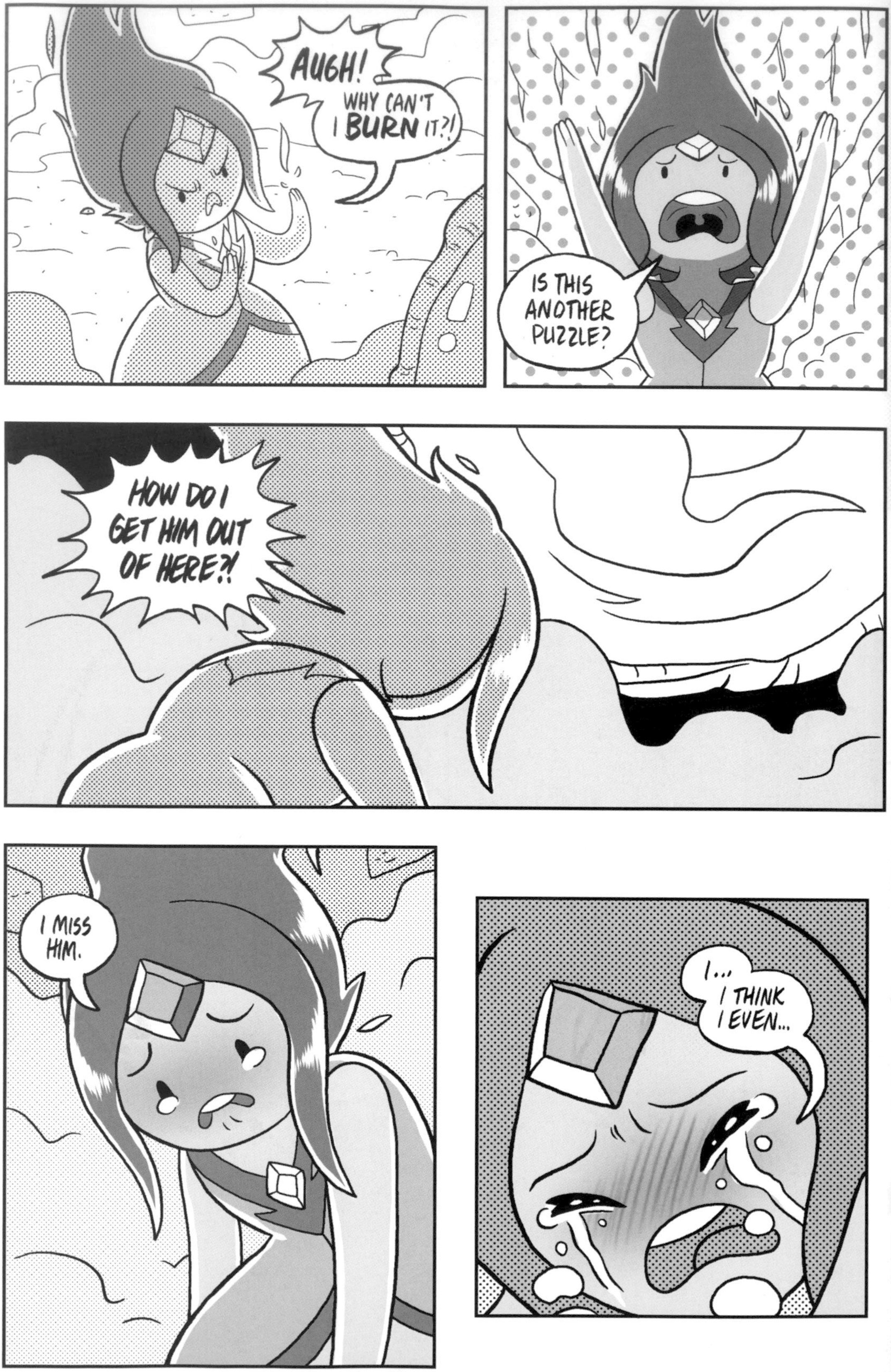
AUGH!
WHY CAN'T I BURN IT?!
IS THIS ANOTHER PUZZLE?
HOW DO I GET HIM OUT OF HERE?!
I MISS HIM.
I...
I THINK I EVEN...

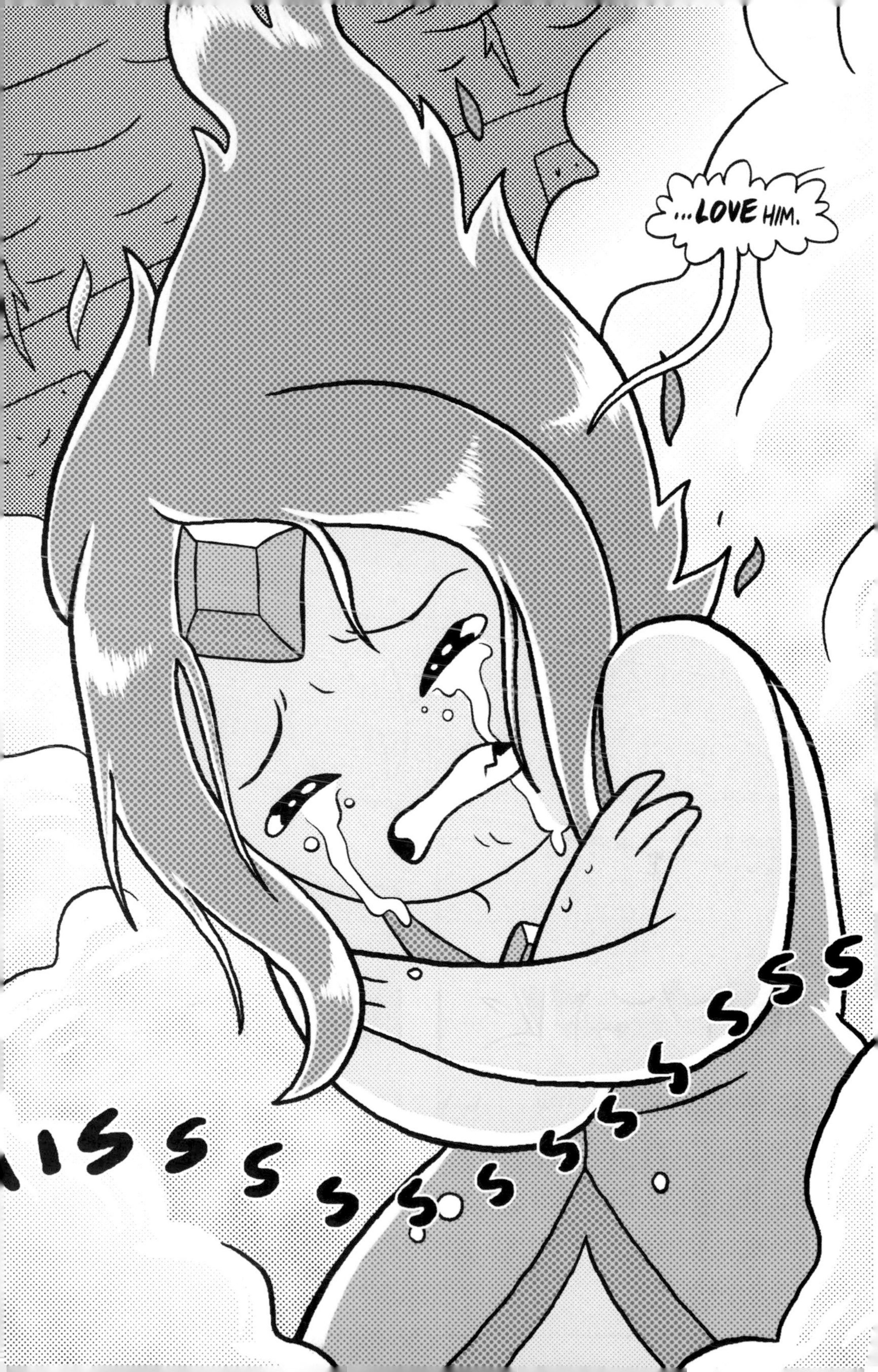
...LOVE HIM.
HISSSSSSSSSSSSSS

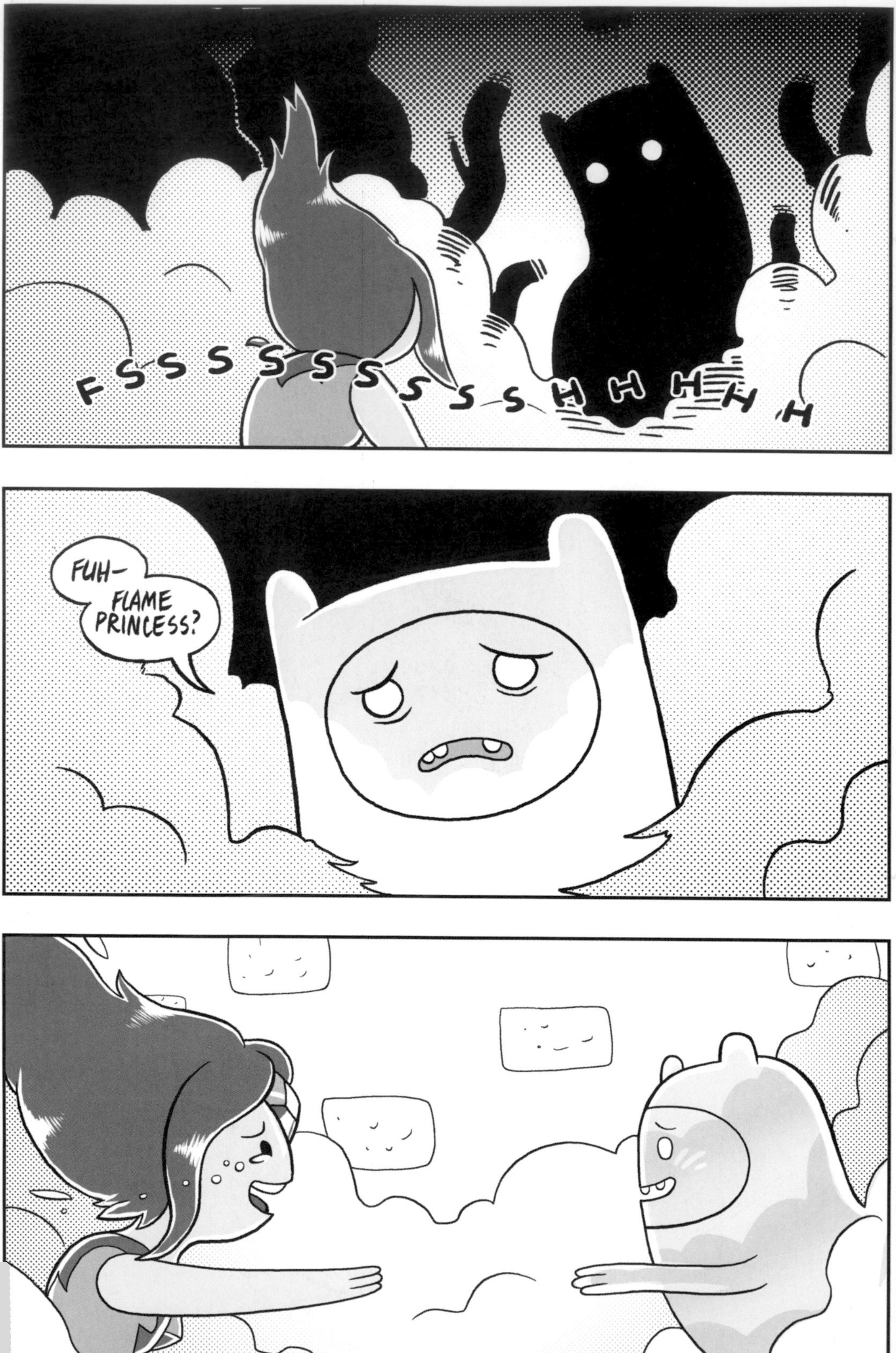
FSSSSSSSSSSSHHHHHH
FUH-
FLAME PRINCESS?

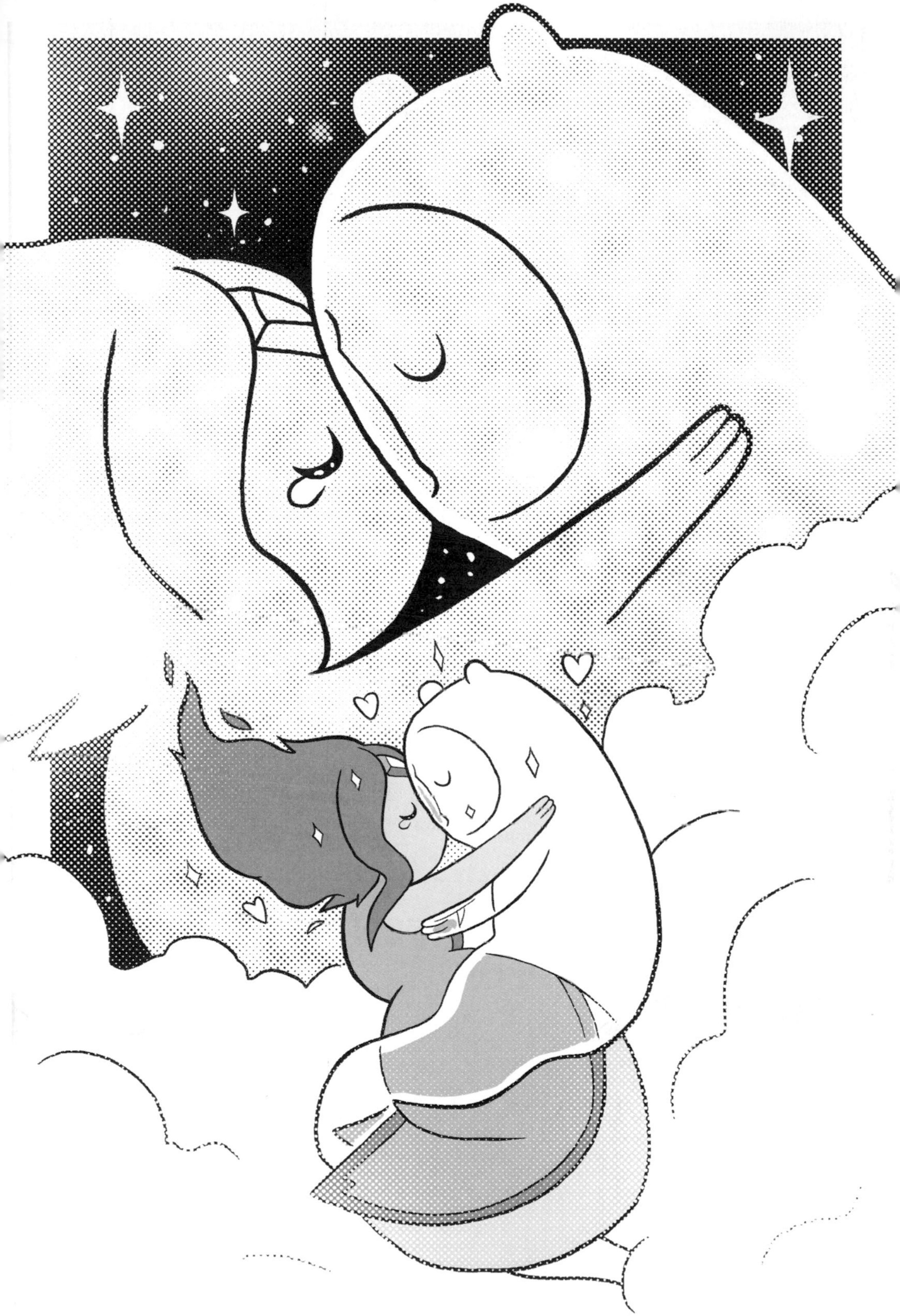

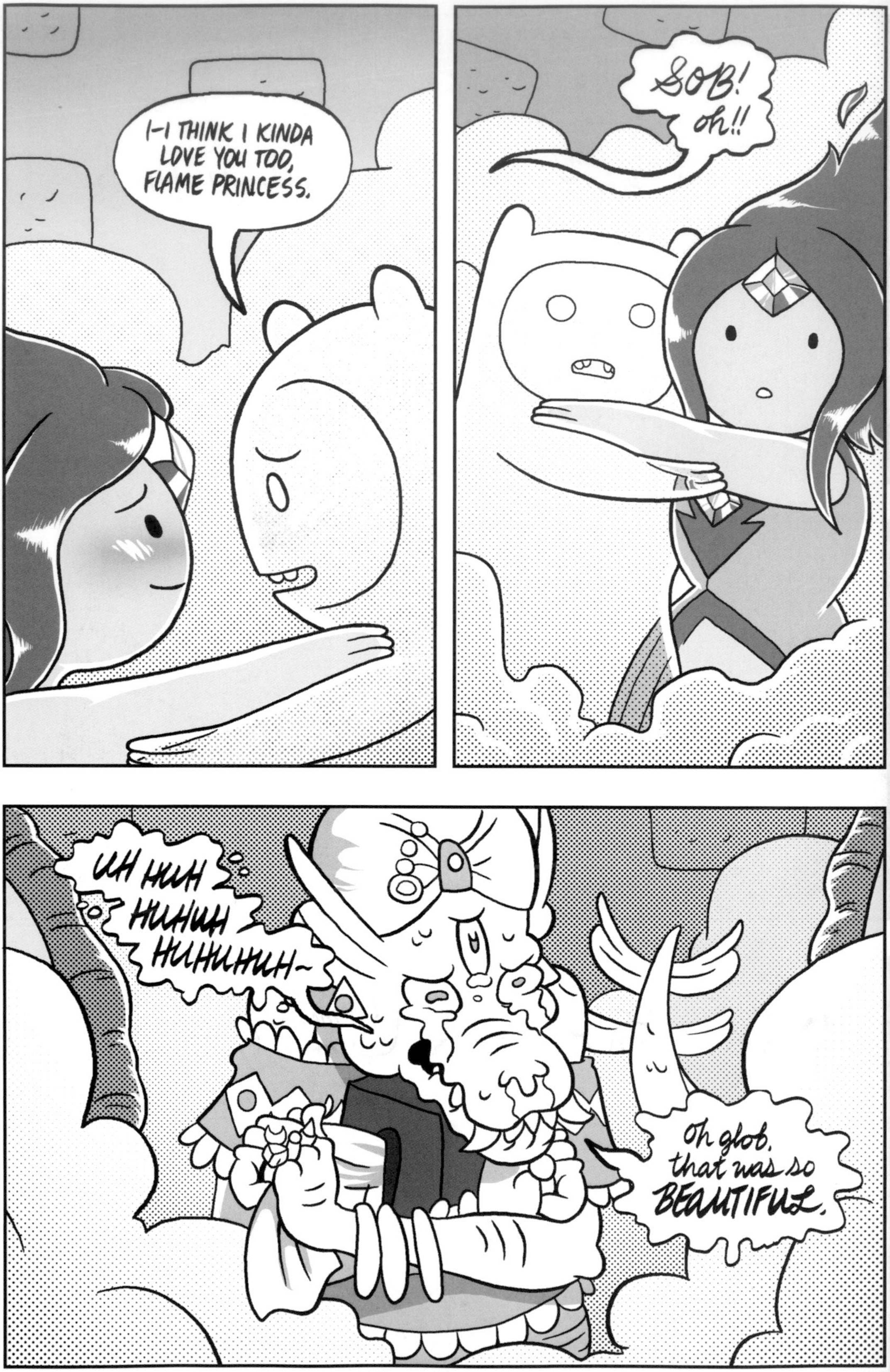
I-I THINK I KINDA LOVE YOU TOO, FLAME PRINCESS.
SOB! oh!!
UH HUH HUHUH HUHUHUH~
Oh glob, that was so BEAUTIFUL.

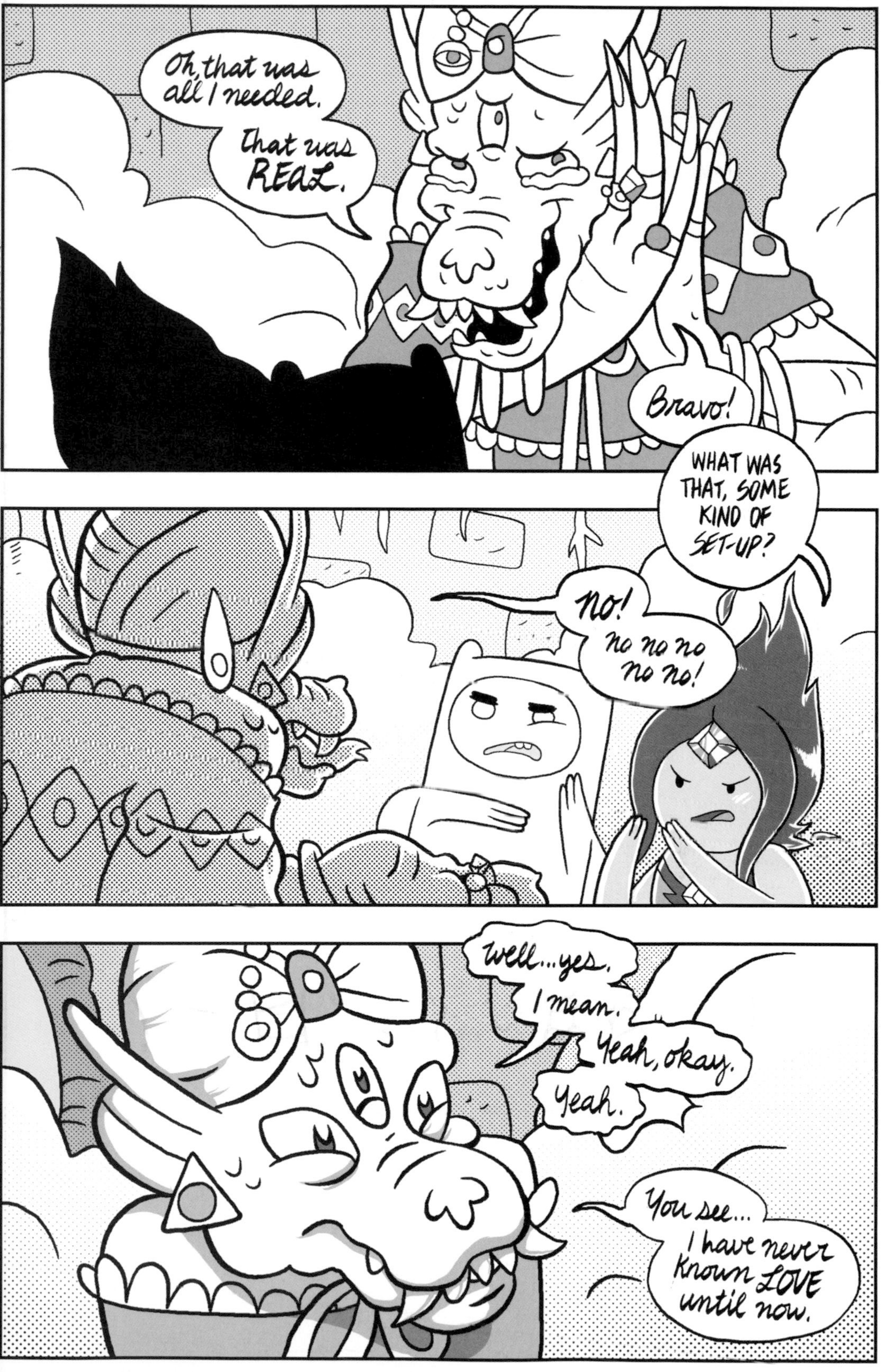

Oh, that was all I needed.
That was REAL.
Bravo!
WHAT WAS THAT, SOME KIND OF SET-UP?
no!
no no no no no!
Well... yes.
I mean.
Yeah, okay.
Yeah.
You see... I have never known LOVE until now.

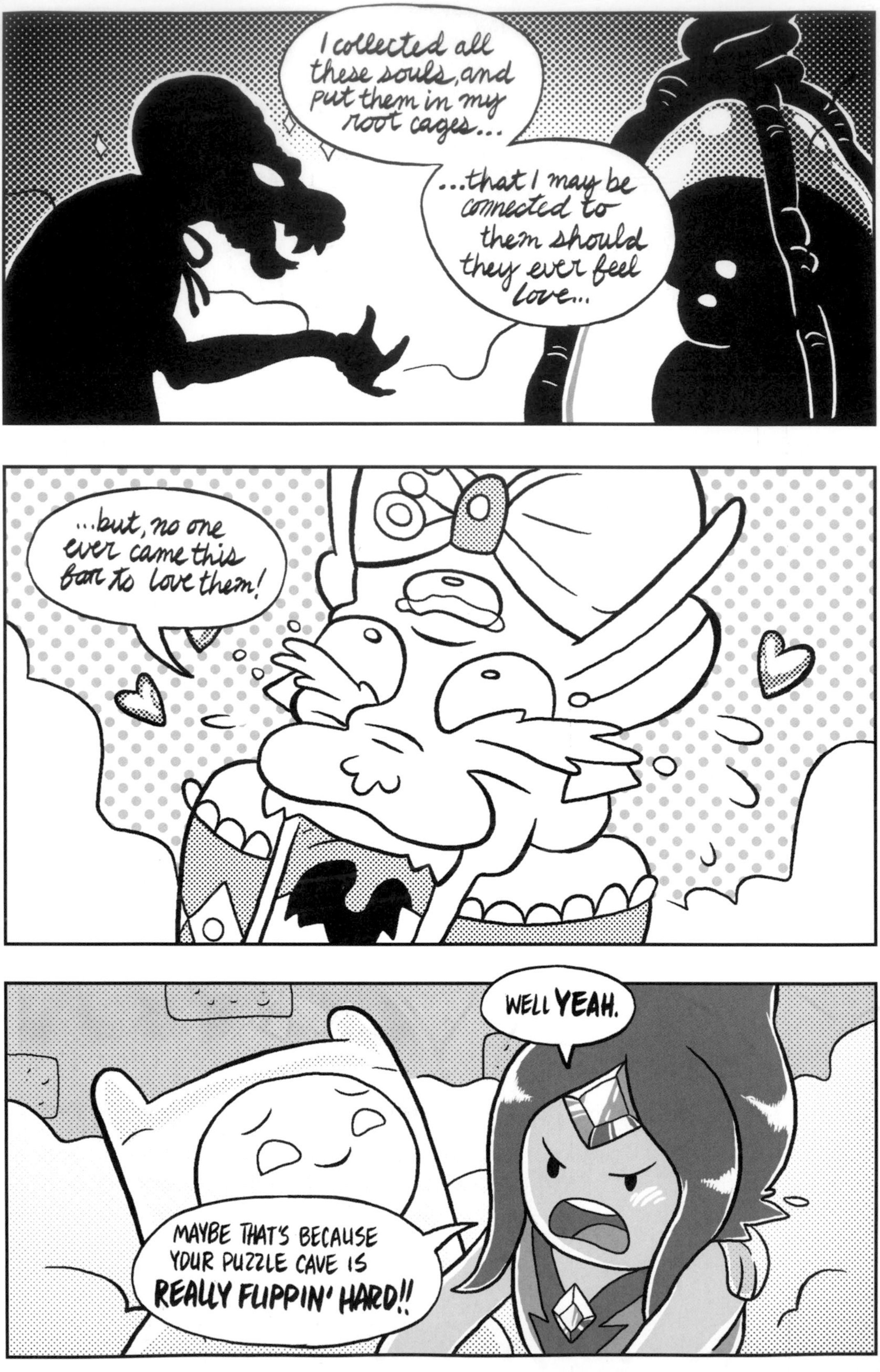
I collected all these souls, and put them in my root cages...
...that I may be connected to them should they ever feel love...
...but, no one ever came this far to love them!
WELL YEAH.
MAYBE THAT'S BECAUSE YOUR PUZZLE CAVE IS REALLY FLIPPIN' HARD!!

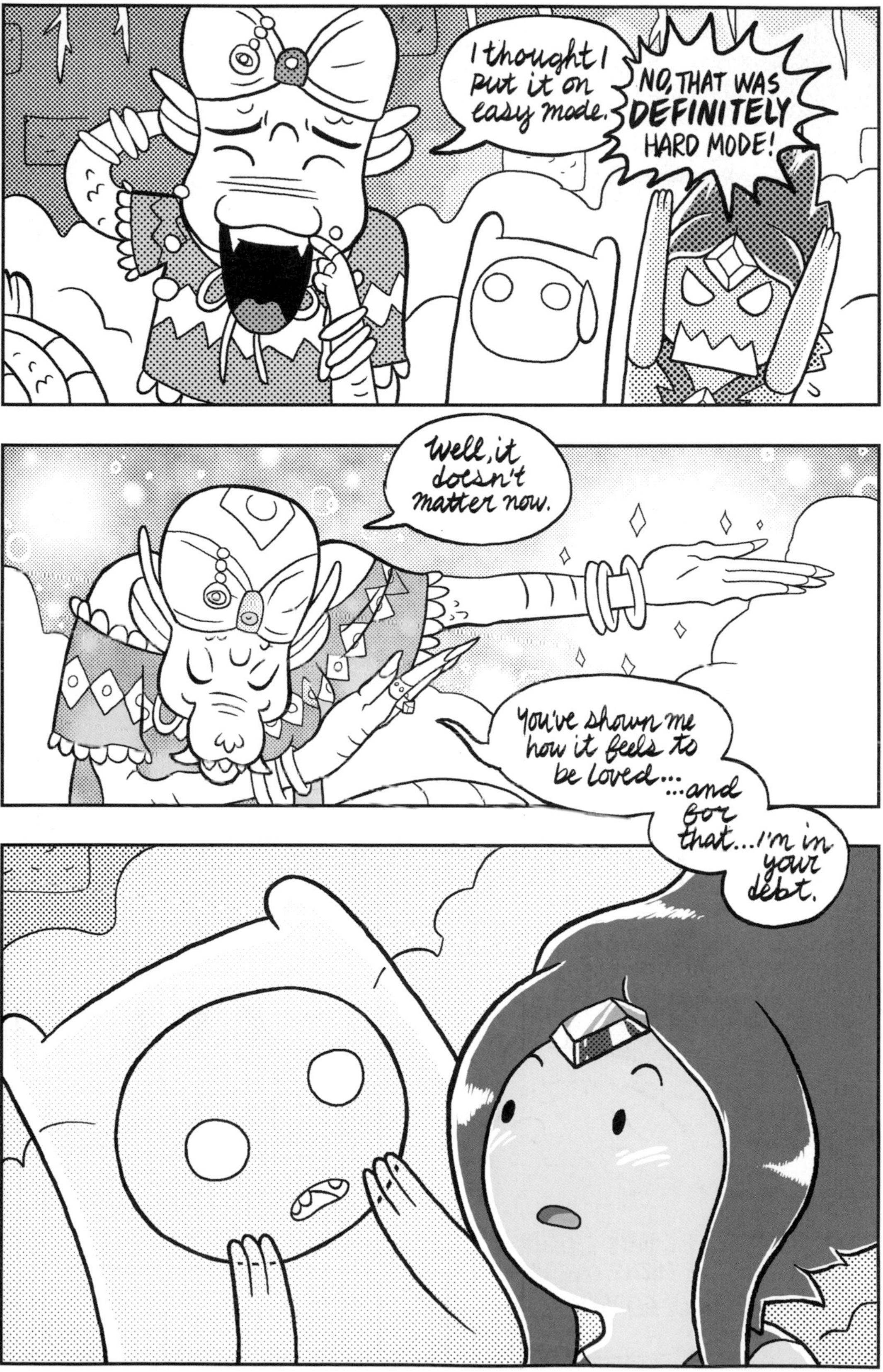
I thought I put it on easy mode.
NO, THAT WAS DEFINITELY HARD MODE!
Well, it doesn't matter now.
You've shown me how it feels to be loved... ...and for that... I'm in your debt.

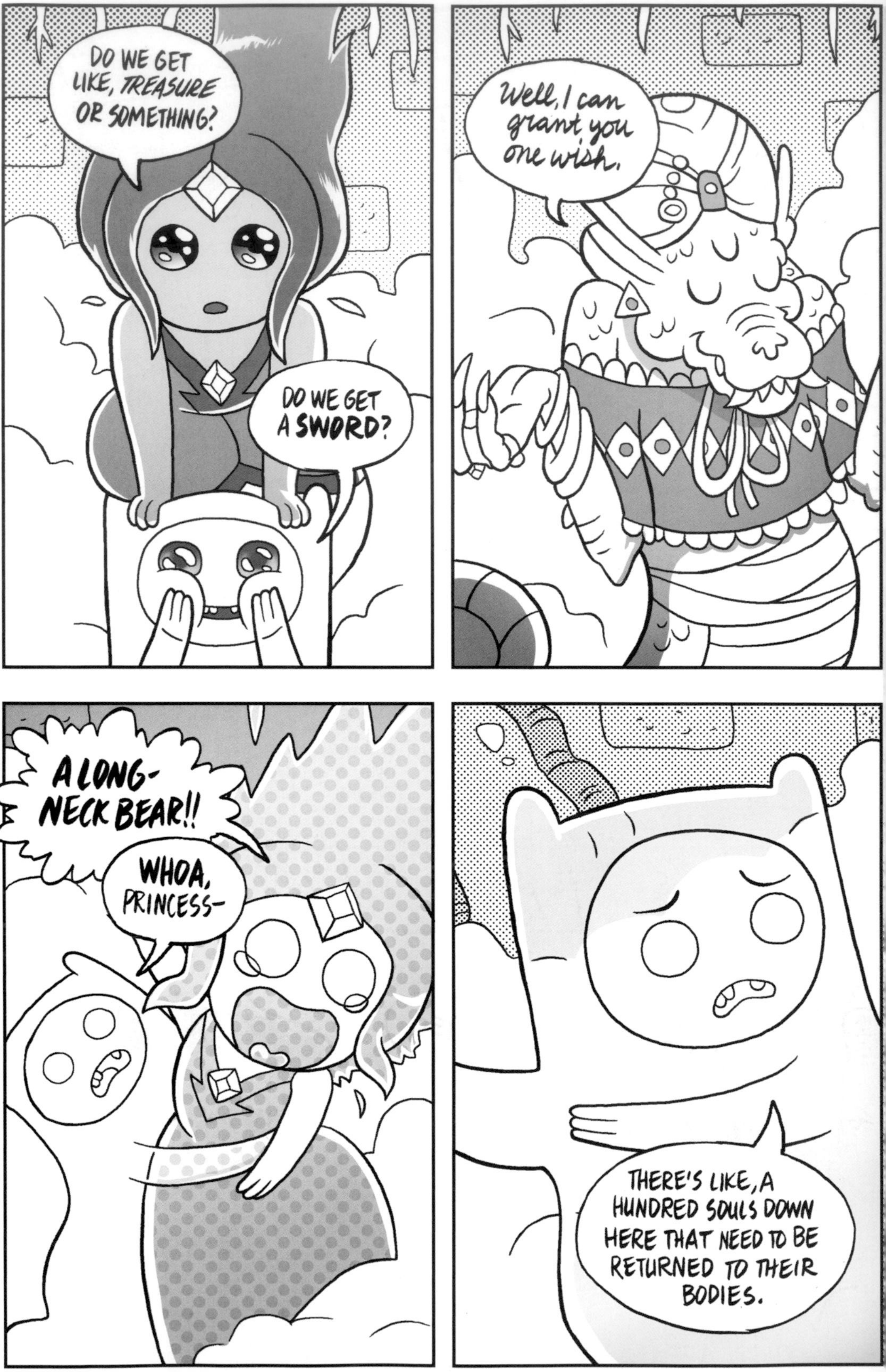
DO WE GET LIKE, TREASURE OR SOMETHING?
DO WE GET A SWORD?
Well, I can grant you one wish.
A LONG-NECK BEAR!!
WHOA, PRINCESS-
THERE'S LIKE, A HUNDRED SOULS DOWN HERE THAT NEED TO BE RETURNED TO THEIR BODIES.

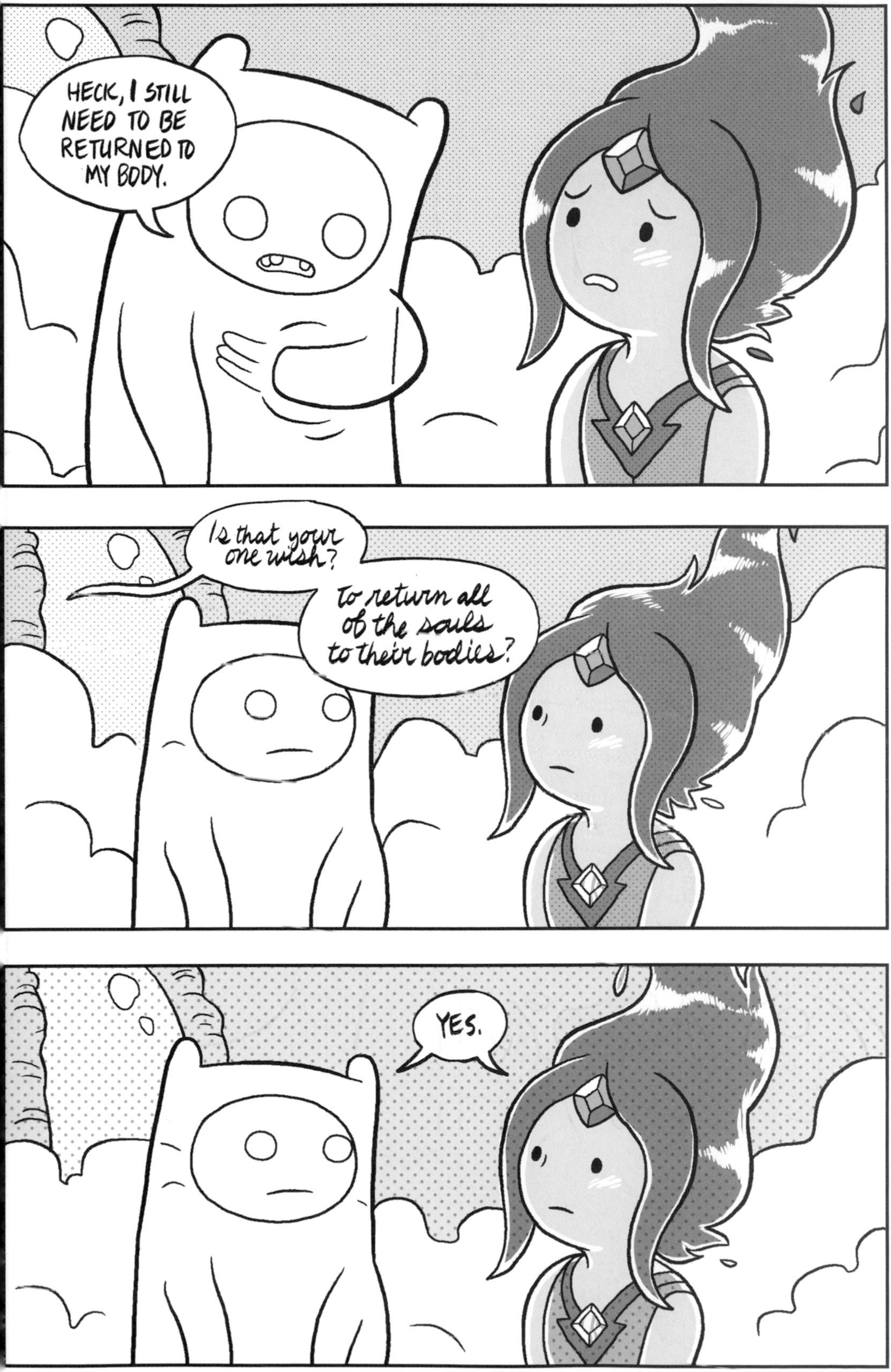
HECK, I STILL NEED TO BE RETURNED TO MY BODY.
Is that your one wish?
To return all of the souls to their bodies?
YES.

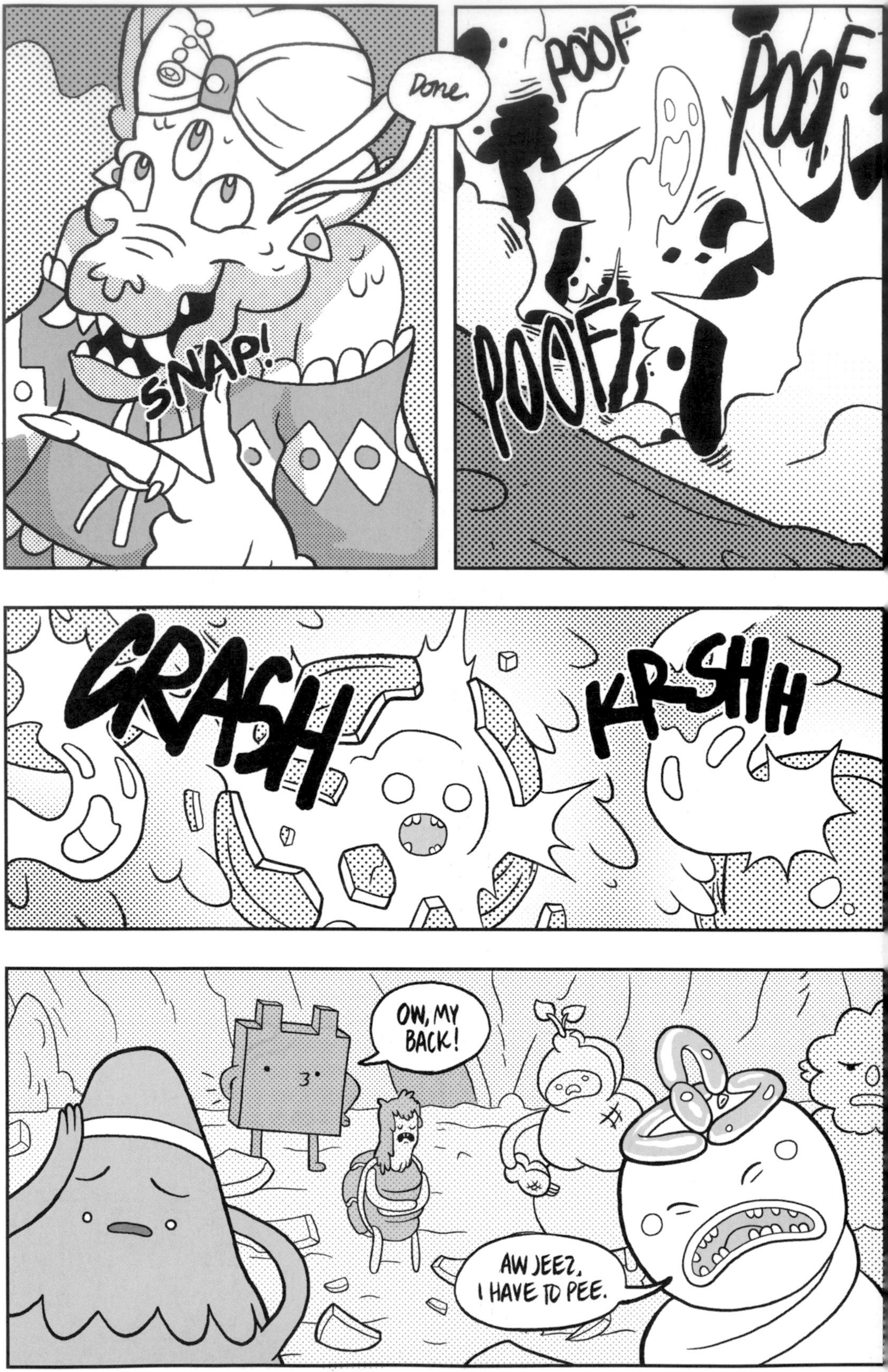

SNAP!
Done.
POOF
POOF
POOF!
CRASH
KRSHH
OW, MY BACK!
AW JEEZ, I HAVE TO PEE.

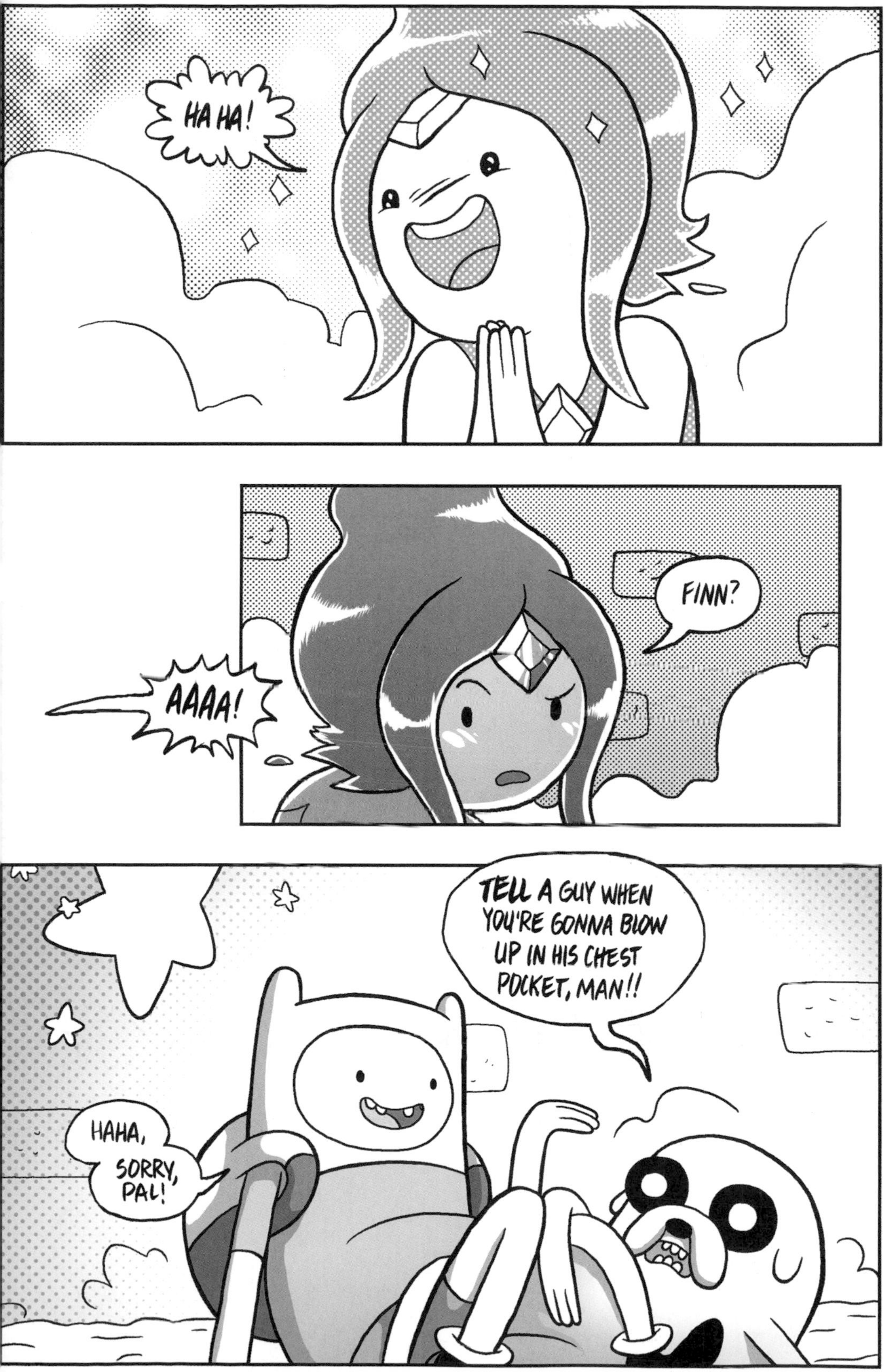
HA HA!
FINN?
AAAA!
TELL A GUY WHEN YOU'RE GONNA BLOW UP IN HIS CHEST POCKET, MAN!!
HAHA, SORRY, PAL!

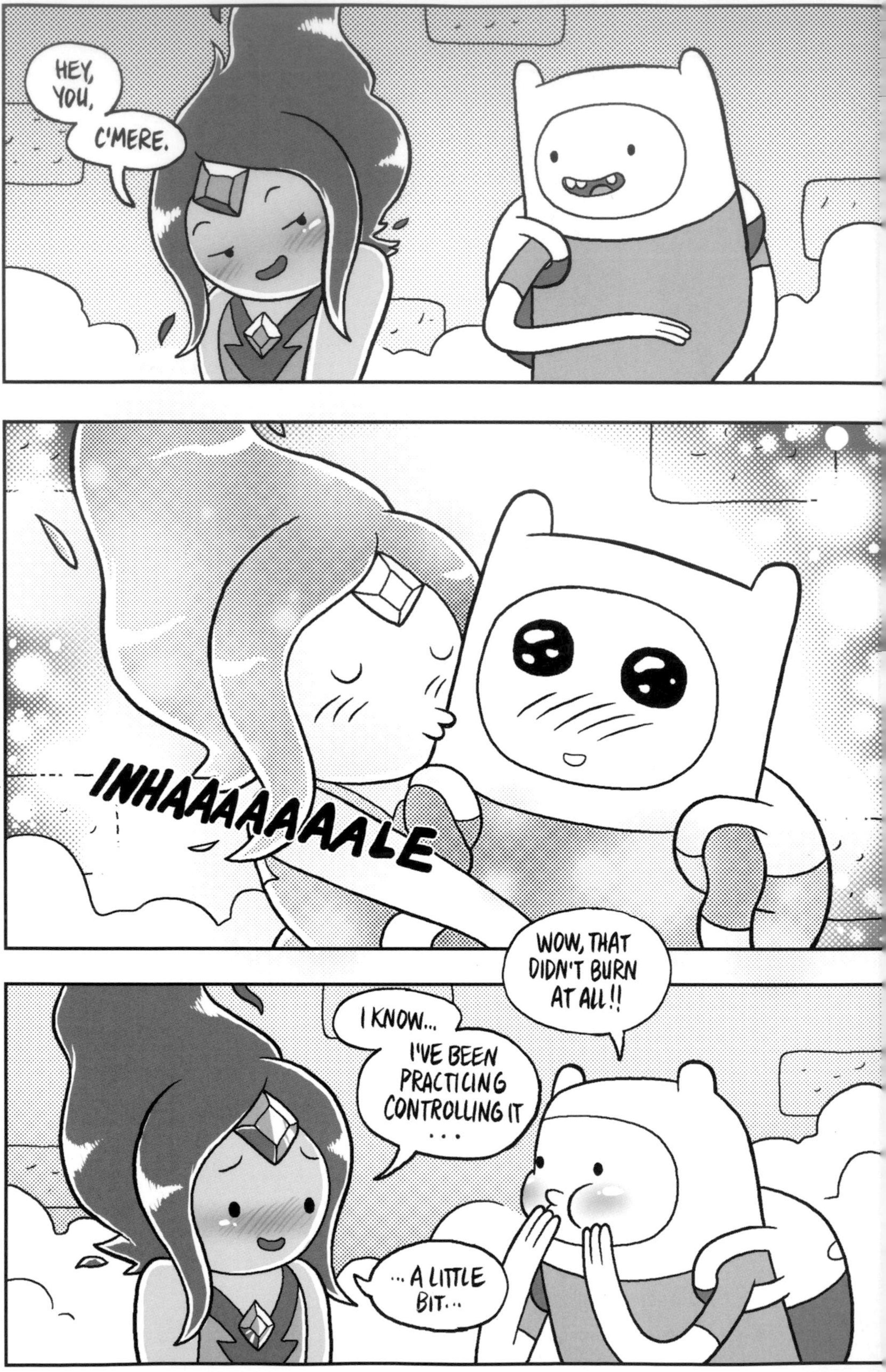
HEY, YOU,
C'MERE.
INHAAAAAAAALE
WOW, THAT DIDN'T BURN AT ALL!!
I KNOW...
I'VE BEEN PRACTICING CONTROLLING IT . . .
...A LITTLE BIT...

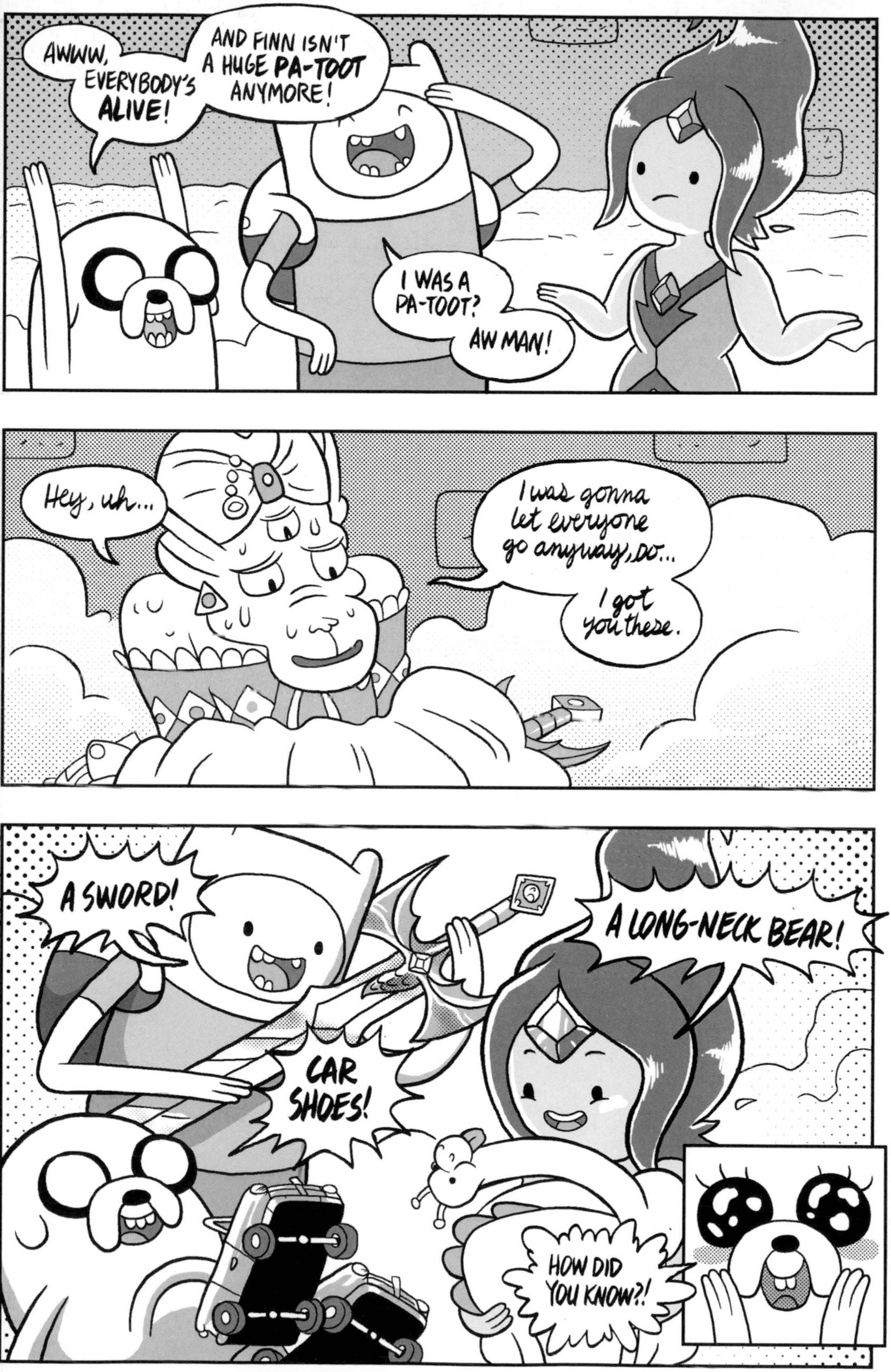
AWWW, EVERYBODY'S ALIVE!
AND FINN ISN'T A HUGE PA-TOOT ANYMORE!
I WAS A PA-TOOT?
AW MAN!
Hey, uh...
I was gonna let everyone go anyway, so...
I got you these.
A SWORD!
A LONG-NECK BEAR!
CAR SHOES!
HOW DID YOU KNOW?!

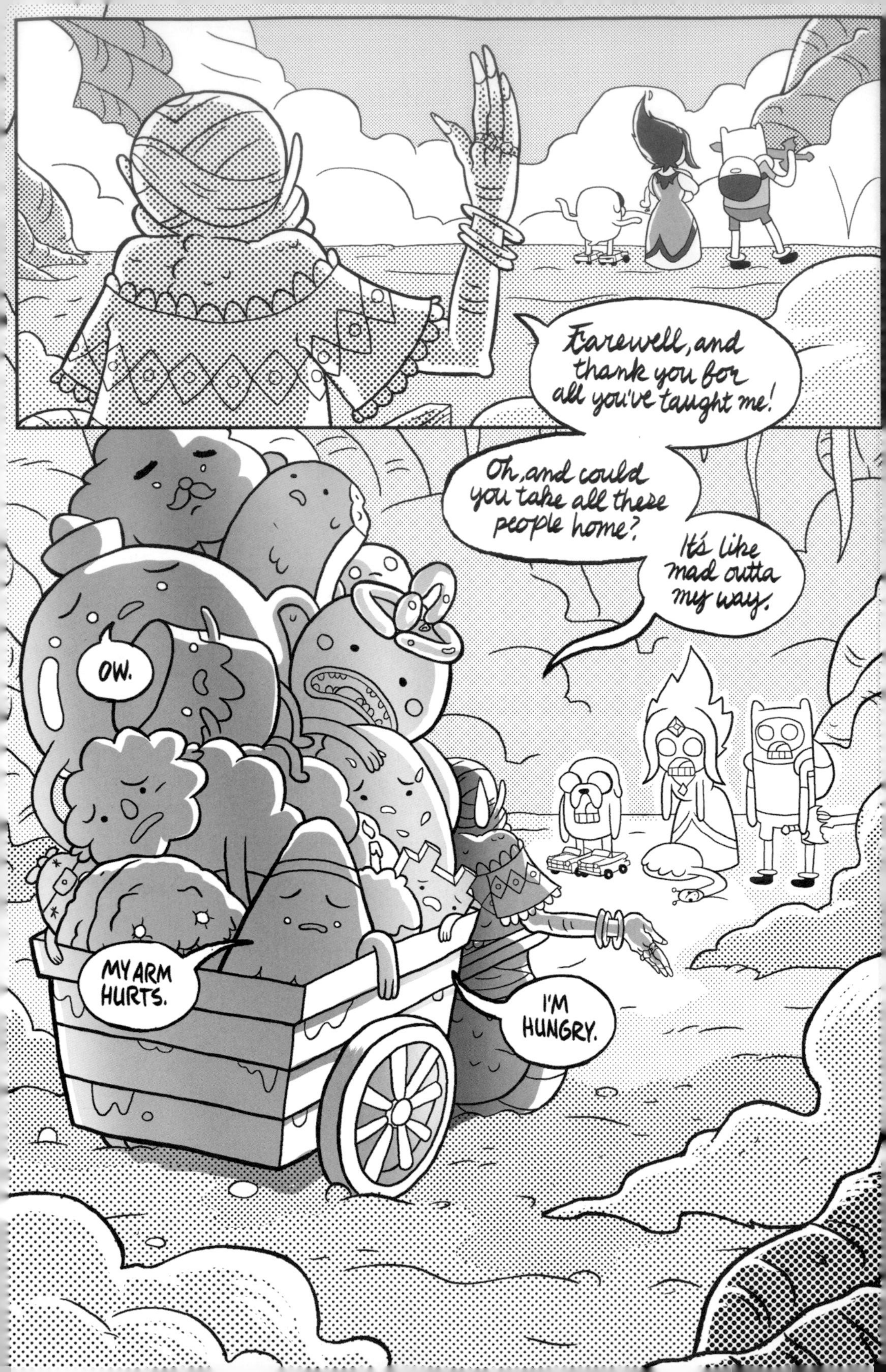
Farewell, and thank you for all you've taught me!
Oh, and could you take all these people home?
It's like mad outta my way.
OW.
MY ARM HURTS.
I'M HUNGRY.

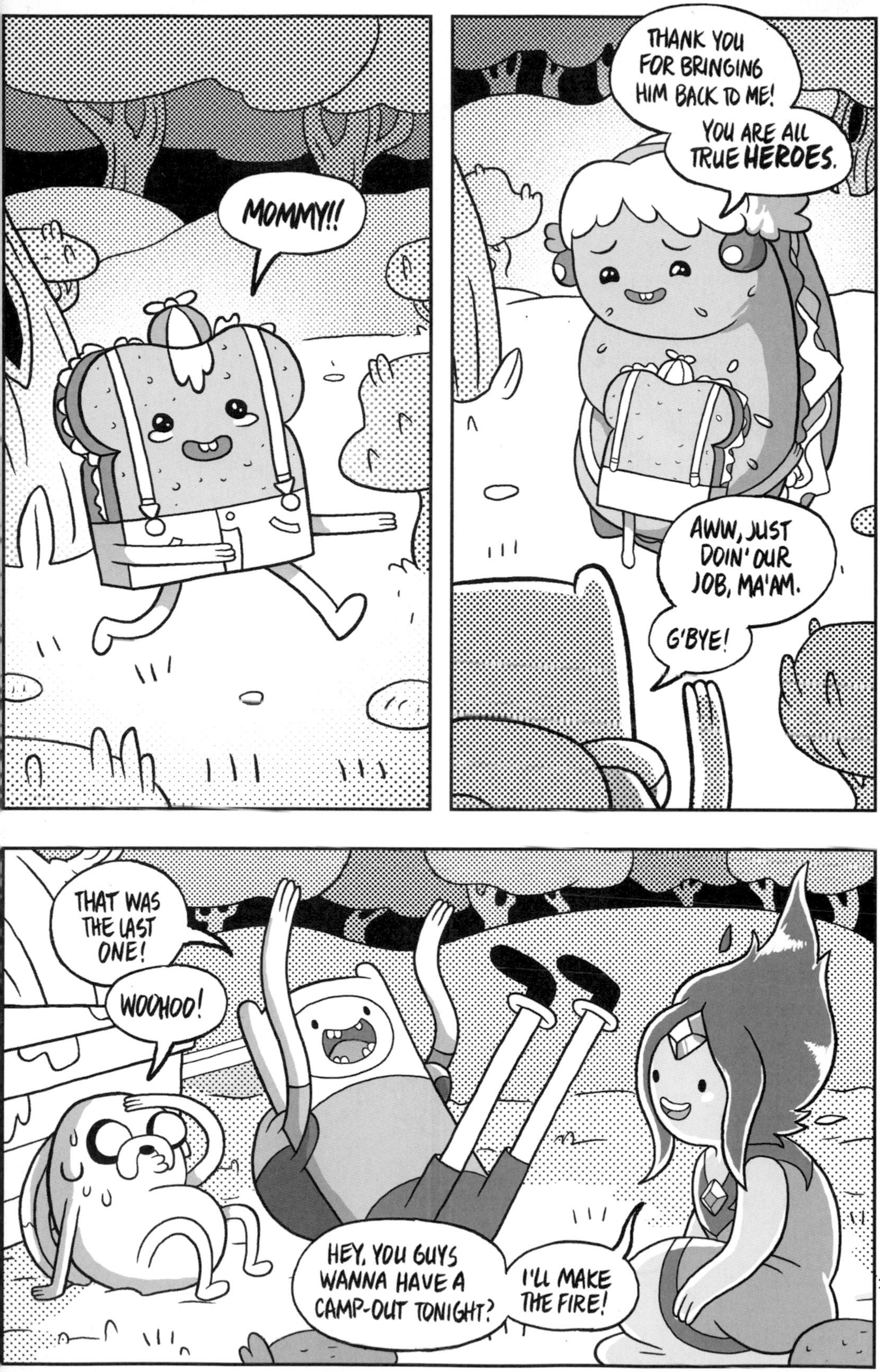
MOMMY!!
THANK YOU FOR BRINGING HIM BACK TO ME!
YOU ARE ALL TRUE HEROES.
AWW, JUST DOIN' OUR JOB, MA'AM.
G'BYE!
THAT WAS THE LAST ONE!
WOOHOO!
HEY, YOU GUYS WANNA HAVE A CAMP-OUT TONIGHT?
I'LL MAKE THE FIRE!

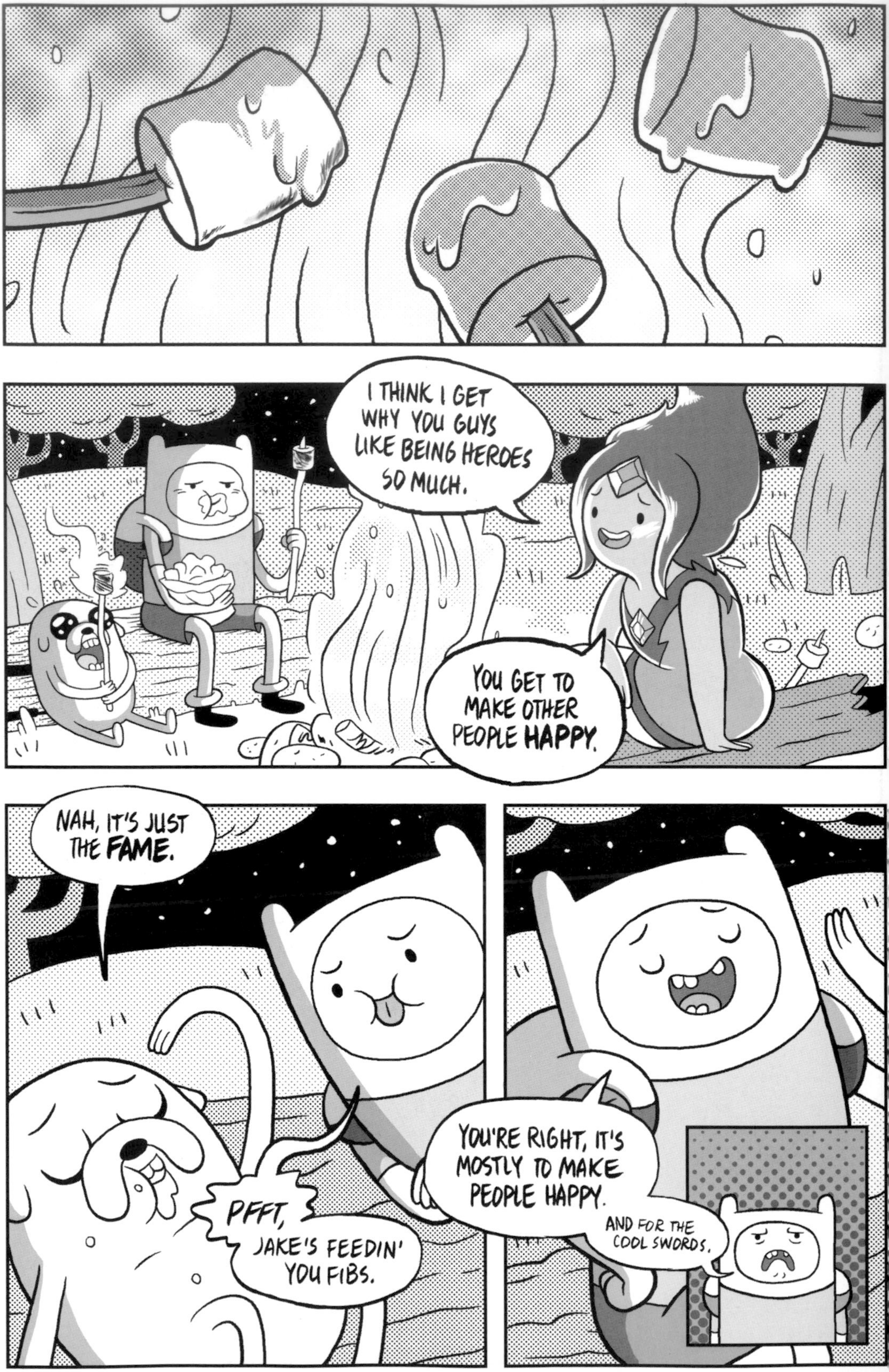
I THINK I GET WHY YOU GUYS LIKE BEING HEROES SO MUCH.
YOU GET TO MAKE OTHER PEOPLE HAPPY.
NAH, IT'S JUST THE FAME.
PFFT, JAKE'S FEEDIN' YOU FIBS.
YOU'RE RIGHT, IT'S MOSTLY TO MAKE PEOPLE HAPPY.
AND FOR THE COOL SWORDS.

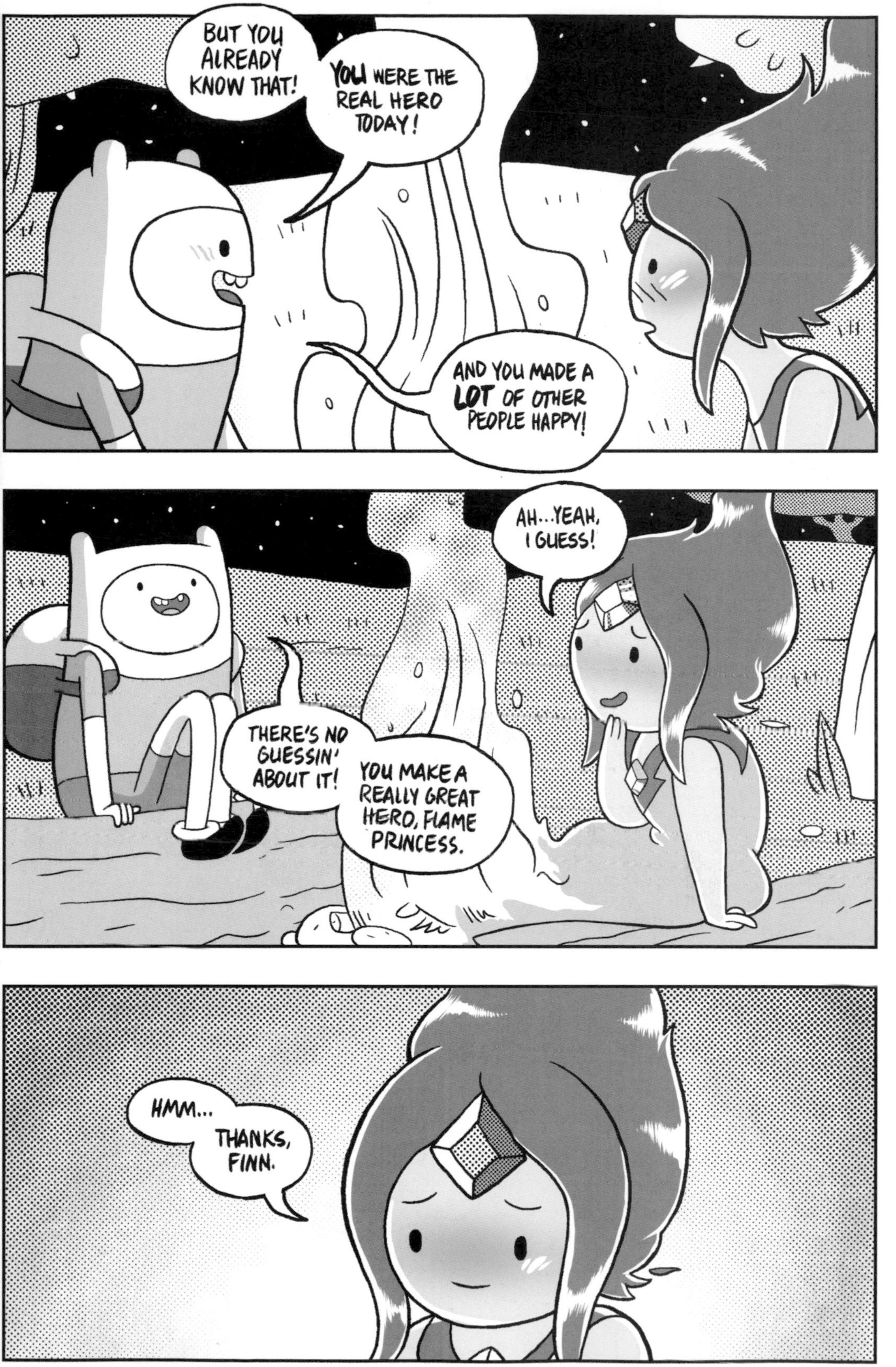
BUT YOU ALREADY KNOW THAT!
YOU WERE THE REAL HERO TODAY!
AND YOU MADE A LOT OF OTHER PEOPLE HAPPY!
AH...YEAH, I GUESS!
THERE'S NO GUESSIN' ABOUT IT!
YOU MAKE A REALLY GREAT HERO, FLAME PRINCESS.
HMM... THANKS, FINN.

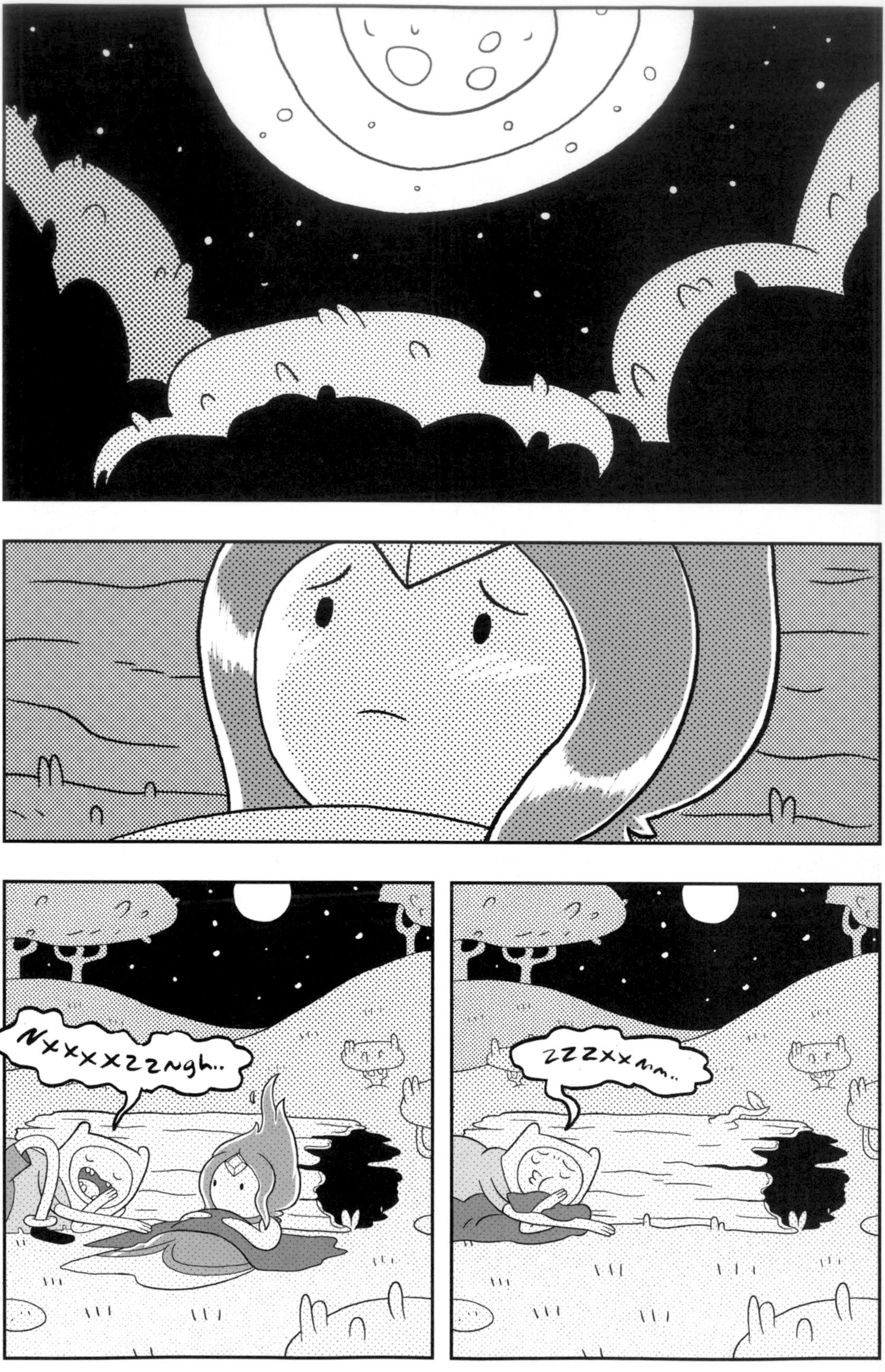
NXXXXZZNgh..
ZZZXXMM..

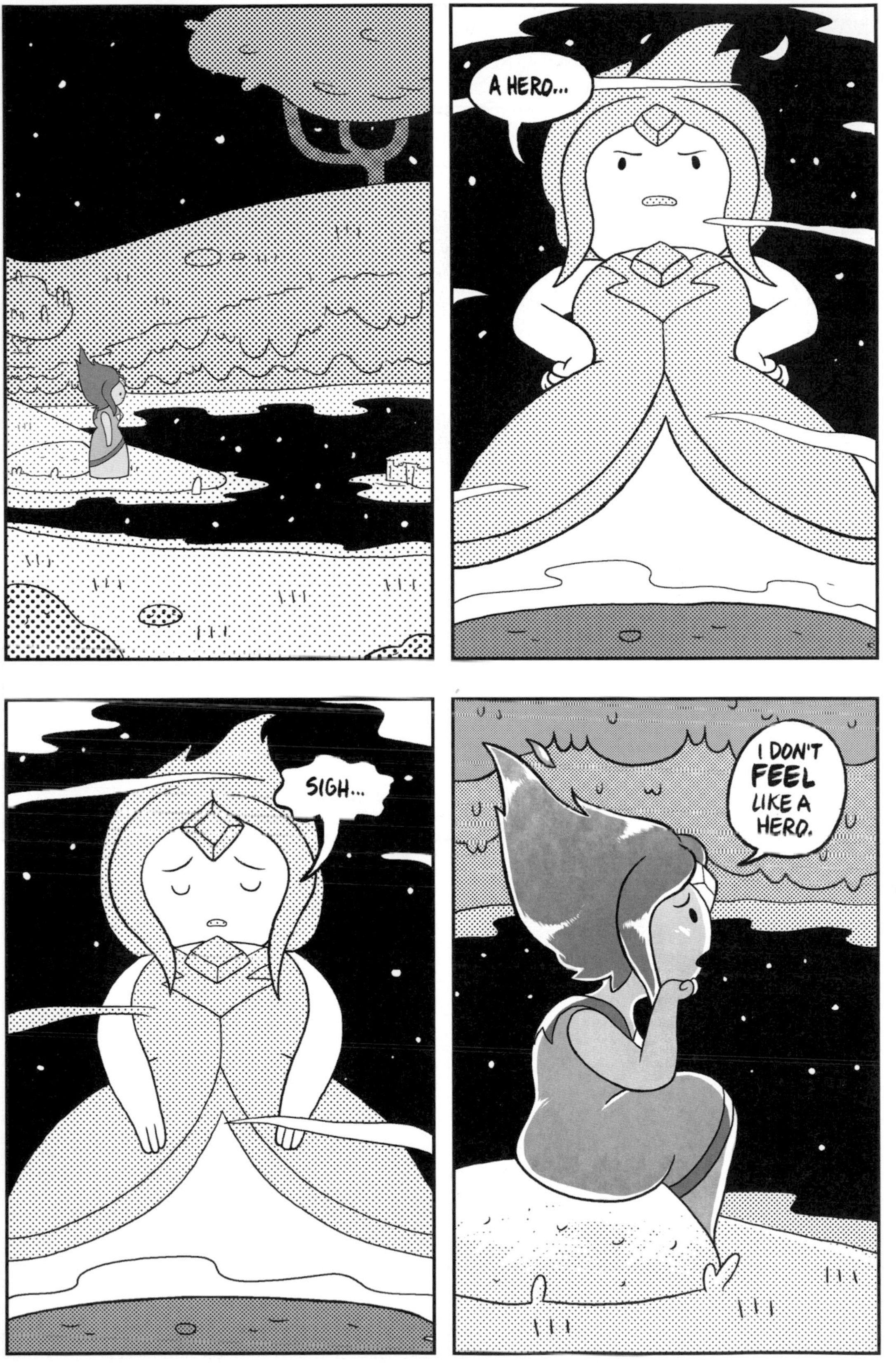
A HERO...
SIGH...
I DON'T FEEL LIKE A HERO.

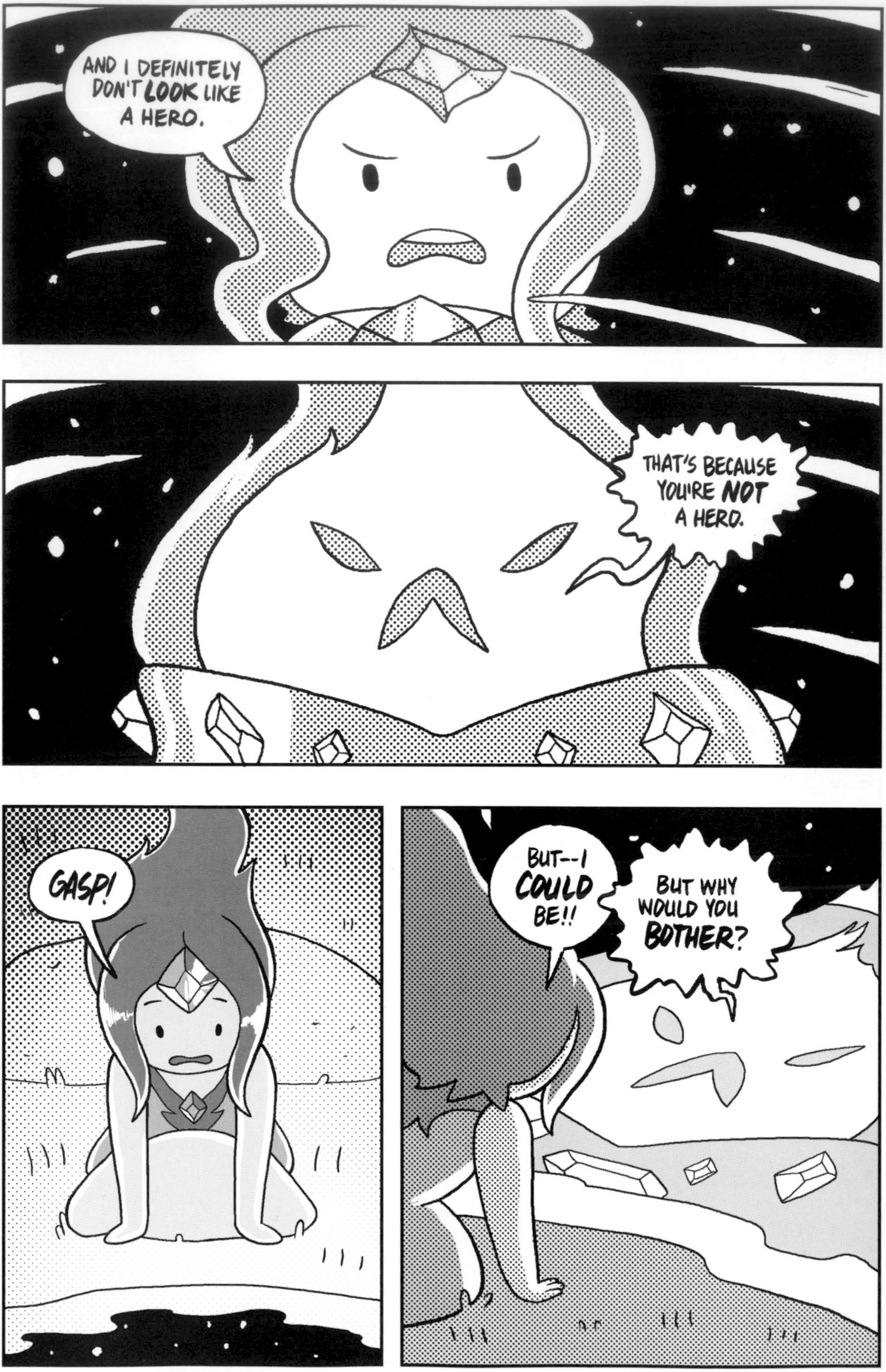
AND I DEFINITELY DON'T LOOK LIKE A HERO.
THAT'S BECAUSE YOU'RE NOT A HERO.
GASP!
BUT--I COULD BE!!
BUT WHY WOULD YOU BOTHER?

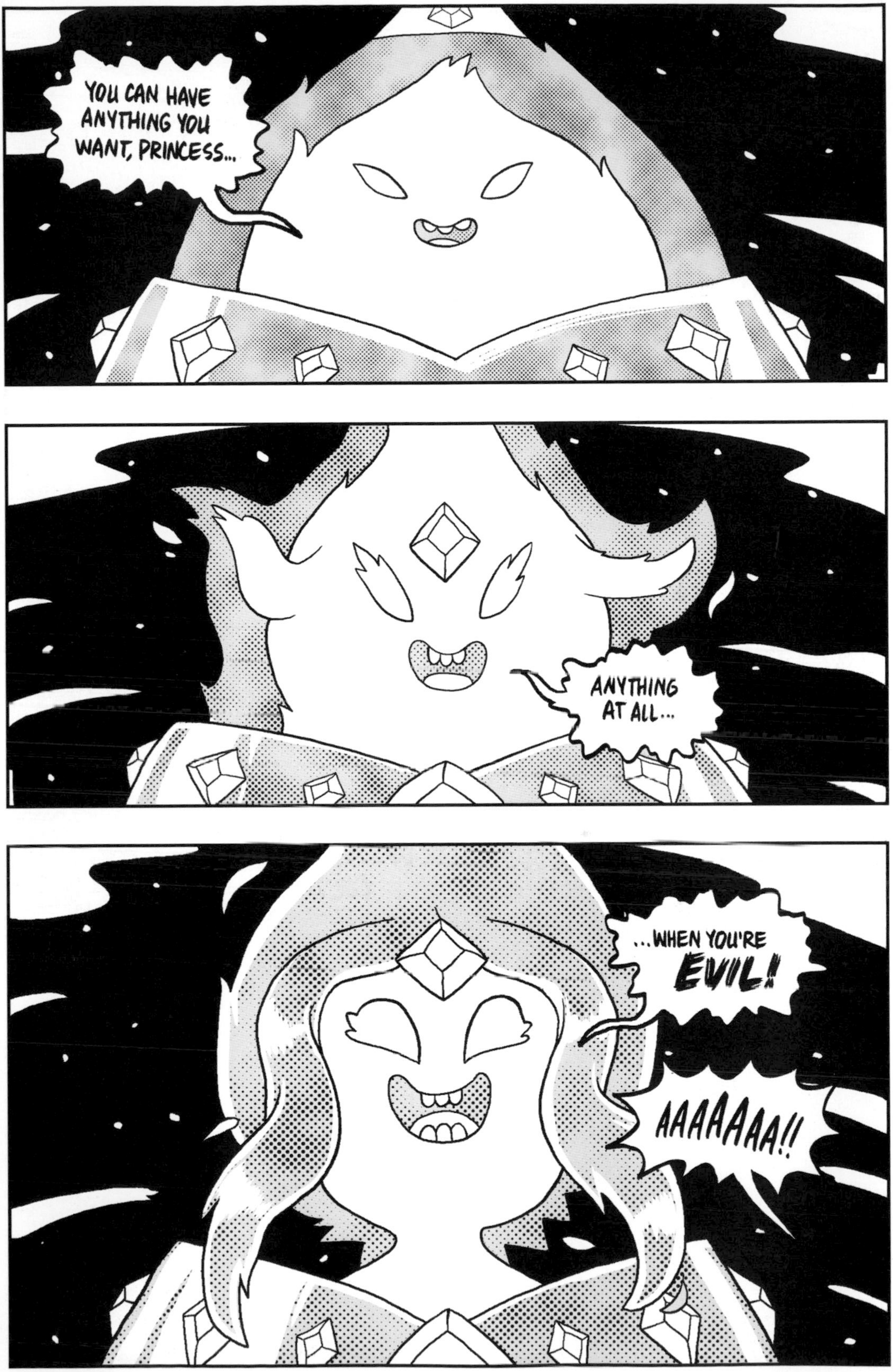
YOU CAN HAVE ANYTHING YOU WANT, PRINCESS...
ANYTHING AT ALL...
...WHEN YOU'RE EVIL!
AAAAAAA!!

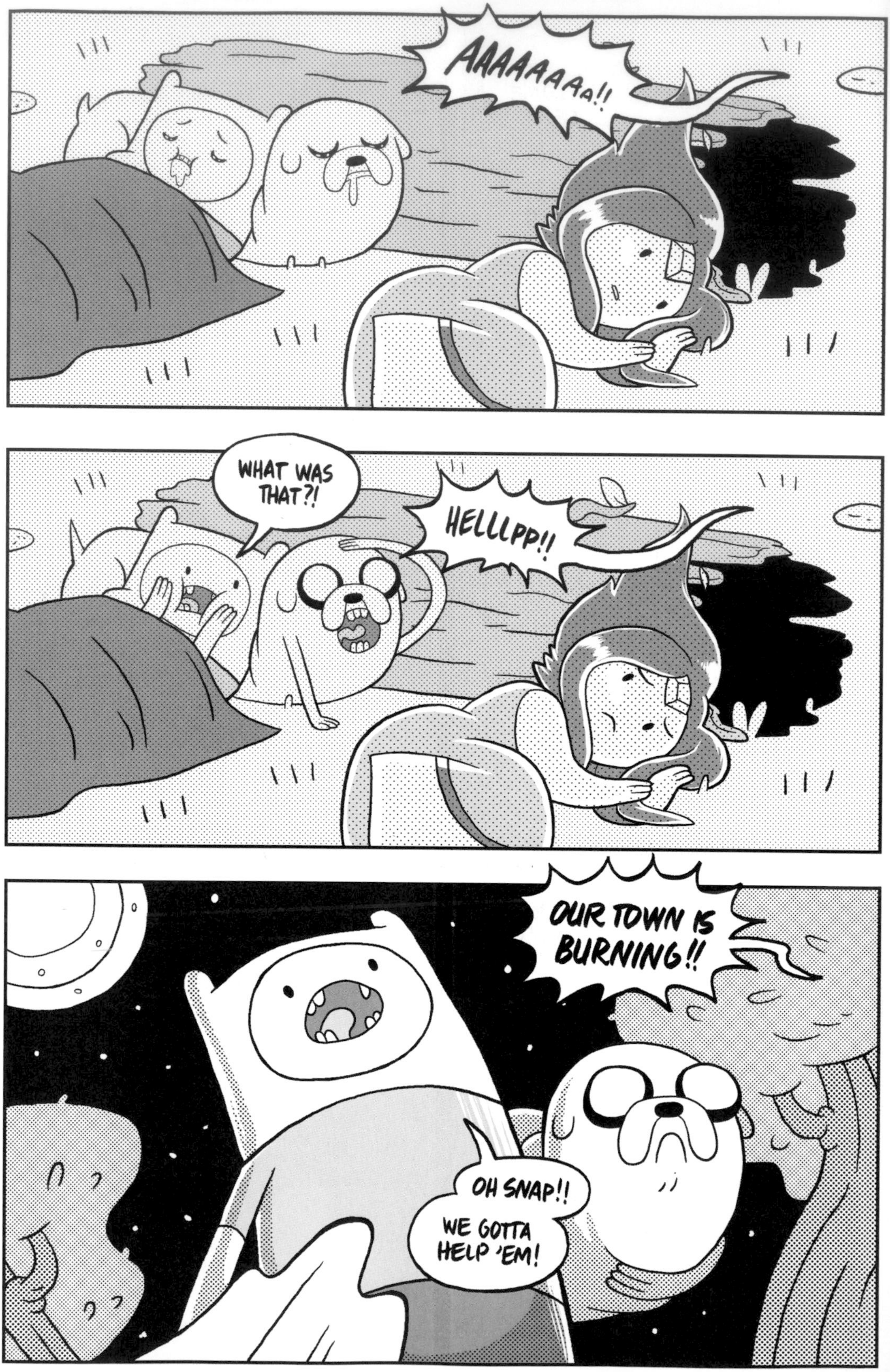
AAAAAAAa!!
WHAT WAS THAT?!
HELLLPP!!
OUR TOWN IS BURNING!!
OH SNAP!!
WE GOTTA HELP 'EM!

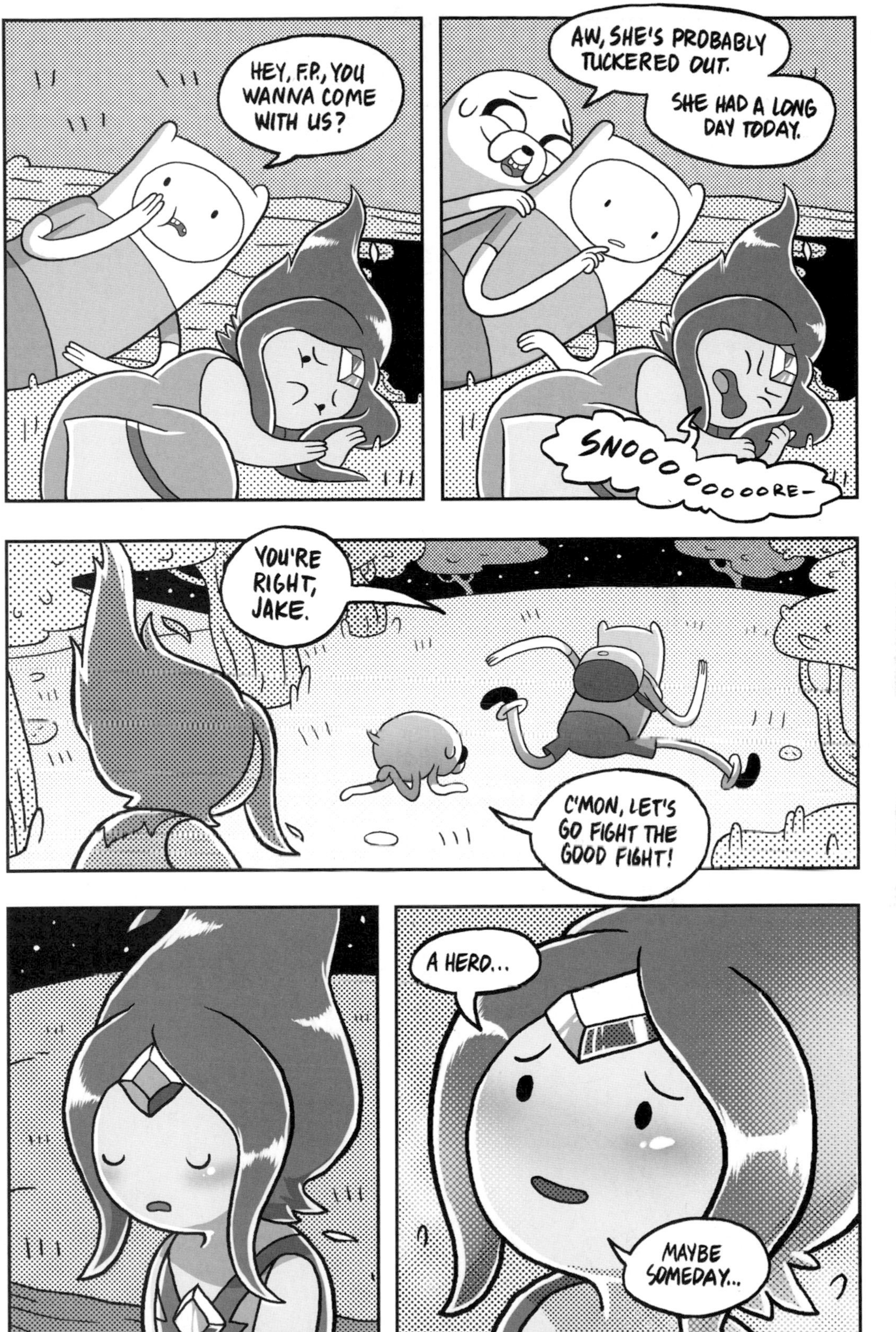
HEY, F.P., YOU WANNA COME WITH US?
AW, SHE'S PROBABLY TUCKERED OUT.
SHE HAD A LONG DAY TODAY.
SNOOOOOOOOOORE-
YOU'RE RIGHT, JAKE.
C'MON, LET'S GO FIGHT THE GOOD FIGHT!
A HERO...
MAYBE SOMEDAY...

THE END

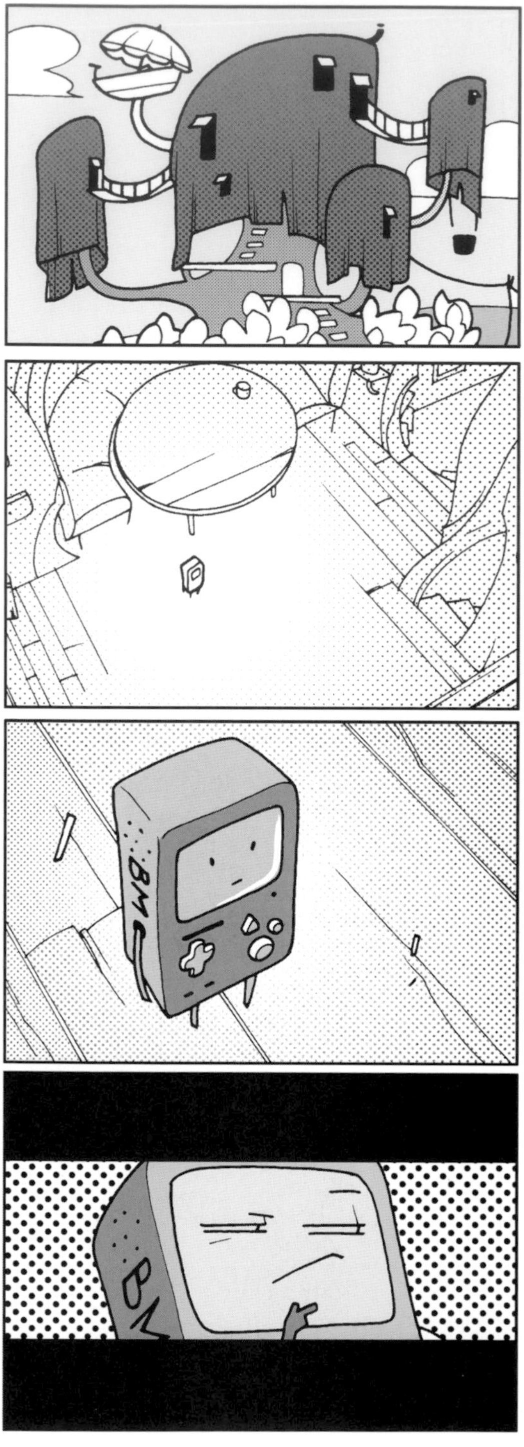

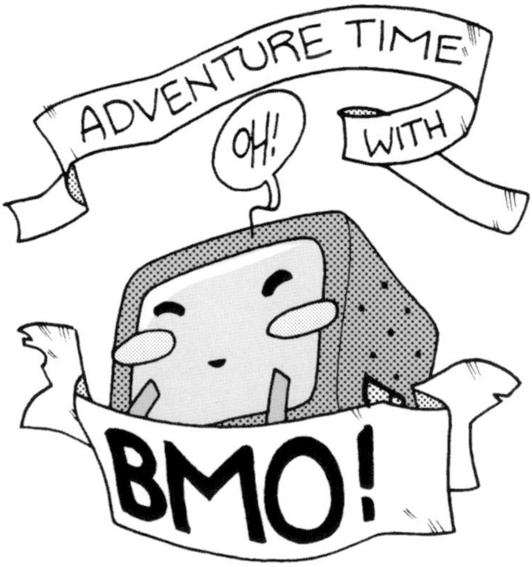
ADVENTURE TIME
OH!
WITH
BMO!

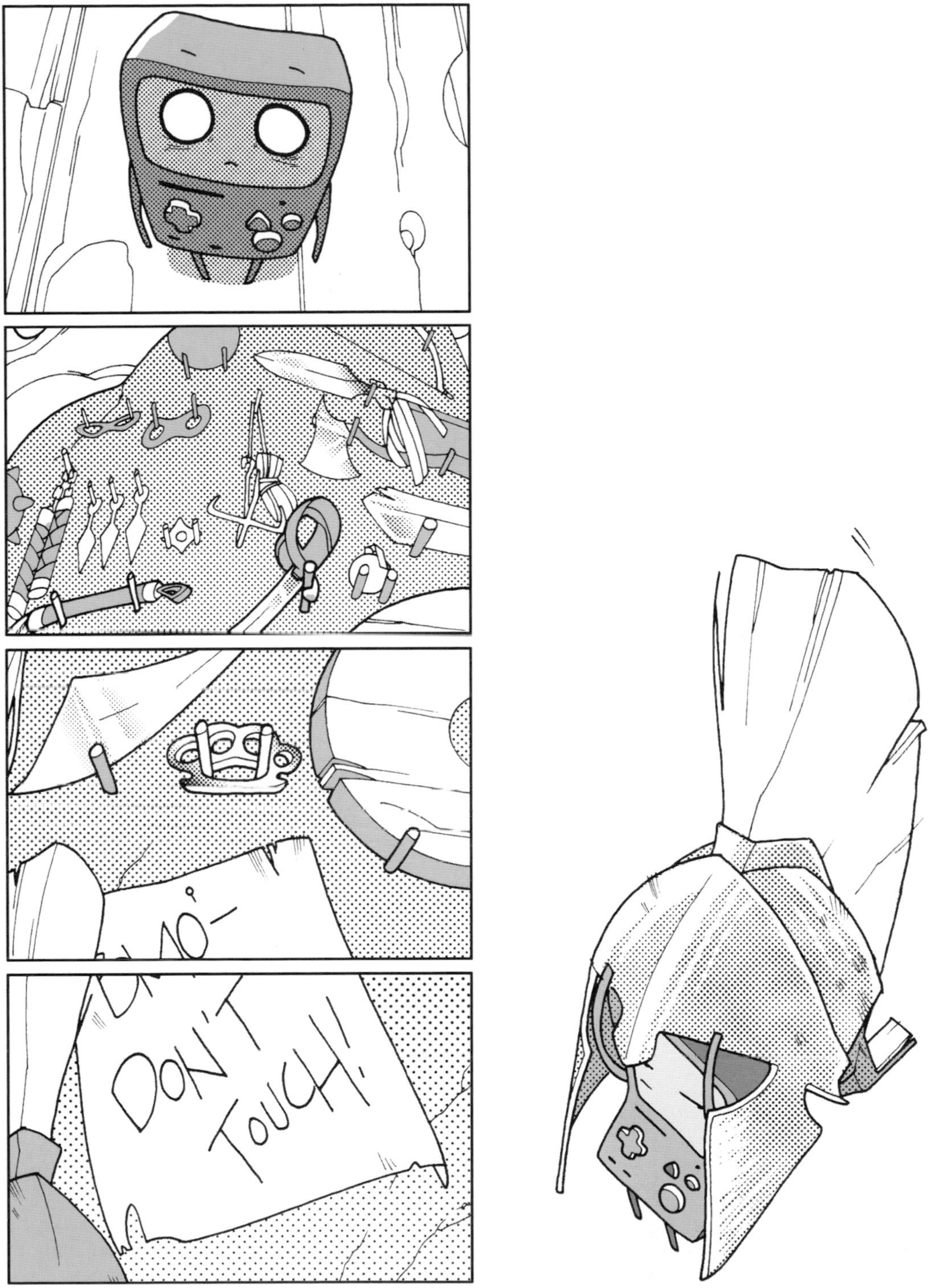
DON'T TOUCH!

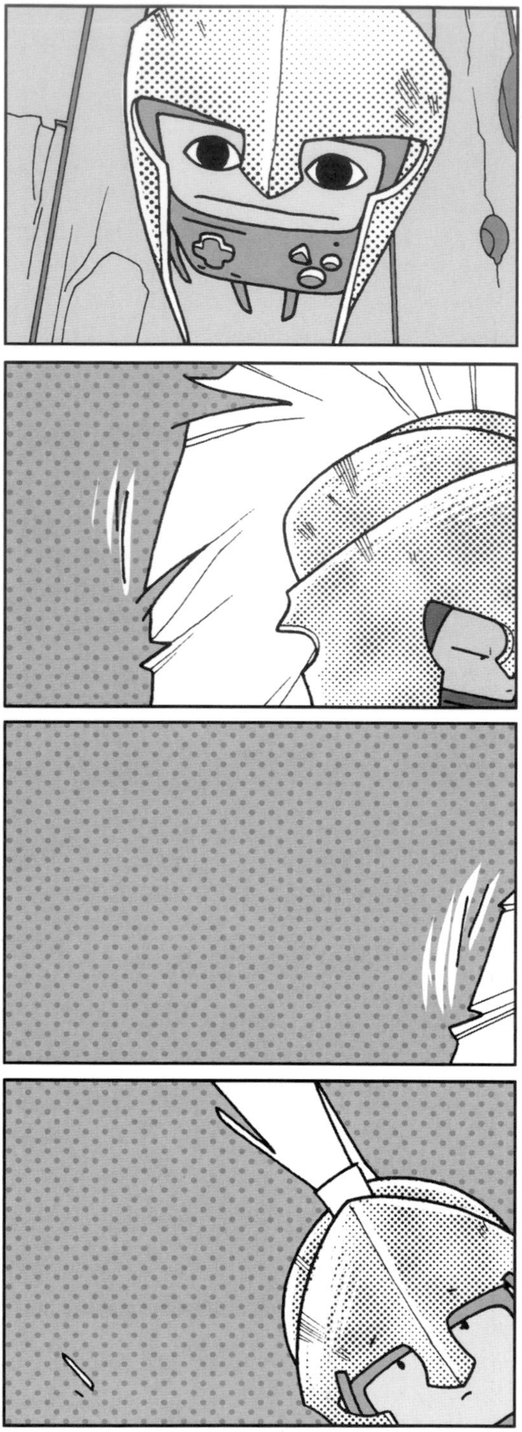

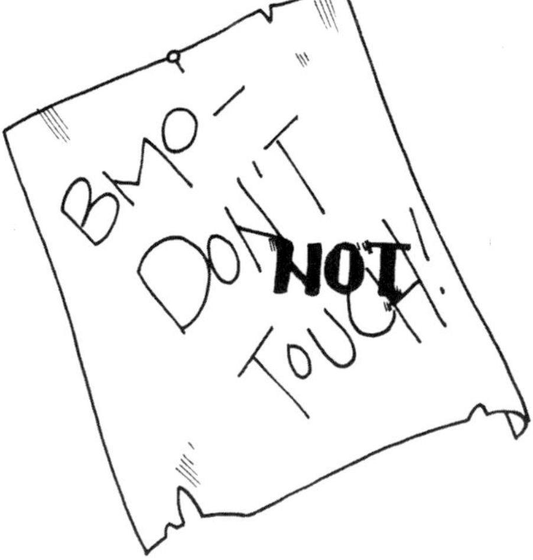
BMO—
DON'T
NOT
TOUCH!

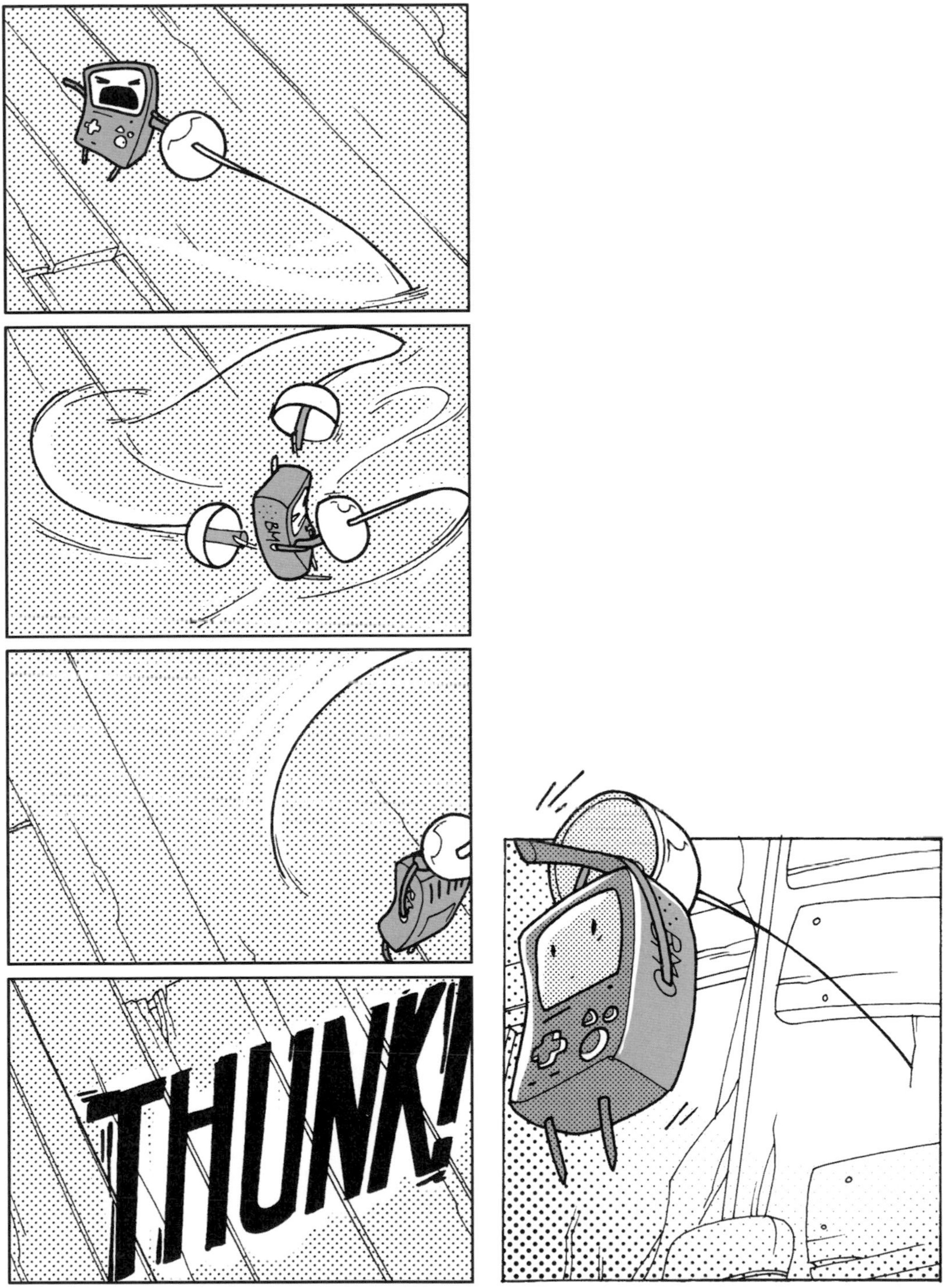
THUNK!

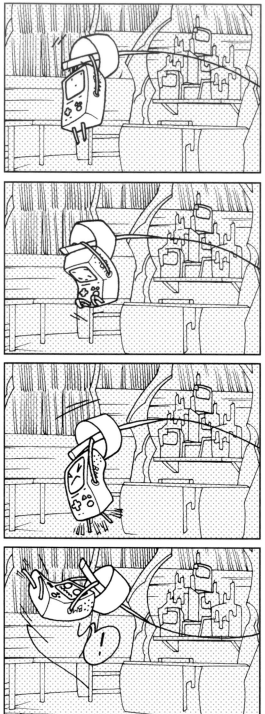

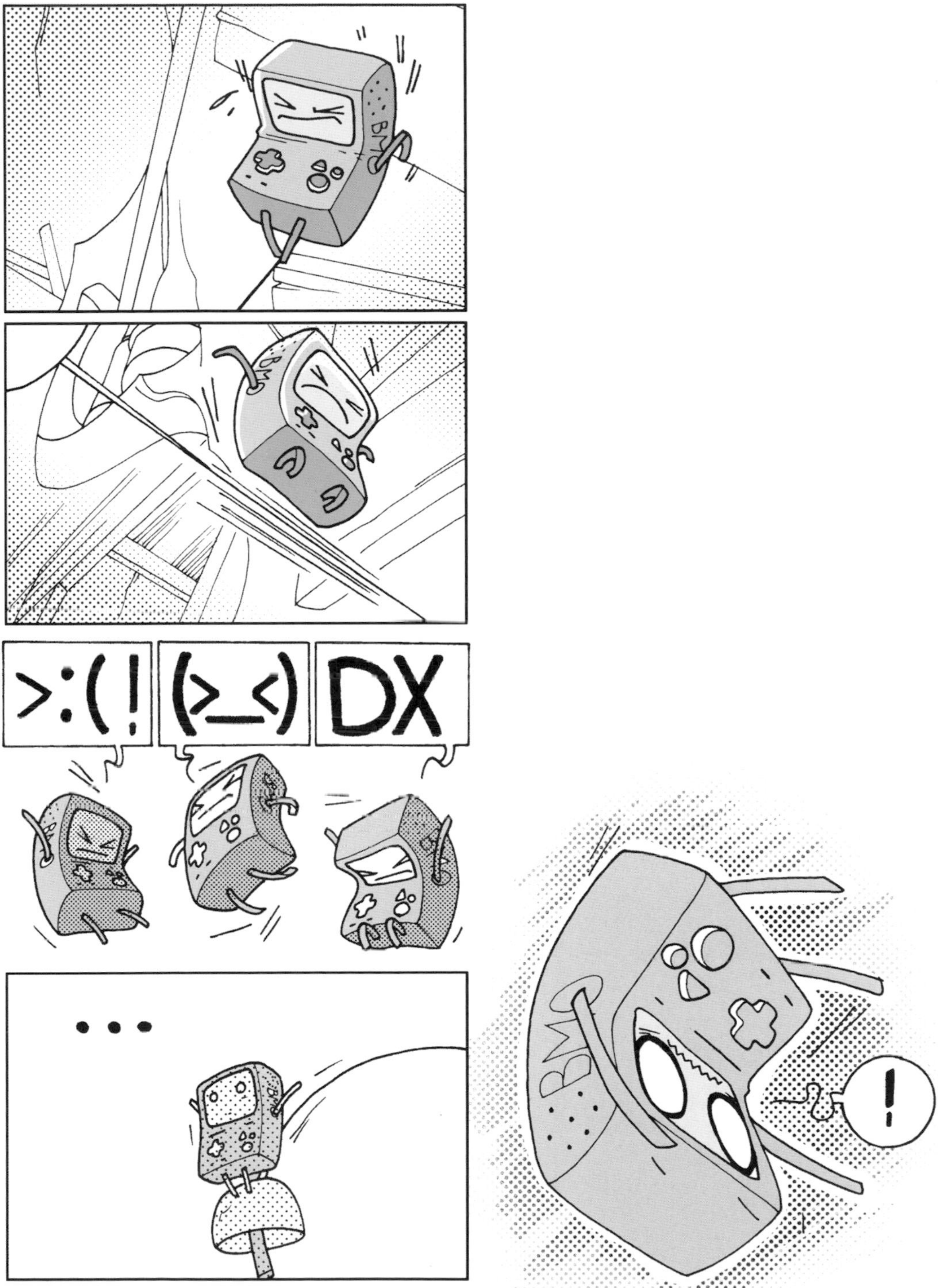
>:(!
(>_<)
DX
...
!

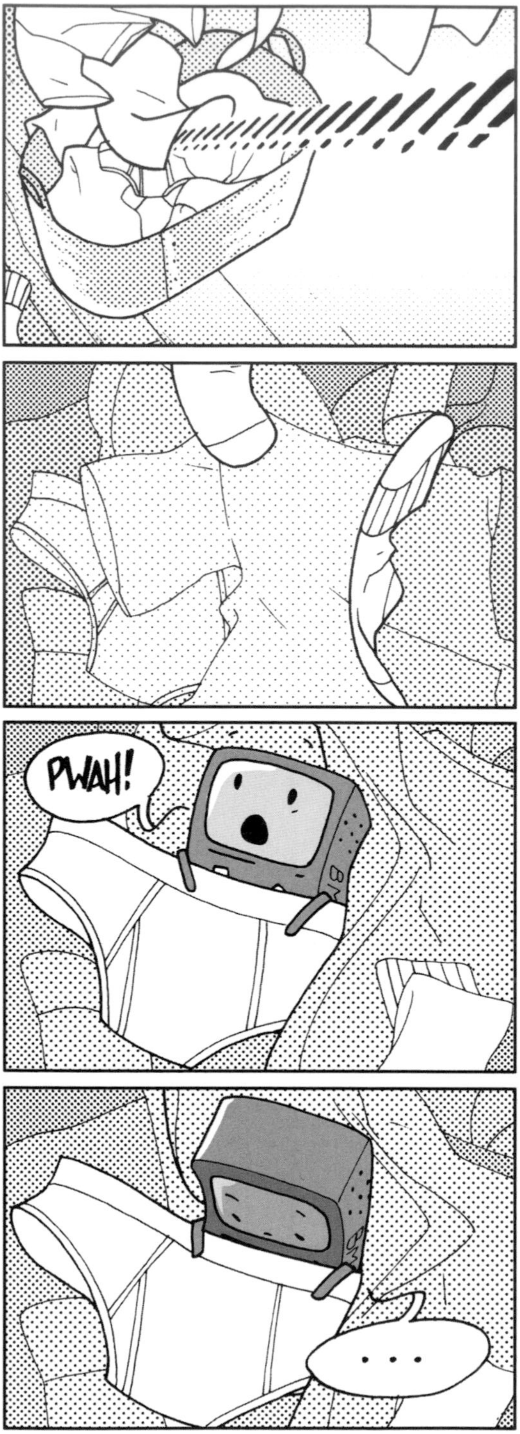
PWAH!
. . .
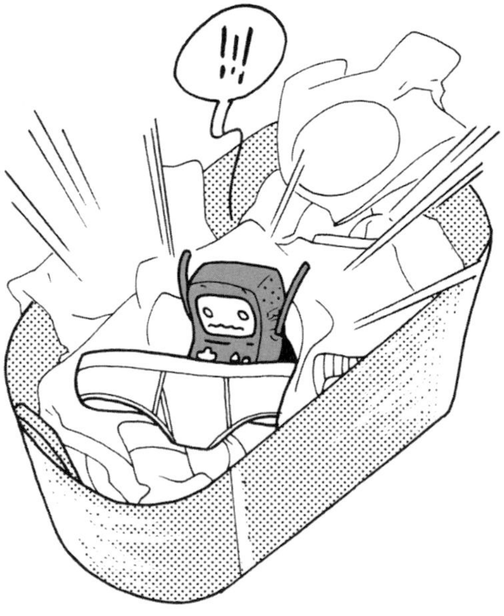
!!!

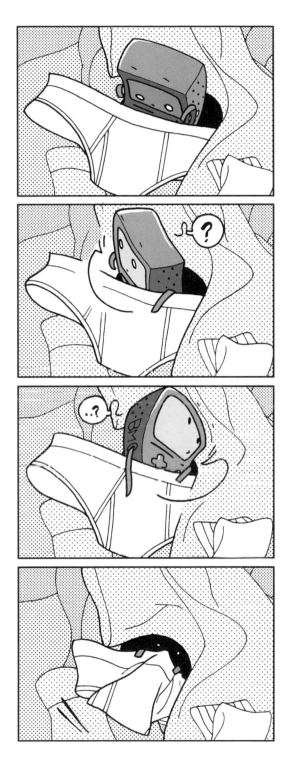

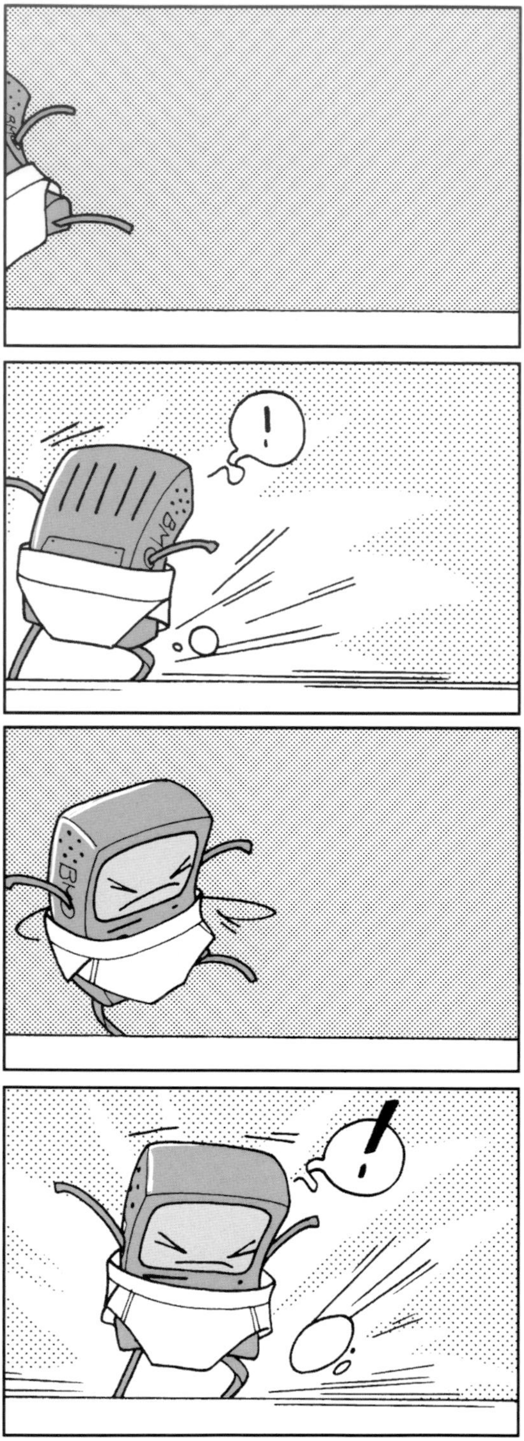
!
!

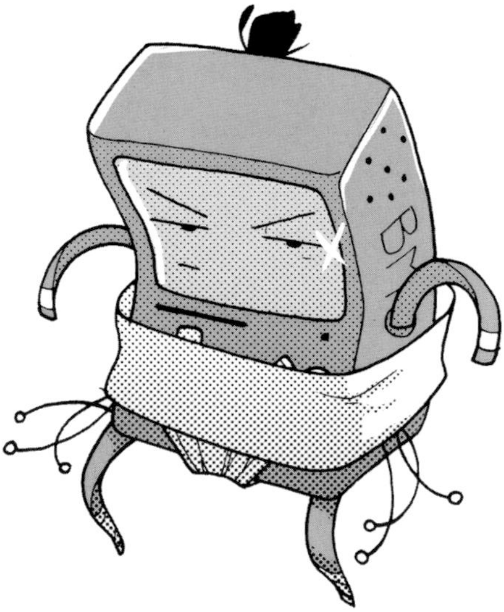

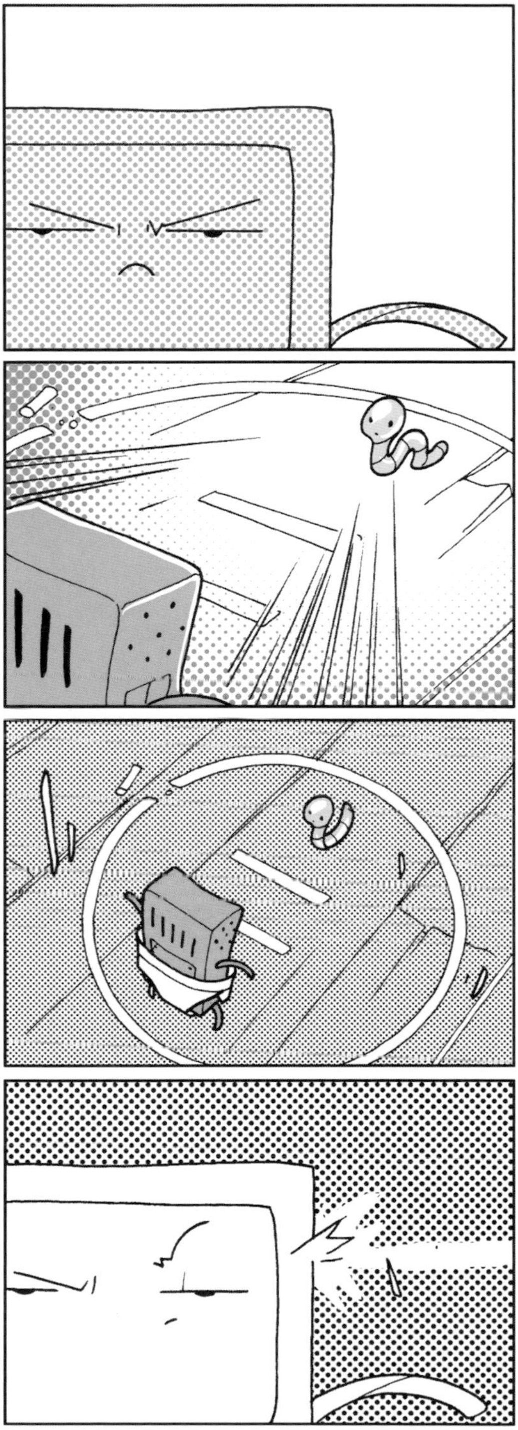

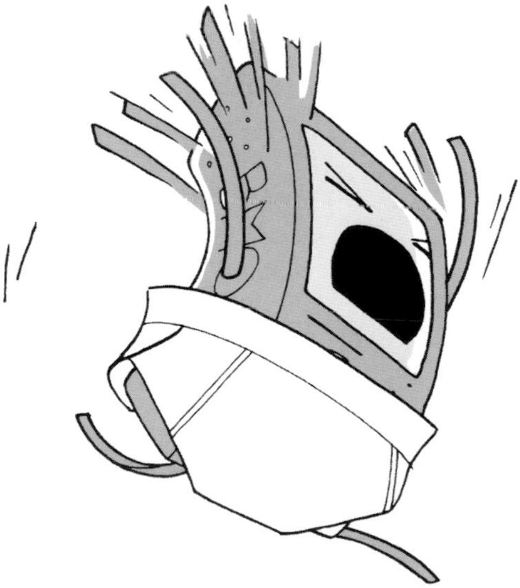

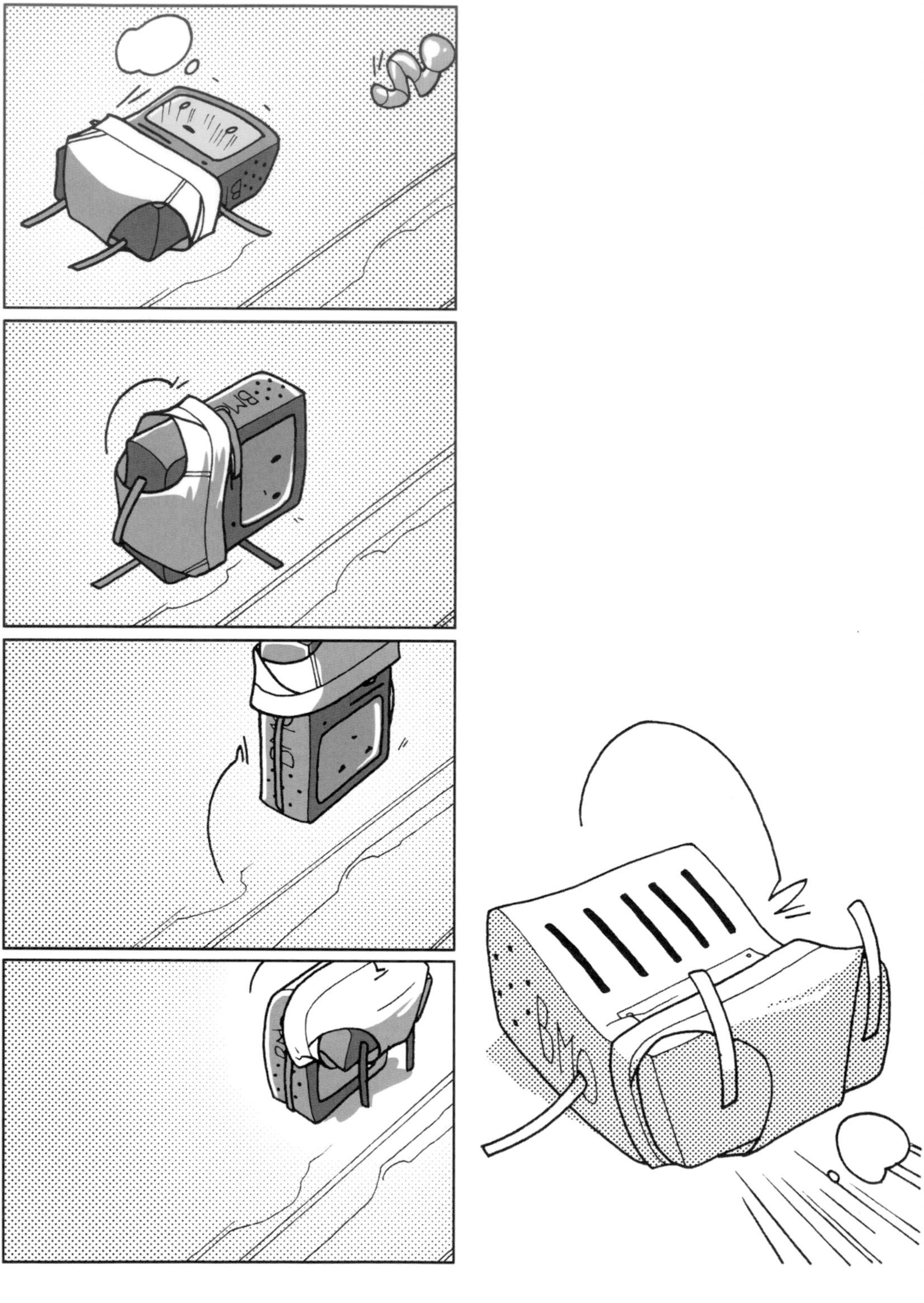
BMO

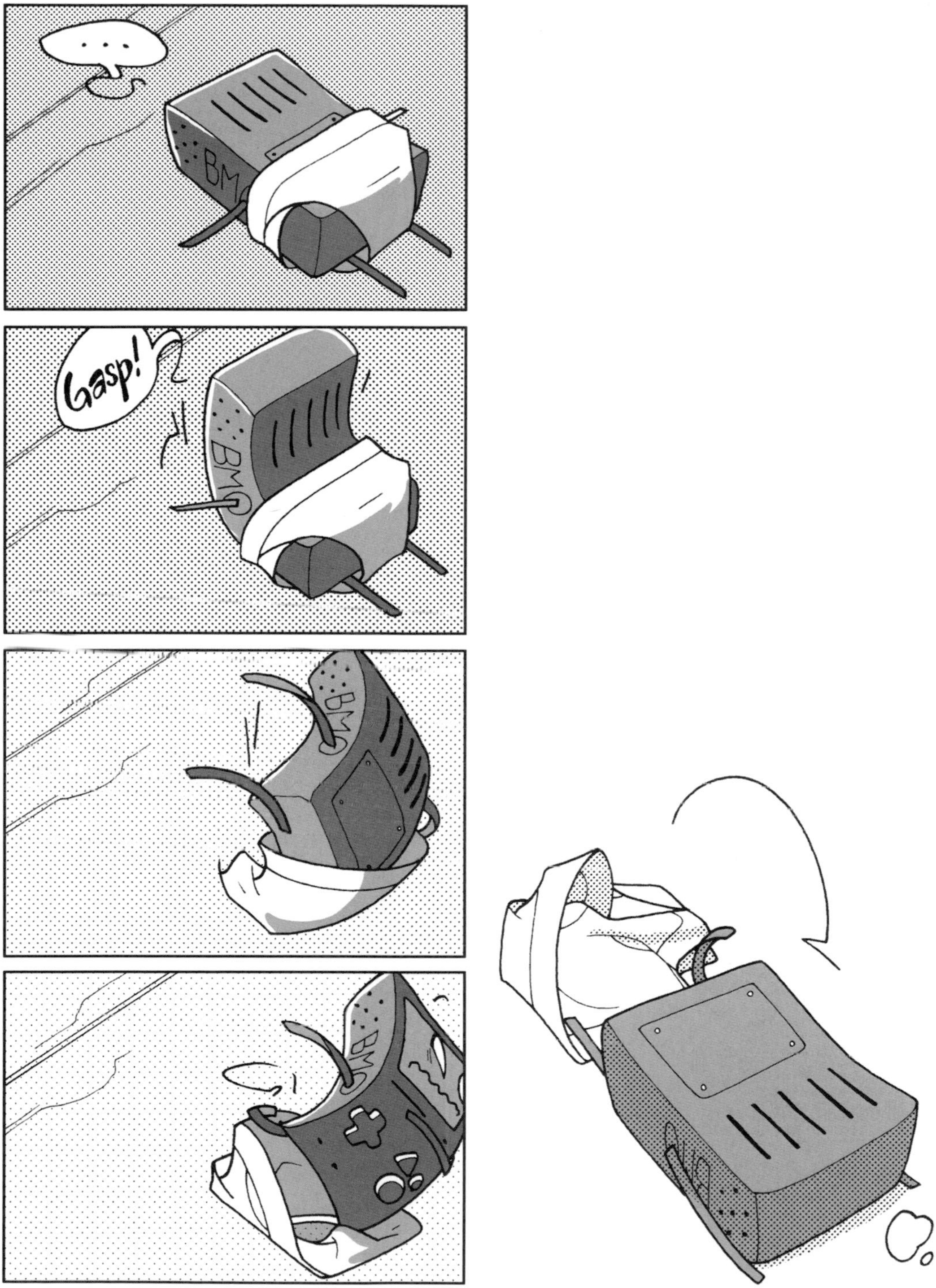

...
Gasp!

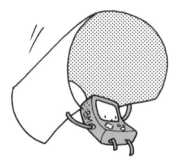

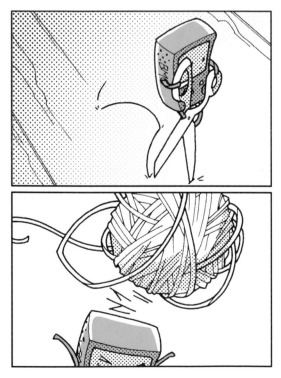

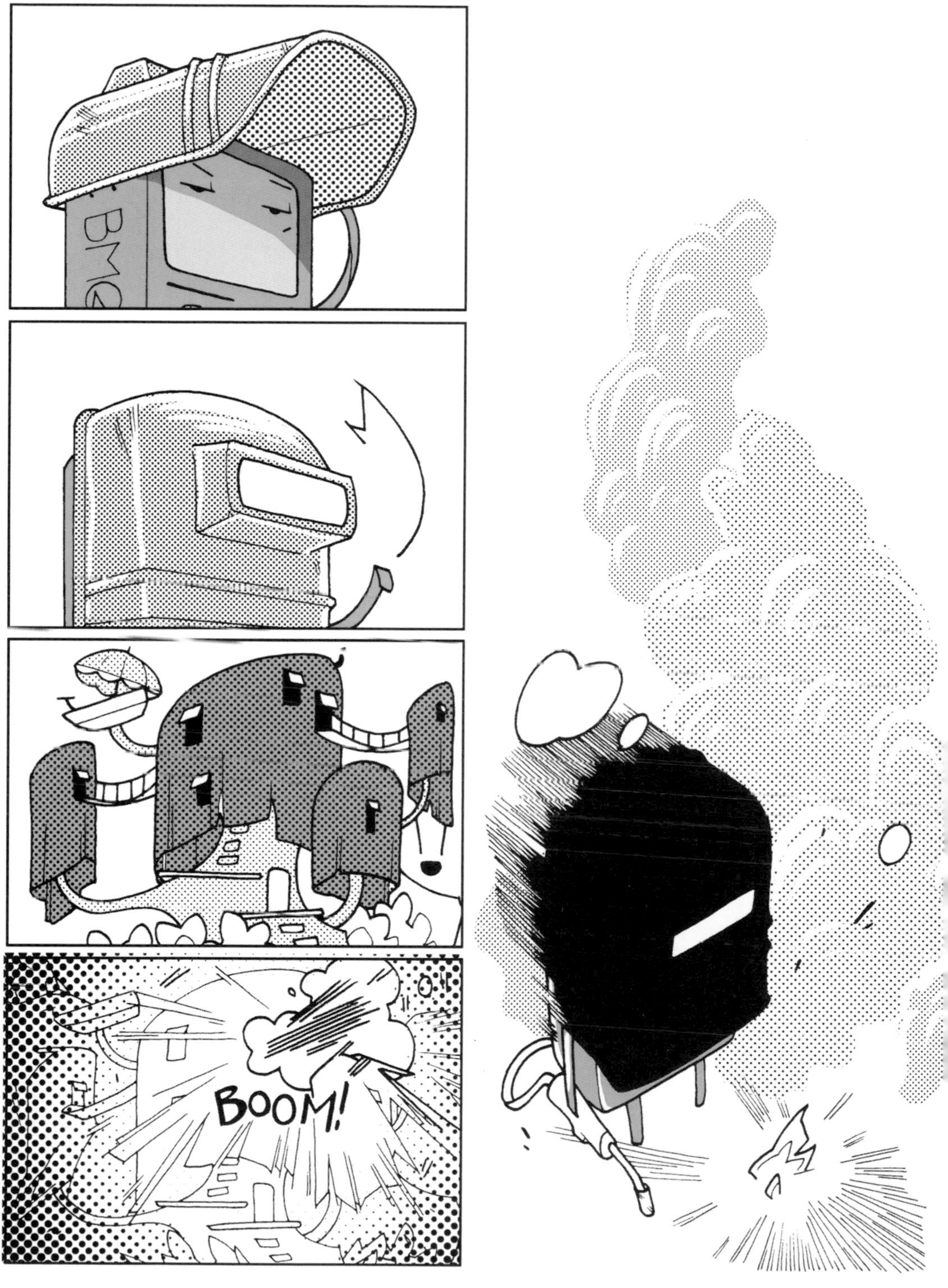
BOOM!

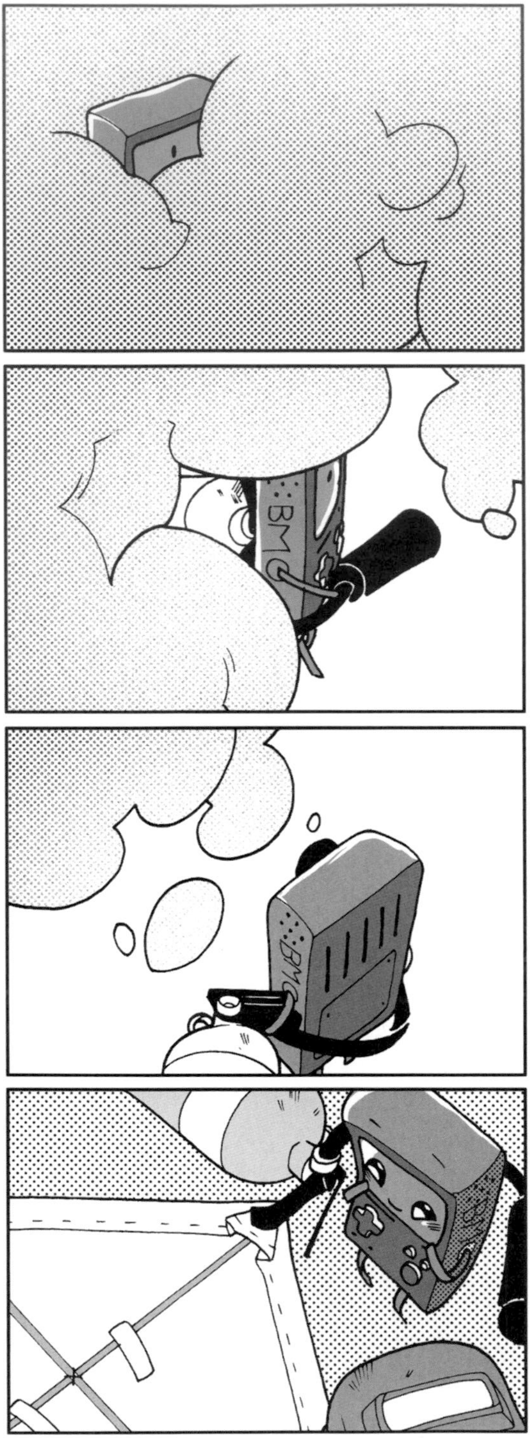

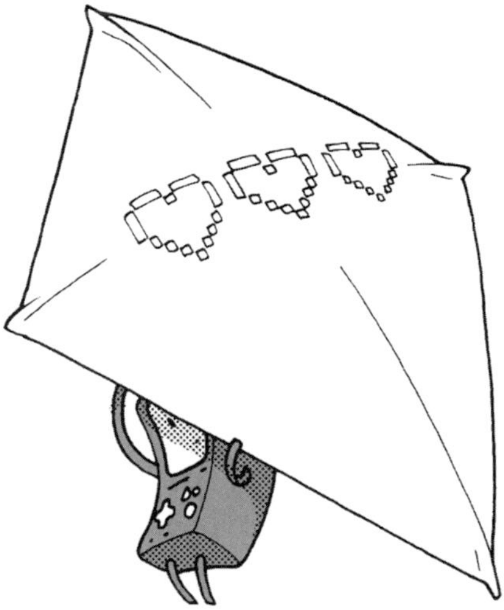

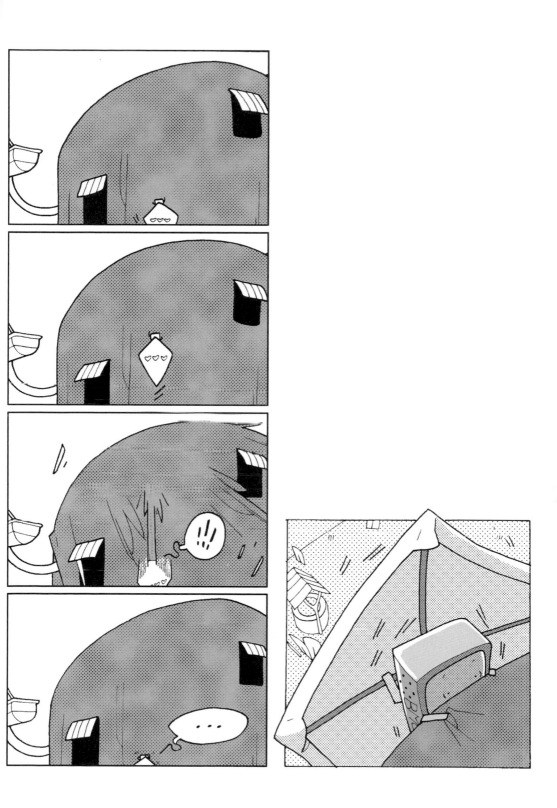

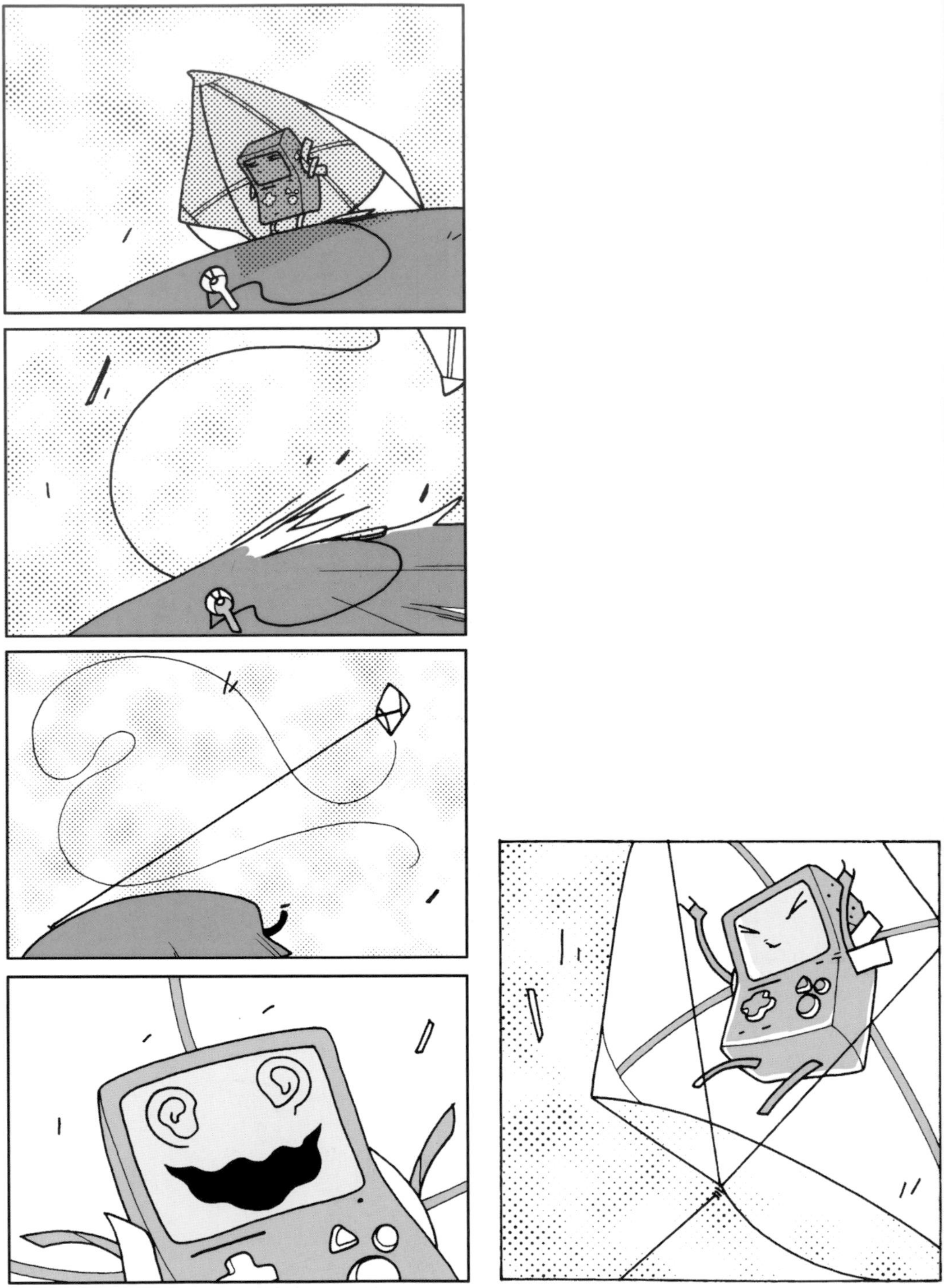

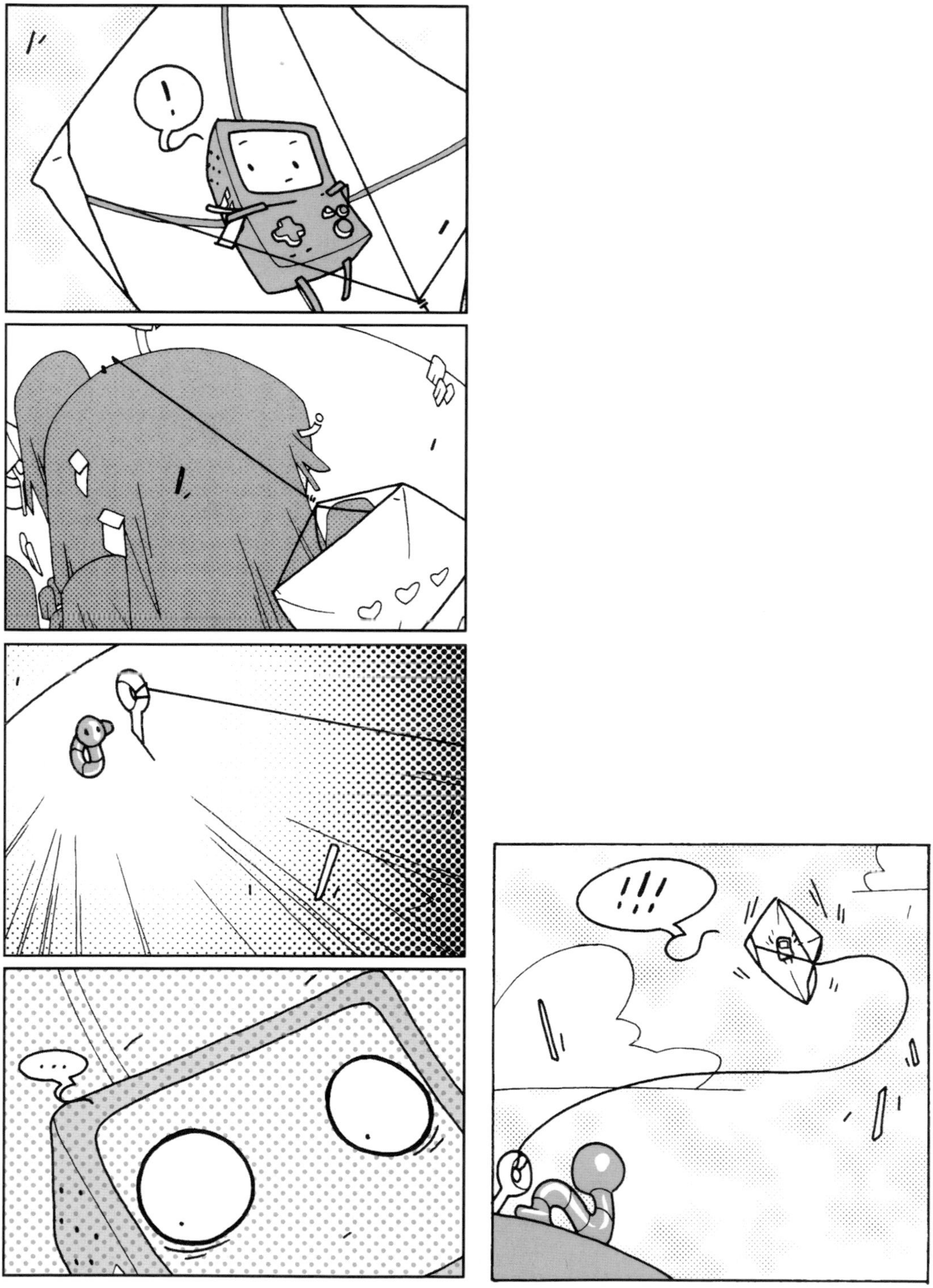
!
...
!!!

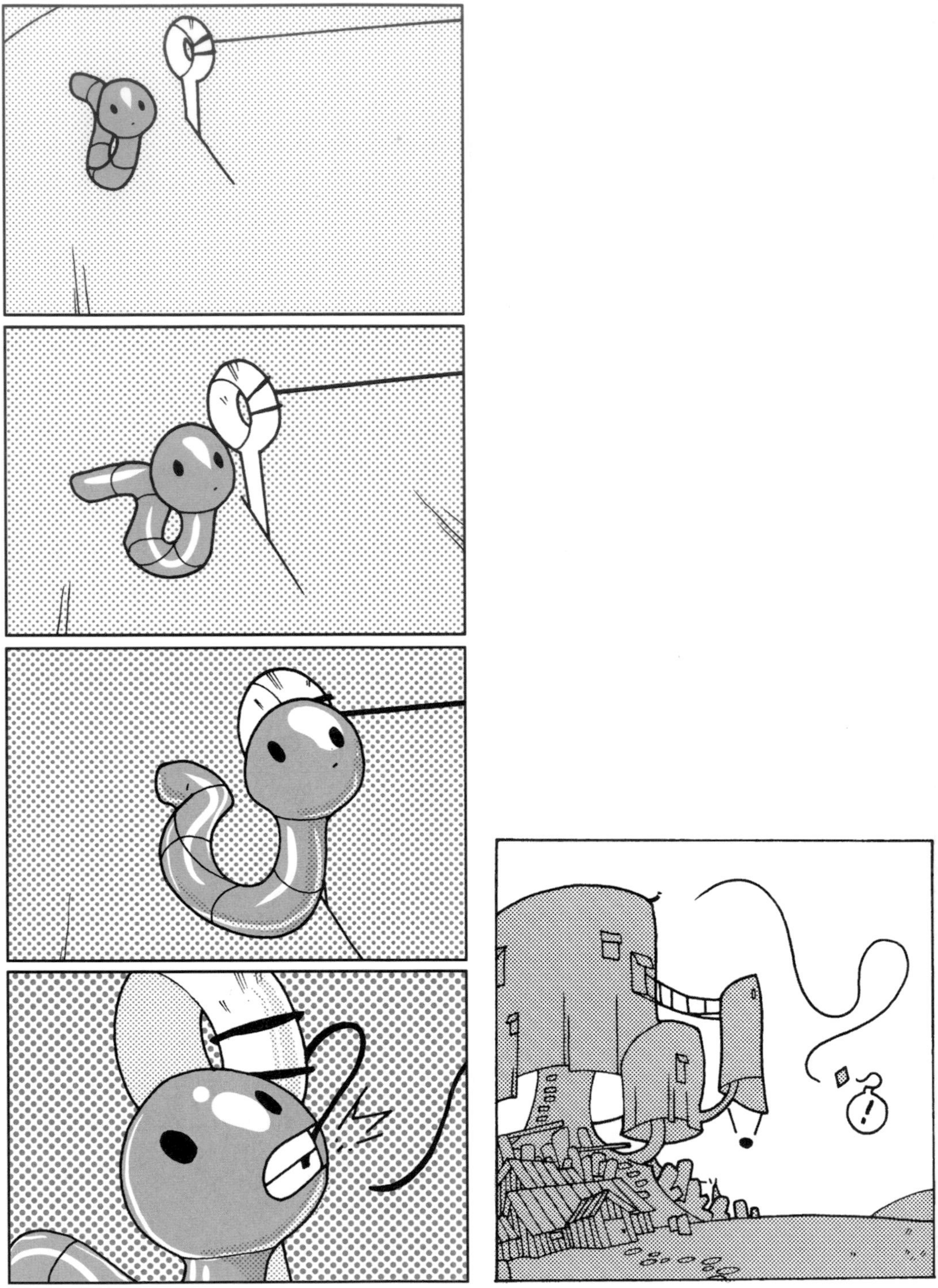

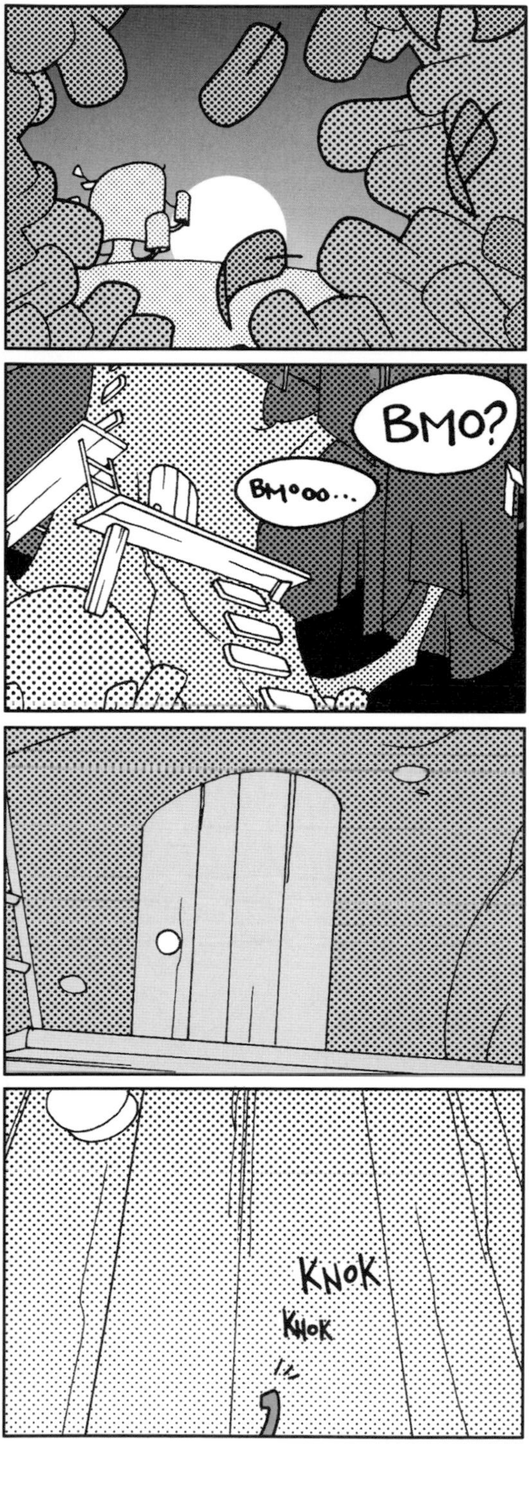
BMO?
BMOoo...
KNOK
KNOK
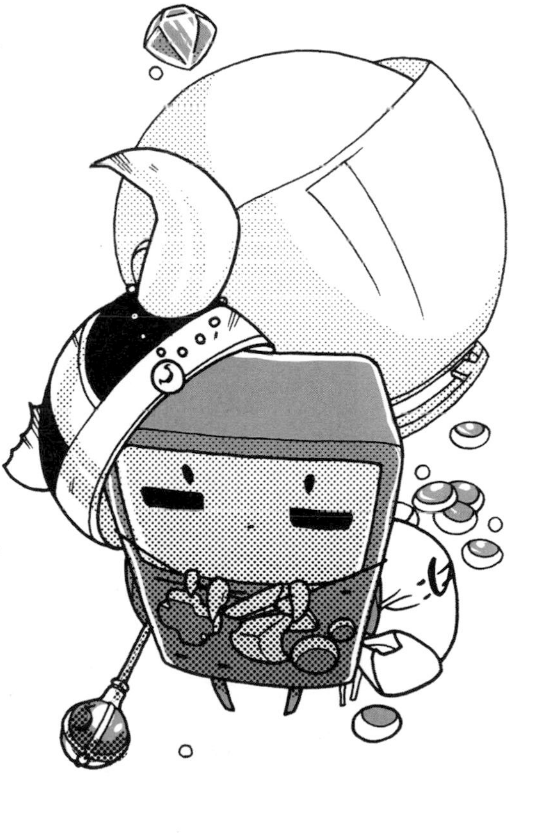

ADVENTURE TIME ™

Volume 2
September 2013

Written by Danielle Corsetto & Illustrated by Zack Sterling